DEAD TO RIGHTS

AN AMOS CARVER MYSTERY THRILLER

JOHN CORWIN

OVERWORLD PUBLISHING

Copyright © 2025 by John Corwin.

All rights reserved. Except as permitted under the U.S. Copyright Act of 1976, no part of this publication may be reproduced, distributed, or transmitted in any form or by any means, or stored in a database or retrieval system, without the prior written permission of the publisher.

The characters and events in this book are fictitious. Any similarity to real persons, living or dead, is coincidental and not intended by the author.

LICENSE NOTES:

The ebook format is licensed for your personal enjoyment only. The ebook may not be re-sold or given away to other people unless expressly permitted by the author. If you would like to share this book with another person, please purchase an additional copy for each recipient. If you're reading this book and did not purchase it, or it was not purchased for your use only, then please go to a digital ebook retailer and purchase your own copy. Thank you for respecting the hard work of this author.

DEADLY RITES

When Carver finds out that Rich Polaski, a man he served with in the SEALS, is on an NSA watch list, he goes to warn him out of a sense of duty.

He arrives in the small town of Bickham, Illinois, a spotless town with almost zero crime, no chain stores, and an aesthetic from a time long past.

That's because the local police run the town like it's their own little kingdom. They take what they want, and no one stops them.

Rich is their latest victim. They used civil forfeiture to take his home and fifty thousand dollars he'd been saving for surgery. But apparently, that wasn't enough. Carver finds out they also plan to take his life.

Carver's arrival stirs up the hornet's nest and puts him on a collision course with the local constabulary. It's a dangerous game, but that's nothing new to him. They're about to find out the hard way that the stakes just got higher.

And the next thing forfeited might be their lives.

BOOKS BY JOHN CORWIN

Books by John Corwin
Want more? Never miss an update by joining my email list and following me on social media!
Join my Facebook group at https://www.facebook.com/groups/overworldconclave
Join my email list: www.johncorwin.net
Fan page: https://www.facebook.com/johncorwinauthor

PSYCHOLOGICAL THRILLERS
The Family Business
AMOS CARVER THRILLERS
Dead Before Dawn
Dead List
Dead and Buried
Dead Man Walking
Dead By The Dozen
Dead Run
Dead Weather Days
Dead to Rights
Dead but not Forgotten
CHRONICLES OF CAIN
To Kill a Unicorn
Enter Oblivion
Throne of Lies
At The Forest of Madness
The Dead Never Die
Shadow of Cthulhu
Cabal of Chaos
Monster Squad

Gates of Yog-Sothoth
Shadow Over Tokyo
Into the Multiverse

THE OVERWORLD CHRONICLES

Sweet Blood of Mine
Dark Light of Mine
Fallen Angel of Mine
Dread Nemesis of Mine
Twisted Sister of Mine
Dearest Mother of Mine
Infernal Father of Mine
Sinister Seraphim of Mine
Wicked War of Mine
Dire Destiny of Ours
Aetherial Annihilation
Baleful Betrayal
Ominous Odyssey
Insidious Insurrection
Utopia Undone
Overworld Apocalypse
Apocryphan Rising
Soul Storm
Devil's Due
Overworld Ascension
Assignment Zero (An Elyssa Short Story)

OVERWORLD UNDERGROUND

Soul Seer
Demonicus
Infernal Blade

OVERWORLD ARCANUM

Conrad Edison and the Living Curse
Conrad Edison and the Anchored World
Conrad Edison and the Broken Relic
Conrad Edison and the Infernal Design
Conrad Edison and the First Power

STAND ALONE NOVELS

Mars Rising

No Darker Fate
The Next Thing I Knew
Outsourced
Seventh

Chapter 1

The front door slammed open.

Men in black fatigues stormed through the door, through the small foyer, and into the small den. They fanned out with expert precision. Three men marched straight into the hallway, three cleared the kitchen, and the last three cleared the dining room.

The house was small, so it didn't take them long to clear the rooms. It didn't take them long to ram through the bedroom door at the end of the hallway and shine rail-mounted flashlights into the face of the man in the bed.

It all happened so fast, Rich Polaski barely had time to sit up in his bed before his bedroom door burst inward and blinding light struck him in the face. He shouted. Scrambled toward the nightstand next to the bed.

A rifle butt struck him in the face. Men shouted, "Hands up! You're under arrest!"

"Under arrest? For what?" Rich tried to raise his hands, but his bad shoulder kept him from raising his right arm much higher than his ear.

Someone grabbed him roughly. Yanked him off the bed and spun him around. Slammed him face down on the bed. They gripped his arms and pulled them behind his back. Rich screamed in pain. His right shoulder couldn't rotate like that anymore.

"Stop resisting!" The man pulled harder on his right arm. "Stop resisting or I'll tase you!"

"I can't bend my arm that far!" Blinding agony raced up the tendons in Rich's arm. It went all the way up his shoulder and into his back and neck. "I'm not resisting!"

"Stop resisting!" the unseen man shouted. He kept shouting it over and over as if that would make Rich's arm do what he wanted it to do.

"Taser out!" another voice shouted. "Clear!"

"No, please stop!" The pain was so bad, Rich could hardly breathe. "I'm not resisting!" He felt cold metal jab into his ribs. An instant later, fifty thousand volts of electricity ripped into his body.

Rich went rigid. His muscles locked. His heart felt like it stopped. He couldn't breathe. Couldn't do anything except wait for the intense pain to stop. A small eternity later, it stopped. He collapsed facedown.

The unseen man jerked his arm again. He still couldn't move it behind Rich's back. "You don't learn, do you? Hit him again!"

More electricity coursed through Rich's body. He hardly felt it this time. His body had gone numb. Just like it had nearly a decade ago when he'd been in an even worse situation. The situation that disabled his shoulder.

Someone laughed. "I think he's telling the truth. Look at those scars."

"Damned cripple." The man trying to handcuff Rich laughed. "Someone dropped the ball on this one." He leaned down and whispered in Rich's ear. "Guess we'll just have to accommodate you."

Rich fluttered in and out of consciousness. Memories flashed through his head. Memories of a time he wished he could forget. He tried to talk, but his vocal chords felt dry as dust. A low groan was the only sound he could make.

"Oh, God." The other guy laughed again. "He pissed himself."

Rich was pulled upright. His knees were so weak he could hardly stand. His knees weren't all that great even on a good day. He felt wet warmth in his crotch. Felt it blossoming out across his boxer briefs. He wasn't wearing anything else.

Another voice joined the chorus. "Hey, I got long chains."

"Great, thanks," the first guy said. "I could cuff him in front."

"Against regs."

"Yeah? Well, long chains aren't exactly regulation either." The first guy huffed. "I'm front cuffing."

"Your call," the other guy said.

"As if it really matters." The first guy snorted. "Look at this guy. He couldn't run if he wanted to."

"His knee looks like cauliflower."

"Cauliflower?" The second guy laughed. "It looks like meatloaf."

"Whatever." The third guy stepped in front of Rich. The flashlight from one of the other men highlighted him. He was of medium build. He wore black fatigues and a helmet with night vision gear mounted on it. He also wore a black face mask to cover everything except his eyes.

His eyes were hidden in shadow. Rich wanted to see his eyes. Not because he wanted to know what color they were, but because he wanted to see how hard those eyes were. How uncaring and cold.

The new guy pulled Rich's hands in front of him. He snapped metal cuffs around his wrists. Pushed them tight enough to dig into the skin. His eyes were visible just for a second. In that second, Rich saw the kind of eyes he'd expected.

They weren't cold and unkind. Even worse, they were amused. Entertained. The man was enjoying this. That wasn't surprising. The man who'd mangled Rich's shoulder and knee had enjoyed his work too.

These men were dressed like SWAT officers. But they didn't have anything printed on their fatigues. They didn't have badges, or anything identifying them. Two were tall and filled out their uniforms as if they were custom tailored to show off their muscles. The third guy was shorter and slimmer.

The first guy grabbed Rich's right arm and yanked him forward. "Let's go."

Rich finally recovered enough of his wits to ask the most important questions. "What in the hell is going on? Who are you people?"

"Shut up. You'll find out soon enough." The man dragged Rich out of the bedroom and into the hallway. Rich couldn't walk very well on the best of days. His bad knee didn't bend like it should. Walking stiff-legged was his norm.

The man didn't care. He pulled Rich along, making him stumble and bang against the walls. The man seemed to enjoy it.

All the lights were on in the house now. Masked men in fatigues searched the rooms. Overturned furniture. Ripped open pillows. Tossed everything in drawers and cabinets. He counted eight men. A man with a crowbar walked past them and into Rich's bedroom.

"Why are you doing this?" Rich said. "I have a right to know!"

"The only right you have is to remain silent," the first guy said.

Someone laughed.

"Get him in the truck." A big man with a gruff voice marched inside. "I want him secure and out of the way."

Rich added him to the count. Nine men.

The first guy stiffened. "Yes, sir." He shoved Rich through the front door and into the night.

"I need clothing." Rich felt the dampness in his crotch. "This isn't right."

There was a black SWAT truck parked on the curb. It had no markings on it. The man opened the back door. There were benches against the left and right sides. A metal wall with a door separated the cab from the rear compartment.

The left bench was shorter than the right bench. That was because there was a metal box at the far end of the left side. The man shoved Rich forward. The truck bumper was low to the ground to make it easier for the police or whoever these people were to get in and out easily.

It was low enough that Rich could step up into it. The man put a hand on his back and guided him to the metal box. There were holes in the metal, like the air holes kids put in boxes so a captured animal could breathe.

There was a sliding bolt on the outside of the box. It bent at ninety degrees on one end so the bolt couldn't simply slide straight out. It had to be rotated upward and then pulled out of the bolt hole.

The man rotated the latch and pulled. The latch slid out easily. He opened the door. He gripped Rich's good shoulder and spun him around to face him. Then he shoved Rich back onto the metal bench inside the metal box.

The man shackled Rich's handcuffs to a metal loop bolted onto the floor. He closed the door, shoved the latch back into place, and rotated it down. The metal was cold against Rich's bare skin.

"Who the hell are you people?" Rich said. "You have to at least identify yourselves. You can't just burst into people's homes for no reason!"

The man said nothing. He banged the butt of his rifle against the metal box and laughed. Then he left the truck. The rear doors clanged shut and Rich was left in darkness. It wasn't total darkness, but it was close enough.

The confines of the metal box and the dark pressed in on Rich from all sides. His heart palpitated. His chest felt as if someone were sitting on it. He couldn't breathe. He flinched violently. Slammed his bad shoulder against the wall.

Pain raced from the shoulder, into his neck, and down into his shoulder blade. It also traveled down into his forearm and radiated out in his hand. It burned through the claustrophobic panic and wrenched his mind back into sanity.

Rich drew in a deep breath. "I can breathe. I can move. I'm alive." He repeated it over and over again, a mantra that was the only good thing to come out of therapy. The psychologist hadn't even been the one who'd recommended it.

It had been another patient who'd told him about it. A man who radiated calm. A man who didn't look like he belonged there. Rich remembered it as clearly as if it had just happened yesterday, though it had been years ago.

###

Rich had just walked out of the psychologist's office. He was agitated. Shaking. Dr. Erickson recommended drugs to treat his PTSD. Same prescription as last time. It was an inhibitor called sertraline. It was the easy way out, for the doctor at least. It treated the symptoms, not the root cause.

There were other patients waiting. Six or seven at least. One of them stood out immediately. He was sitting in the back, his chair angled to fit into the corner of the room so he could face the receptionist and the front door.

His eyes were on Rich for an instant before calmly taking in the rest of the room. Like he was constantly scanning everything and everyone. The other patients reflexively looked up when Rich exited the psychologist's office.

They looked at him differently. They didn't have the same calm about them. Their eyes darted up and around. Some of them flinched. Others stared blankly at him, as if looking right through him.

Rich knew that thousand-mile stare all too well. Their eyes weren't seeing the present. They were seeing the past. Probably the trauma that brought them here same as it brought him.

The calm guy turned his gaze back to Rich. He met his gaze and held it. Most people would avert their eyes. Not this guy. He studied Rich. Not the way a doctor would, but as if he recognized something in the way he walked.

Rich held his ground and studied the other man right back. The calmness emanating from him was very familiar. It was the same calm exhibited by a seasoned soldier just before the next mission. The calm of a man who was very confident in his capabilities and those of the men around him.

That same calm had radiated from Rich on dozens of missions. He'd had absolute confidence in the men around him. They were his brothers in arms. More than family. They would die for each other and no man would ever be left behind.

The receptionist looked up from her computer. "Mr. Polaski, right?"

"Yes."

"Have a seat and I can check you out in a moment."

"Okay." Rich turned back toward the waiting area. He walked boldly to the calm man and sat down next to him. "What are you here for?"

The man didn't look at him for a moment. He was watching a man who'd just entered the office. A man whose arm had been amputated below the elbow. He turned to Rich. Smiled. "Same as you. I'm screwed up."

"PTSD?"

The man shrugged. "Sure. Whatever the doctor says."

Rich blinked. "You don't have a diagnosis?"

"Sure, I do. I have a lot of them."

Rich laughed. "You say that like it's an accomplishment."

"In the military you either collect medals or malfunctions."

Rich laughed again. "That's for damned sure. For every medal a superior officer gets, someone under his command earns a malfunction."

The man's gaze returned to the amputee. "Yeah, well some diagnoses are good for the military. It helps them know who goes where. Who's fit for which duties. Who's unfit for any kind of duty."

"I guess. I never thought of it that way."

The man turned to him. "You've got physical disabilities, that much I can tell even with the long sleeve shirt and pants. You were honorably discharged because of them. From the look in your eyes, I'd guess you were captured. Probably tortured." He shrugged. "No shame in it. It happens to the best of us."

Rich stiffened at his words. He flashed back to captivity. To the coffin his captors kept him in. He could feel the stifling heat. Feel the nausea from the bad food bubbling in his stomach. Smell his own feces and urine trapped in the coffin with him.

He could hear their laughter. Hear the pounding of their feet as they kicked the sides of the wooden coffin. He saw flashes of their feet through the small holes cut in the sides. Dust filtered through the holes, stealing his oxygen.

Rich felt the walls closing in on him. His heart pounded. His lungs felt heavy. He couldn't breathe.

A hand gripped his good shoulder. "You can breathe. You can move. You're alive."

Rich flinched. Looked into the other man's eyes. He knew it was true even if his mind didn't want to cooperate.

"Say it with me," the man said.

"I can breathe. I can move. I'm alive." Rich trembled. The memories faded. "I can breathe. I can move. I'm alive."

The man nodded. "You got it."

"How did you know that would work?"

"Like I said, it happens to the best of us."

"You get claustrophobic too?"

"Let's just say my brain screws with me sometimes. That's all PTSD is. Your brain decides to ruin your day, you know?" He shrugged. "It dumps chemicals into your blood. Turns you into a mess. Sometimes you have to fight back."

"It's hard to fight back."

"Sometimes a man has no choice but to fight back, even if it means battling his own brain." The other man tapped a finger on his temple. "We're all prisoners in our own bodies. But we're also the wardens."

Rich laughed. "Yeah, you're right. Maybe you ought to be a psychologist."

The other man grinned. "I'm psyops. Close enough."

"What's your name?"

"You can call me Tom."

"Is that your real name?"

Tom's grin widened. "Real enough."

The doctor's door opened. Dr. Erickson stepped out. He looked at Tom. "Your turn."

Another man shot up out of his chair. "Hey, I've been here way longer than him! He literally got here ten minutes ago."

"Sorry. Priority case." Erickson went back inside his office.

Tom rose from his chair and followed the doctor inside. The door closed behind him.

###

Rich's mind returned to the present. He was calm again. His shoulder and knee hurt like hell, but he was calm. He didn't know what in the hell was going on. He didn't know why these men had burst into his home.

They were looking for something, that much was obvious. He knew exactly what they would find if they looked hard enough. What he had wasn't illegal. They couldn't send him to jail for it.

It had to be a case of mistaken identity. Maybe they'd planned to raid another house and accidentally come to his instead. Maybe someone was angry with him. Swatting wasn't an uncommon revenge tactic.

All they had to do was phone in an emergency and say Rich was armed and dangerous and had a hostage. The SWAT team would do the rest. Maybe they said he was selling drugs out of his home. That would explain why they were tearing up the place.

A small eternity seemed to pass before he heard sounds of men approaching the vehicle. He heard the rear doors swing open. Felt the truck rock back and forth as men climbed inside. Heard them talking and laughing.

"Hello?" Rich bumped his bare foot against the door to his cage. "What's going on? Why am I here?"

No one answered him. The diesel engine rumbled to life. Doors shut. The truck shifted into motion and drove him toward an uncertain future.

Chapter 2

Carver was being watched.

Maybe. Maybe not. He didn't like the way the man at the beach bar kept glancing at him when he thought Carver wasn't looking. It might just be paranoia. Then again, it never hurt to be a little paranoid for a man in his position.

There were other people the man might be glancing at. For example, the women in bikinis lounging in beach chairs behind Carver. Or the half-naked women sunbathing in front of Carver. In fact, the man might not have even noticed Carver a single time.

It was June. The sun shimmered on the white sands. It was so hot Carver felt like he was baking in an oven. He had a large umbrella shielding him from the sun and a cold beer in his hand.

It was perfect.

The beach was packed with people. There were parents huddled under cabanas while the children raced into the surf or built sandcastles. There were women looking for the perfect tan, men looking for the perfect woman, and then there was this guy.

It was the way he held himself that caught Carver's attention. The way he barely sipped at his drink. The way he barely paid attention to the countless other attractive females in the vicinity.

Maybe he didn't like women. Maybe Carver was more his type. Anything was possible. But it just didn't feel like that was the reason the man kept looking in Carver's direction. There was something else going on here.

It was lunchtime. The perfect time to test Carver's theory about the man's intentions. Carver stood and made a show of stretching. He polished off his beer and put the empty bottle in his cooler.

He stood. Put on his shirt and sandals. Grabbed the wad of cash from his cooler and stuffed it into his left shorts pocket. Put his burner phone in the other pocket. He closed the cooler and started walking.

He left his beach umbrella, the cooler, and his chair where it was. There was no danger of it being stolen. Not here in Myrtle Beach, South Carolina. If he was on the west coast, then he wouldn't dare leave his things unattended.

If you left things lying around on a California beach, those things would get snatched in short order. And if someone did decide today was the day to steal something at Myrtle Beach, it was no big deal. Carver could replace the umbrella, the cooler, and his chair easily.

Besides, finding out if this guy was watching him was well worth the cost of those items. So, he sauntered toward the giant Ferris wheel. There was a restaurant right next to it, Landshark Bar and Grill. He'd eaten there several times since arriving in Myrtle Beach since it was right on the sand.

Carver walked past the rear deck entrance and around to the front of the restaurant. The sidewalk was busy, packed mostly with people in beachwear. It would be easy to blend in if Carver wasn't a head taller than most of them.

A metal fence blocked pedestrians from crossing the street anywhere except for marked crosswalks. There was a crosswalk directly in front of the Landshark. Carver already knew that. He already knew all the best escape routes from the area just in case it ever came down to that.

He crossed the street and kept walking straight into the wide alley between two souvenir shops. He walked at a steady pace, not too fast, not too slow. He turned left at the end of the alley and waited just around the corner.

This was the perfect spot to watch for a tail. It was perfect because there was a large blind spot mirror fixed on the corner of the building right across from Carver's position. It was one of those curved mirrors used in stores to spot shoplifters.

This mirror had been attached under the eaves and was angled so people walking down the alley could see people coming down the sidewalk. Carver didn't know why the shop owner thought it was useful. He was just happy it was there.

The mirror had been dirty when he noticed it on his first night in town. He'd returned the next day with glass cleaner and polished it until it was crystal clear. He'd returned every couple of weeks to clean it again if it looked dirty.

That had been months ago and now his persistence might finally pay off. He leaned against the wall and watched the mirror. The curve distorted the reflection. It made it difficult to differentiate the faces. But he didn't need to see the faces clearly to recognize the man from the bar.

The man from the bar wasn't dressed for the beach. Not even close. He wore a black t-shirt and jeans. He looked like a typical G-man trying to dress like a civilian and failing. He looked like a person who didn't know how to relax if his life depended on it.

And in this particular instance, his life depended a whole lot on blending in.

Carver spotted him at the other end of the alley. The guy was following at just the right distance to keep tabs on the target without falling too far behind. It was like he'd read the official government textbook on tailing a suspect and was following the instructions word for word.

That wasn't necessarily a bad thing. Most people would have no idea he was following them. Unfortunately for him, Carver wasn't most people. Now that he knew for certain the man was following him, what did he want to do about it?

Carver didn't want to leave the beach. He wanted to stick around and enjoy it for the rest of the summer at the very least. Was that too much to ask? For the sake of this guy's health, he'd better hope he had a good reason for following Carver.

Carver was feeling slightly magnanimous, so he decided to be upfront with the guy. Give him a chance to come clean before he cleaned his clock. Normally, he'd turn the tables and follow the guy, but he really wanted to get back to the beach and his beers, not spend the day traipsing around town.

The man rounded the corner. Saw Carver leaning against the wall patiently waiting on him. He flinched back like he'd been struck in the face. "Jesus Christ!"

"Not quite." Carver didn't move from his position. He just stared at the guy. Waited to see if he'd bolt or hold his ground.

The man cleared his throat. Held his ground. "I guess you're wondering why I'm following you."

"Good guess." Carver waited for him to continue.

"Uh, I'm not exactly a government guy, okay?"

Carver kept silent.

The man continued. "My name is, uh... Hmm, maybe I shouldn't tell you that."

Carver just stared at him.

"Okay, fine! My name is Barry and I'm a friend of a friend."

Carver straightened up from the wall. He still said nothing.

Barry stepped back. "Liana sent me, okay?"

"Liana?" Carver raised an eyebrow. "Why?"

"She wanted you to know she's okay. That she's back in the good graces of the powers that be." He looked around as if someone might be listening. "Can we go somewhere more private?"

"No." Carver walked toward him.

Barry jumped back hands raised in surrender. "Don't hurt me, please."

"I'm hungry." Carver nodded toward the Landshark. "Let's go eat."

"Oh, okay." Barry nodded. "Yeah, sure."

They walked back across the street and into the restaurant. Despite the heat, Barry was hardly sweating at all. His skin was pale. No sign of a tan or sun exposure. He looked like a guy accustomed to spending all day indoors.

It jibed with the initial impression Carver had of the guy. He was a G-man, but he was relatively new and inexperienced. Either that, or he was someone who desperately wanted to be a G-man and knew just enough to be a danger to himself and everyone around him.

Barry was packing, that much was obvious from the slight bulge under the waistline of his jeans. He had a small handgun tucked into a concealed carry holster there. Probably a Glock 19 or similar if Carver had to guess. Maybe a Glock 43.

The hostess approached Carver. She glanced at Barry with a slight frown as if trying to decide if the two men were together. She smiled brightly an instant later as if concluding that the men must be together since Barry stood right next to Carver.

"Good afternoon," she said. "Inside or outside seating?"

"First available," Carver said. The restaurant wasn't packed, but the back deck certainly was.

"Is a booth okay?"

"Yep," Carver said.

The hostess led them to a booth on the right side of the restaurant. Barry tried to take the seat facing the door. Carver shook his head and made him sit on the other side. Technically, the doors leading to the deck were now at his back, but he thought it was far more likely any danger would come from the front.

"What's on your waist?" Carver asked.

Barry blinked. "Huh? Oh, my gun?" He grinned. "It's a Sig P365 with a slide mounted sight. Want to see it?"

"No." Carver looked at the waitress as she approached. He ordered a burger and a water. He'd been drinking beer all morning and was a little dehydrated.

The waitress turned to Barry. "What would you like, sir?"

"I'm not ready to order yet." Barry looked flustered. "I would get a burger, but I don't eat beef. It upsets my stomach."

"We have a turkey burger," she said.

"Oh, yeah. Perfect." Barry nodded. "And a Coke Zero, please."

"We only have diet Coke."

He wrinkled his nose. "Gross. Water then."

"Yes, sir." She turned and left.

Carver got straight to it. "Liana is back in her old position?"

"Yes. She told me to tell you everything is good, but she can't tell you in person."

"Good to know. How in the hell did you find me?"

"That's the other thing she wanted me to tell you."

Carver waited.

Barry seemed to realize Carver wasn't going to prompt him and started talking again. "She found a high priority facial recognition search with a runtime of nearly a year. That's the length of time it's been running."

"I know what runtime means." Carver leaned back. "So, I walked in front of a camera somewhere and the algorithm found me?"

"Sort of." Barry looked up as if recalling what to say next. "Liana found out the lake house was wiped out in the hurricane. She figured out from all the news stories that the mysterious big guy who threatened a local assistant fire chief was probably you."

"That's a leap."

"Not coupled with the eyewitness accounts of a big man who supposedly took out several members of a private military company in the middle of the hurricane."

Carver had paid close attention to the news coming out of North Carolina right after the hurricane. His name hadn't been mentioned by any of the locals. They'd kept quiet as he'd hoped. But some had spoken generically of him.

For someone like Liana, that was enough to know who they were talking about. Mainly because she knew that he'd been in the area and had probably tried to leave at his earliest convenience.

"Okay, so she figured I'd left town, right?"

Barry nodded. "She knew you'd head for a beach, but probably not one you'd been to recently. She created a sub-search with her own parameters limited to beaches in the Carolinas and found you a month ago."

Carver did his best to avoid cameras, but in this day and age it was all but impossible to do so. "Why wait until now to contact me?"

"Because she subverted the search by replacing images of you with those of a similar looking man. She wanted to make sure you were safe."

"That's nice of her." The waitress returned with their waters. Carver took his and drank half of it before setting the glass on the table. "Why contact me at all, then?"

"She said there are other searches in the system that might concern you." Barry stared at his water but didn't drink it. "Other former members of your Scion cohort, for example."

That got Carver's attention. "Who, specifically?"

"Leon Fry, Wade Brooks, and Clinton Miller for starters." He took out his phone and unlocked the screen. Turned it so Carver could see a list of names. "There are several also listed as deceased."

Carver read them. Rhodes, Barrows, Menendez, Rocker, Jericho. He frowned at the last name. "Jericho is dead? This is confirmed accurate?"

"I would think so. The NSA doesn't exactly play guessing games."

Carver was a little surprised Barrows was on the list because he hadn't been a Scion regular. Then again, he'd been hot on the heels of Enigma at one point, so that probably got him flagged. As for Brooks and Miller, they'd been straps, not permanent members of Scion.

They'd been strapped onto his team from time to time to assist, then vanished back to wherever they'd come from in the first place. The core team hadn't been large. It had grown or shrank to accommodate the current mission.

The one thing all the temporary operators had in common was that they were almost certainly as far off the books as Scion had been. By contrast, his SEAL team had been deployed with CIA operatives on a regular basis.

If anyone from a legitimate three-letter agency had deployed with Scion, they'd done it without identifying themselves as such. That was just the way black ops worked as far as Carver knew.

He wasn't exactly an expert in black ops administration or planning. He'd just done what he was told to do. Then it had all come crashing down around him when he was framed for using his position for sex trafficking.

He still remembered that day like it was yesterday. Remembered the MPs marching into the cargo hold of the C-17 Globemaster. Remembered them making a beeline for the coffins that arrived on the truck with him.

There were four women inside four coffins. They were sedated and hooked up to oxygen tanks. One of them was dead. Her oxygen had run out during the flight. The coffins were hermetically sealed so once the air ran out inside, that was it.

The women fingered Carver as the man who'd kidnapped them. Scion had been disbanded. Everyone had been dishonorably discharged. And everyone had been mad as hell at him.

Rhodes had died trying to find the truth about the situation. Rocker and Menendez had been behind the setup. Carver had put them in the ground himself. Barrows had been killed by the shadow organization, Enigma.

So, what had happened to Jericho? Why was he on an NSA watch list? It was peculiar. Damned peculiar. The man had survived situations a roach would have died in. He'd also promised to kill Carver if he ever saw him again. At least that was one threat he no longer had to worry about.

Carver took another sip of water. "Does anyone else know where I am?"

"Besides me and Liana?" He grinned. "Nope."

"Okay, so I don't need to leave."

"I guess that's up to you." Barry shrugged. "Liana said that you might be interested in another name. One that's not from Scion."

Carver didn't prompt him for an answer. He just waited for it to come out.

Barry cleared his throat. "Um, a guy named Rich Polaski."

That perked Carver's ears. "He's on the watch list?"

"Yes."

"Why in the hell is he on a watch list?"

"I don't know."

Carver looked up as the waitress delivered their food. He lifted the bun. Put mustard and ketchup on the beef patty. He made sure it had the purple onions he liked. Pickles, lettuce, tomatoes, too.

All the ingredients for a perfect burger were on there. He put the bun on top. Took a big bite. It tasted amazing. The meat was pink where he'd bitten it. As usual, the Landshark chef got it right.

Barry seemed confused. "Um, so that's it? You're just going to eat like nothing has happened?"

"What exactly has happened?" Carver dunked a fry into ketchup. "You found me. You told me that I'm safe."

"Oh, okay." Barry nodded. "Liana said you rarely react the way a normal person should."

"Does a normal person not eat when they're hungry?"

Barry frowned real hard, like he was having a hard time understanding anything. Then he shrugged and tasted his turkey burger. He made a face. "I forgot I don't like turkey that much."

Carver kept eating.

"So, I guess you're going to stay here?"

Carver wiped his hands on the napkin. "Where is Rich Polaski now?"

"I don't know, but I can find out."

"Find out."

Barry nodded. "Will do."

Carver wanted to stay on the beach, but he also needed to know why Rich Polaski was being watched. If Joe Donnely was alive today, he'd go warn Rich about the watchlist. He'd do it in person since that wasn't the sort of thing you did over the phone. Since Joe was dead it was all up to Carver.

Even if it was the last thing Carver wanted to do.

Chapter 3

Rich jerked awake.

As impossible as it seemed, he'd fallen asleep in the metal cage. He didn't know what time it was. For an instant, he didn't know where he was. The truck had driven somewhere. Everyone had gotten out and left him inside.

He'd been there for what felt like hours before falling asleep. The shaking truck had woken him. Men were climbing back inside. They were still in gear, but the helmets and facemasks were off.

Why were they letting him see their faces? Did that mean he was a dead man? Or was this truly a legitimate police or military action?

Rich had nothing to hide. Nothing illegal, anyway. So, why had they torn his house apart? He tried to reason with them again. "Did you get the wrong house? Look, I won't raise any beef if it was a mistake. I just want to go home."

The men took their seats. Some were grinning at each other. Some looked tired. Others leaned back against the wall and closed their eyes. One of them glanced at his phone. Rich caught a glimpse of the screen. It was already noontime.

He thought back to being roused from bed. He'd seen the bedside clock while the cop, or whatever he was, had been yanking his arm. It had been five in the morning. Zero five hundred. They'd driven for a while, the truck had stopped wherever they were now, and an hour or two had passed before Rich fell asleep.

The truck jolted into motion. The diesel engine growled. He wished he knew what in the hell was going on, but for now, he had no choice but to go along for the ride.

The truck had a stiff suspension. It jostled him against the metal walls of his cage. The metal was cold and slick with his sweat and probably his urine. He was in constant discomfort and pain. He'd been out of the military so long that he'd lost the toughness required for his former line of work.

It was shameful, really. He hated to even think about what the others in his former cohort would think about him. All except one. The one who screwed him over. The one who was responsible for Rich's current condition.

He was angry all of a sudden. Furious. It was ridiculous, of course. He was shackled inside a metal cage going to only God knew where, and he was mad at something that happened years ago.

He pulled himself back to the present. *Think, Rich, think!* He'd once been good at something. He'd once been healthy and strong. He'd once been able to endure extreme discomfort and pain. He was barely a shell of his former self. A pathetic shadow of a man.

Rich channeled his anger at the past into the present. He needed to overcome his disabilities. He needed to find out what in the hell was going on. Just a year ago he'd been a man who'd given up.

Then he'd met someone. She was light and laughter where he was darkness and depression. Natalie had shown him he could have a future, but he had to choose it. Things had gone great until they hadn't.

There were times when darkness swallowed Rich whole. When he regretted every choice that led him to this moment. To his crippling injuries. To his crippling depression. To his anger at the people who should have saved him.

Natalie had brought him out of one such bout of depression. She'd done it a second time. The third time, she couldn't take it anymore. She said he had to want to help himself, that she couldn't be the only person in the room trying to lift him back up.

Rich hadn't blamed her. In fact, he'd been surprised she'd stuck around as long as she had. She was a damned good person. He didn't deserve her. Not now. Not ever. Not even if he met her before he'd been crippled.

She believed in him. Now he had to believe in himself. He had to find a way out of whatever this was. It was like he'd been taken prisoner again. Like he was being tortured mentally before they tied him to a metal chair in a room and tortured him physically.

Rich closed his eyes and took a deep breath. He did what he used to do before every mission and calmed his mind. Focused on exactly what he'd have to do to stay alive. He centered himself and gave it a moment to sink in.

He opened his eyes and studied the cage. There were scuffs in the metal. Scratches. It smelled faintly of bleach. There were so many scratches and marks that he concluded a lot of people had been in this very position before.

He ran his fingers along the metal walls, the metal bench, and every square inch he could reach with his hands behind his back. He was looking for anything that might have been accidentally left inside the cage. A sliver of metal or plastic that could help him out of the cuffs.

He found nothing. The cage was clean. The only dirt was what he'd brought inside on his body. The only filth was the urine he'd stained his boxers with after they tased him. It had been hours since then and he had to pee again. Did they expect him to go inside the cage?

Rich touched the waistband of the boxers. They were more like shorts, really, with drawstrings. He abruptly realized they were the answer. Not the drawstrings, but the tips. They were like shoestrings with hardened tips that kept the fabric from unfurling. But in this case the tips weren't plastic. They were metal.

But he had a problem. A big one. His hands were behind his back. The chain was long, so he had some room to maneuver, but not enough to reach the hand on his good arm around to the front where the drawstrings were.

He could stretch to a certain extent, but then his bad shoulder wouldn't move anymore. At least, it wouldn't move any further back. But it certainly could move a little to the front. He moved his right arm forward. The shoulder joint was stiffer than usual thanks to the abuse.

His left shoulder flexed just fine. It gave him enough slack to reach his right hand toward his crotch where the drawstrings hung. He found one. Grasped it. Inched it through his fingers until he found the metal tip.

The tip was round and too thick to do what he needed it to do. He'd have to reshape it. There was only one way to do that. He pulled on the drawstring using what little leverage he had. It resisted at first because the other tip caught on the edge of the hole where the string entered the waistband.

Rich tugged and it finally slipped inside the hole. He got just enough slack so it would reach his mouth, then leaned toward his right hand. His shoulder screamed with pain. He could hardly move it past a certain point.

He twisted sideways, used the cage wall to push his arm just a little further and felt the metal tip touch his lips. He bit the tip. Used his tongue and lips to pull it into his mouth. He got the metal between his rear molars and bit down hard.

He adjusted the position of the tip with his tongue and bit down repeatedly until the metal felt flat. It was hard to tell if it was the right size for the job, but there wasn't much else he could do.

This was something he could do in his sleep with a paperclip. He'd never tried it with a metal drawstring tip. A medium to small paperclip was already the perfect size to fit into the keyhole of a pair of handcuffs. The metal tip wasn't.

He felt the metal tip with his tongue. He adjusted his bite and put a slight curve in the metal. He touched it again with his tongue. It felt about right. Rich didn't know if he could do the next part. He couldn't move his right hand back very far.

Keeping the string clenched in his teeth, he tried to maneuver his left hand closer to his right one behind his back. He had enough flexibility with his left hand to touch the other metal cuff. It still wasn't enough to do what needed doing.

The cage was tiny. There was barely enough room to move. That was all he needed. He shifted to the right and got the handcuff chain under his butt. He did the same for the other side. The chain rattled and scraped against the cage but none of the men said anything about it.

He kept going. The chain was about ten inches long. It was much longer than the standard chain because it was intended for use with hand and leg shackles. Ten inches was just barely enough to work with, thanks to his bad shoulder, but he could make do.

He worked the chain past his butt and under his knees. This would be the hard part thanks to his bad knee. He could bend it just enough to sit down, but it wouldn't bend much further than that.

He bent over as far as he could. Raised his feet. The chain rattled on the metal. The man next to the cage banged a fist on it.

"Quiet down!" He banged again. "What in the hell are you doing in there? Playing with yourself?"

There was a round of laughter.

Rich got the chain under his feet. He sat up straight. The cuffs were in front of him now. He took a moment to catch his breath. He wasn't fat, but he wasn't lean and muscular anymore either.

The drawstring was still clenched in his teeth. He released it. It fell into his left hand. With the cuffs in front of him, what had been a nearly impossible chore became exponentially easier. Provided his improvised key worked of course.

Inside most cuffs are triple stranded ratchets. The key lifts the ratchets out of the way so the cuff can open. That's why handcuff keys are so simple in design. That was why Rich hoped a slightly bent piece of metal would do the trick as well as a paperclip.

He fit the flattened tip into the keyhole. Turned it sideways. The cuff fell open. Rich grinned. He wasn't even remotely free, but this small victory felt like a big one under the circumstances.

Hydraulics hissed. Brakes squealed. The truck slowed and grounded to a halt. The men stirred from their positions. All but three stood and left. One of those three opened the cage. He stared at the open cuff and at the metal drawstring tip in Rich's hand.

He burst into laughter. "You gotta see this."

The other two men crowded around and saw the same thing. They joined in the laughter.

The first guy got in a few words between laughs. "You planning on a big escape?"

"It's like Escape from Alcatraz!" another guy said.

"All right, Clint Eastwood." The first guy yanked him out of the box. "Let's get you somewhere more secure."

He and the others howled with laughter.

Rich was filled with impotent rage. Back before his injuries he could have taken all three of these men. He could have fought them all at once and won easily. Not because he was a martial arts expert, but because he knew how to fight like his life depended on it.

The first guy was lean and muscular. He was about five foot seven inches tall, give or take. Probably in his forties. The other two men were in good shape. They were tall and muscular, with bulging biceps and flat stomachs. They looked strong, but gym muscles weren't the same as the core strength you got from doing hard work all your life like Rich had.

Being young and in shape didn't matter if you didn't know how to street fight. Maybe these guys knew how to fight dirty. Maybe they didn't. Maybe they were overly reliant on their guns and having backup.

Rich could probably take the short one down, but certainly not the two body builder types. Maybe he could have taken them in his prime, but not with a bad shoulder and knee.

They were treating him like he was completely crippled. Like he belonged in a wheelchair. They didn't seem the least bit worried that he might be able to break free and overpower them. And they were right. He wasn't even remotely a threat to them.

They kept laughing and pulled him out of the truck. He saw where he was now, and it filled him with a mild sense of relief. He was at the Bickham police station. He wasn't being taken somewhere by nameless militants for execution.

This had been a police action. But that still didn't answer why police had stormed his home and brought him here.

They took him through the rear doors. Down a long hall to an interrogation room. Sat him down on a metal chair. The short guy slid the loose cuff under a metal loop on the top of the table then ratcheted it on Rich's free wrist with the practiced ease of someone who'd done it hundreds of times before.

He left the room and closed the door behind him. Moments later, a heavyset man walked inside. He looked Rich over and wrinkled his nose. "You reek. I should've had them hose you down first."

"Why am I here?" Rich said. "I haven't broken any laws."

"We can talk about that in a moment." The man sat on the edge of the table. He sat near Rich even though Rich had plenty of slack in his cuffs to jump up and grab him if he wanted to. The complete lack of fear told Rich something.

The man didn't fear him. He wasn't the least bit worried about Rich doing anything to him. If Rich had been an actual criminal, this man would have sat across the table from him where he couldn't reach him. Even with the injured shoulder, Rich could still do some damage if he wanted.

The man was dressed in plain clothes and didn't have a badge. He was either a detective or someone in administration. Rich was certain of it.

The man's next words confirmed it. "I'm Detective Raulerson of the Bickham Police Department. Now, you might be wondering why our men didn't identify themselves or read you your rights."

"I am very curious about that," Rich said.

"That's because you are not actually under arrest. You were removed from the premises for your own safety."

"Being tased and brutalized, then thrown into a metal cage for hours was supposed to keep me safe?"

"Yes."

"Then why am I in handcuffs?"

Raulerson stood from the table and pulled the other chair around. He sat in it. "We have certain procedures. We also wanted to make sure you were not complicit in any of the illegal activities happening in your home."

Rich's mouth dropped open. "I'm sorry, what illegal activities?"

"You are dating Natalie McGillis, correct?"

That question snapped Rich out of his confusion. "Huh? What does she have to do with this?"

"Answer the question, Mr. Polaski."

"I thought I wasn't being interrogated. I thought I was just here for my safety."

"You are not under arrest, that is correct."

"Okay, then I want a lawyer before I answer any questions."

"You are not a suspect in a crime. Therefore, you do not need a lawyer, nor is there a legal requirement for you to have one."

"It's my constitutional right!"

"Only if you've been arrested and accused of a crime." Raulerson tapped a finger on the table. "There's no harm in confirming that you dated this woman, is there? Or should we be looking deeper?"

"Yes, I dated her!" Rich's fists clenched. "But we broke up weeks ago."

"And her teenage son, Alex, regularly came over with her, correct?"

Rich remained quiet. He tried to see where this was going. He couldn't. Alex came over with Natalie a handful of times. He was a friendly kid. Awkward like most sixteen-year-olds. He usually sat on the couch and played games on his phone.

Was Natalie or Alex being accused of a crime? And if so, what did he have to do with it? Rich leaned back in his chair. "I'm not answering any more questions."

"That is your prerogative, Mr. Polaski. Since you don't wish to be cooperative, I will simply tell you what is going to happen."

Here it comes, Rich thought.

"We know that Alex has been storing and selling drugs out of your home."

Rich nearly bolted upright but the handcuffs stopped him. "Are you kidding me? There's no way! That kid is clean."

"I'm afraid he's not. He met an undercover police officer behind your house and tried to sell him cocaine laced with a dangerous amount of fentanyl. So much fentanyl that it would have killed whoever took it."

"You're lying." Rich shook his head. "That's impossible."

"I'm afraid it's true. And we have a written confession from him."

Rich was speechless. He felt like he'd crossed into the Twilight Zone. "Alex McGillis is a good kid. A clean kid. He would never sell drugs of any kind."

"We have a confession that states the contrary." Raulerson sighed. "The most troublesome part is that you apparently allowed this to go on with your implicit permission."

"I did no such thing. Hell, even if it had happened, I had no idea."

"Alex's statement would say otherwise." Raulerson stood and waved a hand dismissively. "It really doesn't matter. You're not being accused of anything nor are you under arrest. But we had a tip that some very dangerous individuals planned to come to your home tonight because they thought you were the reason Alex was arrested."

"Am I dreaming right now?" Rich shook his head. "I feel like I'm dreaming. This can't be real."

Raulerson kept talking like he hadn't heard him. "That was why we evacuated you. Apparently, Alex was storing drugs on your property, also with your implicit consent."

"I never consented to anything or anyone implicitly or otherwise!" Rich pounded a fist on the table. "Remove the handcuffs and let me out of here."

"Absolutely. We just need you to sign some paperwork first."

"I'm not signing anything."

"It's necessary to avoid long legal proceedings, I'm afraid." Raulerson shrugged. "I mean, you don't have to sign anything tonight, but you will certainly have to show up in court if you don't. And if we have to go through all that, then it's going to be a big pain in the ass for all of us."

"How about this?" Rich said. "How about you give me one tiny little clue, one itty bitty inkling as to what this is all about so I can figure out just how much money I'm going to sue you for because you violated my constitutional rights?"

"It's simple, really." Raulerson smiled condescendingly. "Your property was used in a crime. Your property must stand trial in a court of law. Since we have proof and a confession as to the guilt of your property, then the judge will have no choice but to allow us to take this property so it can no longer be used to commit crimes."

Rich's face flushed hot. "No way. This is illegal."

"I'm afraid it's perfectly legal, Mr. Polaski. Now, unless you want to also be charged as an accessory to drug dealing and as an accessory to manslaughter, then I suggest you sign the papers so you can remain a free man."

"Manslaughter?"

Raulerson feigned surprise. "Oh, didn't I tell you? One of Alex McGill's clients died because she didn't know her cocaine was laced with a lethal dose of fentanyl."

Rich wanted to kill the man. But then he'd just go to jail for attempted murder. He couldn't handle this, not in his current condition. He was going to need help.

And he knew just who to call.

Chapter 4

Carver was on a bus.

It was dirty and smelled like diesel and unwashed bodies. There was gum stuck to the back of the seat in front of him. A baby was crying. A little boy ran up and down the aisle slapping the seats as he ran.

Carver felt right at home.

He'd had it good for a while. Some might say too good. He'd had a nice new pickup registered to a fake entity. He'd had a duffel bag full of the best tools a man could want. Tools that were mostly, but not limited to, guns.

One had been a bullpup fifty caliber rifle. It was the kind of tool that you didn't need to use often, but when you did, it was because you needed to take down a helicopter. Unfortunately, the fifty cal was just a twisted hunk of metal along with his other guns and the pickup, thanks to a landslide.

Now he was down to just his Sig and his monocular. And that was all he really needed anyway. The rest was just icing on the cake. Icing that he wished he still had. On the upside, it certainly made traveling a little lighter.

Myrtle Beach was far behind him now. Twenty-two hours and nine hundred miles behind him to be exact. The bus had crossed over from Indiana and into Illinois not long after he woke up from a long nap.

Carver had decided it was too soon to be awake, so he managed to squeeze out another hour of sleep to pass the time and also because it was just good policy to be well rested before walking into an unknown situation.

He needed to be on his toes because the person he was going to see was on an NSA watchlist. Barry hadn't been able to tell him why Rich Polaski had caught the NSA's attention, but whatever the reason was, it couldn't be good.

It was good to know Liana was back in their good graces. Good to know she was watching out for Carver. He would have been just as happy not having the information she'd sent him because then he could have remained blissfully ignorant on the beach.

But once he knew Rich might be in trouble, he simply had no choice. He had to go and see if a former brother in arms needed help. Just like when he found out Cliff Barrows was in trouble. This wasn't quite the same, though. Rich would never call Carver for help no matter how dire the need.

Carver owed his life to Barrows a few times over, but he owed Rich even bigger. He wasn't sure it was a debt that could ever be repaid, but that wasn't why he was going. Responding to a former squad mate in need was necessary no matter the reason.

At least, that was what Rhodes taught him. He could tell that she never thought he'd actually help anyone. He couldn't blame her for feeling that way. Carver wasn't exactly the sentimental type. But he did have a sense of duty even if there wasn't that much sentiment behind it.

For him, it was more about logic. One day he might need someone's help. He didn't want to be the one to say he'd never come to someone else's aid for whatever reason. So, he just did it. That was the way it had to be even if the person he was helping didn't much like him.

The thrum of the diesel engine slowed and grew marginally quieter as the bus slowed. The brakes shrieked with metal-on-metal contact and the bus pulled into the station. Carver was already up and moving down the aisle. He almost made it to the front before the people there stood and got in his way.

The bus had stopped in the city square right in front of the town hall. It was a small, quaint town. It didn't look that much different from every other town he'd seen across the country. They all had their town squares, their town halls, and small mom and pop businesses in old red brick buildings.

The buildings here were old, but the white limestone gleamed brightly like it had been pressure washed. The grass in the square was neatly mown with a visible crisscross pattern. The dark tree bark in the flower beds looked fresh.

The sidewalks were stark white. Not a trace of stains anywhere on them. The flagpole in the middle of the square had an oversized American flag flapping in the breeze. A slightly smaller flag, blue with the black outline of a hawk on it hung just beneath it.

In front of the flagpole stood a large bronze statue of a man, also clean as a whistle. The man had a rifle over one shoulder and a hawk perched on his other arm. His clothing looked like something out of the eighteen hundreds. He was, no doubt, the city founder.

The downtown area was bustling. Carver walked down the sidewalk passing shop after shop full of people. The businesses, streets, and sidewalks were just as immaculate on this side of the road.

A man with a wire brush and a scraper was down on his hands and knees vigorously working on a stain in the sidewalk right near the crosswalk. It was just a small black blotch on an otherwise perfectly clean sidewalk, but the guy was going at it like it was life or death.

Carver felt a little relieved to finally find a clean town without homeless encampments all up and down the sidewalks. It was nice being able to walk without having to dodge drug addicts and human feces.

He found a burger restaurant next to an ice cream shop. Both had a fifties aesthetic to them, with chrome and red leather barstools, a laminate bar top, and black and white checkered vinyl flooring.

It was a little early for lunch, but Carver was hungry. He stepped inside and sat in a corner booth where he could see the door. An overly perky waitress bounced over to him, a big grin on her face.

"What can I get ya?"

"Burger, fries, and a vanilla milkshake."

"Coming right up!" She skipped away.

Carver noticed the other waitresses in the joint were aggressively friendly as well, all of them walking with a skip in their step. Their uniforms mirrored the fifties motif, as did their hairstyles and other personal accoutrements.

The dedication was impressive. Carver just hoped the food was as good as their attention to detail. While he was waiting, he checked the maps app on his burner phone and plugged in Rich's address.

Barry had given him Rich's phone number too, but Carver didn't think calling was the play here, especially if Rich was possibly under surveillance. Barry said there was no evidence Rich was being actively surveilled despite being on a watchlist.

Generally speaking, there were different levels of surveillance. The first and most basic was when an agency checked a person's social media footprint. The next level up was when they investigated things like financial documents and known associates.

Each level up increased the intrusion level. Each level up allowed the agency to dig a little deeper until the agency went into full stalker mode, watching and following the person day and night. Breaking into their house while they weren't home and searching it from top to bottom without leaving a trace of evidence they were ever there.

Barry didn't know which level Rich was at. He might simply be on a watchlist so the agency could keep basic tabs on him, or he might have his own personal field agent assigned to watch him closely.

If that was the case, Carver's appearance at Rich's home was sure to stir things up. It was going to send ripples up the chain of command. Someone was going to know that Carver was or had been on a watchlist as well.

They were going to wonder why in the hell Carver decided to go see Rich, a man he hadn't spoken with for years. Alarm bells would ring, and there would almost certainly be a response. This little town would have its population increased by a dozen or more NSA agents.

That wasn't how Carver wanted to start this visit. Ideally, he could find Rich out and about, but he wasn't sure how likely that was. Once upon a time, Rich had been a real outdoorsman. He loved fishing, he loved sports, and he was an avid biker.

That was almost certainly no longer the case. Barry had told him that Rich once owned a sporting goods store that failed after about a year, during which time his wife left him and took their two kids to Japan where she was originally from.

After that, Rich had lived off disability. He didn't get out much. He'd dated someone briefly but she left him. End of file.

The restaurant was filling up fast even though the clock had just struck eleven. Most of the booths were occupied before it was even eleven thirty. Apparently, everyone around here like to eat their lunch early.

A man took the booth in front of Carver and sat down with his back to him. He unfolded a newspaper and held it up in front of him. It looked small enough to be a local rag and not one from nearby Chicago. The small town headlines confirmed that theory.

Lost Dog Found

Bickham Glory Days Parade This Weekend

Walt's Barber Shop Celebrates 50 Years

Carver's food arrived. The burger was one of the best he'd had in a while. The milkshake was thick and not too sweet. The fries were nice and crispy. The place took its food as seriously as its 50s décor.

He was right in the middle of enjoying it when a pair of uniformed cops entered the restaurant. They stopped inside the door and looked around. One of them tapped the other's shoulder and pointed in Carver's direction.

They were both tall with wide shoulders and trim waistlines. Their uniforms were black with short-sleeved button-up shirts and slacks. The shirts fit them tight like they were tailor made to show off their muscles.

They certainly didn't have typical cop bodies—concave chests, bulging guts, and skinny extremities. They certainly seemed to think they looked good judging by the way they strutted in, arms half bent and held to the sides like they were too large to lay flat.

Carver sipped his milkshake and pretended not to notice them. The end of the bar was a few feet to his left. The hallway to the bathrooms was also just a few feet to his left. The emergency exit was at the end of the hallway.

The officers wore shiny metal nameplates on the left sides of their chests. The nameplates were gold with black writing. The cop on the left was Sutton. The one on the right was Archer. They looked like they could be brothers.

Sutton looked from Carver to the man with the newspaper and back to Carver. It wasn't the kind of look reserved for a suspect or person of interest. He seemed to be coming to an internal decision, but not one of great importance.

Sutton seemed to make up his mind and stopped in front of the guy with the newspaper. He put a finger on the top of the paper and tugged it down. The man flinched in surprise and looked up at the cop.

No words were exchanged at all. The man quickly folded his newspaper, stood, and took his coffee with him to the bar. The cops sat down in the now free booth. The waitress was already halfway to them by the time they took the seats.

She was smiling like her life depended on it, but the smile didn't reach her eyes. Her eyes looked scared. She poured them each a cup of coffee with an unsteady hand. She set the pot on her tray and licked her lips nervously. "What will you be having today, boys?"

Carver pretended to mind his own business. He stared at his phone, putting on the same zombielike gaze as most people mindlessly scrolling through social media. Archer, the cop facing him, glanced at him once, then looked at the waitress.

"The usual, Jen." Archer grinned lasciviously. Looked her up and down. "So, how's that situation with your boyfriend working out?"

Jen didn't seem to know how to answer. She wrote on her notepad and smiled nervously. "Oh, I think it'll work out."

"Probably won't." Archer's grin flattened. "What do you think, Brad?"

Sutton spread his arms out along the back of the seat. "I don't know. He's got some serious problems." Like his partner, he had a strong Chicagoan accent.

"Uh, I'll get your orders in." Jen backed away.

Archer grabbed her wrist and pulled her back. "You sure you don't want my help? We can get the charges dropped."

Jen was shaking now. "I—I just can't do what you want."

He released her. Shrugged. "Hey, I know how it is. Well, hopefully Tommy doesn't go to jail."

"I'll get your orders in." Jen hurried away.

The cops shared a laugh and started talking in low tones. Carver couldn't hear what they were saying. It didn't much matter to him what their topic of conversation was, so long as it wasn't about him.

He overheard bits and pieces. Heard the name of the other cop. It was Brian. Brian and Brad. Archer and Sutton. A cop couple made in cop heaven.

Carver finished his burger. He was about to raise his hand to get the waitresses' attention when he overheard another name. At first, he wasn't sure he'd heard right, but then he heard it again. *Polaski*.

Now Carver was interested. Real interested. He looked down at his phone with renewed fake interest and focused on the conversation. He picked up bits and pieces. Enough to realize that Rich was at the police station.

That didn't sound good.

The waitress picked up two plates from the counter and delivered them to the cops. Archer winked at her. She backed away from the table like prey unwilling to turn its back on a predator. "Anything else?"

"Nah, we're good." Sutton stared at her for a moment. "Just let us know if we can be of service, okay?"

"I will. Thanks."

Carver raised his hand to get her attention. "Check, please."

"Yes, sir. Just a moment." Jen hurried to the cash register. She returned a moment later and handed him a bill for nine bucks and some change.

Carver dug into his backpack and pulled out a twenty. "Keep the change."

"Thank you." A genuine smile crossed her face for an instant. She turned around and walked to the register.

Archer watched the transaction like a hawk. He seemed interested in the backpack, not Carver. Probably because it was a big backpack and it was full to bursting. Carver had stuffed everything he owned into it.

He had two changes of clothing, toothpaste, a toothbrush, his Sig, magazines, and ammo, and about twenty-five grand in cash. He also had a USB drive with cryptocurrency worth another twenty grand or so.

Carver regretted cashing out so much crypto, mainly because it was a pain to carry. But he also wanted plenty of cash on hand in case of emergency. There were so-called cryptocurrency ATMs scattered around the country, but he didn't want to have to count on finding one just to be liquid.

He got up. Went to the restroom.

Archer walked in when Carver was washing his hands. He looked Carver over. "New in town?"

Carver dried his hands. "Yep."

Archer grunted. "You look like a vagrant." He made a show of sniffing the air. "Smell like one too."

"You got a problem with vagrants?"

"We keep our streets clean."

Carver nodded. "I can see that. Cleanest town I've seen in a while."

"We like to keep it that way. First sign of a tent on a sidewalk in these parts gets you community service."

"That's one way to manage the homeless." Carver headed for the door.

Archer gripped his wrist. "What's in the backpack?"

Carver stared at the cop's hand. He resisted the urge to break it. He moved his eyes up to meet Archer's. "Is there a reason you're touching me?"

"I asked you a question, boy."

"One that I don't have to answer." Carver turned to face him dead on. He smiled. "Now, if that will be all, officer, I'll be on my way."

Archer released his hand. Smiled back. "Yeah, you get on your way."

Carver turned his back on the other man. Opened the door and left. He continued toward the front.

Jen passed him going the other way and smiled brightly. "Thank you, sir. Have a great day."

"You too." Carver pushed through the door and stepped onto the sidewalk. He hadn't been in the town more than an hour and while it looked bright and shiny on the surface, it was already obvious that there was something dark lurking beneath the surface.

Maybe Officers Archer and Sutton were just dark spots in an otherwise sparkly clean community. Maybe they were representative of it. It was hard to know for sure. Hopefully he wouldn't be around long enough to find out.

Chapter 5

Carver had to go to the police department.

He didn't want to go there, but from what little he'd overheard of Archer and Sutton's conversation, that was where Rich was. Rich had talked about becoming a cop after retiring from the SEALs. Maybe that was why he was there.

Rich, unfortunately, hadn't retired from the SEALs. They'd retired him. Put him on the permanent disabled list, so to speak. Carver didn't know all the details, but it hadn't been a very clean break.

Despite those injuries, Rich could probably get a job as a cop. Maybe years of physical therapy had fixed his serious issues. Maybe he was chasing down criminals right at this very moment, his bad knee no longer a problem.

Those thoughts renewed Carver's curiosity. Why would Rich be on an NSA watchlist? He was a disabled civilian, not a member of a highly trained special forces unit. Maybe the only reason was because he'd been in the same cohort as Carver. Maybe everyone in his former cohort was on a watchlist.

Carver walked to the edge of the sidewalk. The town hall and town square were right across Main Street from a long line of shops and stores. A catholic church dominated the northern skyline, its gray stone towers rising far above anything else in the vicinity.

The town hall was as tall as the main church building, excluding the towers. It and the neighboring courthouse had been built with white stone, probably limestone. They were the kind of grand buildings you'd expect to find in a big city, not a small town like this.

The buildings' architectural roots were from France. Carver knew that because during a long layover in Paris, Rhodes had taken him on a tour and schooled him in Second Empire design. She knew so much about it not because she loved architecture but because she studied old building designs to learn about their weaknesses.

Stately old buildings were commonplace in many European countries, and most of them hadn't been upgraded to the latest security standards. From Rhodes' perspective, that made them easier to compromise when the time came.

Apparently, Second Empire architecture had been a big influence on the founders of Bickham, Illinois. They certainly hadn't spared any expense on government buildings. It was as if they'd tried to outdo nearby Chicago.

The police station shared the same basic design as the town hall, but the main doorway wasn't arched. There was a large granite statue of an eagle in front of the doors. Maybe it was a hawk. Carver didn't know for sure. The bird of prey was swooping down, talons outstretched as if about to snatch prey from the ground.

A placard answered Carver's question about what kind of bird it was. It was a golden eagle. A very particular golden eagle. The statue was made in honor of Nathan Bickham's hunting eagle, Atos.

Carver couldn't complain about the condition of Bickham. It was clean, the buildings were grand, and the burgers were second to none. It looked like a good place to live so long as you didn't have to deal with Officers Archer and Sutton.

Hopefully they were the exceptions and not the rule.

He pushed through the heavy brass doors of the police station and entered a cavernous lobby with a uniformed policewoman sitting at a large granite counter. She wasn't the typical female officer. This woman looked like a supermodel dressed up as a cop.

She had long blonde hair, striking blue eyes, and her hair and makeup were done to perfection. A welcoming smile spread across her face. "Hello, sir. How may I help you?" She had a foreign accent. Russian or Ukrainian. Carver couldn't quite pinpoint it.

"Yeah, I'm looking for a friend. I think he works here." Carver looked for a nametag, but she wasn't wearing one and there wasn't a placard on her desk either.

"What's his name, sir?"

"Rich Polaski."

Her smile faltered. "He's an officer?"

"Maybe." Carver shrugged. "I'm not sure."

"One moment, please." She tapped on her computer. She stared at the monitor for a moment. Frowned. "I'm sorry, sir, he doesn't work here."

"Where are you from?" Carver said. "Russia?"

Her smile returned. "Sorry, sir, I'm not allowed to discuss personal matters. What I can tell you is that Rich Polaski does not work here."

"Okay, but is he here in the building? Officer Sutton said he was."

"Oh. Are you a family member?"

"Yes."

"Can you wait, please? I think someone else will need to help you." She picked up her phone and dialed. "Detective Raulerson, may I request your help with someone?" She nodded a couple times as the person on the other end spoke. She nodded and replied. "Rich Polaski."

She covered the microphone and turned to Carver. "I'm sorry, what was your name?"

"Bert Polaski."

She repeated the name into the phone. Nodded. "Thank you, sir." She hung up. "The detective will be out shortly."

"What's your name?" Carver asked.

"I'm sorry, sir, but I'm not allowed to discuss personal matters."

"You're a police officer but you can't share your name?" Carver raised an eyebrow. "How about a badge number?"

"Sir, I'm not a police officer. I'm a receptionist and this is simply my uniform." She motioned toward a large wooden door. The brass placard next to it was engraved with the words *Waiting Room*. "Please go through the door and wait inside."

Carver did as he was told. There was a large wood-paneled room on the other side. It smelled strongly of wood oil that had soaked deep into the hardwood over a hundred years of cleanings.

There were rows of long wooden pews in the middle of the room. There was another door in the back of the room. This one was black steel and secured with a keypad and biometric lock. The frame was steel too. The modern door looked out of place in the otherwise antiquated building.

Carver didn't bother sitting down. He had a feeling the detective would be down quickly. Rich did have a brother named Bert. Carver had met him at a cookout at Joe Donnely's house. They'd just returned from a successful search and rescue and spirits were high.

Carver's thoughts drifted back to that day. It felt like a lifetime ago and yesterday all at the same time.

###

Carver opened the wooden gate in the fence and stepped into Joe's small backyard. Most of the cohort was there. Joe's first wife was mingling with the other wives at a picnic table. Little kids were running around wildly. The older kids were tossing a Nerf football.

Joe was at the grill, a beer in hand as he flipped the burgers. He saw Carver and nodded. "Glad you could make it." He held a beer out to Carver.

"It felt like an order." Carver took the beer and twisted off the top.

"You're supposed to use a bottle opener with that."

"Okay." Carver tossed the lid in the trashcan and took a sip of beer. He scanned the area. Took in all the people, their faces, their activities.

"They're not here to kill you, Carver." Joe grinned. "You're not on a mission."

Carver didn't know what to say. "Sorry. I'm not used to family gatherings."

"You're part of a family now." Joe flipped the burgers on the grill. "I know you didn't form any meaningful attachments before you were recruited into the SEALs but it's vital that you do so now."

"Why?"

"Because family looks out for each other. It doesn't matter how good you are if you don't treat every man here like a brother, and by extension, every one of their family members as one of your own." He regarded Carver seriously. "You understand?"

"In theory." Carver's parents had taught him that independence was the only way to survive. That depending on others was a mistake, even if they were family. They'd made sure to beat that into his body and mind.

"Your recruitment was unusual," Joe said. "You didn't even apply."

"No." Carver sipped his beer. He tried to relax his guard but couldn't stop watching every point of entry and every movement of everyone there. *Never relax your guard. Assume you are always in danger.* That was his father's advice.

"You were approached and actively recruited?"

Carver nodded. "They said I caught their attention because of the USS Turing incident."

"You rescued a dozen trapped sailors."

"Something like that. I just pried open a stuck door."

"There was an engine explosion, and the ship was sinking. You swam into the underwater sections of the ship to reach the door and got it open with an underwater torch and fire axe." Joe raised an eyebrow. "That's more than just prying open a stuck door."

"There was someone inside that I didn't want to die." Carver shrugged. "Simple as that."

"So, you do understand personal connections."

"Of course." Carver forced himself to stop watching the others. "I'll do what I'm told. I'll protect everyone in my squad. I don't need to pretend that they're family."

"Who was it that you didn't want to die?"

"I'd rather not say."

A half smile crossed Joe's face. "It was a woman, wasn't it?"

"Yes, sir."

Joe laughed. "There are no women on this team, Carver."

"Unfortunately." Carver nodded at the burgers. "Can I get mine medium?"

"Yep." Joe took one off the grill and put it on a plate.

"Hey, Joe!" Rich entered the backyard flanked by a slightly taller and younger version of him along with his wife and two daughters.

"Polaski." Joe raised his beer toward him. "Better late than never?"

"It's my fault." Rich's wife, Yuki, grinned. "I took too long to get ready." She had a noticeable Japanese accent.

"I'll accept that excuse," Joe said.

Rich introduced the man with him. "This is my brother, Bert."

"Nice to meet you." Joe shook his hand.

Rich nodded at Carver but didn't offer to shake his hand. "Carver."

"Polaski." Carver likewise didn't offer his hand.

Bert studied Carver like he'd been told something about him and was wondering if it was true. Yuki ignored Carver altogether and took the girls to play with the other kids. Rich and Bert walked over to the other men who were standing around the beer cooler.

"That's the kind of cold reception you'll keep getting until you learn to treat your squad mates like brothers." Joe tapped Carver on the chest. "You have to feel it here. Otherwise, they'll know it's not genuine."

"I don't know that I can ever feel it, but I'll do everything in my power to make sure everyone returns home safe." Carver took the plate with his burger. "If that's not good enough, I understand."

"You do good work. You do what you're told. You do it by the numbers." Joe put a hand on Carver's shoulder. "We've just got to work on your personality, son." He smiled to soften the blow. "I think we can accomplish that."

Carver smiled back. It was a genuine smile because he liked Joe. He couldn't help but look up to the man. A small part of him wanted to think of him as the kind of father figure he'd seen in television shows as a kid.

But Joe wasn't that. He was the team leader. A Navy SEAL. He wasn't here to coddle anyone. He was here to squeeze the absolute best out of everyone under his command. Carver had to keep that firmly in mind no matter how he felt.

Carver looked at the other team members. They were in a tight circle, laughing and talking. A couple of them, including Rich, turned to look at Carver. They stared right at him unapologetically, not even pretending they were looking at something else.

They turned back toward each other and kept talking. They'd all applied to be in the SEALs. They'd all worked their asses off to make the cut. Carver hadn't been given any breaks. He'd worked as hard as the next man to earn a spot. But they assumed otherwise because he'd been recruited.

Some thought Carver had received preferential treatment. Many didn't like that he didn't joke and pal around with them. That he didn't treat them like brothers in arms. Carver couldn't blame them.

Emotions were powerful things. His parents taught him how to take advantage of emotional weaknesses and use them against others. Now he had to figure out how to display genuine emotions, so he'd be accepted into this family. It was an uphill battle, but he'd figure it out.

One day.

###

The steel door clanked open, jerking Carver back to the present. A heavyset man with a visible paunch stepped into the waiting room and looked at him. "Bert Polaski?" The steel door shut by itself behind him.

"Yep." Carver stood.

"I'm Detective Raulerson." He stepped into the room and extended a hand.

Carver shook it. "Where's Rich?"

"Your brother got himself into a bit of trouble." Raulerson looked Carver up and down. He was trying to find the resemblance to Rich. Trying to understand how a much shorter guy with completely different features was related to the man in front of him.

"I'd like to see him."

"We're almost finished processing the paperwork and then we'll send him right out." Raulerson pursed his lips. "Can I see some identification?"

"My wallet got stolen."

He looked surprised. "In this town?"

"No. New York."

His lips curled in disgust. "No surprise there. Scum of the earth live in that cesspool of a city. We don't play that game here in Bickham. If you break the rules, you do community service."

"Even for felonies?"

"It depends on the felony." Raulerson shrugged. "Either way, you'll work it off with community service. The only difference is you might have armed guards watching you."

Carver raised an eyebrow. "Like a chain gang?"

"Exactly. Room and board aren't free in these parts. You've got to work for it." Raulerson nodded at Carver's backpack. "What's in there?"

"Clothing. I travel light."

"I see." Raulerson checked his watch. "We'll send him out in a few minutes, and you can take him somewhere."

"Somewhere? As in home?"

"I'll let Mr. Polaski explain his situation." Raulerson went to the keypad and tapped his security badge against it. The lock buzzed and a magnet released. He put his shoulder on the door, pushed it open, and stepped through. The door damper eased the big slab of metal shut.

Carver timed it. Ten seconds from halfway open to fully closed. He could get a foot into it easily before it closed. Not that he needed to do that right now, but it was good to know. The real question was what trouble had Rich gotten himself into?

His plans for becoming a cop hadn't panned out, so what was he doing now? Resorting to a life of crime? Living off disability and getting tossed into jail for being drunk and disorderly? It wasn't any of Carver's business.

But it sure as hell might make things a lot more complicated while he was here.

Chapter 6

Carver didn't like the way this was going.

What kind of trouble was Rich in? Was Carver going to have to deal with something more than just telling Rich about the watchlist? Hopefully not. This wasn't going to be a pleasant visit no matter which way you cut it.

There was a coffee machine at the front of the room. It was one of those fancy types with the little cups. Paper cups were stacked neatly upside down in a plastic organizer next to the machine.

The small containers of coffee were organized by flavor next to the paper cups. There were wooden stirring sticks, various flavors of creamer, and various sweeteners. There was a mason jar next to the organizer. It was half-full of change and dollar bills. A small, printed placard next to it said, *Coffee is free but donations are welcome!*

Carver scooped the spare change out of his pocket and dropped it in the jar. He picked up the pitcher of water next to the machine and poured it to the fill line. He chose a dark-roasted coffee and set it into the socket, then started the machine.

The machine filled the cup within a few seconds. Carver sat down on the front pew and drank the coffee. He considered what he'd say to Rich. Imagined Rich's response. Probably surprise followed quickly by anger.

Carver finished the coffee and made more. He didn't like the way the machine brewed coffee. He preferred making a big pot all at once. Maybe that was wasteful. Maybe this was the new improved way to make coffee. Maybe, but he doubted it.

Thirty minutes passed and Carver began to wonder just how soon Rich would be released. He looked at the camera in the upper right corner of the room and wondered if there was someone on the other side watching him.

There didn't seem to be a way to request an update. The metal door didn't have a doorbell or chime. There was no hardwired phone in the room. It looked like he'd have to return to the receptionist and request Raulerson again.

There was another possibility. Maybe Raulerson told Rich his brother, Bert, was in the waiting room. Rich would have been surprised. He would have asked for a description of the man waiting on him.

Rich would be confused upon hearing the description. He might immediately know it was Carver. Then again, the possibility of Carver visiting him was probably so remote that Rich wouldn't even consider the possibility.

Either way, there were other things Carver could be doing besides sitting in the waiting room. He got up and walked to the door. Opened it. He stepped back into the main lobby. Walked toward the receptionist. Officers Sutton and Archer were talking to her.

The officers were grinning. Flashing their teeth. Leaning on the counter and talking in low tones to the woman. Her body language spoke volumes. The attention was clearly unwanted. She leaned back in her seat, hands clasped in her lap, an uneasy smile on her face.

Carver walked around the large lobby. He noted all the cameras. Noted the heavy metal doors guarding access in the back of the room. The place was locked down tighter than a bank. Even if he could unlock the doors, there was no way past without being noticed by the cameras.

The cops had lanyards with security badges on them. That was how they got into and out of the secure parts of the station. It was normal practice in big police stations, but it was surprising to see this level of security in a small town like this. Bypassing it would be difficult without one of those badges.

Not that it mattered. He had no reason to want to get through the doors. The observation was merely force of habit. He decided to go outside and take a walk. Rich probably wasn't being released anytime soon, and Carver didn't want to risk Rich outing him as an imposter to the detective.

Archer seemed to register that someone else was in the lobby with them. He looked up from the receptionist and blinked when he saw Carver. "What are you doing here?"

Sutton straightened and stiffened. "We thought you was just passing through."

"I am." Carver walked toward the front door. "Just touring downtown for the architecture."

"Yeah?" Archer narrowed his eyes. "We can show you the beautiful architecture of the jail cells if you keep loitering."

Carver kept walking to the front door. Judging from the way these two had spoken with the waitress, these two officers seemed to think they were something special. They seemed to think they could exchange favors to help someone out of a legal jam.

The way Archer had questioned Carver in the bathroom said a lot as well. These two felt like they could do whatever they wanted. It was best not to engage with them any more than was necessary, which was to say not at all.

Carver pushed through the exit and went back out on the sidewalk. He crossed the street and studied the police station. There were cameras on the corners and a camera over the entrance. He walked down the sidewalk and noted that the courthouse and town hall had cameras in the same locations.

There were cameras every few feet mounted on the buildings on his side of the street as well. He'd seen them earlier, but hadn't walked far enough to realize just how many there were. Carver kept walking and kept counting.

The sidewalks were relatively busy for a small town. People neatly parallel parked their cars along the streets. They visited the hardware store, the clothing shops, and the other mom and pop shops as if they had nowhere else to go to buy things.

Carver walked the grid of side streets connected to Main and found cameras on the corners of most buildings and cameras in the back alleys behind the buildings. They were all the same make and model. Probably all installed by the city.

Maybe that was why the city was so squeaky clean. Everyone knew they were being watched and judged and stayed on their best behavior. The fact that the citizenry allowed such a violation of privacy said volumes either about them or their local government.

Carver was itching to get out of town, but he had to warn Rich first. If the NSA's facial recognition system was tied into the city cameras, then they were going to light him up like a beacon. In fact, they probably already had. That was probably how Barry knew where to find Rich in the first place.

The town square, town hall, courthouse, and police station occupied four city blocks along Main Street. Each building sat on a large plot of land with plenty of room between the next building.

A tall stone wall and iron gates guarded the rear of the government buildings. There were cameras mounted on all the corners and above the gates. There were scanners above the gates for vehicles with barcodes on the windshields and keypads for cars that didn't.

The city center had more security than some military bases. It certainly had more security than even larger cities like Chicago. This kind of infrastructure required money. A lot of money. The taxes had to be sky-high in this town.

Carver walked all the way to the Catholic church at the end of Main Street. It was a big building, spanning several blocks all on its own. There was an equally large parking lot in the back. A kids' playground. A long annex that looked slightly newer than the rest of the building.

There were no walls or gates or cameras guarding it. It seemed the church relied on a higher power to protect it from bad actors. It also marked the end of the downtown area. The neatly laid grid of streets beyond the church were residential.

The downtown streets had names, probably the surnames of important people in the city's history. The streets on the north side in the residential area were numbered, First street, Second Street, and so on.

The whole city was so neatly organized that it raised the hairs on Carver's neck. It was just too neat. Too organized. Too squeaky clean. Maybe it was the perfect city. Carver doubted it. Nothing was perfect, and the harder people tried to make something perfect, the worse it got. That was just life.

He headed back toward the police station. The sooner he was done with Rich, the sooner he could get out of town. Hopefully Archer and Sutton were gone from the lobby. He didn't want to encounter them again if he could help it.

He knew their type all too well. They were the kind of men who preened for an hour in the mirror before stepping out of the door. They were the kind of men who thought women should worship them.

They were also probably steroid users judging from the thickness of their jawlines and their aggressiveness. They didn't have facial acne, but their backs might be dotted with it. Carver preferred not to find out.

He pushed through the doors and nearly ran into a man on the other side. The man was wearing what could only be described as a paper jumpsuit. It looked like the sort of thing a painter might wear over his clothing to protect it.

The man in the jumpsuit was none other than the man he'd come looking for, Rich Polaski. Rich was standing alone in the lobby, a miserable look on his face. The receptionist was politely ignoring his presence.

Rich saw Carver. His gaze hardened, but he said nothing. He limped toward Carver. Paused to stare up at him for a moment. Pushed past him through the door. Carver followed him outside. It was a cold reception which was a lot better than what Carver had expected in the first place.

"Who told you?" Rich said.

"Told me what?"

"That I needed help."

Carver paced alongside him. "I'm not here because you're in trouble with the law. I'm here for another reason."

Rich winced and stopped to massage his knee. "I'm beat, I'm starving, and I got nowhere to go."

"What happened?"

"Hell if I know." Rich stared at the burger joint across the road. "You have money?"

"Yep."

"Good." Rich walked to the end of the curb and stepped into the crosswalk. The cars stopped immediately to let him cross.

Carver followed behind him. His nostrils flared. There were no two ways about it. Rich stank to high heaven. He smelled like he'd soiled himself and hadn't showered in a day. "Why don't we get you cleaned up first?"

Rich stopped. Sniffed his armpits. He grimaced. "I don't have any money."

"I'll get you something to go, okay?" Carver nodded at the menu posted on the inside of the restaurant's window. "What do you want?"

"Burger, fries, a large strawberry milkshake."

"Okay, wait here." Carver stepped inside and went to the counter.

Jen the waitress walked to him, a bright smile on her face. "Back already?"

"I need to place a to-go order."

"Absolutely. What'll you have, sir?"

Carver told her. He paid in cash.

"I'll have it out to you right away, sir." She stuck the check on a revolving device in front of the kitchen window, then came back to the cash register. The lunch crowd had died down, but half of the booths were still occupied.

"Looks like this downtown does good business," Carver said. "Most mom-and-pop stores don't do well this day and age."

"Yeah, we just really believe in supporting our local businesses, you know?" Jen smiled. "I hope you enjoy your visit here!" She hurried away and into the kitchen as if talking to a stranger was the last thing she wanted to do.

Carver glanced out the window and saw Rich sitting on a bench. A woman with two children wrinkled her nose and made a face when she saw him. She gripped her children's hands and hurried away.

Rich was too busy staring at the ground to notice. He looked completely defeated. Like he'd just given up on doing anything.

Carver checked the maps app on his burner phone and located motels in the vicinity. There was one in the downtown area, but he preferred to get as far away from downtown as possible. He still didn't understand how Rich had nowhere to go, but figured he'd find out soon enough.

Jen brought him a bag with the food. "Here it is sir!" She set it on the counter in front of him and hurried away as if worried Carver might talk to her again.

Carver took the food. He went outside and handed it to Rich. "I found a motel about half a mile away. Can you walk?"

Rich opened the bag and devoured the hamburger without saying a word. He finished it off in less than five minutes. He wiped his face with the back of his hand, smearing mustard and ketchup. He put the burger wrapper into a garbage can then ate fries straight from the bag.

Carver waited for a response, but Rich took a long draw off his milkshake and didn't say anything. Carver figured he might as well tell Rich why he was here, give him some money for a hotel room, and take off.

"Yeah, I can walk." Rich rose to his feet with a groan. "Let's go."

Carver started walking. Rich hobbled along next to him, his face screwed up in pain. They covered a couple of city blocks before Rich sat down on another bench to rest.

He looked up at Carver. "I would apologize for the inconvenience, but not to you."

"Understood." Carver remained standing upwind of Rich. There was no reason to smell his rancid body odor if he had a choice in the matter.

A black Dodge Challenger police interceptor turned the corner and cruised toward them at a leisurely pace. It had an armor-plated grill guard over the radiator, a low-profile LED light bar, and wide fenders to accommodate the beefy tires.

There was a gold star on the driver's door with the words Bickham PD arching over the top of it in white letters. It was the sharpest looking police interceptor Carver had seen, and it looked like it was built to survive a war zone.

The interceptor slowed and stopped at the curb next to them. The window rolled down. A cop that wasn't Archer or Sutton took off his mirrored sunglasses and looked at Carver for a moment, before dragging his gaze over to Rich.

"I got reports of a homeless man stinking up downtown." The cop stared at Rich. "I suggest you get a move on before you end up doing community service."

Rich stared blankly at the officer while eating his French fries and drinking his milkshake.

"I'm talking to you." The officer opened his door and got out. He was certainly no Archer or Sutton, but he wasn't fat either. He was about five foot seven inches, slim, and athletic. His uniform was neat but didn't look custom fitted.

"My friend's had a long day," Carver said. "I'm taking him someplace to get cleaned up."

"You one of those homeless advocates?" The cop stepped onto the sidewalk downwind of Rich and gagged. "Good lord you stink!"

"Detective Raulerson wouldn't let me take a shower," Rich said.

"Ah, you're the ten eighty-four from last night." The cop stepped away from Rich. "If you need assistance in the short term, the church has a program for that." He stepped into the street just a few feet in front of an approaching vehicle.

The car screeched to a halt. He stopped in the road and stared at the driver. Pursed his lips as if considering something. The driver's eyes widened in fear. He rolled down his window. "Officer, I'm so sorry. I didn't see you there. It's completely my fault!"

The cop stared at him for a moment longer, then walked to the driver's window. "I'll let you off with a warning this time, but you need to be more alert."

"Yes, sir! Thank you, sir!"

"All right, go." The cop stepped away and the driver slowly eased the car down the road, as if afraid to go faster than ten miles per hour.

The cop leaned inside his car's window. He retrieved something and turned around, a business card pinched between his thumb and forefinger. He handed it to Carver. "Get your friend some help, but most importantly, get him off the street."

Carvers studied the metal nameplate on the cop's uniform. He looked at the card. It had an address and a phone number for a charity. "Thank you, Officer Palmer. I'll do that."

The cop nodded. "Okay, time to go."

Rich pushed to his feet. He didn't say a word. He just started walking. Carver plugged the charity address into the maps app. It was connected to the Bickham Catholic Church, but it was about a mile outside of town.

Clearly, they didn't want charity cases wandering the city streets.

The cop leaned against his car and continued to watch them even though his vehicle was blocking the lane. Cars didn't try going around him. They slowed and stopped, the drivers patiently waiting until the cop finally got back into his car and started driving.

The cop didn't seem ready to take Carver at his word and paced slowly behind them, stalking them until they reached the city limits. Then he pulled a hard U-turn, nearly causing a wreck because of the vehicles slowly pacing behind him.

Carver had seen enough in his short time in Bickham to know that something here was off. Way off. And the best thing he could do was crystal clear.

Get the hell out of this town and stay out.

Chapter 7

Nadia Garcia couldn't take it anymore.

She'd lost everything. Her house, her car, her livelihood, all gone in the blink of an eye. And it had all happened thanks to her horrible excuse for a brother.

He'd begged, borrowed, and stolen from her. He'd somehow gotten into her bank account and started withdrawing money. He'd done it in small amounts at first, then taken one of her paychecks all at once to pay off gambling debts.

Nadia had cancelled all her bank cards. She'd changed her passwords. Done everything she could to make sure he couldn't access anything again. She even went to the police and begged them to arrest her brother.

Not just because he'd stolen from her, but because he was going to get himself killed. She hated that she still remembered him as the innocent little brother. The little guy she helped her mother raise after Dad died.

Little innocent Daniel. The light of hers and her mom's lives had turned into a complete nightmare once he started high school. He'd fallen in with the wrong crowd and made nothing but bad choices since then.

The police told Nadia that they couldn't arrest Daniel. They had no proof he'd done anything wrong and being in debt to bookies wasn't a crime. Unless she could prove that he was the one who'd taken her entire paycheck from the bank without her permission, they couldn't do anything.

Nadia already lived from paycheck to paycheck. She couldn't afford to lose that money. She missed a house payment. She couldn't get a loan to cover the cost, and the bank wouldn't work with her to help.

She spoke to her boss. Asked for as much overtime as he could give her. She was already working eight-hour shifts from four in the morning to noontime providing armed security for downtown Chicago businesses. She requested to ride shotgun for the dayshift in their armored transport division.

Her boss told her she wasn't qualified and that he couldn't give her more than a couple of hours' overtime here and there because the company was already fully staffed and running an optimal load.

Desperate, she'd taken side jobs during the day, patrolling a small drug store in Chicago that was experiencing high levels of shoplifting. It wasn't much, but she was slowly lifting herself out of the hole Daniel had dug for her.

Then the cops stormed her house early one morning. They raided Daniel's bedroom. Uncovered a load of illegal weapons and evidence that he'd been using the basement to house an illegal gambling operation.

Nadia couldn't believe it. While she'd been working herself to the bone, Daniel had turned her home into a casino. It had all been going on under her nose. Daniel told her he'd done it at the request of his bookie to help pay off debts.

The Allenton Police had locked down her home. They'd confiscated everything. Then they'd taken her house to court and confiscated it under civil forfeiture laws. She tried getting a public defender to help her but none of them could.

Because Nadia wasn't the one on trial. Her house was, along with all of her material possessions. Everything had been auctioned off except for some few personal items she'd been permitted to keep.

All the proceeds had gone to pay for the city's legal bills. And her brother? He was still walking free. He hadn't seen a single day inside a jail cell. And his debt with the bookie was considered satisfied.

Nadia lived out of her car now. She bathed at the local YMCA. On the upside, she no longer had a mortgage to worry about. But it felt like it was only a matter of time before her employer found out about her legal issues and fired her.

Her employer ran annual criminal background checks on all employees. As a security company, it couldn't afford to hire people who might be compromised. Nadia's background check was due in two months. After that, she'd probably be out of a job.

Now Nadia was staring at a dark future. An abyss with no bottom. She didn't know what to do with herself.

Her phone rang, startling her out of her dark memories. She looked at the caller ID and scowled. She didn't want to answer, but she did anyway.

"Hey Nads. How are you?"

"What do you want, Lief?"

He sighed. "You know why I'm calling. Child support is due at the first of the month and it's the fourth."

"I don't have the money."

Lief huffed. "Look, it's not my fault you keep that loser brother of yours around. You're already behind four payments, and that was enough for me to convince the judge that your wages should be garnished."

"You can't garnish my wages!" Nadia's face burned with anger. "Only in this world could a deadbeat like you get custody of the kids!"

"I got full custody because you're a bad mother. The judge agreed that you created an unsafe home environment. And you're the deadbeat who's not paying child support." Lief blew out a breath. "You're a real piece of work, Nads, you know that?"

"I told you never to call me that again."

"It's a free country, Nads. I can call you what I want."

Nadia put a hand on her gun. She imagined showing up to Lief's house that she helped pay for. Imagined knocking on the door. Imagined his surprised look when he opened it and found a gun in his face. She could pull the trigger, no doubt about it.

Lief kept rambling. "You're also behind on alimony payments. I'm sick of having to call you every damned month only to hear another excuse. Get a better job so you can pay me!"

Nadia ended the call. She resisted the urge to hurl her phone onto the floor. But she couldn't afford to make a scene. She couldn't afford to show her rage. Her side job at the pharmacy might be the only job she had left once her primary employer found out about her home being seized for illegal activities.

The pharmacy paid her as a consultant. They paid her directly and gave her a 1099 form each year. Lief wouldn't be able to touch that income. But there was nothing she could do to keep a judge from garnishing her wages with Bark Security Services.

She had to figure out how to handle this.

"Nadia?"

Nadia blinked out of her thoughts and saw a man standing right in front of her. "Mr. Grimes?"

"Nadia, I need to talk to you in my office, please." Mr. Grimes motioned her to follow.

The tone of his voice told her this wasn't going to be a positive conversation. "Sir, what's this about?"

"I'd prefer to have this conversation in private."

The customers waiting in the checkout line watched them, eager to see drama unfold in front of them. A girl even took her phone out and started recording.

Nadia swallowed her anger and nodded. "Sure, let's go."

Mr. Grimes walked toward the back. He walked with a slight limp because he'd tried to stop a shoplifter himself before hiring Nadia. The shoplifter had been a drug addict and a repeat violent offender.

The shoplifter had punched Mr. Grimes so hard he'd nearly knocked him out. Then he'd stomped on his knee, dislocating it and cracking a bone. That had been enough to convince Mr. Grimes to hire armed security but he still had the limp to remind him.

Mr. Grimes punched a code into a keypad, and they entered the employees' only area. He punched another code into another keypad, and they entered his office. He turned on the light and closed the door.

Nadia didn't wait for him to speak. "Are you firing me, sir?"

He turned toward her. Frowned. "Not exactly, Nadia, although I did want to bring up a couple of things. First, I was contacted by someone who let me know about your legal troubles. They told me your home had been taken along with many of your possessions due to your home being used for illegal purposes."

Her mouth dropped open. "Who told you that?"

"They didn't give a name, but I was under the impression it was someone with the police." He shook his head. "It sounds like a horrible mess."

"My brother used my home for illegal activities without my knowledge. Please believe that I would never do such a thing." Nadia swallowed a lump in her throat.

"Where are you living, dear?"

She was ashamed to answer. "In my car."

He gave her an understanding look. "This meeting isn't about that. I've just decided..." Tears pooled in his eyes. "Nadia, after thirty-two years, I've decided to close up shop. You've done a great job protecting us against shoplifters when you're here, but they've broken in multiple times at night and looted thousands of dollars' worth of goods."

"I can work nights if you'd like," she said. "My day job is probably going to fire me once they find out about me losing my house."

"I-I just can't anymore." Mr. Grimes wiped tears from his face. "This used to be such a nice neighborhood. A safe neighborhood." He sighed. "I was the first black pharmacist in the entire area, did you know that?"

Nadia nodded. "Yes, sir, I know. Your regular customers told me all about it."

"I survived the big box drug stores when they tried to put me out of business. I survived the big discount stores when they opened their own pharmacies and the grocery stores when they did the same."

Nadia felt horrible for Mr. Grimes. This was the place where he'd grown up. He went to medical school and became a pharmacist so he could open shop in his hometown neighborhood.

And now it was over.

"I'm sorry, Nadia." He wiped his eyes. "I'm so sorry. But I'm closing for good at the end of business today. Janet has already contacted the suppliers and is returning all the unsold goods that we can. The rest will be donated to a local charity."

Mr. Grimes pushed an envelope across the desk to Nadia. "That is a month's worth of pay up front. I have been fortunate to accumulate a nice little nest egg over the years, and I didn't want to put you, Janet, Timmy, and Fannie out of jobs without giving you something to get you by for a while."

"Thank you so much, sir." Nadia wiped away tears of her own. "I'm so sorry this has happened to a good person like you. Grimes' Pharmacy is the last business left in the area."

"I know, dear. Nothing can survive the crime in these parts." He sighed. "But what can you do when the criminals run the government?"

He reached over and put his hand on hers. "I'm sorry about your house. All I can suggest is that you move far away from here and never look back. That's what I'm going to do. I've already got a nice place in Florida waiting for me."

"I'm glad, sir." Nadia swallowed hard and stood. "Well, I'll get back to work."

"No need, dear. We're locking the doors at lunch so the suppliers can get their things. Now, you go enjoy the rest of your day." He winced. "If that's possible."

Nadia walked around the desk, bent over, and hugged him. "Thank you, Mr. Grimes."

"You're welcome, dear."

Nadia left the office and closed the door behind her. She went to the front and said goodbye to Janet and Fannie, the cashiers. Timmy, the stock boy, was nowhere to be found. Janet and Fannie were in tears. They were old women, probably long past retirement age, but they just enjoyed working and talking to people.

Now they had nothing left. Or maybe they did. Nadia really didn't know them all that well. She went outside. Grimes Pharmacy was the last place open for two city blocks. Everything else was boarded up.

Everything except the former big box retailer store which was now open as a homeless shelter. Nadia had tried to stay there before, but it was always full. It hadn't much mattered because between her job at the pharmacy and her early morning shift for Bark Security, she hardly had time to sleep.

She walked four blocks to reach her parked car. It was the only free parking place in the vicinity. The first thing she saw was broken glass. The next was all her clothing and possessions strewn out on the sidewalk next to the passenger side door.

"No!" She ran to her car. Someone had broken the window and rummaged through everything inside. Her suitcase was open on the sidewalk. The trunk was open. Her laptop and few remaining valuable possessions were gone.

The trail of clothing and items went toward the homeless encampment not far down the sidewalk. Rage boiled her blood. She was so angry she couldn't even move for a moment. Then she stormed down the sidewalk toward the tents.

This was it. Someone was going to die. She might as well go to jail for life because at least there she could get shelter and three square meals a day. Maybe she could kill her asshole ex-husband before the cops caught up with her.

Hell, she could probably evade the police for days or weeks. Her military career had been all about surviving in hostile locations without being detected. But she didn't care about simply surviving. She'd wanted to thrive. And now, that would never happen.

There were several pairs of women's underwear strewn outside the first tent. Nadia recognized several of them because they were hers. Some sick pervert decided to get his rocks off with her panties.

Nadia drew her knife and slashed open the tent. The razor-sharp blade cut it like butter. A withered husk of a man looked up at her with wide eyes. His mouth dropped open, and he dropped the panties he'd been holding.

"You sick piece of garbage!" Nadia lunged toward him.

A firm hand caught her wrist. "Whoa, hold on!"

Nadia registered a man in her peripheral vision. She automatically twisted sideways, gripped his wrist. Flipped him on the ground. He caught himself. Swept her feet. She jumped up, narrowly avoiding the sweep.

The man backed away, hands up in surrender. "Hey, let's put away the knife."

The homeless man scurried away, howling like an injured dog even though she hadn't even touched him. Nadia quickly sheathed the knife. Her face burned not with rage, but with embarrassment.

She couldn't even kill a homeless guy. And where had this other guy come from? He obviously knew how to fight.

"Are you okay?" The man relaxed slightly. "I thought you were going to slice that guy to ribbons."

"He broke into my car." Nadia calmed herself and tried to play it off. "I just thought he might be dangerous."

The man grinned. "Nah, it's more than that." He shrugged. "Hey, I don't blame you for wanting to scare him. I'd feel the same way."

Nadia stared at her underwear on the ground. Her laptop was in the tent too, but the screen was broken. And her car window was broken. She was homeless just like all the people living in these tents, but she didn't even have a tent.

"Hey, can I help?"

Nadia blinked out of her thoughts and looked at the man. "Who are you?"

"Oh, sorry." He held out a hand. "I'm Keith."

She stared at his hand for a second before shaking it. "Nadia."

"Nice to meet you, Nadia." He released her hand. "How about we get your stuff cleaned up and you tell me how I can help you."

"I appreciate the help, but how else could you help me?"

"I offer drug counseling and other services to people who need help."

"Like these homeless folks?"

"Yes. But only if they want help."

Nadia sighed. "So, you're a homeless advocate?"

Keith laughed. "No, I definitely don't encourage homelessness. But I offer counseling to anyone who needs it."

"Do you drink?" Nadia asked.

He laughed again. "Yes, I don't run AA meetings."

"Okay. You help me clean this up, then we'll go talk over beer."

Keith nodded. "Sounds fair to me."

Nadia managed a small smile. Her day was horrible but at least she had someone to talk to about it. And once she finished talking about it, she was going to go visit Lief.

And she was going to shoot him in the face.

Chapter 8

Carver stopped at the first motel they came to.

It was about half a mile from downtown Bickham. It was laid out in an L shape like every other cheap motel Carver had seen, with the office at the lower part of the L and the rooms along the upper part.

It was a single-story red brick building with twenty-five rooms. The parking lot asphalt was gray and cracked but the building looked cleaner than most motels. Cleanliness didn't matter all that much as long as it had a shower and beds.

Carver patted a bus stop bench and motioned Rich to take a seat. "Wait here. I'll get a room."

Rich sat down without a word. He leaned back and stared blankly straight ahead.

Carver went to the motel office. A bell on the door rang when he opened it.

A middle-aged man emerged from the office in the back. He looked Carver up and down. "Yes?"

"I need a room." Carver pushed three twenties across the counter.

"Gonna cost more than that, son." The man frowned. "I need an ID and a credit card for incidentals."

"How about sixty bucks to fill one of your rooms?" Carver waved a hand at the empty parking lot. "Doesn't look like much is going on here."

The man shoved the money back across the counter. "It's a hundred bucks a night, a credit card for incidentals, and an ID for the record."

"You must not like money," Carver said.

"I don't need it from the likes of you, pal."

"You don't need money to stay in business?"

"I'm doing fine enough not to negotiate with a cheapo like you." The man motioned at the door. "Now, get out of here before I call the cops."

Carver felt mildly irritated. He felt like grabbing the man by the collar and yanking him over the counter. Having a word with him. He let the irritation show on his face.

The man backed up a step. "I said get out!"

Carver turned and left. Rich was still sitting motionless on the bench. He was probably running on fumes after his ordeal. He certainly wasn't the same gung-ho guy Carver had known in the SEALs.

Maybe he'd have a little more pep in his step after a shower and sleep. Carver looked at the map app. This motel had a five-star rating with well over a thousand reviews. In fact, there were only a couple of one-star reviews.

Those reviewers called the office manager extremely rude and said the place was overpriced. That sounded about right. The five-star reviews were glowing. Some of them were almost exact copies of each other. Probably fake reviews.

Other businesses in town also had almost all five-star reviews. There were thousands of reviews for the burger restaurant. All of those seemed well deserved. It was just interesting that every downtown business also had thousands of reviews, even the dry cleaner.

Carver found a motel about two miles outside of town with an overall 2.1-star rating. That was the place he wanted to go. The problem was getting there. He could make the hike, but Rich wasn't going to make it.

He looked at the card the cop had given him. He called the number. A woman answered on the second ring.

"This is Hope House. How can I help you?"

"My friend was referred to you, but I don't have a way to get him there. Do you offer shuttle services?"

"Absolutely! We can send Eddie to pick him up. What's your location?"

"We're near the Stargazer Motel."

"I know exactly where that is. Eddie can be there in five minutes."

"Thank you."

"My pleasure, sir!" She ended the call.

Carver stood upwind of Rich. He didn't see a need to talk or dredge up old memories, so he leaned against a pole and waited for the shuttle.

Rich abruptly pounded his fist on the bench. He got up and glared at Carver. "Why in the hell are you here?"

"I came to warn you."

"That the cops were going to raid my house and take everything?" He shivered with rage. "Too late, Carver."

"No, I didn't know about that."

Rich stepped closer. He looked ready to take a swing. Like he was just barely keeping it together. "Warn me about what, then?"

"I was told that you're on an NSA watch list. I have no idea why but felt that I should tell you."

"An NSA watch list?" Rich laughed hollowly. "Good God, am I on everyone's radar?"

"You're on other watchlists?"

"No, I'm not on other watchlists." Rich balled his fists. "Not that I know of, anyway. Maybe I am. I just meant I was on the local police watch list thanks to some dumb ass kid selling drugs on my property and now the NSA wants a piece?"

"Apparently."

"Let them come and get it, then." Rich banged the bottom of his fist against the bench. "I want to kill those damned cops! I want to cut them to pieces!"

Carver couldn't blame Rich for being furious, but he kept quiet and let the man get it all out.

"How can they do this to me? They took everything!" Rich raised his hands higher and winced in pain. He grabbed his right shoulder. "Not like I can do anything about it. I'm a damned cripple. I'm useless!"

Carver kept quiet.

Rich glared at him. "I'm a cripple and I have you to thank for it because you didn't do your damned job."

Carver said nothing. He just nodded slightly, accepting responsibility for what he'd done, or more correctly, what he hadn't done. He'd apologized before but it wasn't enough. It would never be enough.

"Why did you even bother coming?"

"Because I would do the same thing for anyone I served with."

"You came knowing that I hate you all the way down to my bones?"

"Yes."

"I wish you'd been this dutiful all those years ago."

Carver had no response to that. It was just the truth.

Rich sank onto the bench. "You warned me. Now what?"

"That's up to you," Carver said. "I can go, or I can stay and assess the threat."

"You owe me, Carver."

"I know."

"You owe me for my shoulder, my knee, and the sanity they stole from me." Rich closed his eyes and trembled. "You owe me for two months of my life I'll never forget. Two months of mutilation and torture. Two months of being the plaything for Rahm Abdul Assad."

"I know."

"Okay. Then you're stuck with me until you figure it out." He sighed. "Where were you living before this?"

"An east coast beach."

"You and your stupid beaches." Rich huffed. "We used to call you the beach bum."

"I know."

"Because every time we found a nice beach even if it was in the middle of a mission, you'd stop and look like you just wanted to get a beach blanket and hang out there until we got back."

Carver couldn't deny it.

"Why do you love beaches so much?"

"I don't know." Carver wondered if there was a suppressed childhood memory or trauma that made him long to find a nice beach and relax. Maybe it was because he never got to go play on a beach as a kid. Or maybe it was just because the sun and ocean was something Carver liked deep down.

An old windowless van performed a U-turn and pulled up to the curb in front of them. It was a seventies or eighties model. It still had the original hubcaps and steel wheels. The paint was faded and there were rust spots on the body, but it seemed to be in decent condition.

A man hopped out and walked around. He was thin, had long, stringy hair, and wore a polyester shirt with a huge collar and brown polyester slacks as if he was trying to match the era the van was made in.

"Hey, I'm Eddie. I'm here to pick you up."

"How did you know it was us?" Carver said. "I didn't give our description to the woman who answered the phone."

Eddie waved a hand around. "Uh, there's no one else standing in front of the motel."

Carver had to concede the point. He opened the sliding door on the side of the van. There were cracked vinyl seats inside. Rich climbed in and sat down in the middle row. Carver closed the door and got into the passenger seat.

Eddie went around and got in on the other side. He frowned at Carver. "I usually don't let people sit in the front."

"That's okay." Carver looked at the cracking vinyl on the dashboard. He looked at the hump between him and the driver's seat. The motor was under that hump. There was barely space under the hood to do anything except check the radiator.

He opened the glove box. It was filled with old registrations and insurance documents, all linked to Hope House, LLC.

"How old is Hope House?"

"Uh, you mean how long have they been around?"

"Yeah."

"Ten years, give or take." Eddie shifted the van into drive and waited for a compact car to pass before pulling into the road. "I've been with them for three years now."

"Why do they have such an old van?"

"This is my van." Eddie patted the steering wheel. "She still runs like a champ."

"Just shut up and let the man do his job," Rich said.

Carver ignored him. "Tell me about Hope House."

"Well, they just help people with problems." Eddie cleared his throat uncomfortably. "I needed help a few years ago and they got me out of my depression. Got me working again."

"By giving you a job."

"Yep."

"They provide room and board?"

"Yep, but only to qualified individuals." Eddie glanced back at Rich. "Do both of you need a place to stay?"

"Just him." Carver motioned his head toward Rich. "I'm staying in a motel."

"Alrighty. Your friend will need to fill out an intake form, and then Alicia will want to do an evaluation."

Rich bristled. "I'm not his friend."

"Oh, okay." Eddie picked up a clipboard from an elastic pocket on the middle console. "You can fill it out on the way if you want."

Rich took the clipboard. He started filling it out.

Carver picked up another clipboard and studied it. It didn't ask anything out of the ordinary. Name, address, all the normal things. There was a blank sheet attached for explaining why the person needed help, along with a sheet asking about medical conditions, allergies, and current medications, plus a section asking about any drug use or addictions.

Rich had the form filled out by the time they reached the destination. Hope House was a large single-story building made of white limestone. It looked like a cross between a hospital and a prison.

It was a big building that occupied at least an acre of land. There was a circle drive in front and a paved parking lot on the side. One section of the parking lot was gated. The other section wasn't. There were no fences or perimeters set up around the building itself.

There was an old apartment building across the street on the left, and a church across the street on the right side. The church was made of large gray granite stones from the foundation all the way up to the steeple. It was fenced off from Hope House and had a parking lot of its own.

The sign outside identified it as St. James Catholic Church. The sign in front of Hope House identified it as a mission by the church.

Eddie pulled into the circle drive and put the van into park. He turned it off, got out and walked around to the side.

Rich opened the sliding door and got out. He looked up at the building. "Why do I feel like I'm being committed to a mental ward?"

Carver walked down the sidewalk and pushed through the double glass door entrance. The flooring was old vinyl. The walls had square green tiles. The same kind of tiles people referred to as hospital tiles.

There was a front lobby, a waiting room, and double doors leading to somewhere beyond. The vibe was unmistakable. This place had once been a hospital. Maybe it had even been a mental ward.

The reception area looked like it had once been walled off and protected with heavy glass before someone tore it all out and did a bad job covering the scars on the ceiling with drywall mud.

The counter still had grooves where a thick pane of glass had once protected the receptionist. Now there was just a low wall and a counter behind it. A young woman rose from her chair and smiled at Carver. Her smile faltered a little when she saw Rich.

"Hello and welcome to Hope House! I'm Alicia." She stepped around the counter and held her hand out to Rich. Rich didn't shake her hand. Unfazed, she extended her hand to Carver.

Carver shook her hand. She had a firm grip and looked him in the eye. The friendly smile didn't quite go to her eyes. It was like she was evaluating him. She looked young, but there was something behind her gaze that told Carver she'd seen a lot of crazy things in her time at Hope House.

"He filled out the forms on the way over," Eddie said. He handed her Rich's intake form.

Alicia glanced at the pages. Nodded. "Eddie, show Mr. Polaski to a room so he can get cleaned up."

"Yes ma'am." Eddie bowed his head slightly like he was deferring to an elder though he was clearly older than she was. He turned to Rich. "Follow me, Mr. Polaski."

"Just call me Rich," Rich said.

"Sure thing, Mr. Polaski." Eddie led him down a hallway.

Alicia pursed her lips and looked at Carver. "You're his friend?"

"We served together." Carver glanced at her business cards on top of the desk. The sound of a loud argument pulled his attention toward the hallway. A man and woman were arguing about something. They looked rough. Like they'd just come in on off the streets.

"One moment, please." Alicia hurried down the hall and spoke to the couple. They quieted down quickly and went into a room. Alicia returned to Carver. "Sorry about that."

He shrugged. "I imagine that happens a lot in a homeless shelter."

"That's not what this is." She watched him as if expecting him to have questions. When he said nothing, she nodded. "Okay, well your friend in good hands now. We'll get him cleaned up and find out how to help him."

"Good to hear. I need to talk to him once he's cleaned up."

"Certainly. Eddie can take you to his room when he returns."

Carver looked at the hallway past the desk. "What exactly do you do here? Is this like a halfway house?"

"Not quite." She smiled perfunctorily, like she wasn't interested in answering his questions, but she answered him anyway. "We will provide temporary shelter while he looks for other accommodations."

"And that's it?"

"No, of course not. We provide counseling in a group setting."

"Like an AA meeting?"

"In a sense, yes. It's important for a person to talk to someone."

"No psychiatrists or psychologists involved?"

"No, this is about group therapy and counseling."

Carver nodded. "What's the religious angle?"

"We do not proselytize, nor do we require anyone to attend church or acknowledge a higher being."

"But you're sponsored by the church."

Alicia nodded. "Yes, but we have found that pushing a religious angle on therapy drives some people away. It's best to let people talk and get their issues out in the open. Sometimes our group leader can offer advice or help or connect them with resources that will get their lives back on track."

"Good to know." Carver had been to plenty of sessions like that. They were required after coming home from long missions. It was an alternative to a psychological evaluation. Carver liked that he didn't have to say much of anything during a session.

Unfortunately, it wouldn't help Rich much. Not at this point of his life, anyway. Rich had almost certainly been required to see a psychologist on a regular basis after being rescued. Almost certainly a VA psychologist or someone with experience treating PTSD.

The thing was most people didn't come back from something like that. They were forever changed. Permanently scarred in the places no doctor could treat. Group counseling wasn't going to change a thing for Rich.

CHAPTER 9

Carver wondered what kind of trouble Rich was in.

He'd inferred a few things. Mainly that a kid had sold drugs on Rich's property and Rich had been arrested for it. He'd spent the night in jail, but the charges must have been dropped.

Carver had also inferred that Rich couldn't go home for some reason. Maybe because his home was an active crime scene. Maybe he'd be able to go home in a few days. Then Rich could go back to being miserable or whatever he did in his spare time.

There was no obligation to stay. No reason to stay. But Carver didn't plan on leaving just yet. Once Rich was back in his house then Carver would feel that he'd done what Joe would have wanted.

Alicia still seemed to be evaluating Carver with her gaze. "Do you want to sit in on a group session?"

"When is the next one?" Carver said.

"In about an hour."

"Sure." Carver motioned ahead. "Want to give me a tour?"

"There's not much to see."

"That's okay. I'm easily amused."

She laughed. "Well, if you say so." She waved a hand around the room. "This is the reception area."

"Looks like it underwent renovations."

"Yes, it used to be a hospital."

"A mental hospital?"

Alicia bit her lower lip. "Yes, back in the fifties and sixties. It closed down and was abandoned for decades, and then the church purchased it and repurposed it."

"Did they lobotomize patients here?"

"Probably." Alicia pushed through the double doors to the right of the reception counter.

There was a hallway on the other side. A hallway lined with metal doors. The doors were painted white. The walls had the same avocado green hospital tile as the reception area. The first door on the right was open.

The room was tiny. Inside was a metal bed frame with no mattress. The frame looked rusty and old.

"This is where they kept troublemakers back in the day." Alicia stepped into the room. "We want to tear down the walls between the rooms and open them up, but we haven't had the funds to do it."

"Looks comfy," Carver said.

She laughed. "The doors were bare metal before, but we painted them white to make the space feel more inviting. We thought about removing them, but they're extremely heavy and Eddie can't do it alone."

"Just hire a renovation company."

"We don't have the funds." Alicia shrugged. "We're funded by the church for a very specific mission." She turned and kept walking. "Anyway, this is the main patient ward. They kept low-risk patients here mostly. The dangerous ones were kept in larger more secure institutions."

Carver followed her and took in everything. There were no cameras. No security personnel roaming the halls. No patients. Aside from them, the wing seemed empty. The one thing that struck him was that the lights were on in all the hallways.

Like most buildings its age, it used florescent lighting. At a certain point, the ballasts in the light fixtures went bad and needed replacing. Otherwise, the lighting would flicker. None of the dozens of fixtures were blinking which indicated they were being maintained despite the wing not being used.

It seemed like a real waste of energy and resources to maintain lighting in a wing of the building that wasn't being used. Especially if resources were as limited as Alicia said. In the end, it probably didn't mean a thing.

Maybe there were other reasons the lighting was well maintained. It might be required by city or county code.

Alicia walked past a set of heavy metal double doors and turned left at the end of the hallway.

Carver rapped his knuckles on the doors. "What's back here?"

"It's just a storage area for old furniture. We keep it locked."

"This is a big building with a lot of empty space. Seems like the church could make better use of it."

"I'd like to expand our services, but they haven't been interested in my ideas so far."

"Do they pay well?"

Alicia shrugged. "Well enough. I'm not in this for the money."

"Good to know."

They continued the tour from one side of the building to the other. They reached the side where Eddie had taken Rich. This wing had been heavily renovated. The green tile was gone, replaced by drywall. The white vinyl floor tile had been covered with vinyl designed to look like hardwood flooring.

"This was the staff residence wing," Alicia said. "As you can see, we gave it a makeover. It now serves as temporary residence for people like your friend Rich."

"What about staff?"

"Eddie has a room. He's our driver, our maintenance man, and security guard. Basically, a jack of all trades." Alicia stopped outside a door and knocked. "Rich, are you presentable?"

There was a pause, and the door opened. Rich stood inside wearing gym shorts and a gray T-shirt. He looked cleaner, but certainly not happier. He stepped back and opened the door wider. "Come in."

The room had four white cinderblock walls, a small bed, and a doorway with a bathroom on the other side. There were no windows. The only way out was the way they'd come in. The door didn't have a lock, so there was no danger of being trapped inside anyway.

"Counseling starts in fifteen minutes," Alicia said. "We require anyone staying here to attend all sessions."

Rich shrugged. "Fine. Not like there's anything else to do."

She smiled. "Good. The meeting room is on the other side of the reception area. Just walk through the double doors and it's the first room on the right."

"Thank you," Rich said.

"You're welcome." Alicia left the room but didn't close the door behind her.

Rich stared at Carver. "You can go now. I don't need you around."

"I know, but I'd like to know what happened."

"Why?"

"Morbid curiosity."

Rich snorted. "You're sick in the head."

"Aren't we all?" Carver said. "Look, I'm going to sit in on the first counseling session, so you might as well tell me now before you tell a room full of strangers."

"I wasn't planning on telling them anything."

"When are the cops going to let you back into your house?"

Rich tensed. His jaw tightened. "I'd beat you bloody if I could. I'd stab you in the shoulder and knee so you could know how it feels every time I move my arm or walk."

"Look, it's fine that you hate me. I'm not looking for redemption. I'm just doing for you what Joe would want."

"Go to hell, Carver." Rich balled his fists. "Why in the hell, out of everyone that I messaged, are you the only one to show up? Where the hell is Joe? Why hasn't he even messaged me back?"

"When's the last time you contacted him?" Carver said.

"About a year ago. I needed a favor."

"Did he help?"

"He did his best. It wasn't enough."

"What did you ask him?"

Rich ran a hand down his face. "I asked him to get me approved for surgery to repair my shoulder and knee. But the VA told him it wasn't possible and couldn't be approved. Joe said he'd run it all the way to the top until someone said yes."

"And?"

"He never got back to me."

Carver thought about the timing. "The reason he never got back to you is because he's dead."

Rich's eyes flared. "What?"

"He was murdered. Local politics."

"No!" Rich dropped onto the bed and stared blankly at the wall. "He's the one guy who always kept his word. Always looked out for his men. I thought maybe he'd forgotten about us after retirement."

"Joe would never do that."

"You were his golden boy." Rich scowled. "I never could understand why. He even defended you after you got me captured and tortured."

"I accept responsibility for my failings, but I can't change the past."

"Yeah? And how did you find out about Joe?"

"I went to visit him. I arrived a day too late."

Rich shook his head. "What do you mean?"

"He was murdered a few hours before I arrived. I saw the body."

"I guess you're just not good at helping people, Carver."

Carver shook his head. "I did what I could."

"And what was that?"

It probably wasn't smart to tell Rich what he'd done, but he did anyway. "Let's just say the town's population decreased by a couple dozen."

Rich's eyes flared. He grinned. "Justice for Joe?"

Carver nodded. "Yeah."

"The cops took my house. They took my money I'd been saving for private surgery. They took everything from me." Rich sagged as if getting that out completely deflated him. "I've got nothing left, man. Nothing."

"They took everything but cut you loose?"

"Yeah. Civil forfeiture laws allow them to charge my property with the crime, so they don't even have to take me to trial."

"They were able to do this because some kid sold drugs on your property?"

"Allegedly." Rich made finger quotes. "They tore the place apart. I'd been keeping cash in a fireproof safe under the floorboards in my closet. They found it. Took the fifty grand I'd managed to save over the past ten years."

"Get a lawyer. Go to court and get it back."

"I talked to the public defender. He said he couldn't represent me because I wasn't charged with a crime. He also told me that there's no way to get it back." Rich trembled with rage. "Want to help me, Carver? Kill those crooked cops. Make them give everything back to me."

Carver had heard about civil forfeiture, but he didn't know all the legalities behind it. He wasn't a lawyer, and he didn't want to become one. The easiest way to figure out what to do was to talk to one.

Rich punched Carver's shoulder. "Did you hear what I said?"

Carver ignored the question. "Do you have a list of things they took?"

"Typical." Rich huffed. "You'd kill for Joe but not for me."

"Joe was murdered. You're still alive. Maybe there's a way to get your stuff back without going to war with the city cops." Carver repeated his earlier question. "Do you have a list of things they took?"

"In my head." Rich stared blankly at the floor. "I didn't have much. Money, guns, ammunition, a knife, a crappy old television, and clothing."

"Was Joe the only person you asked for help?"

Rich shook his head. "I messaged a couple of people I met when I was in therapy after my return. I don't know if they responded because the cops took my cell phone too."

"They didn't let you keep anything from the house? Not even your clothing?"

"Man, they took everything. The only thing I have left are a pair of boxer briefs."

"Understood." There was a notepad and pen on the nightstand. Carver gave them to Rich. "Inventory anything you can remember."

"What are you going to do?"

"Find a lawyer and talk to them. Figure out what can be done."

"I told you that nothing can be done."

"Maybe, maybe not." Carver shrugged. "I'll be back later."

"Wait, I thought you were going to session with me."

Carver raised an eyebrow. "Do you really want me there?"

Rich seemed to struggle internally with something. "No, not really."

Carver nodded and left. He walked past reception. Alicia wasn't there. He went outside into the early evening heat. It was already six, but the sun wouldn't set for another few hours. That was good, because he had a checklist to complete.

He looked at the maps app. First thing he needed was a car. The nearest cash lot was fifteen minutes away in the next county over. There wasn't a single one anywhere in Bickham or the surrounding county. There were three regular car dealerships, one right next to the other on the nearby highway, Ford, Toyota, and Dodge.

They all shared the same name, Matheson, right in front of the brand. Matheson Ford, Matheson Toyota, and Matheson Dodge. There were no standalone used car lots nearby. No other dealerships either.

Carver noticed something else. There were no big box retailers anywhere near town. He zoomed out and couldn't find a single one until he crossed the county line. They apparently didn't like outside competition in these parts.

That was inconvenient but not insurmountable. He heard the rumble of Eddie's van. It appeared around the corner of the building and pulled onto the circular drive. Carver waved him down.

Eddie stopped and rolled down his window. Carver went to the passenger side and got in. "I need a lift to the county line. I'll pay you for gas."

"Uh, but I'm not going that way," Eddie said.

"Where are you going?"

"Back into town to pick up groceries."

"Give me a lift first." Carver slid a fifty-dollar bill from his pocket. "That should pay for the gas."

Eddie's eyes widened. "Oh, that'll more than cover it. I'll be happy to take you."

Carver motioned toward the road. "Let's go then."

Eddie pulled onto the road and turned right. He connected to the highway and turned due west toward the county line.

"I noticed there aren't any big retailers anywhere near town or the county," Carver said. "What's up with that?"

"We don't want that trash in our county." Eddie scowled. "They just put family businesses out of business, and they bring crime and low wages to the area." It sounded like he was reciting a line he used a lot.

"So, the local politicians keep them out?"

"Yeah, the county commissioners won't grant them permits and we like it that way."

"What about Bickham? Does the mayor or city council have a say in it?"

"The county commissioners run the city too. The mayor doesn't have any real power."

"That's an interesting arrangement"

Eddie glanced at Carver. "Why are you going to the county line?"

"I'm getting a motel room there."

"Oh, are you already heading out of town?"

Carver stared at the road ahead. "Soon."

Eddie drove below the speed limit, so it took them twenty minutes to reach the county line. He stopped the van in front of Great Lakes Inn. Eddie looked dubiously at the scantily dressed woman standing at the street corner outside. "You sure you want to stay here? You'll probably get AIDS just from touching the bed."

Carver had chosen it because it had a two-star rating and someone in the reviews complained about the number of prostitutes in the area. That meant they almost certainly wouldn't ask for an ID and the price would be right.

"Oh, I don't mind a little AIDS." Carver opened his door. "Thanks for the lift."

"This place is lousy with crime," Eddie said. "All the filth we don't allow in Bickham is here."

"How do they keep everything so clean in Bickham?" Carver asked. "It must cost a pretty penny to keep the town looking like that."

"It don't cost nothing," Eddie said. "If you get caught breaking rules, you get put on community service."

"What kind of rules?"

"They don't hand out speeding tickets or any of that big city crap. Most misdemeanors are punished with community service." He grinned. "They'll put you to work, that's for sure. I had to do it once for littering."

That was ironic. Carver got out. "Thanks for the ride."

"Sure thing, mister." Eddie's gaze locked onto a scantily clad woman walking their way. "Is that a—"

"Yeah, that's a prostitute," Carver said. "I'll buy you an hour with her if you want to give it a try."

Eddie's eyes flared. "What? Hell no!" He gunned the van back onto the street. Carver waited for him to drive out of sight by which time the woman had reached him. She looked young but old at the same time. Probably because of drugs and a hard life on the streets.

"Hey, baby, you new in town?"

Carver nodded. "Yeah. I'll be back later. First, I gotta take care of some business."

"Hey, you come back and ask for Mandy, okay?" She looked him over and flashed a mostly toothless smile. "I'll be around."

Carver walked across the street. He walked down the sidewalk and took a right at the intersection. The used car lot he'd found on the map was located there. He found an old minivan with heavily tinted windows and made sure it ran before buying it for a thousand dollars.

As usual, the dealer wanted him to fill out some paperwork, but he politely declined and added another three hundred bucks to keep the man happy. The license plate sticker still had two months before expiration and that was probably all the time he'd need with the vehicle.

Carver drove off the lot and filled the gas tank at a station. He drove to a restaurant and filled up his stomach next. He went back to the minivan and looked under the dash. There was a lot of wiring in the way, but he found what he was looking for a moment later.

Specifically, he was looking for a space where he could store his Sig. It wasn't registered to him. On the off chance that he got pulled over, he didn't want it to become a liability. He stowed the weapon in a small nook beneath a bundle of wiring. It conveniently held the gun in place.

He stowed his four spare magazines next to it. There was no good place to stow the two boxes of spare ammunition, but there was nothing illegal about having unregistered bullets as far as he knew.

With that sorted, Carver got back on the road and drove toward Bickham. The sun was down by the time he got to his destination and that was good.

Because he needed the dark of night for what he was about to do.

Chapter 10

Carver dressed in dark clothing.

The minivan had plenty of room for him to change clothes and store his stuff. It wasn't the most attractive vehicle, but it had a lot of utility. And the best part was that it didn't stick out too much.

People noticed black SUVs and normal vans. They usually didn't look twice at minivans. That was one reason why Carver liked using them when he wanted to remain incognito.

Carver pushed open the sliding door and slipped out. He was about six blocks northwest of downtown Bickham. The houses here were nice. They were built from limestone and granite much like the other old buildings in town.

He stood on the sidewalk in front of a single-story house. It was probably a couple of thousand square feet with a detached garage. It looked like it had fallen into a state of disrepair. The porch railing was rotting in places and the paint on the wood was peeling.

The white limestone was dirty and moldy. It needed a good pressure washing. The lawn was overgrown with weeds, and the mailbox was leaning an unhealthy forty degrees sideways. The front door looked broken, but that wasn't due to the negligent homeowner.

The police had done that. They'd put a bright red notice on it and police tape across the porch entrance. There was nothing else preventing a person from walking inside.

This was Rich's house. At least it had been. Now it was apparently wholly owned by the Bickham Police Department. The other nearby homes were well maintained. They had black iron fences with gates. They had thick hedges, flowerbeds, and other signs of a caring homeowner.

Rich's place had none of that. Well, it had an iron fence, but it was rusty, and the gate was missing. A house like that was indicative of the mental state of the owner. Carver wondered why Rich had bought a nice house like that in the first place. Why had he moved to such a clean town?

These were questions that didn't really need answering. Carver wasn't here to answer any questions or right any wrongs. He was just here to make sure Rich had more than just the clothes on his back.

The fences made it difficult to sneak through the backyards. Not just difficult, but downright impossible. Rich's house wasn't on a corner lot. It was right in the middle of the other houses.

A full-frontal approach was the only way to do it. Before he strolled past the police tape and up to the front door, Carver would need to do a little recon. He looked the area over with the naked eye first.

The street was quiet and empty. The windows of most houses glowed with light. Most of them were covered with curtains or blinds. The windows of the house next to Rich's weren't covered. The interior of the house was dark.

The lit windows didn't worry Carver. The people inside wouldn't see very clearly outside. They'd be more likely to see their reflections than a man walking down the street. Someone looking out from an unlit room, however, would easily see anyone on the street.

A dark house most likely meant no one was home, but it was still possible that someone was inside. Maybe they were watching a movie or looking at their phones or napping on the couch. Maybe they'd glance out the window and see Carver walking past.

Carver wasn't in the business of taking unnecessary risks. Not if he could help it, anyway. He raised his monocular to an eye and turned it on. It was in thermal mode. He switched it to night vision because glass blocked infrared.

Technically, glass reflected infrared. If you were standing close enough to a window while using thermal, you'd see your own heat image in the reflection. That was why night vision was usually preferred in high stress situations.

The house looked empty. There were no lights on anywhere inside, at least none Carver could see, and no one lurking in the darkness. He walked across the street and studied the houses opposite Rich's.

The houses on that side were mostly lit. The windows weren't covered by blinds or curtains on the house right across the street from Rich's place, but that didn't worry Carver. As long as he didn't stand under a streetlight, no one would see him.

He tucked the monocular in a pocket and walked down the sidewalk like he owned the place. He took a left through Rich's broken gate and ducked under the police tape. He crouched on the dark porch and took another look with the monocular.

He was in the clear.

Carver pulled on his gloves and examined the front door. They'd pulled it almost closed, but the broken frame prevented it from staying that way. They hadn't secured it with anything, so it was basically just hanging open.

He slipped through the front and looked around with the monocular in night vision mode. What little furniture was there was wrecked. The recliner was ripped open, and foam stuffing was everywhere. The small couch was in no better shape.

Carver skipped past it and the other rooms. He went down the hall and found Rich's bedroom at the end. The room was surprisingly large compared to the other rooms in the hallway. There was a metal bed frame against the far wall and a ripped open mattress lying on the floor next to it.

Night vision reflected stains on the mattress. Carver didn't want to find out what those stains were. He was just interested in the closet.

Most of the clothing had been tossed out of the chest of drawers inside the closet. Carver found a large duffel bag on the floor inside and no suitcases. That was typical of ex-military folks.

He unzipped the bag and stuffed it with all the clothing on the floor. He tossed what was left in the chest of drawers into the bag as well. There were flip-flops, sandals, and a worn pair of tennis shoes in the closet too, plus a very worn set of service boots.

Carver tossed everything into the bag and still had plenty of room left. The closet was all but empty now because there was nothing on the hangars. The only thing left was a blanket and pillow piled in the back corner.

The duffel bag still had room so he rolled up the blanket to stuff it inside. When he moved it, he noticed a hole in the floor beneath it. Next to the hole was a neat square made from the hardwood flooring. The square was a trapdoor designed to blend in with the hardwoods.

Carver looked inside the hole. It was empty. It was a good-sized hole. Large enough to fit a safe inside. Probably the same safe Rich used to store his cash and other valuables. None of the other hardwoods in the closet were broken or touched.

It looked like the cops knew exactly where to look for the trapdoor. If they'd known where it was, why had they torn up the rest of the house? Was it to put on a show or had they suspected Rich might be hiding something else?

Carver put his head into the hole and looked around with the monocular. There was a crawlspace under the house. It was a finished crawlspace, the kind with heavy plastic over the dirt and spray foam on the granite foundation.

It looked clean. No bugs, no dirt. There was an indentation in the plastic a few feet over from where the hole in the floor was. The safe had been there. Judging from the depth of the indentations, it was a heavy safe. There was also a pile of blankets and a pillow there too.

The hole in the floor was big enough for Rich to fit through. It was barely big enough for Carver to fit through. He pulled his head out of the hole and put the trap door in place. He closed the closet door, turned off night vision, and turned on the light.

The trap door fit seamlessly, using the natural lines between planks to hide the seams. The top and left side fit under the baseboards. A picture formed in Carver's head. A picture with the blanket, the pillow and Rich.

Rich had been sleeping in the closet. Maybe not all the time, but definitely some of the time. He was suffering from PTSD. The bedroom probably felt too insecure, so he'd go into the closet. When the closet didn't feel secure, he'd go into the crawlspace. That was why there were blankets and a pillow down there.

Someone had clearly known all about it. They'd told the cops where to find Rich and where to find the safe. At least, that was what it seemed like. Rich must have told someone about the safe. That someone told someone else and so forth and so on until it reached the ears of someone who wanted to take that money.

Carver wasn't here to find out who or why. He was just here to warn Rich about the watch list. Now that he'd done that, he could leave with a clean conscience. Once he gave Rich the duffel bag with his clothing, it would be time to move on.

He turned off the closet light and picked up the duffel bag. He opened the door and went into the bedroom. He stepped into the hallway. The floor creaked and it wasn't because of him. The floor creaked again twice in a row.

Someone was in the house, and they weren't being quiet about it. Carver stepped across the hallway and into the room across from Rich's. The room was bare. No furniture, nothing. No place to hide.

The lights turned on in the front room. A man spoke. "What do you think?"

"I love it!" a woman replied. "With a little cleaning, it'll be perfect for my mom!"

"Yeah, I thought so too, honey." The man spoke with a heavy Chicagoan accent. "I'll get the boys to clean out the inside once the proceedings are done. I'll get Jodie Granger to come pressure wash the outside and fix the front door."

"You still have him by the balls, Daddy?"

"Honey, I got the whole county by the balls." The man laughed. "Now, come show daddy some proper appreciation. I think the kitchen table would do nicely."

"Anything you want, Daddy!"

Carver got the feeling the woman wasn't really his daughter. He looked down the hallway and saw a portly man in a rumpled white suit. A young woman in a short skirt led him by the hand.

They walked past the hallway and into the kitchen. More lights came on. That was going to be a problem. The kitchen was right next to the den. The hallway from the bedrooms went right past the kitchen door.

The only back door was in the kitchen. Carver had noted all of that when he came inside. It was habit to know where all the exits were. The windows were the original ones, single-paned and wooden. The ones in the bedroom were nailed shut.

Carver looked at the ones in this bedroom and confirmed they were also nailed shut. They also looked painted shut. That left the front door as the only real way out. That was unless Rich had given himself a way out of the crawlspace.

He probably had, but Carver wasn't ready to take that route just yet. He picked up the duffle bag and slowly stepped into the hallway. Porcine grunting echoed from ahead.

"You like that, Daddy?"

The grunting paused for a second. "Yeah, honey, I love it." The grunting resumed.

Apparently, someone had a deviated septum or a lot of fat in the back of their throat because he was raising a racket. And that was a good thing. Carver walked slowly down the hallway in time with the grunts.

He stepped into the den. Looked to the right. Saw the man leaning against a rickety kitchen table. He saw the woman's blonde hair bouncing about crotch-high to the man, but the door frame blocked the details.

He was grateful for that.

The next part was risky. Carver was going to be fully visible stepping out of the doorway. Hopefully, Daddy didn't have a bodyguard or driver waiting on him. He peered through the crack in the door and didn't see anyone waiting on the porch.

Carver opened the door and stepped outside. He walked quickly but confidently down the porch stairs and down the sidewalk to the gate. A white Corvette was parked facing the wrong way on the curb.

He looked at the license plate when he passed it. It was a custom plate that simply read *BIGD*. That could mean a lot of things, but Carver narrowed it down to Big Daddy or a wishful description of the owner's manhood.

Carver kept walking. He crossed the street to the left and reached the minivan where he'd parked it. He opened the sliding door and tossed the duffel bag inside. He scanned the area with his monocular to make sure no one else was around.

Big D and the woman exited Rich's house. She was wiping her mouth with the back of her hand and he had his hand around her waist. Apparently, Big D hadn't lasted more than sixty seconds.

Big D might also stand for Big Deal. Because apparently this guy thought he was a real big deal if he could give his girlfriend's mom a house that had just been seized by the police. Not even the police chief could do something like that as far as he knew.

He might be a city councilman, or he might be rich enough to own the city council. Carver was very curious about this man. He needed to know more about him, and the best way to do that wasn't by approaching him and asking him questions. No, the best way to find out the answers to Carver's questions was simple.

Carver was going to follow him home.

Chapter 11

Carver got into the minivan.

The Corvette's taillights blinked on. It squealed away from the curb, tires burning rubber. Carver eased away from the curb. He didn't want the tires to screech or to risk blowing up the minivan's engine.

He turned the corner and drove in the same direction as the Corvette. He stopped at a four-way intersection and watched the Corvette's taillights getting farther away by the second. Apparently, Big D didn't have to worry about speed limits or stop signs.

The car turned to the right about four intersections ahead of Carver. By the time he reached the intersection, the Corvette was nowhere to be seen. That was okay. A white Corvette probably wouldn't be too hard to spot in a town this size. He'd just have to keep his eyes open.

Provided he stuck around. He had mixed feelings about that. Rich could take care of himself from here on out. He should still be getting disability payments and a twenty-one-year retirement pension.

It wasn't much, but it was enough for him to start over. It was the whole starting over thing that stuck in Carver's craw. He didn't like what the local cops had done to Rich. Maybe they were done with him. Maybe not.

The whole thing reeked of a setup. They'd known about the hidden trap door and the safe hidden underneath. That much was obvious because they hadn't randomly torn up the hardwoods anywhere. They'd gone straight for the prize.

The situation bugged Carver more than it might have before Joe's murder. If he'd had even a hint that Joe was in trouble or dealing with something dangerous, he would have been there to help in a heartbeat.

Now he was in a similar position with Rich. The only question was whether the cops were finished with him, or if they planned to threaten or jail him so he wouldn't challenge them in court.

Rich didn't like Carver, and for good reason. Carver was ambivalent about Rich in most ways except for the one that mattered. They'd served together. They'd fought together. Protected each other. They were brothers in arms.

Carver owed a duty to Rich just because of that. He also owed him big time for a whole lot more. It was a debt that really couldn't be paid back. Or maybe it could. At least partially. He'd have to talk to Rich about it.

He turned the minivan around and got on the highway leading to Hope House. He parked a short distance away, so no one saw him exiting the minivan. Not because he was ashamed of his new ride, but because he didn't want anyone to know about it.

Carver hefted the duffel bag and slung the strap over his shoulder. He hoofed it the short distance to Hope House and went through the front door. The receptionist was gone but the lights were still on.

It was almost ten and the hallways were quiet and empty. The lights were off in all the hallways except where the residences were. There didn't seem to be any form of security. It seemed like they didn't care if the residents stayed or left.

Most halfway houses had security and curfews. They didn't want occupants coming and going because separating them from the outside world was part of their treatment. This place apparently wasn't like a typical halfway house. Maybe it wasn't even one to begin with.

Carver went to Rich's room and knocked on the door. Rich opened it a moment later, a grin on his face. The grin vanished immediately.

"Carver? What are you doing here?"

Carver patted the duffel bag. "I got your things."

Rich blinked rapidly. "You did what?"

"Can I come in?"

Rich paused. Frowned. "Yeah, sure." He backed away and opened the door wider.

Carver went inside. He set the bag on the floor. "I cleaned out your closet. If anyone asks, you bought this clothing."

Rich sat down on the edge of the bed and unzipped the bag. He pulled out clothing. Sighed. "Thanks."

Carver nodded.

Rich looked up at him. "I know you're only here to try and make things right between us, but that's never going to happen. I just want you to have realistic expectations."

"Agreed." Carver sat on the chair next to the table. "It's a debt that can't be repaid. But I have a question for you. You mentioned surgery. How effective was it going to be?"

Rich remained silent for a moment. "Shoulder replacement would give me ninety percent or more of original mobility. The knee replacement would be eighty to ninety. And the pain would be gone."

"And the VA refused to pay for it?"

"Yeah. They literally prescribed ibuprofen for the pain. Told me that was all they'd approve."

"What's the cost for the surgery?"

"Over two hundred grand."

Carver frowned. "I know medical care is expensive, but that sounds way overpriced. Did you shop it around?"

"Yeah. I even tried getting private insurance, so they'd pay for it." He gritted his teeth. "They're supposed to allow for preexisting conditions, but said it wouldn't be covered since it was supposed to be covered by the VA."

"After shopping it around, two hundred thousand was the best you got?"

"I talked to a lot of places. The surgery cost ranged from a hundred grand and up, but the guarantees were a lot different depending on the surgeon. Most said range of motion and everything would be seventy percent of what it was. Only the top tier places said they could guarantee close to full recovery."

Carver hadn't had to deal with private healthcare. Aside from a few gunshot wounds, knife cuts, and other minor scrapes and bruises, he'd been lucky. Rich was like this because of him. The least he could do was scrounge up a couple hundred grand.

He already had fifty and some change. He could contact Leon and reestablish a connection to the offshore bank account Leon had linked him to. There was enough in there to cover the rest of the cost.

Rich watched him closely. "Why are you so quiet?"

"I can pay for the surgery. I just need to contact a friend."

Rich's eyebrows rose. "How are you going to get that much money?"

"I just will." Carver stood. "I'm going to get some rest. I'll touch base tomorrow."

"You're really trying hard, aren't you?" Rich kept staring at him. "Why? You haven't developed a conscience somewhere along the way, have you?"

"I owe you. No other reason than that."

"You don't value my friendship? You don't personally care about me?"

"We were never friends," Carver said. "That's not what this is about. I screwed up, you got screwed. I can't make it totally right, but I can at least get close."

"Yeah, you can get close." Rich nodded. He reached his hand toward Carver.

Carver shook his hand. "Okay."

Rich nodded. "Okay." He released Carver's hand. "Thanks."

"Yep." Carver left. He went back outside and headed toward the minivan. He noticed a dark sedan that hadn't been there earlier. It looked like an old Chevy Caprice. Probably a 90s model.

The paint in the center of the front passenger-side door looked newer than the paint around it. Like something had covered the paint for a long time and then been removed. Decals maybe. Probably police decals. It was almost certainly a retired police car.

It was dark inside the car, but Carver could see the outline of a person in the driver's seat. He could get a better look with the monocular but didn't want them to see him looking. He pretended not to see them and kept walking.

He turned right at the corner instead of walking to the minivan. A wooden fence concealed him from the driver of the Caprice, so he took out the monocular and peeked around the corner. The car was coming his way, and the headlights were off.

Carver zoomed in with night vision. The driver had a ballcap on pulled down low. From what Carver could see, the face was masculine. The jawline didn't match either of the cops he'd met in the diner.

The driver had broad shoulders but didn't look overly muscular. The night vision made it hard to tell the driver's age. The best Carver could tell was that the driver was middle-aged. Maybe forty.

The man's clothing was dark. Nothing identifying him as a cop. Just plain civilian clothing. There was no passenger in the car. Just him. The car had probably been sold at auction after it was retired. Just because it used to be a patrol car didn't mean the driver was a cop. It might be a civilian who liked to play cop, though.

Carver tucked away the monocular and jogged down the sidewalk. He crossed the road and ducked behind the building on the other side. He poked his head around the corner and watched. The car turned onto the street.

The car stopped. The driver looked around. He gunned the engine and reached the next stop sign. He paused there and looked both ways down the street. He seemed to come to a decision and turned left.

Carver waited for the hum of the engine to fade in the distance. He doubled back to the main road and turned right at the intersection. He crouched there, watching and waiting just in case the car returned.

The area where Hope House was located was mostly residential. The Caprice driver might assume Carver had gone into one of the nearby houses. If he was the suspicious type, he might assume Carver saw him and hid.

Why had he followed Carver? Had he seen Carver with Rich? Had he taken an interest for some reason? It just seemed strange to follow someone for no reason. As far as Carver knew, he hadn't drawn any undue attention since arriving here.

Maybe he had. Maybe just showing up at the police station and asking to see Rich had raised all kinds of red flags. There was no doubt that Rich's situation was a setup. Maybe they'd planned to leave him alone after they were done with him but then Carver had shown up.

Carver was an unknown factor. If they knew Rich had once served in the military, they might think Carver had also served and that they once served together. They'd be right, of course. And they'd be right to worry about what that meant.

The car hadn't been there when Carver arrived. He habitually looked at his surroundings wherever he went. There had been no cars parked on the street across from Hope House. That car had arrived sometime after Carver went inside.

Carver had been inside for maybe twenty minutes. No more than that. Maybe someone saw him enter. Maybe someone made a phone call, and someone else scrambled to get over there. A person could easily get from downtown Bickham to Hope House in ten minutes.

Maybe they hadn't gone there because of Carver. Maybe they'd arrived for another reason. They saw Carver. They knew he was connected to Rich somehow and decided to follow him. But he wasn't their primary objective.

Rich was. He was their objective because Carver had shown up to town. They'd expected Rich to remain quiet. To do nothing about being legally robbed blind. But now they had doubts because Carver had shown up. Now they had to talk to Rich and get answers.

Carver blew out a breath. He couldn't go back to the motel until he figured out what the man in the car was up to. He walked across the main road. He walked between the red brick buildings there and went to the alleyway behind them.

He turned left down the access road and passed two buildings. He stopped at the next alley and looked between the buildings. Hope House was visible across the road. He walked down the alley and crouched near the corner.

The Caprice appeared down the road to his right. Apparently, the driver had circled back, gone around the streets behind Hope House, and given up the search. He parallel parked where he'd been earlier, facing toward Carver's left. He rolled down the window and turned off the car.

The car was just fifteen feet from Carver's position. He used the monocular for a better look. The driver removed his ballcap to sweep back his hair and put it back down low on his head. That was long enough for Carver to identify the man.

It was the officer who'd escorted them out of town. The one who'd given Rich the business card for Hope House. Officer Palmer. That was interesting.

Palmer sat in the car doing nothing. He didn't look at his phone. He didn't smoke a cigarette or read a book. The only thing he did was raise a cup to his lips and drink from it. It was a to-go mug. It probably had coffee in it.

This looked like a stakeout. He'd seen Carver, a known associate, show up and then followed him. He'd lost him, returned to the scene and was now watching the place again. But why?

Rich wasn't exactly a flight risk. He didn't have a vehicle and couldn't walk very well with his bad knee. The stakeout was probably because he was waiting for Carver to show. At least, that was the only logical reason Carver could think of.

It meant Palmer was going to be waiting for a long time for no reason. And that was okay. Maybe he'd be too tired to harass people tomorrow. Or maybe he enjoyed that part of the job so much that it didn't matter how tired he was.

Carver didn't think he had to watch the guy but decided to give it another thirty minutes just in case. The alley was nice and dark, so he stayed put and watched from there. There was a stack of old wooden pallets against the wall just high enough to serve as a seat.

He got comfortable on the pallets and watched. He'd barely settled in when another car drove up behind the Caprice and parked. Carver switched on the monocular for a better look at the newcomer. It was a man. Medium build. Lean but with a bulging belly. Carver didn't recognize him.

The driver of the second car got out. He walked around to the passenger side of the Caprice and got in. Carver slid off the pallets and crept closer until the car was just ten feet away. He didn't dare leave the alley because there was enough ambient light from streetlamps to reveal him.

The driver's window was down but the two men spoke in low tones. Carver couldn't make out a word they were saying. The cop, Palmer, pointed down the street and gestured with his hand. He was probably talking about seeing Carver and following him.

The other guy replied with a shrug. He jabbed a thumb over his shoulder toward Hope House. It was frustrating not knowing what they were saying. It was also potentially dangerous for Carver not to know.

He risked getting closer. He got right up to the edge of the alley and cupped a hand around his ear. This time he caught bits and pieces of the conversation.

"It doesn't matter right now," the cop said. "Do this and we'll worry about the other guy."

"Fine by me," the other guy said. "This guy's a cripple, so it'll be easy. The other guy, not so much. I want double."

"I'm not the one to negotiate with."

"I know. I'll talk to him after this."

Palmer nodded. "You do that. Here's your payment." He moved his arm like he was handing the other guy something, but it was concealed by the seat.

The other guy raised a paper sack up to his face and looked inside. He nodded. "I don't need to count it."

"You know we're good for it." The cop said something Carver couldn't quite hear, then something about a suicide.

"Oh, it'll be convincing." The other guy laughed. "Crazy where life leads you, huh?"

"Sure." Palmer adjusted his ballcap. "Give me fifteen minutes to get out of here, then you can head in."

"All right." The second guy got out of the car and walked back to his. He leaned against it and lit a cigarette.

The cop drove away. The second guy, the presumed hitman, remained where he was. He thoughtfully faced Hope House instead of the alley which made it easy for Carver to sneak up behind his car.

It was time to have a word with this guy and find out exactly what was going on.

Chapter 12

Carver put his Sig to the man's head.

"Hi."

The man froze. He raised his hands. "What the hell is this?"

"Tell me why you're here, and don't lie."

"I'm just out for an evening smoke. Are you mugging me?"

Carver kept the Sig steady against the man's temple and frisked his pockets. He found a wallet in the front pocket. Tugged it out and flipped it open in his palm. The ID was in a plastic windowed pocket.

There was an old flip phone in the other front pocket. It didn't even have a color screen or a screen lock for that matter. There were no text messages on the phone, just a series of calls, all of them from restricted or blocked numbers. It was the perfect burner phone.

Carver frisked the man's back pockets and beneath his shirt. The man didn't have a gun or a knife on him unless it was in an ankle holster. Carver wasn't going to risk bending down to check. If the man had to bend down to draw a gun, he wasn't going to be alive to stand back up again.

Carver examined the name and address on the wallet. The guy lived in Chicago. "Tony Sullivan of Chicago, I'm going to ask you one more time why you're here."

"I told you I'm just out for a smoke break." He had an accent reminiscent of Italian mobsters from a bygone era. He looked and sounded like a hitman.

"All the way from Chicago." Carver nodded toward the car. "And the sack full of cash is so you can buy milk and bread for your mom?"

"Yeah. Milk and bread. Maybe some eggs, too."

Carver backed up a step. He could shoot the man well enough from five feet if he had to. This guy put off serious mobster vibes. He had olive skin, dark hair, and acne scars on his cheeks. He talked like a tough guy even with a gun to his head.

"You were hired to kill Rich Polaski and make it look like a suicide."

Tony's eyes flared. "What the hell is this? Some kind of shakedown? You idiots have a death wish?"

"This isn't a shakedown. I want to know why they hired you to kill him."

Tony's eyes narrowed. "Who are you?"

"I'm someone who's prepared to make you talk, Tony." Carver didn't want to be forced to shoot the man. Mainly because the shot would alert anyone in the vicinity, and it would be difficult to conceal the killing.

If Tony had to go down, it needed to be quiet and as bloodless as possible. A cop had hired this hitman to kill Rich. A cop that was almost certainly tied to the raid on Rich's house. Which meant this was an official act of the local PD.

It meant if Carver wanted to keep investigating, he had to keep Tony's death a secret. A mystery for the police to solve. That was almost certainly where this conversation was heading, especially if Tony didn't answer any questions.

"You think you can make me talk, big guy?" Tony laughed. He still had his lit cigarette which was saying something about his character. The man hadn't lost his cool when he felt a gun to his head. "People have tried to make me talk in the past and it didn't turn out so well for them."

"I'm guessing you were hired to kill Rich and make it look like a suicide because the local cops are nervous about me. They were fine letting Rich live, but I threw a wrench into the plans." Carver paused a beat to gauge Tony's reaction, but the other man took a long draw on his cigarette to finish it off.

Tony tossed the cigarette butt on the ground and ground it out with his foot. "That's going to be you before the night is over."

Carver blew out a breath. "Okay, you're a tough guy. You're not going to answer questions. I guess that means this conversation is over."

"Yeah?" Tony grinned. "You going to shoot me now?"

"Probably."

"Let me tell you a few things you ought to know." Tony slowly reached a hand toward his shirt pocket. "Mind if I get another smoke?"

Carver already knew the man didn't have a weapon concealed in his shirt pocket or anywhere beneath his shirt, so he nodded. "Go for it."

Tony smacked the cigarette pack against the palm of his hand. He pulled out another cigarette and put it in his mouth. He pulled the lighter from his shirt pocket and lit the cigarette. Took a long draw and stared at Carver.

Carver kept the gun steady. "I'm waiting breathlessly for you to tell me what I should know."

"First of all, I know who you are. You're on my list." He pointed toward Hope House with the two fingers holding the cigarette. "Your buddy is on my list but only if I couldn't get you first. If I got you first, then your buddy gets to live."

"Because they're worried I might discover something."

Tony nodded. "Yeah, that's usually how it works. So, you could spare your buddy's life right now by hanging yourself." He grinned.

Carver grinned back. "Excellent plan. Is that all you wanted me to know?"

Tony shook his head. "No, there's more." He sucked down another lungful of smoke and blew it toward Carver. "I've been doing this since I was a teenager. I've been in more close calls than you could imagine. I can count on one hand the number of times I've failed."

"Why would the local cops hire you? Are you connected somehow?"

"No, there's no connection. I'm an independent contractor."

That made sense. "So, you basically answered my questions despite saying you weren't going to."

"I just thought you should get a little background on the situation. Maybe it would alter your perspective."

"You almost convinced me to kill myself, but I'm going to make a counteroffer. How about you forget this job and go home? I'll disappear and Rich gets to live." Carver shrugged. "Sound fair? You can claim you found me and did the job."

"And risk you showing back up?" Tony laughed. "That would ruin my reputation. I'm an honest businessman, okay? And that's why—" Tony didn't finish the sentence. He flicked his cigarette at Carver's face.

Carver had seen the shift in the other man's stance. He'd seen the telltale signs that Tony was about to resort to a desperate last-ditch effort to survive. Maybe Tony had survived similar situations before and thought he had a chance.

Tony lunged. He wasn't a big guy but that didn't mean he wasn't dangerous. Carver took the safe way out and dodged to the side. Tony's arms grasped thin air. He stumbled forward. Carver rammed the Sig's butt on the back of Tony's head.

Tony crashed into the ground. He rolled onto his back, remarkably nimble for a guy who should be unconscious from the blow. He lifted his right leg while reaching a hand toward his ankle. Carver saw a low profile ankle holster beneath the cuff of Tony's pants.

Carver stomped on Tony's leg. Tony cried out in pain. Carver dropped all his weight onto Tony's chest. Air exploded from the other man's lungs. Carver wrapped his hands around Tony's throat and squeezed.

He hated strangling someone this way. It left obvious marks, and Tony's throat was thick for a guy his size, making it harder to squeeze. In fact, the man's throat felt like it was all bone and gristle.

Tony bared his teeth in a grin. Blood stained his teeth and lips. His eyes widened maniacally. It was a look Carver had seen before. The look of a man who'd faced death and wasn't going to give up until the last breath left his body.

Tony's neck tensed. The man had some serious neck muscles, that was for sure. Carver also noticed a thick scar at the base of Tony's throat. Like someone had tried to slit his throat before and failed.

It was a shame to kill a survivor like this. This was a hard man. Someone who'd fought many battles and somehow come out on top each time. He was just a self-employed contract killer trying to get by like everyone else.

It was a damned shame he'd run into Carver. Carver gave up trying to strangle Tony, but he kept a grip on his neck. He raised Tony's head and bashed it against the asphalt. Tony tried to roar in defiance, but the choking had made him hoarse.

His legs flailed. He tried to free his arms, but Carver had them pinned beneath his knees. Carver bashed his head once more against the asphalt. Tony's eyes fluttered and rolled up into his head.

Carver stood. He yanked Tony up by his shirt. There was surprisingly no blood on the back of his head. The blow had been just hard enough to knock him senseless, but he was already starting to recover.

Carver spun Tony around and put his hands on his head. He gripped the jaw on one side and put his hand on the other side of the head. He twisted savagely and heard a satisfying crack. He prevented Tony from falling and put fingers on his neck.

Tony's weak pulse quickly faded to nothing. Tony was dead and it was a shame, really. He wasn't exactly a top-level assassin, but he certainly had been a tough guy. The fact that he hadn't been alert or had a gun within easy reach told Carver that Tony had become complacent. Probably overconfident.

Carver opened the back passenger side car door and sat Tony in the back. He buckled him in but that didn't keep the corpse from slumping. It was all good. He didn't need to stay there for long.

Carver still had his gloves on, so he wasn't leaving any fingerprints. It also meant he wouldn't have gotten Tony's skin under his fingernails or left fingerprint bruises on the dead man's throat.

He hadn't even realized he still had the gloves on. He'd put them on to enter Rich's house and never taken them off even when he delivered the duffel bag to Rich. It was just a force of habit to leave as few traces behind him as possible.

These were habits he hoped he would always maintain, because slipping up even once meant he might end up like Tony, dead in the back of a beat-up old Ford Fusion. It was probably Tony's burner car.

Now it was going to be his final resting place. At least until someone found the car and the body. On the other hand, the car might be something Carver could keep and use for himself. He slid into the driver's seat and reached into the glove compartment.

There was an old nine-millimeter handgun inside. A Smith and Wesson Bodyguard, according to the inscription on the side. The serial numbers were filed off nice and smooth. It was a professional job for sure.

There was also paperwork and two boxes of ammunition in the glove compartment. The car was registered to Sally Smith. The address was in Chicago. There was an Illinois driver's license in the center console.

Tony's face was on the driver's license, but the name was Joe Smith. It seemed real dumb to have his real wallet and ID on him instead of the fake one. He'd obviously thought since he was being hired by cops that he didn't need to worry about faking his identity.

There was no other phone in the car. The burner phone was the only phone Tony brought with him. Maybe it was his real phone. Maybe he left his real phone at home and forgot to leave his wallet and real ID along with it.

The sack of cash was on the passenger seat. Carver decided it was best to count that elsewhere. He needed to make Tony disappear as soon as possible. First, he needed to figure out how to make that happen.

The car keys were still in the ignition. He cranked the engine and pulled away from the curb. He drove down a few streets and parked in a residential neighborhood behind another car. Carver searched the map app for an ideal place to hide a body.

He hadn't seen many abandoned buildings in the area. At least none that were remote enough to hide a body for a long time. The problem with bodies were that they rotted and decayed. They attracted scavengers like vultures and predators of opportunity.

They also attracted dogs, so if someone was walking by and their dog went crazy, they might let the dog follow its nose to a corpse. It was important that Tony remain concealed for a while.

Deep bodies of water were always good options, but sinking a body and keeping it down required too much work for Carver's tastes. Digging holes also worked, but Carver didn't have a shovel, and holes also required a lot of work.

He considered several options. There was a waste meat processing plant that ground up inedible waste from the butchering process and used it for fertilizer. Turning Tony into fertilizer so he could feed families sounded kind of nice.

But it would require breaking into a facility. Carver had used similar facilities in other countries to dispose of bodies, so he knew how to use the equipment, but he didn't feel like infiltrating a plant in the dead of night to do it.

He also considered dumping the body in a trash compacting dumpster behind a restaurant. The smell of rotting food would cover the odor of the body, and it was likely that the body would be hauled to the landfill, buried, and never found.

There was an even better option, but it required driving an hour and a half to Chicago. It was still the easiest option by far, so he decided to take it. He got on the highway and drove a little faster than the speed limit to cut a few minutes off the drive.

He pulled up a website and found Tony's forever home. The website marked all the homeless encampments in and around Chicago and categorized them by size and whether the inhabitants were locals or illegal immigrants.

Apparently, the native homeless population hated the homeless immigrant population, so the two groups were typically found in separate encampments. Carver stopped near one encampment underneath a large highway overpass.

It was late but there were still inhabitants out and about. There were barrel fires and open campfires dotting the area. Many of the tents were of the same design, probably given to the homeless by an organization to make their living space more comfortable.

Carver got into the back seat with Tony. He stripped the man down to his underwear, a tasteful pair of red bikini briefs. There were multiple bullet-wound scars, knife scars, and a messy scar low on the abdomen typical of an emergency appendectomy.

Tony was a survivor. Well, he had been a survivor. No matter how good or lucky you were, there was always someone luckier or better. You just had to avoid meeting that person as long as possible.

Carver bundled the clothing under an arm and walked toward one of the barrel fires. He dumped the clothing on the ground. Maybe someone could use it.

He tossed Tony's real and fake driver's licenses into the fire. He watched the laminate melt and made sure they burned to ashes. He did the same with the credit cards, and everything else in Tony's wallet.

None of the encampment occupants approached him or came near him while he took care of the task. They seemed determined to mind their own business at any cost. That was the way it usually was in the big encampments for some reason. Maybe because it was dangerous to poke around in other people's affairs.

Once everything was properly incinerated, Carver went back to the car. He drove around the encampment until he found a nice dark spot. He got out and used the monocular in thermal mode.

He crept around the tents and investigated the ones that weren't zipped up. Most were occupied. Most stunk to high heaven because the occupants hadn't showered probably for weeks or even months.

One tent had a slightly different odor. Carver spotted used needles. He spotted the occupant. The occupant was deceased, and judging from the stench, his death hadn't been all that recent. Carver went back to the car.

He scanned the area to ensure no one was out and about. The tent fabric blocked infrared, so he could only see people who were outside of the tents. He didn't see anyone in the vicinity, so he hefted Tony's body and carried him to the tent with the drug addict's body.

He laid Tony down next to the dead man and draped an arm suggestively across his back. Almost like a lovers' embrace. That would make it seem more likely the two died of a drug overdose together.

Carver stepped back to look at the scene. It was acceptable. Once the bodies were found and recovered, Tony would probably be processed as John Doe. Case closed. His disappearance would be quite a mystery to everyone that knew him.

Tony was dead and gone, so Rich was safe for the time being. But he was far from being in the clear. In order to ensure his continued wellbeing, Carver would have to get to the root of the problem and rip it out of the ground.

He was going to have to take on a town full of bent cops.

Chapter 13

Carver went back to the car and mulled over what came next.

Bickham was obviously full of bent cops and a sugar daddy named Big D. They wanted him dead. Failing that, they wanted Rich dead.

Tony's mysterious disappearance and Rich's continued survival was going to stir up some kind of reaction. Maybe it would be a little reaction. Maybe it would be an overreaction. Whatever the case, Carver would observe and learn something from it.

Such an observable event wouldn't take place until the morning, which gave Carver some time to rest. He needed to figure out what to do with Tony's car first. Leaving it parked somewhere in Chicago would be best, but then he'd have to catch a bus back to Bickham.

There were multiple bus services in the area but none of them offered service this late in the evening. The next bus going to Bickham left at six in the morning and took three hours to reach the destination due to multiple stops along the way.

There was also train service, but it wasn't any better or faster. It was too far to walk, and he never had much luck hitchhiking. He'd think it over. In the meantime, he had a couple of things he wanted to check out while he was in town.

He'd memorized Tony's real driver's license. It was a long shot, but maybe there was something at Tony's house that would tell Carver exactly who had hired the hitman. Maybe Tony's real phone was there too.

He could always drive back to the tent and use Tony's face or fingerprint to unlock it if need be. Until he confirmed that there was a modern phone at Tony's place, he was going to leave Tony's fingers attached to his body.

Carver plugged the address into the maps app. Tony lived on the south side of Chicago in a neighborhood called Bronzeville. It was a twenty-minute drive from his current location. Traffic was light at the late hour, so he made it there in fifteen.

The streets were lined with limestone and brownstone rowhouses. The front yards were little more than five square feet of grass. In some places it looked like a neighboring rowhouse had been demolished, leaving a single narrow building on a plot of land.

Tony's rowhouse was a red brick affair attached to a long line of identical houses. His house was at the end of the row. There was a single rowhouse on a full-sized lot next to his. The side of the single rowhouse had no windows, probably because that wall had once been shared with another house.

That meant no one could look out of a side window and see Carver walking up to Tony's house. The windows in most of the nearby homes were dark. Everyone was probably asleep since it was just past midnight.

Carver parked the car down the street from Tony's place. He strolled down the sidewalk noting all the dead and broken streetlamps along the way. There was only street parking in the neighborhood, even at the house with the full-sized lot.

There was broken tempered glass on the sidewalk. The cars next to the broken glass didn't have broken windows. Someone must have gone down the street breaking into cars at some point and the mess they'd left behind had never been cleaned up.

He wondered if there was etiquette to parking cars in neighborhoods like this. Did the homeowner have a claim on street parking in front of his house, or was it every man for himself?

There were two empty spaces in front of Tony's house. Tony had probably driven his real car to pick up the Ford. Maybe he had a girlfriend or wife who drove another car. Maybe that was why there were two spaces. Or maybe everyone in the neighborhood gave Tony a wide berth because he looked like a mobster.

The answer was probably the latter.

There was a narrow walkway between Tony's house and the neighbor's chain link fence. Carver turned onto the walkway and followed it to the back of the house. Tony had four keys on his keychain. One was for the Ford. One looked like a padlock key. The other two were house keys.

Carver tested the first house key. It unlocked the deadbolt. The other key unlocked the bottom lock. He wondered why people did that. What was the point of having two separate keys for just one door?

It was one of those mysterious homeowner things that he would never understand. A reinforced frame with deadbolts at the top and bottom and hinges with anti-kick pins were the way to go.

Of course, none of that mattered if the windows were within easy reach. Windows were the weak point of any secure structure as the thief who'd broken into the cars along this road had proven.

Carver unlocked the bottom lock and eased the door open a crack. He didn't think Tony was the kind of guy to set booby traps, but he didn't know for sure. He used his monocular's night vision to check for tripwires and saw nothing.

He pushed the door open. The strong scent of garlic hit him. Carver stepped inside and found out why the odor was so strong. He was in the kitchen and there was a string of garlic hanging from a spice rack.

The kitchen was clean—remarkably clean for a hitman. That raised all sorts of red flags. It meant Tony almost certainly had a wife or girlfriend who enjoyed cooking. She might be in the house.

That meant he couldn't turn on the lights until he confirmed it was empty. He wished he had a pair of night vision goggles. The monocular was great, but it wasn't exactly meant for close quarters.

Carver used it anyway.

The kitchen was long but narrow like the house. The appliances looked old but well kept. There were all kinds of pots and pans hanging from a rack over the gas stovetop. The pantry was full of dry goods. There was definitely a woman in this household.

There was a single door leading out of the kitchen. It led to a hallway. There was a dining room on the right and a family room on the left. The family room had a leather couch. It might be brown or black, but it was hard to tell with night vision.

There was a large TV mounted on the wall. A recliner sat directly in front of it. There was a small end table on the left. It was clean but there were marks and stains on the surface as if something hot had been placed on the surface and left a mark.

There were also salt and pepper shakers on it. It looked like Tony liked to eat while he watched TV. Nothing surprising there. There was a small fireplace with a mantle. There were pictures on the mantle.

The pictures were of a younger version of Tony and a woman about his age. Another picture showed a slightly older Tony and the woman with a young girl and a boy. There were portraits of the same girl and boy hanging on the wall across the room.

There were no portraits of the woman or Tony. There were no pictures of the boy and girl as they aged. Maybe they'd split up. Aside from that, there wasn't much else in the room besides an antique record player and an equally antique cabinet filled with vinyl records.

The record from the top was labeled 1930s club music. Albums from Bing Crosby, Dean Martin, Frank Sinatra, and so forth were stacked neatly on top of the cabinet. It seemed that Tony liked the classics.

Carver liked Tony's music selection. Rock from the sixties and seventies was good. Old jazz was relaxing. Modern music just wasn't his thing. He could listen to any of Tony's preferred artists while relaxing with a beer and gazing at the ocean.

Except he wasn't going to see the ocean anytime soon if he sat here looking at Tony's record collection. He returned to the hallway. He put his weight on the first stair. It creaked loudly. He paused and went motionless, waiting for someone upstairs to say, "Tony, is that you?"

No one did.

The air conditioning thermostat was on the hallway wall. It was the old kind with an analog dial. It was set to seventy-two degrees. Carver set it down to sixty-nine. The air kicked on. The vents rattled. The floor vibrated slightly. The unit was probably down in the basement.

Carver found a door beneath the stairs. He opened it and found a stairway leading into the basement. He left it for the time being and went upstairs. The stairs creaked but the sound of the air conditioner would drown that out for anyone upstairs. Or so he hoped.

There was a landing and a short hallway at the top. There were several doors. Three of them were open. The two that weren't rose to the top of Carver's priority list. He went to the first open door. It was a bedroom. It was fully furnished.

The furniture looked old. The room smelled a little musty like it hadn't been used in a while. There was no clothing, no pictures, no books on the nightstand, or anything to indicate anyone used the room.

The door next to the bedroom was for the hallway bathroom. The door across the hallway went to another bedroom. It looked a lot like the first one. The next door was closed. Carver slowly turned the doorknob. The air conditioner was loud, but a clicking latch would be audible to anyone inside the bedroom.

The latch clicked. He eased open the door and found a linen closet. It was full of blankets, towels, and supplies. He closed it. The next door was open and went to a small office. There was an old wooden desk, shelving, and an ancient computer.

The next door was closed. Carver eased it open and found yet another hallway closet. This one was jammed with coats and other clothing hanging on the rack. The clothing smelled old. It looked old.

Carver closed the door and went to the last door. It was a bedroom. This one had books on the nightstand. It had an open closet door with clothing hanging in it. It had a bed with rumpled sheets.

No one was in the bed. No one was hiding in the corners or in the closet either. Carver went into the master bathroom. It was spacious and like the rest of the house, looked like it had all its original parts. No one was using it to hide.

If Tony had a woman, she wasn't here. Most of the signs indicated Tony lived here alone. Maybe he was divorced. Maybe he liked to cook and kept the kitchen well stocked.

Carver went into the closet. He turned on the light. There was a clothes rack filled with nice suits. There was a chest of drawers with socks, T-shirts, and all the usual items. The underwear drawer was filled with colorful briefs. Apparently, Tony had a wild side when it came to underwear.

There was a metal cabinet on the other wall. Inside the cabinet was a double-barrel sawed-off shotgun. There was a pump action Mossberg Persuader. There were two stainless-steel Colt Anaconda revolvers.

All of those were fine weapons. But the one that won Carver's heart was the H&K MP5. More specifically, it was an MP5SD. It looked like any other MP5 except for what looked like a big suppressor on the end.

The suppressor wasn't separate though. It was an integral piece of the barrel. Combined with the other German engineering inside the barrel, it was about as quiet as a submachinegun could be.

The firing selector on the side rotated between safety, single shot, and sustained fire. There was no serial number on the side, confirming Tony hadn't acquired this thing legally. It was a real nice submachinegun. A work of art.

There were four magazines, all loaded with 9x19 Parabellum rounds. The magazines were nice and slim and relatively lightweight compared to a magazine holding 5.56 rifle rounds. It was ideal for close quarters combat and not so great for sniping at a distance.

Then he saw why Tony hadn't kept this thing by his side just on the off chance that he could use it in a big firefight. The suppressor had a thin crack in the side probably from too much heat buildup. Tony must have abused the full auto feature one too many times.

A cracked suppressor hinted at other problems lurking deeper below the surface. The barrel might be compromised. A warped or bad barrel could lead to rounds exploding in your face. What could have been a great addition to Carver's toolchest was unfortunately not meant to be. He patted it affectionately and set it down.

The other weapons looked good too, but he wasn't interested in the Anacondas. The sawed-off double barrel shotgun was fun but not practical at all. He decided to take it anyway. There was a duffel bag at the bottom of the cabinet. Carver stuffed the shotgun and available ammunition into it.

There was also a large safe in the closet with a combination lock. The safe was old like everything else in the house. It was also far too heavy to move. Tony might have stashed all his cash inside this thing. Unfortunately, Carver wasn't getting into it without some serious tools.

He finished searching the closet, then hefted the duffel bag and carried it to the top of the stairs. He went into the office and turned on the computer. It was an ancient machine running an operating system that hadn't been in use for probably twenty years.

Unsurprisingly, there was nothing of note on it. It looked like it hadn't been used for much of anything in a while. There was a filing cabinet that was well kept. There were paper bills, tax returns, and other items in there.

There was also a folder with several faded newspaper stories in them. One was an obituary for Thomas Sullivan, Tony's son. He'd died in a car accident about ten years ago in his twenties. There was another folder with divorce papers.

Between those two folders, Carver knew about all he needed to about Tony. He also learned that Tony's reported income was about forty thousand a year. He almost certainly wasn't including his income as a hitman in that total.

In fact, his day job was listed as a chef. He was the head chef at an Italian restaurant down the road. That explained the kitchen and all the ingredients. It also told Carver something else important.

If Tony worked for organized crime, they were almost certainly connected to that Italian restaurant. Carver took a picture of the name and address of the restaurant. He didn't plan on visiting it unless he absolutely had to.

Tony might have told him the truth. He might be an independent contractor. Or this might go much deeper than that. The cops in that town might not be ordinary cops. They might be connected to organized crime.

It would be nothing new for the Chicago area. It wouldn't be anything new for Illinois in general. He'd seen and heard enough to know that the political apparatus in the state was far from squeaky clean.

In fact, some Chicagoans prided themselves on the mobster history of their city. Carver couldn't blame them. Old school mobsters were kind of cool in their own way.

He'd dealt with organized crime plenty of times in other countries. The Russian mobsters were some of the most dangerous and well organized, but they weren't unique. There were still plenty of Italian mafiosos doing real well in this day and age. Plenty of them were still thriving in Chicago and the northeast.

And if they were thriving in the town of Bickham, then Rich's situation just got a whole lot more complicated.

Chapter 14

Nadia woke with a pounding headache.

She'd talked long into the night with Keith. He'd listened more than talked. He hadn't said much about himself except that he ran a counseling service. He'd invited her to come and talk through her problems.

Then he'd taken her to a shelter run by the counseling service. It was a nice place. A single-store brick building in south Chicago. She had a room of her own. A bathroom. And for the first time in a while, a bed to sleep in.

She sat up and winced. Pressed her hands to her temples. She looked at the time. It was almost three thirty in the morning. She gasped. She was going to be late for work. She got up, used the bathroom and took a quick shower.

Nadia put on her Bark Security uniform. It was wrinkled and needed a wash. She'd go to the laundry after work today since she no longer had a job at Mr. Grimes' pharmacy.

She stuffed her things into her suitcase. Most of the clothing inside was filthy thanks to the homeless man dragging it into his tent. Keith told her she could stay for a few days in the shelter, but she took everything she owned with her anyway, just in case.

She wished she had something to take for the headache, but that would just have to wait. She ran to her car and took out her phone to plug in the address of the construction site she'd been assigned to guard for the past three weeks.

There was a missed call from Bark Security and a voicemail. She listened to the voicemail.

"Nadia, this is Jerry. I need you to swing by HQ this morning at zero five hundred. Thanks."

Dread filled her stomach. They almost never asked her to come into the office. She had a feeling it was related to her legal problems. It couldn't be anything else. Not unless they were planning to switch her to a new client.

She plugged in the address and pulled onto the road. Traffic was light, so it only took her twenty minutes to reach the front gate. She showed her badge to the guy in the security booth, and he opened the gate to let her in.

Nadia parked and stared at the two-story building. The lights were on in most of the windows even though it was four thirty in the morning. This place ran twenty-four hours, seven days a week. They kept fast-response teams on call for emergencies and monitored every client's security cameras remotely.

The pounding in her head was relentless. She squeezed her eyes shut and pinched the bridge of her nose. It didn't help. She decided to go inside and stop by the infirmary. They'd probably have ibuprofen.

She was also dead tired and probably still a little drunk. A bad combination for reporting to work. Maybe they had something that could freshen her breath a little.

Nadia went to the front door and pressed her badge to the card reader. It beeped and let her in. The lobby was a large square room that rose two stories. There were no other entrances or exits except for the front door.

There was a front desk where a guard sat, and a waiting area just past him. The vinyl seats were avocado green. The table in the center looked like a relic from the seventies. There was nothing else in the minimalist space.

She walked past the front desk. The guard on duty looked up from his computer screen and at her. Her face automatically popped up on his screen when she unlocked the door. He must have decided the picture matched her face because he went back to looking at his computer screen and tapping on the keyboard.

Nadia walked past the waiting area and to a heavy metal door that also required her badge. It buzzed open when she presented it to the card reader. There was a wide hallway on the other side. The walls were gray, and the vinyl flooring was white. It was like that through most of the building, boring and utilitarian.

The infirmary was down the hallway to her left. She went inside to the waiting area. A nurse at the desk looked up from her iPad. "How can I help you?"

"Do you have ibuprofen? I've got a raging headache."

"Absolutely." The woman walked into the supply room at the back and returned with three orange pills. "Six hundred milligrams ought to make it better." She filled a paper cup with water and set it on the counter.

"You're a lifesaver." Nadia downed the pills. "Do you have any mouthwash?"

"Sorry, no. I have gum." The nurse pulled a stick of gum from her purse.

"Thank you so much."

"You're welcome." She smiled. "Anything else?"

"I think that'll do it." Nadia popped the gum in her mouth and felt peppermint sting her tongue. Hopefully it would mask any alcohol still on her breath. She stepped into the hallway and nearly ran into a young man in a black security uniform.

He did a doubletake when he saw her. "Nadia Garcia?"

"Yes, that's me."

"I was sent to retrieve you. Anderson says you can come on up to his office."

Nadia's stomach knotted so fiercely she almost doubled over.

"Are you okay?"

Nadia straightened. "Yes. I'm just nervous about why he wants to see me."

"I'm afraid I don't know, ma'am." He gestured toward the stairwell door. "This way, please."

Nadia followed him into the stairwell and up the stairs. She followed him down the hall to the left, past the monitoring center, the gym, the training rooms, and to the offices. He stopped in front of Anderson's secretary, a rail thin middle-aged woman with a stern look on her face.

"Nadia Garcia for Anderson," the escort said.

The secretary nodded. "Nadia, you can go right in."

"Thanks." Nadia put on her best face and walked around the desk and through the door on the other side. Anderson's office wasn't huge, but it wasn't small either. It was just large enough to convey to visitors that this was an executive's office, nothing more.

His office furniture was minimalistic like everything else. There were two black leather seats in front of the plain wooden desk. Anderson rose from the computer chair on his side of the desk.

He was six feet tall, lean and muscular. His gray hair was cropped short military style, and he wore a black T-shirt and black cargo pants as if he planned to spend the day in an active battle zone. A Sig P226 was holstered to his right thigh.

Anderson stepped around the desk and held out a hand toward Nadia. She shook it. He smiled. "Good morning, Nadia."

"Good morning, sir."

He motioned her to sit down. She took a seat. He sat on the edge of the desk and pressed his lips into a thin line. "I'll cut straight to the point, Nadia. I was made aware of your legal issues. I ran it by our legal department, and they agreed there are compromising elements to them."

"Sir, who told you that?"

"A clerk at the Allenton Police Department. Patty Henderson is her name." His gray eyes focused on her. "Now, before you explain the situation, I'll tell you everything they told me. Your house and other possessions were taken by civil forfeiture proceedings because your brother was utilizing the premises for illegal purposes."

Nadia was unable to repress a shiver of rage. Hopelessness curdled in her stomach. "I had no idea he was doing that, sir. I've done nothing wrong."

"We know you haven't personally done anything wrong, Nadia. But it has created an opportunity for bad actors who are aware of your problems. It means you could potentially be easier to bribe or coopt." He sighed. "In this business, we can't afford to have chinks in the armor. I have therefore assigned our legal department to begin proceedings."

Nadia gritted her teeth and resolved not to show her anger. She would keep her cool and walk out of here without shame. None of this was her fault, but she was paying the price for it.

"Nadia, are you okay?"

She blinked and looked at Anderson. "Yes, sir. Sorry, what were you saying?"

"I said I asked legal to study the situation and see if there's a way to have your home and your things returned to you. Civil forfeiture is an often horribly misused tool in the fight against crime, and we plan to let the police know that we won't just let them take everything from a valued employee."

Nadia's mouth hung open. She hadn't expected this at all. "Really?" She jolted to her feet. "Thank you, sir!"

Anderson held up a hand. "It's not all good news, I'm afraid." He sighed. "Nadia, I have to take you off assignments and put you on suspension for the time being."

She dropped back into the chair. "But—"

"I'm sorry. We'll do everything we can to help with your legal situation, but I'm going to put you on suspension with half pay. It's the best I can do right now."

"Is there a small client I can be assigned to? Maybe someone that only requires shoplifting prevention?"

"I can't keep you on active duty at all. Our insurance requires us to terminate anyone who might potentially be compromised. For example, if we learned you had huge gambling debts or major debt issues in general, we'd have to terminate you."

Anderson stood and walked around his desk. "Your situation is a little different. You're not necessarily burdened with debt, but your home has been taken away, and with it any equity you built into it. You're also still responsible for the mortgage payments since civil forfeiture doesn't alleviate that responsibility."

"Wait, what? I'm supposed to keep making payments on a house I no longer own?" Nadia laughed hollowly. "That's insane!"

"I agree." Anderson held out his hand. "Please give me your badge and your company sidearm."

Nadia pulled the badge from her pocket and handed it to him. She unsnapped the holster from her belt and gave it and the gun inside to Anderson. "What about the uniform?"

"You paid for the uniform out of your first paycheck."

"Oh, I didn't realize that."

"It's stated in orientation."

Nadia nodded. "I guess I was too excited to start work."

Anderson smiled wanly. "With any luck, we'll have your issues settled and have you back on track, okay?"

"Thank you, sir."

He put her things in his drawer. "You asked several times to be promoted to armored truck services, right?"

"Yes, sir."

"Maybe you could use this downtime to take certification courses. As you know, we offer them on our training campus."

"Yes, sir, but I couldn't afford the fees at the time, and there's no discount for employees."

Anderson nodded. "Yes, unfortunately those courses are far too expensive for us to give them away for free. But the pay raise for armored car division makes it worthwhile."

"Provided I can actually keep my job."

"True." He pressed his lips together. "I've asked Troy to escort you out. We'll keep you notified, okay?"

"Thank you again, sir. I was honestly very surprised you'd do that for me."

"I reviewed your evaluations, and they're all glowing, Nadia." He walked around the desk and to the door. "Your military service and record tell the story of a skilled and brave individual I would like to keep in the Bark Security family."

"I appreciate that, sir."

Anderson opened the door. "We'll keep you notified of our progress, okay?"

"Thank you, sir." Nadia stepped out of the office. Anderson closed the door behind her.

Her escort from earlier stepped forward. "I'll escort you outside."

"Thank you, Troy."

He didn't seem surprised that she now knew his name. They took the stairs to the first floor and exited the front door. Troy didn't go outside with her. Nadia turned and watched the door swing shut. The magnetic lock clicked and hummed.

She turned toward the parking lot and walked toward her last remaining possessions, her car, her clothing, and a broken laptop. Nadia dropped into the driver's seat. She opened her wallet and looked at the cash inside.

Mr. Grimes had given Nadia her final paycheck in the form of cash since it was easier that way. It was just over eight hundred dollars. Maybe enough to pay for a new passenger side window. Maybe enough to let her live in a cheap motel for a week.

She still had car payments to make. She also apparently still had mortgage payments to make. Her mortgage was almost three thousand dollars. Her car payment was four hundred. It was all automatically drafted from her bank account each month.

Her salary with Bark Security was fifty-one thousand a year or four thousand two hundred dollars a month. After taxes, she took home about three thousand. Cutting that in half would reduce her tax withholding but she'd be bringing in maybe fifteen hundred a month.

She definitely couldn't cover the mortgage. There was no choice but to let it go into default and keep making the car payments.

Nadia logged into the mortgage website and disabled the automatic draft. She received an email a moment later from the bank telling her that automatic draft was required due to her credit score and that it would not be disabled.

Her checking account was with the same bank she had her mortgage with. That was a problem. She needed to make sure her paychecks didn't go to that account anymore. She was still sitting in the parking lot but without her badge, she couldn't just go back into the building.

Knocking on the door to be let in was embarrassing, so she called the main number and pressed the options to take her to the payroll department. She asked to pick up her checks in person instead of having them electronically deposited. The woman in payroll set it up and said her next paycheck would be available at the end of the week.

With that settled, Nadia drove to the nearest ATM and emptied the remaining five hundred dollars from her bank account. She went to a hardware store and purchased metal tape and heavy-duty clear plastic to cover her passenger side window.

Without work, she didn't know what to do with herself. It was barely six thirty in the morning and she had nothing to do and nowhere to be. Her best next move would be to find employment somewhere else because the legal proceedings to recover her property could take months.

Nadia drove back to the shelter. She could look for employment tomorrow. She was exhausted from staying up late and drinking. What she needed now was sleep. She hunted around for street parking and finally found a slot uncomfortably close to a homeless encampment.

Her car already looked trashed with the plastic covering the window, and she wasn't going to leave anything inside the car anyway. Maybe no one would mess with it. She got her suitcase and closed the car. She left it unlocked since the plastic wouldn't stop anyone from breaking in if they wanted to.

She headed down the sidewalk toward Hope House, wending between the tents and garbage in the homeless encampment. There was a flash of movement to her right. A body slammed into her.

Nadia lost her grip on the suitcase and fell hard. Her head bounced off the concrete and stars flashed in her vision. She saw a man in filthy clothing standing over her. He punched her in the head.

She blacked out for an instant. The man dug through her pockets and yanked out her wallet. He grinned and shivered in pleasure. Anger burned through Nadia's disorientation. She grabbed the man.

He tried to punch her again, but she threw up her other arm in defense. His fist struck her elbow. He howled in pain. Fury overcame Nadia. She reached into her uniform's leg pocket. Pulled her knife.

She thrust it sideways. It plunged into the man's side. The blade hit bone and twisted sideways before going in deeper. The man screamed. Nadia pulled the knife out. The man toppled sideways off her.

Nadia pushed herself upright. She grabbed her wallet and money. She stood. Kicked him in the ribs. She abruptly came to her senses and stopped. There was blood. So much blood. The man was going to die, and she was going to be charged with murder.

This was Chicago. They prosecuted people for killing in self-defense. Nadia looked around. It was still dark and none of the other homeless people had come out of their tents. They were still asleep at this early hour. But they probably wouldn't be for long after all this noise.

Nadia jumped back from the bleeding man. She grabbed her suitcase and ran down the sidewalk toward Hope House. She dodged between tents and garbage. She looked around for anyone who might have seen what she did, but no one else was there.

She went into the building. No one was at the reception desk. She hurried back to her room. Closed the door. It didn't have a lock. She went into the bathroom and washed the blood off her hands and the knife.

Her uniform was spotted with blood, so she took it off and soaked it in the sink. She could take it to the laundry later.

Nadia took a shower. She was filthy from her tumble to the ground and the fight, and she had blood on her face. Once she was cleaned up, she stared at herself in the mirror. She saw a crazy woman looking back at her. A killer.

She'd killed before but that had been in the service of the country. Now she'd killed a man who tried to rob her. An unarmed man. There had been low spots in Nadia's life, but this was as close to rock bottom as she'd ever been.

"What in the hell is happening to me?" Tears streamed down her face. "What am I going to do?"

There was a knock on her door. She wrapped the towel around her and stepped into the room. The door opened and Keith stepped inside. He blinked when he saw her in the towel. He looked at her shoes and back to her. "Sorry, but can you come look at something?"

"I'm not dressed."

"Can you get dressed?"

"Okay. Wait outside."

Keith left the room. Nadia threw on jeans and a T-shirt. She picked up a shoe to put it on and saw blood on the tip. She grabbed toilet paper and wiped it off. She stepped into the hallway.

Keith was leaning against the wall outside. He blew out a breath. "Follow me. He led her to the lobby and pointed at the floor.

There were bloody footprints leading from the door and into the hallway.

Chapter 15

Carver went to the basement stairs in Tony's house.

He went down the stairs and found a metal door at the bottom. The door was padlocked shut. Carver used the padlock key on Tony's keychain to open it. He pulled the padlock off, swung the hasp off the latch, then hung the padlock on the latch hole.

The door opened silently on well-oiled hinges. There were metal shelves inside and dusty cardboard boxes stacked on the shelves. It looked like Tony had stuck all his random junk down here like any other normal person.

Carver turned on the light and looked around. He was ready to leave when he noticed scratches on the floor next to one of the shelves. It looked like the shelf had been moved repeatedly.

There were felt pads glued to the bottom of the metal shelf legs. It was the only shelf that had them. Moving it must have kept scratching the concrete until Tony put the felt pads on the bottom.

Carver pulled the shelf away from the wall. This shelf had a board attached to the back to conceal what was behind it. Behind the board was another metal door. There was a heavy barrel bolt on this door, but it wasn't engaged.

The door opened easily and quietly. There was a slab of pink foam glued to the other side of the door. Carver stepped into the room and found a light switch. There were thick foam panels glued to all the walls.

In the middle of the room was an iron box with a slit cut into a door in the front. Carver opened the door and looked inside the box. It was maybe four feet tall, six feet wide, and six feet long.

There was a thin, dirty mattress inside. The mattress had all kinds of stains on it. Probably blood. Probably other bodily fluids. There was a metal pail inside too. It looked clean, but it had probably been used as a toilet.

The box was one thing, but what really caught Carver's attention was the wall on the left side of the room. It was covered in photos. More specifically, photos of young men. Men who looked eerily similar to Tony's son.

There were several pictures of each subject. One when they were unconscious. One when they were inside the box. Several pictures documenting the decline of the young men into hopelessness and insanity.

Each series of pictures was a story. Each story ended with a knife in the chest of a young man. The pictures were laid out like the storyboards for a particularly gruesome movie, except these events had occurred in real life.

Carver counted thirty-one such stories. Thirty-one young men imprisoned, tortured, and murdered. Tony hadn't just been a hitman; he'd been a serial killer. Apparently, he captured young men who reminded him of his son.

He kept them caged in the basement for weeks or maybe months before killing them. Maybe he felt like they were temporary replacements for his lost son. Maybe they were the sons of enemies or the sons of someone he'd killed and taken as a trophy.

Carver looked around but didn't find a journal or anything explaining the abductions and murders. Whatever the reason, it went to the grave with Tony. It wasn't all that important to know anyway.

Tony had been a stone-cold killer. A professional hitman. But he'd also had an unprofessional side to him. A side that apparently enjoyed killing. In some cases, it was just business, nothing personal. And in the cases of these young men, it looked entirely personal.

There were no dossiers. No handwritten notes about jobs past, present or future. Tony apparently just kept it all in his head. It was safer that way. No paper trail for the cops to find if they nabbed Tony one day.

It looked like Carver was done here. Almost done. There was one more thing he could do to throw a wrench into the works. Maybe a way to give the families of the murdered men some closure.

It seemed like a good idea. Carver thought it through as he walked upstairs and decided it was better than good. It was great. He went to the old landline phone in the kitchen. It was an old-school push-button phone.

Now that he was here, his plan seemed less great. He'd considered calling 911 so the cops would come investigate Tony's place. They'd find the secret room and the pictures. They'd find all the evidence painting Tony as a serial killer.

It was bound to make the news. Thirty families would finally have closure on their missing boys, provided there were surviving relatives. Maybe the bodies were buried in the backyard. It was highly doubtful. Tony had probably been too careful to do that.

But bringing down the law on Tony's house would also alert Palmer and the Bickham police that Tony was dead or missing right away. It would raise the heat level. He wasn't prepared to do that just yet. Maybe later he would.

Carver left the house. He hopped back into Tony's burner car and searched the maps app for an electronics or security store. He found what he was looking for just a few blocks away, but it was closed at this late hour. There was a twenty-four-hour big box store twenty minutes away, so he went there.

The big store was almost empty of people. The shelves were also mostly empty and those that weren't were secured with cages and padlocks. The store didn't have parabolic mics or the really good stuff he wanted, but they had small security cameras.

He found an employee to unlock the cage guarding them and purchased a few along with a hub that could wirelessly upload the footage. Carver didn't have a specific use in mind for them, but they might come in handy.

When he was finished there, he drove back to Bickham. Rich was safe for the time being, but there was more to be done. The next thing he needed to do was track down Palmer, the cop who'd paid Tony to kill Rich.

The order to do that had obviously come from higher up, but Palmer would be a good starting point for an investigation. The problem was, Carver couldn't directly question him. He'd have to shadow him and see where that led things.

Then he would decide just how far he needed to go to protect Rich.

Rich stared blankly at the TV.

A show was on, but he hadn't watched a minute of it. He'd been lost in thought. Trying to wrap his head around what Carver had told him. Could he really pay for Rich's surgery? Would he?

Carver wasn't the kind of guy to make idle statements. He wasn't the kind of guy to talk unless it was part of a mission or unless he felt he had something important to say. That was why he hadn't had many friends in their unit.

Despite that, he'd always been a reliable guy. He'd always been there for his cohort. Always done what he was told. Never left a brother behind. At least until he'd left Rich behind.

It had been a straightforward mission. Get in, abduct the target, get out. He could see everything just as clearly as the day it had happened.

###

The UH-60 Nighthawk ran silent through the darkness. The baffles were fully engaged, directing sound skyward. It was still loud inside the cabin, but to people on the ground it would be faint, almost unnoticeable.

"Thirty seconds to LZ," the pilot said. "Beginning rapid decent."

"Roger that." Joe Donnelly gave a thumbs up to everyone. "In and out. I'm on point. Carver you're rear guard. Keep track of your buddies. Make sure everyone gets out."

Everyone returned the thumbs up. Everyone already knew their assignments. They knew the layout of the building. They knew exactly how this was going to go down because they had good intelligence.

Akim Jabar was the target. He wasn't a terrorist leader, or a soldier. As far as they knew, he hadn't killed anyone. But he was responsible for laundering billions of dollars and secretly diverting it to terrorist groups.

Most importantly, he'd been diverting huge sums of money to Rahm Abdul Assad, a former prince turned terrorist. Akim was onsite visiting one of his favorite women and he likely had a laptop with him that had access to many of his secret accounts.

That was all Rich knew. That was all anyone in the unit knew. They were just there to kidnap the money man and get out.

The Nighthawk swung hard right and touched down. Everyone piled out. The chopper was in the air a split second after the last man's boots hit the ground. They were just inside the walls of a compound.

There were no guards patrolling the grounds. Terrorists learned the hard way that having a heavy guard presence just made them more noticeable to satellites. They opted to keep guards indoors with vantage points.

A place like this didn't have many guards anyway. It was just a place Akim kept one of his favorite women so he could visit her whenever he wanted to while keeping a low profile.

The target building was in the middle of several outbuildings. They were all made of hardened and reinforced concrete. The buildings could have been demolished by missiles, bombs, or any other means, but capturing the target and his laptop was what the big boys wanted.

They hurried toward the nearest outbuilding in single file. There were no streetlamps or exterior lights in the compound, so they relied on night vision to see where they were going. They reached the outer building.

Joe edged to the door. He signaled the go-ahead. Jefferson tested the doorknob. Nodded. He eased it open. The two rushed in. The rest of them followed. The building was small. There were two men inside.

They neutralized them with their suppressed HK416s. They cleared the small building. Returned outside. Moved to the next building. This one had a window. The lights were on inside. A lone man sat on a couch watching Happy Days with Arabic subtitles.

They stacked up on the door. Jefferson tested the doorknob. Nodded. He eased it open. Joe went in first. His HK coughed. Brains spattered the TV screen. The guy watching Happy Days never got to see Fonzie jump the shark. Maybe that was for the best.

There were two large rooms with bunk beds in them. There were two men asleep in two of the beds. They neutralized them. Cleared the building. No one spoke. No one made a sound even though it was probably safe to. It was best to maintain silence and keep going.

The target building was right next door to this one. If there were active guards, they'd be right inside and presumably more alert. More often than not, these guards had performed their boring routines for so long that they'd become complacent.

They were about to find out if that was true here or not. The target building had three doors, all made of heavy iron. All were buttressed with iron bars on the inside. They could be blown open with enough C4, but thankfully, they didn't have to resort to that.

The reason for that was simple. There was a secret exit from the target building. That secret exit was an underground tunnel. The bedroom Akim slept in was also deep underground. Terrorists had learned that sleeping on the top floor of house just made you an easy target.

Joe took point and led them down a flight of stairs and into the basement. There were shelves filled with dry goods and other ordinary household supplies. Joe went straight to a shelf loaded with what looked like heavy burlap sacks.

He pressed his hand against a sack. It was like pushing a pillow. The contents were something soft. Joe pulled on the shelf. It slid easily to the side as if it weighed almost nothing. The sacks didn't move or fall off because they were glued to the shelf.

Behind the shelf was a curtain. Joe pulled it to the side to reveal a dark tunnel. He signaled to advance and took point. Jefferson stacked up behind him, a hand on his shoulder. The others followed.

Rich looked behind him and saw Carver staring at the opening. He seemed to be hesitant to go inside. Rich moved out with the others. He glanced back and saw Carver following.

They went down a slope into the tunnel. The tunnel branched off in different directions. Joe took a left, then a right, ignoring the other branches. They entered a room with multiple tunnels connected to it.

Joe hugged the wall to the right. He pointed to the three tunnels in the wall. Held up two fingers. Motioned forward. Jefferson and Sanchez stacked up on the middle tunnel. It was just wide enough for them to proceed shoulder-to-shoulder.

Rich stacked to the right side of the tunnel. Carver should have touched him on the shoulder to let him know he was there, but there was nothing. He looked back. Carver wasn't there. Where in the hell was he?

Carver appeared from one of the tunnels. He ran past Rich. Ran straight to Joe. Said something to him. There was no hesitation. Joe signaled a retreat. Jefferson and Sanchez took point and returned the way they'd come.

Joe said something to Carver and chopped his hand forward. He ran after the others. Carver nodded. Rich was confused but he took his position behind Porter and hurried after the others.

Gunfire erupted. There was an explosion. Rich looked back. Carver wasn't there. Something struck him. He crashed against the wall. The ceiling fell on him and everything went black.

Consciousness returned slowly. Painfully. His head felt like it was split open. His mouth was dry. His tongue felt like sandpaper. His eyelids felt glued shut. He could hardly feel his hands or feet. He tried to move but he was tightly bound.

Someone spoke in Arabic. Cold water splashed in his face. He was finally able to open his eyes. The first thing he saw was a grinning face. A face he knew well from dossiers and mission briefings. The face of his soon-to-be torturer.

Rahm Abdul Assad.

Chapter 16

Nadia stared at the bloody footprints in horror.

They faded out just inside the hallway, so they didn't lead directly to her room. She tried to play innocent. "Is that paint?"

Keith sighed. "Nadia, I was down the street picking up breakfast from the café. I saw you running inside with your suitcase. You looked scared. I saw the bloody footprints and followed them here."

Nadia felt sick to her stomach. "A homeless guy tried to mug me! He got on top of me and started punching me! It was self-defense!"

Keith put a hand on her shoulder. "It's okay. You wouldn't be the first person who was attacked by someone from that encampment."

"So, you're not going to tell anyone?"

"I would never report a fellow veteran for an act of self-defense."

Nadia felt weak with relief. "Thank you. I don't know if I could handle even one more problem."

"I think you're already past the breaking point." Keith stepped back. "There's a group of us who meet a couple times a week just to unload our problems on each other. It's nothing formal and definitely not like an AA or addicts meeting. Just former vets who have to live in a civilian world."

Nadia wiped tears from her cheeks. "I could use something like that. But more than anything, I need a job. I need money."

"Don't you have a job?"

"I did. At least until yesterday." She told him about the pharmacy and her paid suspension with Bark Security.

"Man, that's tough." Keith bit his lower lip. "Maybe someone at the meeting can help. Some of them have their own companies."

Nadia didn't have high hopes of keeping her job at Bark Security. Even if she did, she couldn't survive on half wages in the meantime. "I'm willing to consider anything." She laughed. "As if I have a choice."

Keith took out his phone and tapped on the screen. "I think there's a meeting today. Let me confirm."

"Sure. Great." Nadia tried not to get her hopes up but couldn't help it. She felt like she was at rock bottom. Like she had nowhere to go but up. She'd had low points in her life, but it felt like everything was piling on top of her at once.

"In the meantime, let's get this cleaned up. Follow me." Keith walked down the hallway. Nadia followed him. He stopped in front of a door, pulled out a ring of keys, and unlocked it. He opened the door to show her a supply closet.

There was a large utility sink inside and shelving with various cleaning products on them.

Keith pointed to a rolling mop bucket and mop. "Take that, some of the general-purpose cleaner, and clean up the blood inside and outside. We don't want a blood trail leading here, okay?"

Nadia nodded. "I'm on it."

Keith nodded. "Get to it, soldier."

She put water in the bucket. Poured in a generous amount of pine-scented cleaner. This was nothing new to her at all. She'd had kitchen duty more times than she could remember during basic. She'd had to learn how to do it properly or get dressed down by the sergeant.

Nadia mopped the hallway. She pushed the bucket outside and mopped the footprints on the sidewalk. It felt surreal mopping up the trail of blood all the way through the homeless encampment. No one emerged from the tents to bother her or ask what she was doing.

The non-homeless residents glanced her way as they went about their business, but they probably thought she was just cleaning up feces and urine. That wasn't too far from the truth. The sidewalk was caked with urine and human waste.

The homeless man wasn't where she'd left him. There was a trail of blood leading into a tent. She stopped mopping and looked inside. The man was face down in his tent. A rusty old table knife protruded from his back.

Nadia flinched in surprise. Had someone else attacked the man after she left him for dead? In a place like this there was no telling. With the bloody footprints gone, it looked like someone had stabbed the man and he'd crawled into his tent to die.

The police might take one look and think another homeless person did it. They'd investigate. Question the other inhabitants of the encampment. Check nearby security camera feeds.

It was the last possibility that sent chills down her spine. She immediately looked up and around for cameras. She didn't see any. She pushed the mop cart back into the shelter. She emptied the water into the utility sink and washed the bucket and mop to remove all traces of blood.

She went back outside and looked carefully at all the nearby buildings. None of the buildings on this side of the street had cameras. There was a camera on a bodega across the street, but it was pointed down at their door. It wouldn't see anything across the street.

Nadia walked up and down both sides of the street. She found two more places with cameras, but none of them were pointed in the direction of the homeless encampment. She might be in the clear.

Keith was waiting right inside the door when she returned. He smiled. "Good job."

Nadia blinked in confusion. "Thank you?"

"I saw how thorough you were. How aware you were of your surroundings. What kind of military duty did you have?"

"Grunt work mostly."

"You ever see combat?"

She nodded. "Yeah."

"Kills?"

"Four confirmed. There might be more, but it's hard to know in the middle of a firefight."

"Why'd you get out? Too heavy?"

"I don't really like to talk about it."

Keith patted her shoulder. "Totally understandable." He looked at his phone. "There's a meeting starting in an hour."

"Really?" Nadia checked the time and was shocked to discover it was nearly noontime. She'd completely lost track of time. "Where is it?"

"Not far. I can drive us there."

"Yeah, sure." Nadia looked at her hands and realized they were filthy from cleaning the mop and bucket. "I'm going to clean up. I'll meet you out here in fifteen."

"Sounds good."

Nadia showered. She threw on comfortable cargo pants, a T-shirt, and tennis shoes. She left the room and stared at the doorknob. The lack of a lock was concerning but she didn't want to lug her suitcase everywhere with her.

There wasn't much of value in it anyway. She walked down the hallway to the lobby. Keith was there talking to a young man wearing a Dodgers ballcap backwards. Keith looked at her and smiled. "Doug here will be joining us. He's a former Marine."

"Sure." Nadia shook Doug's hand. "Nice to meet you." She smirked at his ballcap. "You must love losing."

Doug grinned. "Hey, this is their year for sure."

Keith laughed. "That's what we say about the Red Sox every year."

"Still plenty of season left for them to make it into the NLCS," Doug said.

Nadia wasn't all that into sports, but she knew enough to banter with others. It was a learned trait in the military. An easy way to break the ice and get to know people.

"All right, better get a move on." Keith motioned them to follow him and led them outside. They walked a block to an old white van with Hope House painted on the side.

Nadia took shotgun. Doug pushed open the sliding door and got into the back without complaint. Keith started the engine and wheeled around in a U-turn. They drove about fifteen minutes to a big community center.

It was a big building from a bygone era. It looked like one of the giant gymnasiums from the fifties or sixties, a giant concrete building with a little something for everyone inside. There was enough parking for hundreds of cars, but the parking lot was nearly empty aside from a handful of cars.

"Now that's one big building," Doug said. "It looks abandoned."

"It was closed down a few years ago," Keith said. "Hope House bought it thinking they could revitalize it, but I guess it cost more money than they could afford to sink into it." He pulled into a parking space next to a blue Toyota with a missing bumper and heavily dented rear fender.

They went through double glass doors to the inside. There was an admissions desk where people used to pay a fee or verify membership before being allowed in. They turned right and followed the curving hallway. Faded signs pointed to locker rooms somewhere ahead.

They went left through a large opening and entered a huge open area. The place was massive, boasting two basketball courts, an Olympic sized swimming pool, a gym with free weights and machines, and more.

The gym looked clean and well maintained. There were fresh nets on the basketball court goals, and a cage with new balls inside. The Olympic pool, however, was empty.

Doug whistled. "Man, that's some nice gym equipment."

"We used it sometimes," Keith said. "But obviously it's expensive trying to keep a place like this maintained."

Doug nodded. "I'll bet."

Large signs pointed to the men and women locker rooms and restrooms which were walled off from the open interior of the gym just beyond the pool area.

Right in the middle of the vast space were rows of chairs and a foldout table with a coffee machine and donuts on it. There were seven people standing near the table. Keith led them to the group and shook hands with a man. He turned to Nadia and Doug. "This is Tom. Tom, this is Nadia and Doug."

"Nice to meet you." Tom shook their hands. He was a little taller than Nadia. Maybe five feet, ten inches. He was lean but his arms were nicely toned. His thick black hair was neatly combed to the side. He looked like a businessman that had thrown on jeans and a shirt just to fit in with everyone else.

Nadia noted his firm grip. "Nice to meet you too, Tom."

Doug shook his hand. "What service were you in?"

"Army," Tom said. "And you?"

"Marines."

Tom grinned. "Semper fi."

Doug raised a fist. "Semper fi."

Tom pointed at the donuts. "Make yourselves at home."

Nadia's stomach was growling. She really wanted lunch, but donuts would do for now. She chose a jelly donut and chased it down with a cup of black coffee.

Tom clapped his hands. "Okay, everyone, let's find a seat and get started."

Keith found a seat. Nadia sat next to him. She studied the faces of the men and women present. There wasn't a sad face among them. They were all grinning and talking like they didn't have a care in the world.

Group therapy wasn't normally like this. The mood was almost always grim. There were few smiles and even fewer laughs. Maybe getting together with fellow vets was the best medicine for people who couldn't adapt to a civilian life.

"If you're new here, raise your hands," Tom said.

A young man with a thick scar on his cheek raised his hand. Nadia reluctantly raised hers. She hated introducing herself to a crowd no matter the size.

"Excellent." Tom rubbed his hands together. "You can tell us a little about yourself if you want, but you don't have to."

The young guy looked at the woman next to him. She nodded encouragingly. He stood. "I'm Jordan. I was in Afghanistan during the withdrawal. I caught a bullet in the face." He touched the scar. "Somehow it just tore a hole in my cheek." He swallowed hard. "My two buddies weren't so lucky. Neither was our unit translator and guide, Ali. He brought his family, and they refused to take him."

Tears welled in his eyes. "Those idiots in charge just let them die. They didn't even try to help. I took two other translators onto the plane, and they kicked me out because of it. Dishonorable discharge."

The woman next to him patted his arm. "You tried to do the right thing."

"They threatened to court martial me if I didn't take the discharge." Jordan's jaw clenched. "All I can think about is how I want to go face-to-face with those smug bastards and put them in the ground."

Jordan took deep breaths. He bit his lower lip. "Sorry. I get emotional when I think about it." He sat down.

Tom pursed his lips and nodded. "Jordan, we get it. The bureaucracy always wins."

A muscular man with a heavy beard raised a fist. "It shouldn't!"

The others in the circle raised their fists and shouted in agreement.

"Amen, brother." Tom turned to Nadia. "No pressure."

Nadia felt emboldened by Jordan's story. He'd outright admitted how she felt a lot of the time, and everyone was so supportive. She took a deep breath and stood. "I'm Nadia. I was an Army grunt. I was also in Afghanistan, but I got kicked out long before the withdrawal."

The woman next to Jordan grinned. "I like you already."

Nadia smiled back. "We were doing routine patrols guarding poppy fields for a local tribe. None of us knew why, exactly, but we figured it had something to do with winning hearts and minds."

There were laughs and groans all around.

"We had similar duty," a man said. "You were in the northeast?"

"Yep," Nadia said. "The CIA had a heavy presence there too. They'd show up in trucks during harvesting, load up, and pay the villagers with goats, chickens, and food."

"Same!" the man said.

"Brad, let's hear the rest of her story," Tom said.

The man nodded. "Sorry, I talk a lot."

The others laughed.

"There were rumors about a withdrawal," Nadia said. "It was supposed to happen within a month. The local CIA implants didn't like that at all. They didn't tell us directly, but I overheard them talking about it a lot."

Her hands shook as she thought about the night it all went down. "The CIA team pulled out two days later. They didn't say a thing to us. No one knew why they left. They'd been the ones giving us the orders, so we asked for an update from our forward operating base commander, but the satellite signal was gone."

Brad nodded as if he'd heard it all before.

"Our team leader felt like something was off, so he made the decision to pull out under cover of darkness. The problem was, we'd been left high and dry without wheels, so we'd have to hoof it."

Nadia's heart beat harder and faster as the story got closer to the worst part. "We left at nightfall, but it was already too late. Taliban forces must have been converging on us all day, because they flooded into the village that night. There were a hundred of them and forty of us."

The others were leaning forward in their chairs. Brad nodded as she spoke.

"We were already geared up and ready to go. It was obvious they hadn't expected that, because they were rushing us on foot." Nadia smiled grimly. "If you served time there, you know they never just rushed a position unless they knew for certain they could catch us off guard. It was like they expected us to be tucked in for the night with minimal guards."

Brad laughed. "I wish I could have seen the looks on their faces."

"Oh, we did. And what shocked us was that these hundred fighters had helmets and night vision goggles, all of them U.S. Army issued."

"Are you kidding me?" the woman next to Jordan said.

"Anyway, we started blasting." Nadia made finger guns. "We would have taken them all down with minimal casualties, but then the villagers attacked us from the rear. It was a well-planned ambush, clearly designed to wipe us out."

"It was the CIA, wasn't it?" Brad said.

Nadia took a deep breath. "We lost almost half our team by the time it was all said and done. But the tangos were dead as were all the men of fighting age in the village." She bared her teeth. "We interrogated the other villagers with our translator. They claimed they didn't know anything about it. But one of the village elders finally admitted under torture that they'd been told to wipe us out."

"By the CIA?" Brad said.

Nadia couldn't answer. She saw the muzzle flashes. The blood. The bodies of her brothers in arms lying all around her. She felt a hand squeezing her shoulder and turned to see Keith there.

"Hey, you don't have to keep going."

"No, I want to." Nadia steeled herself and continued. "We didn't leave anyone alive in that village."

Brad stood and clapped. Others rose and clapped and cheered.

She flinched because she hadn't been expecting that reaction. "We were full of rage and fury. We blamed every adult for what happened."

The woman next to Jordan nodded. "And the kids?"

"The boys in the village attacked us alongside the older men. The really young kids were nowhere to be found. We think they sent them somewhere safe until the attack was over."

"Sons of bitches." Brad smacked a fist into his palm. "Our team was in the northeast too. We were guarding opium fields. There was no CIA team there and we were reassigned during that first mention of a full withdrawal. I wonder why they targeted your team specifically."

"I don't know," Nadia said. "But I think about it every day. I'd love to get my hands on those bastards." She took a few deep breaths. "The Taliban had driven several Toyota Hilux trucks and parked them in a valley not far from the village. They'd left them to approach quietly on foot. We took those trucks and made it back to FOB Dyer."

Brad frowned. "That's not even an Army base, is it?"

"No it was a Marine FOB." Nadia shrugged. "It didn't matter to us. We just needed to get somewhere safe. The next thing we knew, we were transported via Osprey to FOB Halifax and then taken out of country with absolutely no explanation."

Her fists clenched. "We were all dishonorably discharged for multiple violations, but mostly because they said we abandoned our duty posts. There was no mention of the village or anything. We were also threatened with court martials if we didn't agree."

Nadia blew out a breath. "Anyway, that's it in a nutshell. I think about it every day. I want to hunt down the people responsible for it. But instead, I force myself to work in a civilian world that feels completely alien to me." She sat down.

Tom nodded. "Thank you, Nadia. In one way or another, most of us identify and agree with you."

Murmurs of assent rose around the room. Nadia could hardly believe it. It felt like she'd finally found a place she belonged.

Chapter 17

Carver had to hunt down a cop.

More specifically, he was looking for Officer Palmer. He had a few questions for the man, the most important of which was why was a cop using a mafia hitman to take out a man the police had taken everything from?

Carver had an hour and a half to think on his way back to Bickham. The town was squeaky clean. It spared no expenses keeping everything in top notch condition. The few cops he'd seen were feared by the locals. Bickham PD demonstrated that power by stripping Rich of all his earthly possessions.

Was Rich the rule or the exception? Did BPD exercise this power frequently, or rarely? Did the money from civil forfeiture pay for the town's maintenance? Big government buildings required a lot of upkeep. Carver was no building maintenance expert, but it seemed like common sense.

They couldn't rely entirely on people doing community service. There had to be permanent professionals doing certain jobs. There was no way the town didn't spend millions of dollars in annual upkeep.

The town wasn't that large, at least on the map. Maybe the population had deep pockets. Maybe if everyone was shopping locally and the government was paying local companies to provide maintenance and upkeep, they had enough tax receipts to fund the town.

All of those considerations were way out of Carver's wheelhouse. He didn't know a thing about building upkeep or governmental budgeting. All he could do was make assumptions about those things.

Things like extortion and ruling through fear were certainly well inside his wheelhouse. From his perspective it looked like those kinds of things were certainly happening in this town. Maybe it was limited to a small subset of the police department. Maybe it was widespread. Maybe this Big D guy was at the center of it.

Officer Palmer probably had most of the answers. Tracking him down and questioning him was right at the top of Carver's priority list. Palmer had probably gone home to bed after handing off Rich's assassination to Tony. It would probably be hard to find him at this late hour, but Carver decided to try anyway.

He drove back to Hope House and parked Tony's car where it had been earlier. He didn't need to wipe it down since he'd worn gloves. He put the keys in the center console, closed the door, and went down the alley.

Carver returned to his minivan. He drove back into town. Drove up and down the grid of streets. Everything was closed at this late hour and the streets were empty. It was like a ghost town. There were almost no cars parked anywhere downtown except in front of the police station.

The Caprice wasn't one of those cars. It wasn't anywhere visible. Carver thought it might be behind the gate at the police station, but he wasn't going to try climbing the wall to look over it. There were cameras covering the gate and the wall so he couldn't get close to the place without being seen.

Carver drove through the nearby neighborhoods. He didn't see the Caprice. Maybe it wasn't Palmer's daily driver. Maybe he just used it when he was meeting with mafia hitmen. Either way, it didn't look like Carver was going to find Palmer tonight. He'd have to wait until the officer was on duty and follow him when he left work.

The only thing to do now was get some sleep. Carver got on the highway out of town. He passed the Stargazer Motel along the way. The parking lot was just as empty as it had been earlier. He wondered how it stayed in business without any customers.

He followed the highway a little over two more miles and found Big Value Inn. It was still in the same county as Bickham but didn't have the sky-high ratings like the Stargazer. Maybe you had to be related to someone in the government to get all the fake reviews.

This place had a 2.5 star rating. It was better than the one across the county line, but not by much. The half-empty parking lot also indicated there were plenty of rooms available. Carver parked at the far end of the motel and walked to the office at the bottom of the L-shaped building.

The place looked old. It still had design elements from the fifties and sixties, like a big neon sign and a concrete lattice wall. It seemed like all the motels back then were cookie cutter versions of each other, at least with the general layout.

There was a grumpy-looking woman behind the counter in the office. She had stringy gray hair and that same tired look most motel managers had permanently etched on their faces. She took his sixty bucks, no questions asked and gave him a physical key to the room he requested.

Carver walked back to the room. He got his backpack from the van and took it inside. He'd already put Tony's money in the backpack with his own. It was a lot of cash to carry around, but he wasn't about to deposit it in a bank.

Maybe he should just give it to Rich right away. It was best if Rich went into hiding somewhere just in case Palmer decided to send another hitman after him. But to do that, he'd need a place to stay. He'd need money.

Carver could give him what cash he had. It would pay for a motel for the time being. Then Carver would contact Leon and get the encrypted banking app so he could access his slush fund. Hell, Leon had taken close to a billion dollars in crypto from the cartel in El Fuerte. He could spare enough cash to get Rich settled elsewhere.

He used his burner phone to navigate to the SecMail website. He logged in. There was an email from Paola that was three months old. Carver had lost his cell phone in North Carolina along with the encrypted messaging app he used for secure SMS messages.

Paola had probably texted him on that phone and then sent him the email when he never responded. Carver tried not to be a little excited by the email, but he couldn't help it. All the time and distance in the world hadn't lessened his feelings for Paola and it probably never would.

For some reason, Carver was okay with that. He opened the email. It simply said: *Everything is going well. We are all okay. I hope you are also okay. I sent a text two months ago and never heard back. I wanted to make sure that you received my message.*

Carver sent back a message telling her he was okay and that he'd lost his phone. He was going to sync back up with Leon again soon. He sent that email and then sent one to Leon asking for a hash key that would allow him to access his messaging account again and for another key to allow him access to his offshore bank account.

He didn't expect a quick answer, but hopefully Leon would get back to him in the next few days. In the meantime, he'd use his meager resources to get Rich out of town until something more permanent could be arranged.

Carver took a shower. He unloaded his backpack and inspected his clothing. The shirts and pants looked ratty. It was time to replace them. He bundled Tony's money with the rest of his cash and stuffed it back inside then put the clothing on top of it.

He put on a pair of boxers and turned out the lights. He took the lone chair in the room and wedged it beneath the door handle. He looked through the window at the parking lot. He saw the same seven cars outside that he'd seen earlier.

He saw an eighth car that hadn't been there before. A police car. It was parked near the office. Carver threw on pants, shirt and shoes. He removed the chair from beneath the door handle and eased open the door.

Carver looked toward the office. He saw two cops inside it. He used the monocular for a better look. Saw Archer and Sutton, the cops from the diner, talking to the manager.

The woman had the same tired look she'd had earlier. She looked down at something. Nodded. Pointed in the general direction of Carver's room and said something. That was all Carver needed to see.

He tossed the motel key on the bed. He gathered his things and left the room, locking and closing the door behind him. He hopped into the minivan. The dome light was already disabled so it didn't come on. The daytime running lights were also disabled.

There was a large pickup truck parked between the van and the office, so no one would see the van until they got to the other side of the pickup. They would, however, see the back of the minivan. The reverse lights and taillights also weren't disabled, so they'd see those too.

It couldn't be helped. Carver backed up the van just enough so he could turn right and looped toward the parking lot exit at the far end opposite the manager's office.

It would have been smarter to just hoof it out of there, but Carver didn't want to waste more money on another car. He kept an eye on the cops in the manager's office. For some reason, they hadn't immediately gone to Carver's room.

It looked like Sutton was on his phone. Maybe he was awaiting further instructions. He definitely wasn't looking at Carver's minivan as he eased out of the parking lot and onto the road. Carver drove across the road and into a bar's parking lot.

It was late, but the bar was still open. He parked so he'd have a good view of the motel. It looked like he'd be sleeping in the van tonight. Even with the rear fold down seat that formed a bed, it wasn't quite large enough for Carver. That was fine. He'd slept in plenty of worse places.

Sleep, however, wasn't on the current agenda. He took out his monocular, watched the motel, and waited. Thirty minutes later, a familiar Chevy Caprice pulled into the parking lot. Sutton and Archer left the motel office.

They went to the driver's side window and spoke to the person inside the Caprice, presumably Palmer. Sutton held up a room key. A decision was reached. Archer and Sutton nodded. Palmer parked the Caprice. The trio walked toward Carver's room with all the confidence in the world.

Sutton walked right up to the door. He slid the key slowly into the lock. Archer put his back to the left side of the door. Palmer stood on the right with his back next to the room window. Sutton drew his sidearm and slowly twisted the lock.

He twisted the doorknob, shouted and shoved inside all in one fluid motion. Carver couldn't hear him but he could tell the man was shouting "Police!" over and over again. They went inside the room and looked at the bed.

When they didn't see Carver, Sutton hurried into the bathroom. He returned a few seconds later shaking his head and talking to the others. Carver wished he had a parabolic microphone so he could hear what they were saying.

It might be hard from this distance and with a highway in between, but it would be worth a shot. The men returned to the front office. They spoke with the manager. She shook her head. Shrugged. Pointed at the parking lot. It looked like she was pointing at the truck the minivan had been parked behind.

She shook her head again and sighed. The manager nodded almost deferentially at the cops. Like she feared them just as much as everyone inside incorporated Bickham did. Gone was her tired look, replaced with stress and concern.

Carver typed *Bickham* into the maps app. It outlined the borders of the city. The motel was about a mile outside the city limits, but it looked like the fear for the Bickham police didn't end at the city line.

Most people showed respect for the police. It was a natural reaction most people had to so-called authority figures. But this wasn't the same reaction. This was something else. Almost like the same kind of fear people experienced when they ran into a mugger in a dark alleyway.

That was interesting. Real interesting.

It made Carver even more certain that he had to get Rich out of town. First thing in the morning would be good. He also gently chided himself for not doing a better job picking out a motel.

This place was on the same highway as the Stargazer Motel. It was just a couple of miles down the road. All the cops had to do to find him was go from motel to motel asking managers if they'd seen a big guy with his features.

This motel also wasn't that far from Hope House. It had probably been the most logical place for them to check, making it the dumbest place Carver could have chosen. Then again, there weren't that many nearby motels meeting his exacting standards of bad ratings and no ID requirements.

Sutton and the others emerged from the motel office. They circled up and spoke for a while. Sutton waved a hand around as if indicating the general vicinity. He pointed to the bar. The others nodded.

That meant one of two things. Either they were going to get drinks, or they thought Carver might be inside the bar. It was possible they thought he was still on foot since he hadn't had a car earlier.

Carver got out of the driver's seat and sat on the second row bench seat. He watched the men walk to the sidewalk, look both ways, and then cross the four-lane highway. There was still plenty of traffic, but it all ground to a standstill to let the men cross the road.

The car drivers watched the men carefully, as if afraid the slightest movement could draw their attention. It was like watching prey remain still to avoid predators. What made these people so afraid of their supposed protectors?

Sutton, Archer, and Palmer went into the bar. Carver watched them through the windows. They went to the counter. The bartender flinched when he saw them. He stopped what he was doing and hurried over to them.

Sutton spoke to the bartender. The bartender looked at something Sutton was holding. Probably a picture of Carver. He shook his head and looked hopeful that the cops would accept his answer and go away.

Sutton turned and looked around the building. He walked out of sight of the windows. Archer and Palmer went in different directions. The bar was about the size of an average restaurant. They'd take a few minutes to search it. They wouldn't find Carver, so they'd leave.

Carver wondered what they'd do next. Were they really all that eager to lay hands on Carver, or were they just making sure he'd left town? The only way to know for sure would be by asking them.

It seemed likely that they wouldn't go after Rich for the time being because they thought Tony had killed him. Once they found out Rich was alive, then they might go after him again. But not tonight.

Which meant Carver had the luxury of sleeping, or he could do something a little more dangerous. He could follow these men. Archer and Sutton seemed to be on duty tonight. Palmer wasn't.

They were obviously working together. They all knew Tony had been hired to kill Rich. They all wanted to either have a word with Carver or kill him. Probably both. And that led Carver right to the best decision.

He was going to stalk Palmer.

Chapter 18

Carver watched and waited.

Archer, Sutton, and Palmer took their time sweeping the building. Carver caught glimpses of them through the windows. He saw the looks of apprehension on the faces of the patrons. Saw the looks of relief when the cops finally left.

The trio stood outside and spoke for a moment. They nodded a few times. Gestured in different directions. One of them limped and held his shoulder as if mimicking the way Rich moved. He mocked a look of surprise and went limp as if he'd died. The others burst into laughter.

They were probably imagining how Rich looked when Tony killed him. They were mocking his surprise and fear in his final few seconds of life. Well, the joke was going to be on them when they found out he was still alive.

Rich wasn't Carver's buddy. He wasn't his friend. He was a former brother in arms that he owed big time. Watching those men mock someone who'd paid a high price defending his country made Carver angry.

He felt the urge to go have a word with them right then and there. Maybe show them what it felt like to be crippled. Maybe let them know that their plan to kill Rich hadn't gone so well. They would face a reckoning someday. Maybe someday real soon if Carver had something to say about it.

It was best to get Rich out of the picture. Get him somewhere safe. Once Carver had access to his slush fund account, he could get him the medical attention he needed. Then he could decide if it was worth the effort to teach these boys a lesson.

The three men walked across the road to the motel. Sutton and Archer climbed back into their patrol SUV. Sutton wheeled it onto the road and gunned it back toward town. It seemed they weren't going to continue searching for Carver.

Palmer slid into his old Caprice. He backed it up, turned it around, and backed it into a parking space right across the parking lot from Carver's room. He leaned the seat back and settled in. It looked like he'd been assigned stakeout duties.

That told Carver the pecking order of the trio. It looked like Sutton called the shots. Archer was his partner or maybe even his best buddy. Palmer did what he was told. It was also possible someone else had given the orders. Maybe that Big D fellow.

Carver considered his options. Sneaking up on the Caprice wouldn't be easy. It was backed into a parking space next to the highway and right across from Carver's room. The parking lot was wide open. There was no cover at all.

Another option was to park right next to the car. Back into the slot so close to Palmer's car that the door couldn't open. Then Carver could get out and train his handgun on the cop. Make him get out nice and slow. He could take Palmer somewhere and interrogate him.

And then what? What objective would he accomplish by capturing Palmer and interrogating him? He might get a few answers, but what did that really do except alert the entire police force that he was onto them?

Intelligence gathering was a test of spy craft. If you could gather information from observing the target without his knowledge, that was far preferable to capturing the target and trying to force information from him.

Information gathered from interrogation and torture had a higher likelihood of being bad or outright false. Sometimes the prisoner could resist and refuse to say anything. Sometimes the prisoner would tell you whatever you wanted to hear to avoid torture.

Gathering information through observation was the best course for now. He was already on the cops' radar and all he'd done was visit Rich. If one of them went missing or reported being interrogated, then they'd probably go nuclear. He didn't want that. He wanted to keep them blissfully unaware of his activities for now.

His primary objective was to get Rich out of town and that was what he'd do. As much as he wanted to introduce Palmer and friends to the business end of his fists, he needed to focus on the objective and get it done.

Carver folded the rear bench seat into a bed. All the van windows except the windshield were heavily tinted so no one could see him inside. The front bench seat would conceal him from anyone peering through the windshield.

He wanted to keep an eye on Palmer but didn't want to stay awake all night, so he set up one of the cameras he'd purchased earlier and placed it on the dash. He plugged it into the cigarette lighter with a USB to 12 volt adapter and used an app to link the camera wirelessly to his phone using Bluetooth.

The camera was high resolution and had a decent zoom feature. He trained it on Palmer's car and set it to record. With that done, it was time to get some shuteye.

He stretched out diagonally across the folded down seat for maximum space. It wasn't quite long enough but it would do. He went through his relaxation routine and fell asleep quickly. He woke up when a rowdy group of bar patrons got into the cars next to the van.

Carver checked the time. He'd slept for two hours. Palmer's car was still across the road. He looked through his monocular. Palmer wasn't moving. He might be asleep. He might be staring at his phone. From this angle, it was hard to tell.

The bar was closed but there were still several cars in the parking lot. Patrons too drunk to drive had probably gotten rides home. No one would think twice about the minivan still sitting there.

Carver went back to sleep. He woke up at zero six hundred feeling reasonably refreshed, but a little stiff from the cramped quarters. Palmer's car was gone. Carver connected his phone to the camera and looked through the footage.

Palmer had given up about thirty minutes after Carver went back to sleep. The time-stamp showed a little after zero three hundred. That told Carver something about the man. He did what he was told, but only to a certain extent.

The Caprice had gone back in the direction of Bickham. That told Carver that Palmer probably lived in town or close to it. It wasn't a lot of information, but it was something.

Carver searched for a diner outside the city limits. The closest one was in the next county, fifteen minutes away. It was worth the drive to be out of Bickham's jurisdiction, so he went there.

The atmosphere inside was relaxed. Everyone seemed happy and normal compared to what he'd seen at the burger restaurant. Probably because Bickham's finest were nowhere to be seen. The food was pretty good, too. Not the best or the worst he'd ever had, but it filled him up.

After breakfast, he filled the minivan's gas tank and went to Hope House. He parked down the street and scanned the area. Tony's car was still parked where he'd left it. There was no sign of Palmer and friends anywhere. All looked calm and quiet.

That was going to change real fast once Palmer found out that Rich was still alive. He might not discover that for hours, or he might wonder why no one had called 911 to report a death at Hope House.

He might call Tony to ask for an update and grow suspicious when Tony didn't answer. Maybe Tony was supposed to have texted him after it was done, and he was already wondering if something had gone wrong.

Or he might still be asleep since he'd been up most of the night watching Carver's hotel room. There was no way to know for sure.

Carver went into the building. Alicia looked up when he walked in. She watched him cross the room as if assessing a threat. Her voice, however, was friendly. "Are you here to see your friend?"

"Yep." Carver turned left into the hallway and went to Rich's door. He knocked twice and opened the door. Rich's duffel bag was open on the floor, but Rich wasn't there.

Carver returned to the reception area. "You know where he is?"

She shrugged. "He might be in the cafeteria eating breakfast."

"Thanks." Carver walked to the other hallway. The cafeteria was a couple of doors down on the left. There was a small buffet with bacon, eggs, hash browns, and pancake batter to make your own waffles in the waffle iron.

Rich was seated inside eating a waffle. He glared at Carver.

Carver sat down across from him. "After breakfast, I think we should get you out of town."

"Why? They've already taken everything from me and now you want me to just leave?"

"You almost had a visitor last night." Carver told him about Tony.

Rich dropped his fork and stared at his waffle. "I guess my house, my nest egg, and everything else wasn't enough for them. Did Tony tell you why he was sent to kill me?"

"I think they were prepared to leave you alone until I showed up. I'm an unknown variable."

Rich sighed. "Bad things happen when you're around. Maybe you should leave and then they'll leave me alone."

"It's probably too late for that."

Rich worked his jaw back and forth. "You want me to run away and let these assholes win?" He shook his head. "Not a chance. I'll take them down with me if I have to."

Carver nodded. "Sure, if that's what you want to do. But there's no shame in retreating until you form a plan of attack."

"You're quoting Joe, aren't you?"

"Probably." Carver shrugged. "He taught me a lot."

"Do you know what it's like seeing you again, Carver? What it's like having the guy who left me for dead helping me just so he can soothe his conscience?"

"Looks like it makes you angry and conflicted. Probably brings back bad memories."

"Yep. All of the above." Rich clenched his trembling hands. He winced and massaged his shoulder. "All last night I dreamed about being captured. It played in an endless loop in my head. I haven't been able to stop thinking about it all morning."

Carver didn't say anything when Rich paused to look at him. Sometimes it was best to listen.

"I don't want your money, Carver. I don't want your help. I want you to go. If they come for me again, I'll be ready."

"Do you want weapons or ammo?" Carver said.

Rich laughed hollowly. "Did you hear what I said? I don't want you around. I want you to leave. Do it publicly so those assholes know you're gone and will leave me alone."

"I owe you," Carver said. "That's why I'm here. I can't make it right, but I can help, okay? Maybe I'll end up taking a bullet for you. Maybe I'll end up dead. Maybe we both end up dead."

"What's wrong with you?" Rich tapped a finger on his own temple. "Can you not understand what I'm saying? Can you just respect my wishes and leave me alone?"

Carver nodded. "Okay. Once I get access to the money, I'll send it to you. It doesn't make things even. It's not payback. It's just restoring what they took from you."

Rich nodded numbly. "Okay. Now go."

"Okay." Carver stood. He turned and left. He was going but not leaving. Maybe that wasn't exactly honoring Rich's request, but sometimes you had to help people who didn't like you or want your help.

That was something else Joe had told him. He'd also said that everyone in his cohort was a brother even if they didn't like him.

"Yeah, but don't you need unity in a squad?" Carver said.

"Unity is a bond forged either with friendship, a sense of duty, or a common purpose," Joe said. "SEAL teams rely on a lot of people and resources. Not everyone gets along or agrees with each other. Hell, I can't stand our CIA liaison. He's an absolute idiot. But we are unified in our common goals." He grinned. "Most of the time."

Carver blinked out of the memory. What he wouldn't give to have Joe alive and well right now. It would be nice if just one more or of their former cohorts would show up and talk some sense into Rich.

He didn't have anyone else's contact information. He hadn't left the SEAL team with many friends except Joe. The incident with Rich had only made them ostracize Carver more. It made him wonder what Joe had seen in him. He still didn't know the answer.

It hadn't been long after the Akim Jabar mission failure that he'd been recruited into Scion. Carver had taken the opportunity right away because it felt like his continued presence with the SEALs would just be a distraction.

Joe had warned him about taking the job. He said they would see Carver as a disposable tool. He said they didn't believe in the no man left behind creed or in brotherhood. He didn't even agree with Carver's reason for leaving. He said that the mission had been a setup. That the intel had been faked or planted and that what happened to Rich wasn't Carver's fault.

Carver had been the rear guard. Setup or not, he'd been responsible for making sure no one came up behind them. The intel said no one else would be in the tunnels. Carver had left his position to confirm the intel was right.

Joe liked to say, "When the intel looks perfect, it ain't." In other words, don't trust even the best intel. Always be alert.

Carver thought back to those final moments before it all went to hell.

###

Joe led the squad through the tunnels. He knew exactly which ones to follow and which ones to ignore. Carver didn't like ignoring tunnels even if the intel said they were clear. It was like not clearing a room and leaving your six open to anyone who might be hiding inside.

They were on a tight schedule. There was no time to clear every single tunnel they passed. Joe still looked into each tunnel they passed. All of them did. But they didn't take time to go through the tunnels, around the corners and bends and confirm that they were as empty as intel claimed they were.

Carver paused at the first tunnels that branched from the one they followed. He jogged to the first corner and looked around it. The tunnel beyond was clear. He ran down the next one and cleared it as well.

He caught up to the others at a five-way junction. He waited for Joe to clear the corners and proceed. Then Carver did a quick check of the other tunnels. It looked like several tunnels doubled back on one another or were dead ends. Anyone without a map could easily get lost.

Carver realized he'd gone in a circle and ended up back at the main junction. It had taken him far longer than expected to clear the last tunnel, so he had a decision to make. Did he catch up to the others or clear the other branches?

He went to the tunnel Joe had taken. It was long and straight. If an ambush was going to come from the rear, this wasn't the tunnel the enemy would come from. He decided to catch up with the others. He passed another large junction and saw the mark Joe had left to indicate where they'd turned.

Carver looked into the other tunnels. He saw movement. He put his back to the wall and peered around the corner. A group of men were coming down the tunnel, using a dim flashlight to guide their way.

He counted six bogeys with AK-47s. They weren't just casually patrolling the tunnels. They were moving slowly and quietly to avoid detection. They were flanking his team. Thankfully, they weren't as well equipped as he was.

They couldn't see him, but he could see them clear as day with night vision. He shifted to the other side of the tunnel for a better angle. He aimed at their rearguard. He practiced a sequence of shots, then he executed them.

Carver pulled the trigger. His HK coughed. The rearguard dropped with a bullet in the skull. The man in front of him flinched and looked back. The next bullet punctured his temple. The bullet whined off the concrete wall.

Carver aimed center mass for the remaining four. The 5.56 rounds ripped through their insides, incapacitating them before they could raise their rifles or fire. They cried out in surprise and pain. He silenced them with headshots.

There could be more of them coming from the other tunnels. More of them who'd heard their comrades' screams. Carver couldn't take the time to investigate. He ran past the other tunnels, sparing only quick glances into them.

He didn't see anything, but he was moving too fast to get a good look. It took him precious seconds to reach the others. He ran past Rich. Ran straight up to Joe. The others stared at him from behind the NV goggles. They looked confused. They probably wondered what in the hell Carver was doing.

Carver spoke in low tones to Joe. "It's an ambush. I caught a squad coming up behind us."

Joe didn't waste any time. He signaled a retreat. The line doubled back on itself. Jefferson and Porter took point. Joe was right behind them. Carver saw movement down an adjacent tunnel. He went down on one knee and opened fire.

Men screamed and went down. Muzzle flashes lit the tunnel. The AK-47s spat 7.62 rounds at Carver. He ducked around the corner. Explosions boomed. Concrete and rock collapsed. Carver hurried after the squad but the tunnel in front of him had collapsed.

No one had thrown a grenade or explosive device. The explosive had already been there. It had been rigged to blow. If Carver hadn't warned Joe, the explosive probably would have been detonated when the team passed that point. The soldiers would have finished off or captured anyone left alive.

He worked his way through an adjacent tunnel. The enemy didn't have night vision. They had flashlights. That was all the advantage he needed. He saw three of them creeping around a bend. He took the first two down before they knew what hit them. The last guy tried to run. A 5.56 round turned his brains to porridge.

Carver followed the tunnel to a ladder. It took him aboveground to a different building in the compound. He was in a small room with a square hole in the floor and the ladder leading down into the tunnels.

There was a small opening in the wall that was only three feet tall. He ducked through it and pushed past a rug that was covering the hole on the other side. He was in a small room with rugs and mats on the floor. There was a long low table in the middle.

He left the room and walked down a short hallway. A metal door hung open on the right. He looked through it. No one was in the room. There were several open wooden crates in the room. There was a large table in the middle with an AK-47 and several magazines on top of it.

Carver ran past the room and to the last room in the building. There were no windows, so he had to ease open the door to look outside. He was about a hundred feet from the building his squad had originally entered to access the tunnels. If Joe was leading them back the way they'd come, they'd soon exit that building.

That was going to be a big problem because there were twenty men lined up outside the door waiting to mow them down when they did. Carver decided to break radio silence. He activated his comms and got shrieks of static. Something was jamming the frequencies.

He was down to his last magazine, and it was half empty. He didn't have enough to take down twenty men. He ran back inside the building and picked up the AK-47 from the table. He snapped in a magazine and pulled back the charging handle on the side.

There was a lot of resistance in the handle. Too much. Something was wrong with it. That was probably why it had been left on the table. There was a weapons rack on the wall, but no rifles left. He ran to a crate and found something that might work even better.

Potato mashers. Soviet hand grenades. They looked like the old Soviet RKG-3 grenades, but they might just be knockoffs. Either way, they were guaranteed to do the job he needed. They were basically RPGs but thrown by hand.

He grabbed two of them. He exited the building. Joe and crew would be exiting the building anytime now, so he didn't have time to clear the area. He might be seen by other enemies. He might get shot in the back. He was okay with that.

Carver ran forward. He pulled the pins on the potato mashers. He threw them at the men waiting to slaughter Joe and his squad. One grenade struck a man in the head. He cried out in surprise. The other grenade landed right behind the group.

Someone else shouted a word. Probably, "Grenade!" in their native tongue. It was hard to tell over the sound of the explosion. Carver used the last rounds in his magazine to clear a path. An instant later, Joe and the rest of the squad burst out of the door.

"What the hell!" someone shouted.

Joe didn't take time to show surprise at the carnage. The chopper was already swooping down to get them. They boarded the chopper. Everyone was accounted for, or so they thought. One man was missing. The man Carver should have been right behind until the tunnel cave in cut him off.

Rich had been left behind.

Chapter 19

Rich had lost his appetite.

He'd reached out to so many people for help and the only one to come was the last person he wanted to see. He hadn't even reached out to Carver and yet fate decided to spit in his face and send him anyway.

It was almost laughable. Almost.

Rich stared at his half-eaten waffle. He didn't even see it. All he could see was the face of his torturer. All he could think about was how Carver hadn't done his duty and left him to be captured and tortured.

He was just a hollow shell of a man. Not even a shadow of his former self. The rage ignited a spark deep in his soul. It burned so hot that he could barely think straight. He was ready to die. Ready to take down his tormentors with him.

Raulerson and his cops would be a good start. Taking Carver down with him would be even better. But that would be too difficult. Carver had the instincts of a lone wolf. He wouldn't go down with the pack. He'd live to fight another day.

Taking out Raulerson and his ilk would be enough. Even taking just one of them down before dying would make him happy. Rich just had to figure out how to do it. He might be a cripple, but he could still take down the bad guys, couldn't he?

If only some of the other guys from the squad had come to his aid when he called. Together they could take down these asshole cops. Make them pay. But it looked like Rich would have to do it himself.

He'd taken down international terrorists and thugs. He'd infiltrated some of the most dangerous countries in the world. He'd sabotaged enemy facilities and rescued political hostages. He'd been a damned SEAL. Taking down a few corrupt cops should be no problem even if he was a cripple.

Rich felt a little better. He felt like a man with a destiny. A man who'd decided his own fate and wasn't the least bit afraid. His appetite returned. He was going to hell, and he was going to take his tormentors with him.

He sensed someone standing near him and snapped out of his thoughts. He looked to the left and saw the receptionist watching him with concern. He couldn't remember her name.

"Rich, are you okay?" She sat down across from him. "You look angry and upset."

"Wouldn't you be if you were in my position?" He frowned. "You're just the receptionist. Why does it matter to you?"

"I'm the coordinator for this chapter of Hope House, not the receptionist." She laughed. "I do wear many hats around here, however."

"I'm sorry. I didn't mean any disrespect."

"It's okay, Rich. Is it okay if I call you by your first name?"

He nodded. "Yes. Sorry, I don't remember yours."

"I'm Alicia." She extended her hand. "I'm sorry we didn't formally meet when you first arrived."

He shook her hand. It was soft but her grip was firm. Despite the smile on her face, her eyes looked calm and serious. "Well, I stank and looked homeless." Rich smiled. "Nice to meet you again."

"How are the group sessions?" she asked.

"Meh. They're okay. Seems like most of the attendees have really minor problems, though."

"The sessions are open to anyone in the community free of charge."

Rich didn't have a response to that, so he cut into his waffle and took a bite.

"We do have other chapters. The one in Chicago sees quite a number of serious issues."

"I'll bet." Rich poured syrup on his waffle. "How much longer can I stay here?"

"Your situation is more serious than most." Alicia smiled. "We can extend your stay, but I'd like to put you in contact with our Chicago chapter. I think they might be more effective at helping you."

"How am I supposed to get there?"

"I can drive you. I've already spoken with their coordinator, Keith, and he's excited to meet you."

Rich laughed. "Excited? I doubt that."

"It's true." She put her hand over his and squeezed it. "Please get cleaned up and dressed right after breakfast. We'll leave in thirty minutes."

Rich frowned. "You're trying to get rid of me, aren't you?"

"On the contrary, Rich. I'm trying even harder to help you."

"Your driver, Eddie, isn't going to take me?"

"No, it's better if I take you." She released his hand and stood. "Please be ready in thirty minutes. I don't like to be kept waiting."

"Um, sure." Rich was a little surprised by the authority in her voice. "Were you in the military?"

Alicia gave him a half-smile, turned and left.

Something about the exchange felt very strange but also very familiar. It felt like he'd been ordered to prep for a mission and that well trained part of him was ready and willing to comply. Despite the passage of years, those parts of him were still strongly implanted like muscle memory.

Curiosity also played a part in it. What kind of people would he meet at the Chicago chapter of Hope House? Maybe some with an experience similar to his? He wasn't sure if he wanted to meet someone like that or not.

He was well aware that his disabilities had made him a bitter, sad man. He'd just accepted that the new him was nothing like the old him. He would never be one of those inspirational people who rose from the ashes and made the best of their situation. Meeting someone like him would be depressing and he certainly didn't want to meet someone who'd lost more than he had and was still kicking ass and taking names.

Despite those misgivings, Alicia really hadn't given him a choice. He'd just do this to make her happy so he could stay a little longer and plot his revenge. All he needed was a little more time and then he wouldn't be a problem for anyone.

Rich went to his room and closed the door. He went to the bathroom and stared at the unkempt mess that was him. Thanks to Carver retrieving his things, he now had his toiletries. His beard looked like a bird's nest and his hair looked like it hadn't been combed in months. Since losing his girlfriend, he hadn't even bothered.

He found his beard trimmer and cleaned it up. He trimmed his bushy eyebrows and buzzed the hair off his ears. He showered and washed his hair. He dried off and combed his hair neatly to the side.

Rich put on jeans and a black T-shirt. He looked at himself in the mirror and hardly recognized himself. He couldn't remember the last time he'd groomed himself. The last few months were just a blur.

He wasn't even sure why he'd felt the need to groom himself. Maybe because he wanted to impress Alicia. Maybe he wanted to not look like a complete monster to the people he was supposed to meet today.

Whatever the case, it felt good to look human again.

Alicia was waiting in the reception area. She smiled at him, a genuine smile this time. "You clean up nicely, Rich."

He couldn't help but smile back at her. She was an attractive woman with an air of authority around her. Not that she'd ever be interested in a loser like him.

She walked around him. Picked a piece of fuzz off his shirt. Straightened out a wrinkle. She looked him up and down and nodded. "Let's go."

Rich felt a chill of pleasure as she inspected him. It was so bizarre and sexy at the same time. He followed her outside. A black Tesla Model X was parked in the circle drive. It looked like Eddie had just finished washing it because he was drying the hood with a towel.

Alicia went to the driver's side and got in. Rich waited for Eddie to remove a bucket of soapy water from in front of the passenger door.

"You're going to Chicago today?" Eddie said.

Rich nodded. "I'm supposed to meet some new people."

"I think you'll like them a lot. Everyone who goes does."

Alicia rolled down the passenger side window. "Eddie, what did I tell you about that?"

"Oh, I'm sorry, Miss. Alicia." He backed away ducking and bowing like a whipped dog. "I forgot, I promise."

"Get in, Rich."

Rich had been so self-absorbed during the initial ride here that he hadn't noticed Eddie obviously wasn't the smartest guy on the block. He didn't sound retarded, but he was certainly in the double digits when it came to IQ.

He got into the car. Alicia rolled up his window and shifted the car into motion. She gunned it out of the circle drive and onto the street. The Tesla surged forward quiet as a ghost. She rolled through the next stop sign and did fifty miles per hour in a twenty-five zone.

She almost ran the next stop sign. Rich's heart froze when he saw a Bickham PD patrol car sitting at the same intersection. The cop just watched them go and didn't even try to stop them.

Rich turned to Alicia. "You have an agreement with the cops or something?"

"What makes you say that?" she asked.

"I mean, you just blew through that stop sign and the cop didn't even care."

"He's probably on a donut break." She laughed at her own joke and checked the rearview mirror. "Maybe we just caught a break."

"Around here?" Rich barked a laugh. "Never."

"Have you had many interactions with the local police?"

"Not really until recently." Rich checked the sideview mirror to make sure the cop hadn't decided to chase them.

"Is Bickham your hometown?"

"No. My parents moved here from Chicago after they retired. They said it was a nice, quiet town. I inherited the house after they died."

"Did they die peacefully or screaming?"

Rich barked a laugh. "That's one hell of a way to ask that question." He couldn't tell if she was serious or not but answered the question anyway. "Dad died of a heart attack about eight years ago. Mom died three years ago. My brother, Bert, and I inherited the house. He signed his half over to me since he figured I needed it more than him."

"Because of your injuries?"

"You're blunt, aren't you?"

Alicia nodded. "It's all part of my charm."

"Yes. I was on disability and seeing a shrink at the VA. I didn't have a job or any prospects, so he gave me his part of the house." Rich stared out the window. "I didn't grow up in that house, but it was mine, you know?"

"I understand."

"One of my former brothers in arms helped me get disabled veteran status so the property taxes were reduced to almost nothing. Another helped me get my disability pay increased. I felt like I was finally saving enough money to get the surgery I needed."

Alicia nodded. "I like it when vets help each other out."

"Ah, so you are former military."

"Naval aviator. Helicopter sea combat squadron."

Rich whistled. "I was a SEAL."

She smiled. "We gave your boys a ride or two back in the day."

"You were NSW?"

"I was briefly in special warfare, yes. I took a promotion and was assigned to NAS Whiting Field as an instructor."

"Is that really a promotion?"

Alicia laughed. "Believe it or not, yes. It's a lot safer than NSW, I can tell you that."

"Yeah, for sure." Rich enjoyed the conversation. He couldn't remember the last time he'd liked talking to someone. It was almost enough to make him forget his suicide mission against the Bickham PD.

"Tell me how you're feeling now," Alicia said. It sounded more like a command than a request.

"Better than earlier."

"You had the look of a man with nothing to lose."

Rich looked away from her and at the road ahead. "What makes you think that?"

"Because I've seen it plenty of times before." Alicia reached over and patted his hand. "Rich, be honest with me. Are you thinking about suicide?"

He bit his lower lip.

She squeezed his hand. "Answer me."

"Not really. I just want to do unspeakable things to the local cops."

"Do you think you could actually go through with something like that?"

He turned to her. "No, of course not."

Alicia seemed to look deep into his soul. "I don't believe you. You were a SEAL. You did unspeakable things to people before. What's to stop you from doing it one last time before suicide by cop?"

Rich turned away. "Just because I was a SEAL doesn't mean I'm capable of doing that in the civilian world."

"Once a SEAL, always a SEAL."

"Where'd you hear that?"

"From a SEAL."

He laughed. "You're something else, you know that?"

"Yes." There was zero doubt in her voice. She sounded absolutely sure of herself.

"I don't like many people, but you seem okay."

"I'm on your side, Rich. You can tell me anything and I won't tell a soul."

"You're a psychologist too?"

"No. I'm just a soldier fighting for the person next to me."

A lump formed in Rich's throat. He hadn't heard that for a long time. "You must be a shrink, because you know how to push my buttons."

"I can just identify with you. That's all."

"I don't really want to talk about my feelings if that's okay with you. I like you and respect you, but I'd prefer to keep you out of my head."

"Understood." Alicia squeezed his hand one last time and released it. "I would like to talk about your goals, though. What plans do you have for the future?"

"Now that I've lost my house, my nest egg, and my dignity?" Rich laughed hollowly. "I wanted to get surgery so I could regain some mobility. Now that's out of the window." He didn't mention Carver's offer. He didn't even want to think about Carver.

She frowned. "You're not getting it done through the VA?"

"They said it wasn't covered."

"Did they offer you a lifetime prescription of ibuprofen?"

Rich laughed. "Basically." He sighed and stared out the side window. "It's fine."

"It's not fine. Maybe someone has connections and can get you approved."

"Doubtful." Rich didn't want to think about it. "Can we talk about something else? I feel like I've done nothing but talk about my problems. I'd rather keep the conversation light."

"Sure. You have a favorite sports team?"

He grinned. "Yankees all the way."

Alicia made a gagging sound. "I knew there was something wrong with you."

Rich laughed.

They arrived in Chicago a little before lunch. Alicia drove to a bad part of town near homeless encampments and abandoned buildings. She parked right outside a massive building. It looked like one of the old community recreation centers from the seventies. She didn't seem the least bit worried about her Tesla.

Alicia led Rich inside and walked him straight down the hallway and into a cavernous gymnasium. A small group of people were gathered in the middle of the giant space not far from the pool. There were foldout chairs and a foldout table with coffee and donuts on it.

It looked like a standard group therapy session except for the participants. Many of them had the stiff postures of former military. Several seemed constantly alert, like they were waiting for something bad to happen. Many had one thing in common. They looked like they were putting on a happy face to cover whatever was going on in their heads.

Rich knew that look all too well. He'd long since stopped covering it up. Then again, he'd long since stopped going to therapy sessions. At least until recently. As they neared the group, the participants parted to let them through.

Rich saw a face he hadn't seen in years on the other side of the group. A face he knew all too well from previous therapy sessions. It was the same man who'd set him up in Bickham. He stopped in his tracks, hardly able to believe it.

It was Tom.

Chapter 20

Carver sat in his minivan outside Hope House and watched for trouble.

He didn't know how long it would take for Palmer to realize Tony hadn't killed Rich. Most of the time the killer would send a message to let the client know the target was dead. Maybe Palmer was wondering why he hadn't received that message yet.

Then again, Tony might not send texts or make phone calls. The flip phone Carver found in Tony's pocket hadn't had any texts or outgoing phone calls on it. Only incoming calls. Maybe Palmer would call him to confirm the job was done.

That phone call probably hadn't been made yet. Palmer had stayed up all night staking out Carver's motel. He might still be asleep. There was no way to know for sure, so it was best to keep an eye on things from a distance and see how it played out.

A sparkling clean Tesla SUV pulled into the circle drive in front of Hope House about twenty minutes later. Eddie got out. He wiped down the hood with a towel and walked around the car inspecting it.

Alicia stepped outside. She was still the young, confident woman he'd met before, but there was something different about her. She walked a little taller. A little straighter. Like an apex predator surveying its domain.

Rich emerged from the building right behind her. He wore jeans and a T-shirt. His mess of a beard was neatly groomed, and his hair was combed. He looked like a different man. He was still limping and favoring his bad shoulder, but he looked pretty good for a guy who'd all but given up just thirty minutes ago.

Alicia said something to Eddie and got into the Tesla. Rich climbed into the other side. The car lunged forward and sped out of the circle drive. One thing was certain. Alicia drove like a bat out of hell.

Carver cranked the minivan's ignition and waited for the Tesla to get some distance between them. Alicia was practically running all the stop signs, so it didn't take long for that to happen.

In fact, she was driving like she owned the road. In a town like this, that seemed like a really bad idea unless you had an understanding with local law enforcement. Carver certainly didn't, so he came to a complete stop at each one.

Alicia ran the last stop sign and turned onto the highway right in front of a police car. The cop didn't even try to pull her over. He just watched her go and then casually turned left in Carver's direction.

The police car was a Mustang. A souped-up muscle car outfitted with an LED light bar and all the other police goodies. Palmer drove a Challenger. Sutton and Archer rode around in an SUV. Apparently, the traffic cops in these parts got to pick and choose their own vehicles.

Carver made sure he was under the speed limit and kept driving. He leaned his seat back a little so his face wouldn't be visible through the windshield. He came to a complete stop at the next intersection, counted to three, and then accelerated.

The last stop sign was at the intersection with the highway. He looked in the rearview mirror and saw the police cruiser pull a hard U-turn. The front end lifted slightly as if the driver had jammed down the accelerator.

The Mustang roared up behind him in no time flat. The cop looked at the minivan then looked at something to his right. He was probably looking up the license plate with his onboard computer.

He was going to see that it was registered to the car dealership. The sticker on the plate was still good for a couple of months so there were no problems with that. Hopefully at that point he'd decide everything was aboveboard and go about his day.

The lights on top of the cruiser flashed and the siren whooped twice in quick succession. Carver considered his options. He really didn't have any. The minivan definitely couldn't outrun the police car. The only thing he could do was pull over.

Carver pulled onto the shoulder. He put the minivan in park and turned off the engine. The cop got out. He unsnapped his holster and put a hand on his gun. His partner got out of the car and did the same. They approached from both sides.

Carver was glad he'd taken the time to stow the Sig and its magazines under the dash. If they found that, then he was cooked. He didn't recognize either of the cops. Unless there was an APB out on him, it meant they wouldn't recognize him either.

Both cops looked slim and fit. The patrol car driver was Hispanic his partner was Caucasian. Both wore their hair cropped short and had no facial hair. They were just under six feet tall and dressed in Bickham PD blacks. Their uniforms fit well enough but didn't look tailor fitted like Sutton's and Archer's.

Carver rolled down the driver's side window and put his hands through it. The driver of the patrol car circled out a few feet from the window, remaining out of Carver's reach.

The cop kept his hand on his gun. "Roll down your passenger side window halfway."

Carver read the man's nameplate. "Did I do something wrong, Officer Morales?"

"Do as I instruct, and I'll tell you."

"I'm rolling down the passenger side window." Carver pushed down on the switch and the other window rolled down. He stopped it at the halfway point as instructed. He looked at the other cop's nameplate. *Officer Davidson.* Carver raised his hand again. "How's that?"

"I pulled you over because the tint on your vehicle is illegal." Morales watched him closely. "Your vehicle is also licensed to Quality Used Vehicles. Do you work there?"

"I just bought the car. They said it'd take thirty days or so for the paperwork to process." Carver shrugged. "And they said the tint was legal."

"Not in our jurisdiction it isn't." Morales shook his head.

Davidson pulled out a tool and put it over the window. "We got thirty-five percent VLT."

"That's way over the limit," Morales said.

"I don't know what that means," Carver said.

"It means your tint blocks sixty-five percent of all light transmission through it."

Carver frowned. "What's the limit?"

"Seventy percent VLT," Morales said. "You can only block thirty percent of light transmission."

"Way over the limit." Davidson smirked. "That's an expensive fine."

Carver figured it wasn't the worst thing in the world to get a ticket for. "Sorry, officers. I'll remove it."

Davidson made a show of sniffing. "Do you smell that, Morales?"

"Yeah." Morales sniffed a few times. "You been smoking pot?"

"No, sir." Carver sensed a shakedown coming. There wasn't even a trace of pot odor in the minivan, just the scent of the pine deodorizer hanging from the rearview mirror. "In fact, I chose this minivan because the previous owner was a nonsmoker."

"I don't know." Davidson sniffed loudly. "Definitely smells like pot."

Morales pulled his gun from his holster and backed up a step. "Step out of the vehicle."

Carver did as he was told. He kept his hands raised. "Okay."

Davidson walked around the vehicle and frisked him. He found Carver's driver's license and a clip with a hundred bucks in it. That was about all Carver carried in his pockets. The driver's license was real, but it had a fake name. Carver had paid a lot for it, and this was just the reason why.

Morales looked at it. "Chuck Grayson. What kind of name is that?"

Carver said nothing.

Davidson opened the sliding door. He looked at the empty interior. He looked under the bench seats. He stepped inside and looked at the back row seat. "Aha!" He hefted the backpack from the back seat with a grunt. "Damn, this thing is heavy."

He set it on the floorboard. "Is this yours, Mr. Grayson?"

"Yes."

Davidson seemed to repress a grin. "Do you want to declare anything before I look through it?"

"I don't give you permission to search it." Carver stared at him. "Doing so is a violation of my fourth amendment rights."

Morales laughed. "I smell pot and Davidson smells pot, so we have probable cause."

Severe injuries were certainly becoming more probable for both cops if they did what Carver thought they were about to do, namely open his backpack and empty out the contents.

Davidson did as predicted and unzipped the backpack. He pulled out the clothing. He wrinkled his nose at the torn and dirty garments. "Jesus, these stink. What the hell is wrong with you?"

"That's where I keep my dirty laundry," Carver said. He hoped that would be enough to dissuade Davidson, but it wasn't.

Davidson turned the bag upside down and shook out the contents. The dirty laundry, the cash, the monocular, and two boxes of 9mm ammunition spilled out.

Morales whistled. "Will you look at that?"

"I'm definitely looking at that." Davidson picked up a stack of bills and rifled through them. "I think we found ourselves a dealer."

"Based on what evidence?" Carver said.

Morales made a show of sniffing again. "The vehicle smells like pot and you're carrying weapons and a bundle of cash."

"That's just ammunition, not weapons." Anger knotted in Carver's stomach. He didn't take kindly to being robbed and he certainly wasn't above pounding a couple of bent cops into paste if they wanted to steal from him.

"Where's the gun?" Morales said. "Is it inside the vehicle?"

Carver decided not to answer.

Morales sighed. "Look, I'm feeling generous today. We'll have to confiscate the cash, but I'm willing to let you off with a warning for the tint."

Davidson snorted in barely repressed amusement. "That seems more than fair to me."

Carver noted that Morales still had his gun drawn but it was down by his side. Davidson's gun was still in the holster. Both men were within striking distance. He was itching to make them regret ever pulling him over, but doing so would probably cause bigger problems in the near future.

He took a gamble and bluffed. "Look, I'm just helping out Hope House because Eddie's van got a flat. Maybe you'll want to have a chat with them first."

The smiles faded and the officers looked at each other. Davidson scowled and scooped the cash into the backpack. "Yeah, I don't think so. We're taking this and Alicia can come talk to Raulerson if she has a problem with it."

Morales got in Carver's face and poked him in the chest. "What the hell do they have going on over there, huh? What's with all the cash?"

"I have no idea." Carver was itching to grab the other man. "I'm just an errand boy."

"Yeah?" Morales backed up and bared his teeth. "We'll just have to talk to Bo about that."

Carver asked a risky question. "Who's Bo?"

Morales raised his eyebrows. "You an outside contractor or something?"

"I'm from out of town," Carver said.

Davidson frowned. "Are you from the Chicago branch?"

"Yeah."

"Well, you're going to find out real fast who Bo is if we find out you've been running unauthorized business through our territory." Davidson prodded Carver in the chest. "Real damned fast." He picked up the backpack and walked it back to the patrol car. He tossed it into the back seat.

Morales holstered his gun. He tossed Carver's money clip and driver's license onto the ground at Carver's feet. "Go to Chicago and tell them what we said. Tell them Bo will want an explanation immediately."

Carver was just as curious as he was angry. He hadn't expected that response from them. He'd expected them to think the money was from charitable donations. He'd expected them to give it back. Instead, they revealed that there was some kind of arrangement between them and Hope House.

He tamped down his anger. He was going to get his money back no matter what he had to do. But now he also wanted to know what kind of dealings Hope House had with Bickham PD.

Something stank to high Heaven in Bickham, and he'd just discovered the tip of it. With all the cash they'd just taken, it seemed like they owed him more than just the tip. They owed him a steak dinner and a full explanation.

At least they'd left Carver's money clip. It wasn't much money, but he didn't need a lot. At least not for now.

Morales whipped the Mustang onto the road and gunned the engine. He rolled through the stop sign at the intersection with the highway and turned left toward town. Carver considered following them, but it seemed almost certain that they'd go straight to the police station to turn in the money and talk with Bo, whoever that was.

Maybe Bo was Big D. Carver would have to find out, but he'd have to do it without being spotted. Too many cops knew his face now and at least three of them wanted him dead and gone. Unfortunately, he didn't have a good way to conceal his face or his size. And his cover about working for Hope House wouldn't hold up to any scrutiny. The moment Alicia was confronted about it and given Carver's description, she'd almost certainly know it was him and deny it.

One thing was certain. He wouldn't let this go unanswered. He was going to get his money back even if he had to go through the entire police department to do it. But he'd do it the smart way.

If the cops in that car had been Sutton and Archer or Palmer, then this would have gone down much differently. He would have had to come out of the van gun drawn just to make sure they didn't try to get the drop on him.

It probably wouldn't be long until Morales and Davidson bragged about their cash haul to their buddies at the station. They'd describe the big guy in the minivan. Someone might put two and two together and realize they'd pulled over Carver. Davidson or Morales would say they told Carver to go to Chicago and the hunt would be on.

The minivan would be a known vehicle. The license plate would be reported. But it would be a needle in a haystack in Chicago. That gave Carver four to eight hours before he had to get himself another ride. He wasn't sure how he'd afford it without his money.

Carver turned right on the highway and headed for Chicago. He was a good fifteen minutes behind Alicia. There was no reason to believe she'd follow the speed limit judging from the way she drove in town. There was plenty of reason to believe she'd drive at least eighty miles per hour.

In other words, Carver wasn't going to catch up to her unless he pushed the minivan to the limit. He didn't want to risk getting pulled over for speeding. He also didn't need to catch up because it seemed likely that Alicia was taking Rich to the Chicago branch of Hope House, wherever that was.

He searched for an address and found it on the south side. It was twenty minutes southeast of Tony's house and about fifteen minutes west of the homeless encampment where he'd stashed Tony's body.

The drive gave him an hour and a half to think about everything. He imagined a whiteboard with names on it. He put Bickham PD at the top on one side and Hope

House at the top of the other. He put Bo directly under Bickham PD and Alicia under Hope House.

He drew a line between the two. They were connected but not exactly affiliated. They had an agreement but not an alliance, that much was certain from what Morales said. That was why Alicia could drive like a banshee and not worry about the cops.

It was also clear that Hope House didn't have free license to do whatever they wanted. Was Hope House a criminal organization? Did they have an agreement with the local government? Was Bo also the head of a criminal organization with a lot of power in the police department? Or was he a powerful politician?

The possibilities were endless.

Alicia ran Bickham Hope House. Someone else probably ran the Chicago branch. Maybe they were equals or maybe she was the subordinate. Maybe she ran both branches and preferred the Bickham location over the Chicago one.

She hadn't seemed the least bit surprised to see Carver nor had she seemed nervous or concerned that Rich was still among the living. In fact, it seemed like she had plans for Rich because she was taking him to Chicago.

That meant it was unlikely that Alicia knew about the hit on Rich or that she had anything to do with Tony. Which meant the Bickham PD faction had no problems taking out someone that Hope House was interested in.

But why was Hope House interested in Rich? They were a charity. They didn't even offer full-time accommodations like a halfway house did. And Rich was no good to anyone physically or mentally right now, so what possible use would they have for him?

There were too many puzzle pieces missing to even guess what was going on between the two factions. There were just barely enough facts to piece together anything. Carver knew Bo was at or near the top of the Bickham faction, and that Alicia was at or near the top of Hope House. At the very least, she had a supervisory role.

Bickham's police officers might just be pawns or they might be full-fledged players. When it came to things like this, it was best not to take guesses. It might also be best not to ask direct questions because someone might be ready to kill to protect the answers.

That didn't leave Carver a lot of wiggle room. And now that the cops had his cash, he couldn't exactly go out and invest in good spy equipment. The only things they'd left behind were his dirty laundry, his monocular, and the surveillance cameras.

Leon hadn't responded to Carver's email yet which meant Carver would most likely have to acquire cash by other means. Until then, he'd have to rely on his monocular, his eyes, his ears, and the security cameras.

And if those weren't enough, he always had his gun.

Chapter 21

Carver arrived at Chicago Hope House.

Most of the nearby buildings were boarded up. A couple looked like they'd burned down to the foundation long ago. Apparently, no one wanted to rebuild. There was a large homeless encampment occupying the sidewalks along the street that ran perpendicular to Hope House. There were several smaller encampments scattered on the sidewalks and in the nearby alleys.

The highest concentration of tents was near a large red brick building with no signs on the outside indicating what it was. The windows were bricked up and the front doors were solid metal.

Carver checked the map app and saw it was a homeless shelter and soup kitchen associated with a local Methodist charity. Places like that normally required their guests to vacate during the day so they could clean up the mess left behind. It looked like it was locked down for the day.

It looked like no matter where he parked, there was a high probability someone would break into his minivan. He drove around the block to examine Hope House from all directions. There were alleys on either side and a service street with a dumpster and rear exit directly behind it. It wasn't nearly as large as the Hope House in Bickham.

Carver didn't see Alicia's Tesla. There didn't seem to be an employee parking area but there was a parking deck a block down. He drove there. A liftgate arm blocked the entrance. He pressed the button on a kiosk next to the gate to get a ticket. The gate raised and allowed him in.

The rates were outrageous. Thirty dollars for the first half hour and sixty for an all-day pass. Maybe it was the only place safe for vehicles to park and that commanded the high premium. The only cars parked on the first level were old service vans. They looked very well used.

Two had small stickers identifying them as Hope House vans. There was a black high-top van with no identifying stickers on it. The tires were dirty, and the undercarriage was caked with dried mud. The last van had two flat tires and a thick coat of grime on it.

The next three levels were empty except for a strange looking red car. All four tires on the car were flat and the body had an even heavier coat of dust and grime on it than the van on the first level. The badge on the side said EV1. Carver hadn't heard of it before.

He drove to the top of the deck. Alicia's Tesla wasn't there. Maybe she hadn't brought Rich here. Maybe she'd taken him out for a day in the city. Maybe they were at the Big Bean or going out for Chicago-style pizza.

Carver drove to the bottom of the deck and put his ticket into the kiosk there. Since he'd only been there five minutes, it released him without charge. He'd been prepared to smash through the gate arm if it tried to charge him.

He parked in front of Hope House and went inside. There was a man in the reception area. He was looking down a hallway expectantly as if waiting on someone. He turned to Carver. "Can I help you?"

"I'm looking for my friend," Carver said. "He was staying in Bickham but said Alicia would be bringing him here today."

"Oh, sorry." The man shrugged. "I haven't seen Alicia here today. Are you certain?"

"Yeah."

"And your name is?"

"I'm Bert Polaski." Carver watched the other man to see if Rich's last name elicited a response.

The other man smiled and extended a hand. "I'm Keith. Maybe I can help you find your friend. What's his name?"

"Rich."

Keith blinked twice rapidly then furrowed his brow. "Hm, doesn't ring a bell."

The blinking told Carver that Keith knew the name. The fact that the name Polaski hadn't gotten a reaction told Carver that Keith knew Rich's first name but not his last. Keith was feigning ignorance. He didn't want Carver to know that Rich was here, or if not here, somewhere with Alicia.

A young Hispanic woman exited a room in the hallway and walked toward them. She wore her hair in a tight bun on top of her head. She wore form-fitting cargos and a T-shirt that outlined a lean, muscular body. She had a deep scar on the left side of her chin. It followed her jawline and curved up to her ear.

She was staring right at Carver and Keith but seemed to be looking right through them. Carver had seen that look a thousand times. The look of someone plagued by internal strife. She blinked out of it and smiled at Keith.

"Sorry it took me so long." She had a plain American accent. "I lost track of time."

Keith checked his watch. "It's fine."

"I don't want to keep the others waiting." She glanced at Carver. "Who is this?"

"Uh, it's Bert, I think?" Keith said.

Carver extended a hand toward her. "Bert Polaski."

"Oh, that's an interesting name." She took his hand in her firm grasp and shook it. "I'm Nadia Garcia. Are you coming with us?"

"No, he's looking for a friend."

"A guy named Rich," Carver said. "He's supposedly coming here with a woman named Alicia."

Nadia's expression didn't change. "Sorry, I haven't heard of him."

"She's a supervisor from another branch of Hope House." Keith checked his watch. "We've really got to get going."

"Where are you going?" Carver said.

Nadia opened her mouth to answer, but Keith cut her off. "It's private, I'm afraid. Shall we go, Nadia?"

"Yeah, sure." She nodded at Carver. "Nice meeting you."

"Likewise." Carver left the building before Keith asked him to leave. He took a right and walked around the block to where he'd parked the minivan. He figured Keith and Nadia would go to the parking garage and take one of the vans there because there were no vehicles parked near the Hope House entrance.

He hopped in the van and drove it around the other side of the block. He drove behind the back of the parking garage, crossed the next street, then turned right on the next one. He turned right again at the next street and pulled to the curb. Now he had a clear view of the front of the parking garage.

Keith and Nadia had plenty of time to walk to the garage. They were probably in the van by now. That proved true a moment later when one of the old vans with the Hope House logo on the side pulled out of the garage. It turned left towards Carver.

The traffic in the area wasn't very heavy, but it was enough to use as cover for the minivan. Carver pulled into traffic behind a sedan and stopped at the traffic light. The Hope House van stopped across the intersection at the same traffic light right behind a motorcycle. It didn't have a turn signal on.

The light turned green. The van turned to its right. Carver waited for the car in front of him to go straight then waited for several cars to go past before he could turn left across the intersection. The van was ahead by two intersections, but that was okay. The logo on the sides and rear made it easy to see even from a couple of blocks back.

Carver followed it at a distance. The van moseyed along at the pace of traffic, stopping frequently for the absurd number of traffic lights in the area. It traveled three miles in about fifteen minutes which was normal for city standards.

It turned left and into a community recreation center. There were a handful of cars parked in front of the large building. Carver counted eleven cars, three of which were Hope House vans, and one of which was Alicia's Tesla. There were four Hope House vans if he included Keith's.

He parked curbside across from the rec center and examined the cars through his monocular. The Hope House vans looked similar. Two had Illinois license plates. One had an Indiana plate and the other a Wisconsin plate.

Keith and Nadia exited the van and went inside. The lost look on Nadia's face was gone, replaced with one of excitement. She didn't exactly have a skip in her step, but she looked happier than earlier.

Another Hope House van drove past Carver's position and pulled into the parking lot. This one had a Michigan plate. It looked like vans from all over the place were coming here. The van parked and three men exited.

One wore olive green cargo pants and a black T-shirt. The other two wore jeans and T-shirts. They all wore their hair short but not buzzed. Nadia's attire and hair had caught Carver's attention immediately. The way she walked told him she was almost certainly former military.

These guys had the same look about them. Everything about them told Carver they'd done some time in the service. Keith had likewise put off military vibes, though not as strongly as Nadia. Maybe he'd been out a while. Either way, it highlighted the theme of this so-called private meeting.

It certainly piqued Carver's interest. Why had Alicia spirited Rich away from Bickham and all the way to Chicago? Why had these other vans apparently driven from neighboring states to get here? Was it some kind of PTSD convention? Was it something else?

There was one way to find out. Carver pulled a U-turn and pulled onto the road in front of the rec center. He turned right into the parking lot and parked between two Hope House vans. He got out of the minivan and tested the doors of the other vans. They were unlocked.

He checked the glove compartment and found a registration to Hope House in Milwaukee, Wisconsin. There was nothing else of interest. He checked the neighboring van and found the registration for a Hope House in Indianapolis, Indiana.

Carver walked to Alicia's Tesla. It was locked and there was nothing visible on the seats or dash. Oddly enough, the second row seats were gone and it looked like the last row had been modified. The tint was too dark for him to see the details.

He investigated the other cars and found license plates from Indiana, Wisconsin, and Michigan, but most were from Illinois. He didn't see anything identifiable in any of the cars and they were all locked.

With that bit of the investigation done, he strode confidently up to the entrance and walked in. He entered a large, empty hallway. He heard voices echoing from the left, so he followed the sound and found a large gymnasium. The room was easily half the size of a football field. The place looked and smelled old. It looked like one of those huge all-in-one buildings from the sixties or seventies.

There was a swimming pool, a basketball court, a playground, and other assorted recreational sections inside the large building. Everything looked old, but functional. In the middle near the pool was a cluster of chairs and small groups of people milling around and talking.

Rich stood on the outskirts of the group next to Alicia, but he wasn't talking to her. He was talking to Nadia. They looked like they were talking about something they were passionate about, maybe even angry about, but they both seemed in agreement about it.

Carver estimated there were about twenty people, but he didn't have a good view from here. He considered walking straight up to them and pretending he was supposed to be there, but Rich would almost certainly call him out as would Alicia and Keith. Due to the wide-open design of the building there was no way to slip into the group unnoticed.

There were long maintenance ladders leading up to the steel rafters in several places around the cavernous space, but they were all in plain sight, so anyone climbing them would be visible. There were giant stadium lights near the tops of the ladders, and large overhead lights hanging from the rafters that could serve as concealment, but Carver would have to get to them unseen first.

Carver walked across the large hallway and skirted past the doorway leading into the gymnasium. He walked until he found another door leading into the center area. He had a slightly different angle on the small crowd from there.

There was a stack of old chairs, tables, and other odds and ends near the door that gave him a decent place to watch from without being seen. He just wasn't sure if he could hear anything from this distance. He crouched and walked along the stacks of furniture to the right. He found a narrow space and followed it between the stacks until he was about fifty feet closer to the group. It wasn't great, but it was better than nothing.

He got down on his stomach and watched between the table and chair legs. He had a decent view but couldn't see everyone. That was okay. He just wanted to hear what they were discussing. Judging from the circle of chairs and the table with the coffee and donuts, this was going to be a group therapy session.

Except it didn't make sense to bring people from so far away to meet in a place like this for group therapy even if the theme was military folks only. Hope House seemed geared toward helping people no matter where they came from, be they ordinary civilians or the military. Maybe they decided it was better to hold special sessions for former soldiers.

The buzz of conversation quieted immediately, as if a drill sergeant just walked into the barracks. People found their chairs quickly and quietly.

A man spoke in a clear baritone. "Thanks, everyone. We've got friends visiting from other branches today, so we've got quite a crowd. If you're new here, I'd like you to stand and introduce yourselves. If you're not comfortable with that, you can just raise your hand."

Two men stood. Someone raised their hand. Carver zoomed in with the monocular and saw it was Rich.

One of them spoke. "I'm Allen Baker, a proud Marine."

Shouts of "Semper Fi" rose from the crowd.

"Semper Fi, brothers." He smiled. "I did my duty and got dishonorably discharged for refusing the command of a superior officer and rescuing a non-com who was under fire from local forces. I've got no regrets and would do it all over again if I had to."

"That's what we're here for!" someone shouted. Carver couldn't see who it was.

"Superior officer my ass!" someone else added.

Baker nodded. "I wanted to go career, but now I'm stuck in civvy land and can't get a job thanks to my status." He shrugged. "So, I'm here, brothers."

The man who'd called the meeting to order spoke. "Thank you, Allen." Carver tried to get a look at him, but he was on the other side of the circle and out of sight.

There was brief applause, and then the next man standing spoke.

"I'm Jamie Lewinsky, former Army grunt. My life has been a complete shitshow since I got discharged. I feel like I'm at rock bottom, you know?" He rubbed his hands nervously. "I was ready to off myself after I lost everything but then Hope House took me in and made me reconsider."

He turned to the man sitting next to him. "Thanks to Kyle here, I'm in a much better place."

Kyle stood and hugged him. Others applauded. Rich seemed to gain some confidence from watching the others and stood.

"I'm Rich Polaski, former SEAL, now a disabled veteran with nothing going for me thanks to a supposed brother in arms falling down on duty."

A few people booed.

Rich flashed a brief smile. "Yeah. I was doing okay. Trying to save up money to get my shoulder and knee fixed, but then some neighborhood kid got caught dealing drugs on my property. The cops used that as justification to take everything from me. Now I've got nothing." He dropped into his seat.

"Same thing happened to me," someone else said.

"Me too." Nadia stood. "My brother was hosting illegal gambling parties in my house and the cops took it."

"I'm sure a lot of you have experienced the worst of the civilian world," the meeting leader said. "We're here to get it all out, okay? I know some of you have heard all the stories before, so you can share if you want but you don't have to. I'd like whoever wants to speak to do so. Let's get it all out in the open, okay?"

And that's what they did for the next two hours. Most of the people present had been dishonorably discharged for what they considered unfair reasons. Some had bad run-ins with CIA liaisons, some had disobeyed direct orders, and some had no idea what exactly they'd done.

Many had been thrust unwillingly into civilian life. Many had been doing okay only to lose everything. Some of those cases involved local police and civil forfeiture, but others had simply gotten into trouble the old-fashioned way and gone to jail for it.

Some of them accepted the consequences of their actions while others proclaimed innocence. It was like any other group therapy session Carver had ever seen except this one was limited to former soldiers of all persuasions. It was nothing new and certainly nothing interesting.

Carver began to back out of his hiding spot. It was time to go. It was almost certainly time to leave Rich to his own devices. He'd done everything in his power and now he was fifty grand poorer for having done so.

One thing was certain. He wasn't leaving town without his money or at the very least giving it to Rich for his surgery whether he wanted it or not. Then he was going back to the beach and forgetting this ever happened.

He reached the door and heard the voice of the meeting leader telling his story, so he slowed to listen. The story was that of a man in a covert unit that was disbanded and everyone in it dishonorably discharged due to the actions of one man.

Carver had heard this story before. He knew it all too well because it sounded a lot like his story. Except he was the supposed criminal in his own story. The one who'd destroyed his covert unit, Scion. Hearing the same story from the mouth of someone else got his attention.

The meeting leader was standing in plain view now. Carver put his monocular to his eye and looked at the man. He was familiar. Too familiar. An instant later recognition set in. He knew the man. Seeing him alive and well was quite a shock.

Because that man was supposed to be dead.

CHAPTER 22

Carver was staring at a dead man.

He didn't look exactly the same as the last time he'd seen him. He had a beard and slightly longer hair. A few new wrinkles. The deep scar on his forehead was gone, reduced to an almost unnoticeable line even with the monocular zooming to maximum.

He wasn't the skinny tech Carver remembered. He was a little bigger now, more muscular in the upper body but not so much that it affected flexibility and agility. There was one thing that hadn't changed. His eyes. They still looked dark and soulful. Almost angelic. Women fell for those eyes every time. Some men had done the same. Most had paid with their lives or been captured and interrogated.

Someone in the group called out the man's name, Tom. That wasn't the name Carver had known him by. He'd only known him by his last name, or at least what he'd always assumed was his last name. It might have been a nickname for all he knew because no one told him otherwise.

The name was Jericho.

Carver had a healthy respect for the other members of Scion. They'd supposedly been the best of the best while simultaneously being the worst of the worst because they'd do anything, follow any orders, no questions asked.

Rhodes had been the brilliant strategist. Leon had been the dependable sniper. Menendez and Rocker had been pros at demolitions and bombs. Carver had been the infil and exfil expert. The one who'd done the dirty work in close quarters, quickly and quietly. Jericho had been a skinny tech guy.

The first thing most people would do was look at him and think they could take him down easily. The second thing they'd do was die with a surprised look on their faces. Jericho wasn't skinny. He had lean, wiry muscle. He was an expert in hand-to-hand combat, something Carver hadn't discovered until they'd been assigned to infiltrate a building together and install surveillance equipment.

Carver felt confident he could have taken most Scion members in a close quarter fight whether it was with fists or bladed weapons. He didn't have that level of confidence with Jericho. In fact, he was fairly certain Jericho could puncture an artery with a lightning-fast thrust before he even knew what hit him.

After Carver had been framed for using his position with Scion to sex traffic women, Scion had been disbanded, and everyone had been dishonorably discharged. The last time Carver had seen Jericho was when Rhodes told everyone the bad news.

Carver had been in military police custody at the time. He'd been taken to the meeting in shackles. The other squad members had hurled angry insults at Carver. Rocker and Menendez hadn't been all that angry and Carver later found out why. It was because they were the ones who'd framed him.

Jericho had been livid. His absolute favorite things in the world revolved around his duties in Scion. Seducing people with his innocent good looks, surveillance, assassinations, and especially psyops and regime change.

The last thing he'd said to Carver was very straightforward. "If I ever see you again, I will kill you." And there was little doubt in Carver's mind that he was one person who could follow through with that threat.

The NSA had listed Jericho as dead, at least according to the list Barry had shown Carver. And yet, Jerico was obviously alive and well and apparently leading a group therapy session. That was strange. Real strange. Jericho wasn't the kind of guy to do charity work unless he had an ulterior motive.

Jericho was an expert at manipulation. He knew all the pressure points. He knew how to apply pressure to them. His technical expertise blended with his personal skills made him a master at convincing people to do what he wanted them to do and making them think they were doing it of their own free will.

It wouldn't surprise Carver in the least if Jericho had manipulated him into being here. Barry might not be with the NSA. He might be with Jericho. Or he might also be a victim of Jericho's manipulations.

Jericho might have breached the NSA's computers and used them to locate Carver, then put Carver and Rich on the NSA watchlist. Liana saw the flag and sent someone to tell Carver. Carver saw Rich on the list and did what Jericho knew he would do, namely come see Rich in person and warn him.

Somehow, Jericho had manipulated events to get Rich to this location and by extension, get Carver to come here. How he'd done that, Carver couldn't imagine. There were too many vectors to plot. Too many things that could have gone wrong.

First of all, Jericho would have to know about Liana and her connection to Carver. To know that he'd have to have an inside track at the NSA. Maybe he'd manipulated someone at the NSA to list him as dead while also giving him useful information. Maybe he'd hacked into their systems and done it himself.

There was no telling. Carver had no idea how Jericho had pulled this off, but in this case, knowing wasn't half the battle. In this case, the battle might already be over. He was within Jericho's reach in a room full of former soldiers who would probably help him capture Carver.

They might be circling his position even now and he didn't even know it. Everything leading Carver to this moment had been a masterful manipulation, leaving him completely unprepared for his reckoning.

Be that as it may, Carver wasn't going to take it lying down. He quickly made his way out of the maze of stacked furniture and got back to the doorway. He ducked around the corner, gun drawn, and studied the hallway. It was empty.

He half-expected Jericho to taunt him. To say, "Hello, Carver. Where do you think you're going?"

But that didn't happen. Jericho kept droning on about the importance of everyone supporting each other and sticking together. About how they would stick it to the uncaring civilians who didn't value the sacrifices they'd made protecting the country.

It had gone from being a pep talk to inciting shouts of anger and agreement from those present. In other words, it was just an ex-military pep rally. But appearances could be deceiving, so Carver didn't let down his guard. He followed the curve in the hall toward the front door and reached it moments later.

No one was in sight. There were no good hiding places, so no one was hiding either unless they were just inside the doorway leading toward the inner gymnasium. Maybe this was all part of the manipulation. Maybe Jericho wanted Carver to see him. Maybe he wanted Carver to run and to feel hunted. It was just the sort of thing Jericho loved to do.

There was also the possibility that Jericho had absolutely no idea Carver was here or that he even knew of a connection between Carver and Rich. Occam's Razor told him that the simplest explanation was usually the best, the simplest being that this was all a coincidence.

But Jericho had a way of completely subverting that principle. He excelled at sending rats through the most complex of mazes and having them end up exactly where he wanted them to be.

So which situation was this?

It was hard to say. The only way to know for certain would be by walking into the meeting and saying hello to Jericho. If Jericho abruptly stopped speaking, drew a knife, and charged Carver, then that would answer that.

That wasn't how Carver wanted the question answered. He preferred a more controlled environment. He also wanted a chance to tell Jericho that Rocker and Menendez had set him up on the sex trafficking charges. That Scion had been disbanded at the behest of a private military company and other unknown players because they wanted to privatize the black ops business.

Maybe Jericho would believe him, but that seemed unlikely. He would, however, believe Leon, provided Carver could reach him. The best option for now was to wait and watch the situation. To see what unfolded next while keeping a close eye on things.

He really wanted to know what connection Hope House had with the Bickham police. At the very least they had an agreement or an understanding. They certainly weren't close business partners, but they tolerated each other.

Another more urgent problem suddenly occurred to Carver. Rich hadn't mentioned Carver by name during his testimony, but once he started talking to others, he'd almost certainly tell them that the man who was responsible for his condition had shown up in town pretending to care about him.

Rich would say the name Carver, and Jericho's ears would perk up. Jericho would ask him how he knew that name. He would find out Carver was in town. And then the hunt would begin. Jericho would at first use Rich to draw out Carver. Except Carver now knew about Jericho's presence and wouldn't be manipulated into showing himself.

That was, of course, if this entire thing wasn't a setup. Jericho was good, but he wasn't all-knowing. Maybe he really didn't know Carver was here. It was seeming more and more likely that he didn't.

Getting out of town and far away was the best thing Carver could do. Or maybe it wasn't. Maybe it was time to bury the proverbial hatchet with Jericho and make things right, so he no longer had to worry about him.

Because now that he knew Jericho was alive, he wouldn't be resting easy no matter how well he thought he was hidden. Carver stood near the entrance and listened to Jericho's pep talk while he thought about his next moves.

He still had a bone to pick with Bickham PD. They had his money, and he wanted it back. At the very least, he'd give it to Rich for his surgery. Then there was Jericho. If Carver could get Leon on the phone, then he could settle that issue once and for all as well.

It would also be nice to know what Jericho was doing here. Was this another one of his psyops, or was he genuinely trying to help these people? The former was almost certainly the real reason. Jericho didn't help people unless it furthered his own goals. It was a core part of the man and not something that was bound to change over time.

The only way to know for sure was through observation. Talking to Rich or interrogating Alicia and Keith probably wouldn't yield many results. They might not be aware of the manipulation, or they might be part of the process.

Carver hadn't been prepared for the can of worms this trip had opened, but it presented an opportunity he hadn't known he needed. Jericho was alive. Jericho wanted him dead. Now he could set the record straight and live with one less major threat to his life.

He settled in next to the doorway and listened to Jericho's speech. He was too far away to hear the softer parts clearly, but when Jericho's voice rose with emotion, he could hear the payoff and the resounding cheers.

There were no calls to action. Nothing specific, anyway. It was mostly about keeping a positive mental attitude and putting former military folks above lowly, ungrateful civilians. Jericho might be laying the foundation for a psyop, or he might really be trying to help these people. It was impossible to tell.

Jericho ended the meeting by inviting everyone to gather at a local bar for drinks and pool. Someone jokingly asked why there wasn't a pool table in the gymnasium, which drew a round of laughter.

Jericho replied that it was important for them to gather in a civilian environment. He said isolation was part of the disease and he aimed to cure it. That drew a loud round of applause.

Then it was over, and people dispersed into smaller groups to talk. Carver peered around the corner. He zeroed in on Rich to see if he approached Jericho or vice versa. The two men made eye contact and strode purposefully toward each other. They shook hands and grinned like two long-lost friends.

They spoke for a few minutes. Jericho patted Rich on the shoulder and said something, probably along the lines of, "Let's catch up later." Rich nodded and replied, then went back to Alicia. Nadia and Keith joined them in conversation.

Rich spoke with Nadia. Carver watched his expressions with the monocular. For the first time in a while, he looked genuinely happy to be alive. He tried to raise his right arm too high and winced when his bad shoulder stopped him. His smile faded, but he didn't look angry or resentful.

Maybe this was a good thing for him. Maybe this would turn his life around even if he was being manipulated by Jericho. Considering the life he'd been living until now, anything was an improvement.

Carver considered his next move. He could go to the bar and possibly observe Jericho and the others, but he'd have to gather some preliminary information first. He'd also need a top-notch disguise. Gathering the most useful intel would require a parabolic mic and some surveillance tools.

He didn't have the funds for those unless he recovered his money from Bickham PD. That would require a very well-planned operation to succeed because the police station was built like a fortress. He was going to get his money back, but first he needed to solve his Jericho problem.

Carver's only surveillance equipment was the cameras, his monocular, and his eyes and ears. Unless he found an easy mark like a drug dealer with a wad of cash, the equipment on hand would have to make do for now. It was also possible that there was cash hidden at Tony's place, but he'd have to find it.

Carver left the building. He got into the van and steered it out of the parking lot. He pulled into another parking lot a few blocks away and plugged in the name of the bar the group would be visiting later.

The place was named Red Shoes. It had mostly positive reviews. It was open until zero two hundred. Carver drove there and parked. He went inside and looked around. It was a typical pool hall with twenty tables, a full bar, and food service.

The place was mostly empty at this time of the afternoon, but it would probably fill up at night. It was in a strip mall right next to a well-maintained middle-class neighborhood. The single-family homes were newer unlike the old rowhouses in Tony's neighborhood.

If everyone from the group came here, they'd easily fill up half the pool hall, maybe more depending on how many wanted to play and how many wanted to drink beer and talk. If the place was packed, that would make it easier for Carver to fit in but harder for him to eavesdrop.

He checked the time. He had three hours before they planned to arrive. That gave him time to get ready and time to put his meager budget to good use. He looked at the attire of the other patrons. They were mostly men. Mostly wearing jeans and T-shirts. One man wore a suit and one of those old flat caps from the thirties or forties.

He looked pretty dapper, but he stuck out because of it. Carver wanted to do the opposite, but he would need more cover than just jeans and a T-shirt. Unfortunately, it was too warm to wear a hoodie, and no one was wearing surgical masks these days.

Remaining unnoticed was of vital importance. Because if Jericho recognized him, there would be trouble. There would be violence.

It would be game over.

Chapter 23

Rich couldn't believe Tom was there.

Tom saw him and did a doubletake. "Rich? Rich Polaski?"

"Tom!" Rich limped over as fast as he could and held out a hand.

Tom ignored it and hugged him, careful to avoid his shoulder. He stepped back. "I'd say you're looking good, but I'd be lying."

Rich laughed. "Believe me, I know how bad I look."

"How many years has it been?"

"Hell, I don't know." Rich shrugged. "I kind of lost track of time." He waved a hand around. "So, what are you doing here? Are you involved with Hope House?"

"Not directly. I interface with organizations that provide counseling and therapy. While they deal with the public at large, I deal more specifically with veterans."

"How did you get into this line of work?"

Tom chuckled. "Let's just say I wasn't impressed with what the VA offered me. And when I tried to push back against the system, the system pushed back against me. I came up with an organization that bypasses the red tape and gets straight to helping people."

"Hell yeah, brother." Rich held out a fist. "It's about time we took control of our own lives."

Tom bumped his fist. "Thanks, Rich. It means a lot coming from you."

"Yeah? Why me?"

"Because you're one of the reasons I felt inspired to leave the system behind."

Rich laughed. "I was that much of a basket case?"

"Yes." Tom grinned. "Yes, you were."

Rich looked at the gathering crowd. "How's it working out so far?"

"It's going better than expected. We collect funds from multiple charities, and we also managed to backdoor some funding from the federal government itself."

"Whoa, how'd you do that?"

"You'd be surprised at how easy it really is as long as you pretend your organization supports one of their pet projects."

Rich shrugged. "I don't get it."

"Did you ever deal with organizations funded by USAID overseas?"

"Yeah, of course. That agency is a backdoor for regime change in multiple countries. They come in pretending to be a relief organization spreading medical care, food, and so forth but they're really running psyops."

"Exactly." Tom smirked. "But the politicians in power also fund countless pet projects through the agency that have nothing to do with any of that. We just find out what's politically popular and apply for aid under that pretense."

"Aren't you worried you'll be found out?" Rich said.

"It's a federal agency used to launder billions of dollars. It'll never get audited."

Rich whistled. "That's brilliant, actually."

"It wasn't my idea." Tom grinned. "Let's say I was inspired by the people who ran our covert unit. They know all the tricks for leeching off the government teat."

"Hell yeah, they do." Rich liked the idea of turning the government's tactics against itself. "Those assholes have betrayed us for way too long. First they manufacture fake intel to send us to places we shouldn't be in and then when we get injured, they claim there's not enough money to help us."

"That's the game, man." Tom sighed. "In fact, the budget for just one small federal agency would be more than enough to take care of every veteran alive today."

Rich scowled. "They're lucky I'm a cripple, because I'd love to teach those folks a lesson."

"You and me both, Rich." Tom's expression grew serious. He put a hand on Rich's good shoulder. "There will be a reckoning, but it needs to be smart and decisive. Politicians need to learn that betraying veterans comes with a steep price."

"Amen, brother." Rich loved what he was hearing. "Damn, what I wouldn't give to have my shoulder and knee fixed so I could do something about it."

"It might just be in our budget." Tom looked around. He made eye contact with a woman and waved her over.

She hurried over, a smile on the left half of her face. Her mouth on the right side looked like it was trying to smile and failing. "Hey, Tom. Who you got here?" She spoke with a quaint southern accent.

Tom put a hand on her shoulder. "Amy, I'd like you to meet Rich."

"A pleasure." Amy shook Rich's hand and seemed to notice him looking at the side of her face. "You can ask if you want. I don't mind."

"Did you have a stroke?" Rich asked.

"Half my face was almost blown off," Amy said. "I had major reconstructive surgery."

"The VA paid for it?"

She laughed. "Hell no. Tom got the government to pay through a back door."

Rich suddenly felt hopeful. "That couldn't have been cheap."

"You'd be surprised how much of a cash discount we can get," Tom said.

Amy pointed to scars along her jawline and above her hairline. "I didn't think it was possible to do what they did. I don't have feeling in some areas and my facial muscles on that side don't work as well as they used to, but I also don't look like a monster anymore."

"It's amazing." Rich shook his head in wonder. "The VA could do this for all of us. But they choose not to."

"Exactly." Amy bared her teeth, or at least half of her teeth since the lips didn't curl up quite as far on one side. "And there will be a reckoning one day."

Rich nodded. "That's exactly what Tom said."

Tom looked around. "I think everyone is here. Guess we'd better get started."

Rich nodded. "Damned good seeing you again, Tom."

"Rich, you've come to the right place for help." Tom squeezed his good shoulder. "I'm glad you found us."

Rich looked at the circle of chairs. They were almost all taken. Alicia waved him over and pointed to an empty seat between her and Nadia. He hobbled over and sat down.

Alicia raised an eyebrow. "You know Tom?"

"Yeah." Rich massaged his bad knee and winced. "His VA shrink appointments were usually right after mine, so we'd talk for a few minutes in between my session and his. We kept in touch a little bit over the years, but it's been a long time since I last heard from him."

"He's a good man," Alicia said. "And he knows how to leverage our experiences so we can help each other."

"You sound like a corporate boss when you talk like that."

"I talk like I was trained to talk." She shrugged. "It is what it is."

"Yeah, sorry."

"Don't apologize. I accept who I am. You need to accept who you are and use it."

"A cripple?" Rich laughed. "I don't know how to use that."

"You're a SEAL." Alicia looked a little disappointed. "Act like it."

"I haven't been a SEAL in ages. I'm barely even a man anymore."

"Keep thinking like that and that's all you'll ever be." She turned her attention to Tom.

The chairs were arranged in a circle just like most group therapy sessions, but this circle was wider than normal because there were around twenty people present. Tom took his seat on the opposite side of Rich.

"It's good to see everyone," Tom said. "It's good to see the circle expanding."

"Hell yeah," someone shouted.

Others shouted and applauded.

Tom grinned. "Our efforts are finding more and more people who were all alone and without help. What you see here is just a small part of what's happening across the nation. What you see here is just the beginning."

There was more applause, more shouting. Rich found himself shouting along with everyone else.

"Now, before we go any further, I'd like everyone to introduce yourselves. I'd also like you to tell your stories. I know some of you don't want to, but it's important that we get to know each other and what brought us here, so let's get started." He looked around. "Who wants to get us started?"

Amy stood. "I'll do it."

Tom clapped. "Thank you, Amy."

After the applause died down, Amy told her story. It was a story Rich had heard before. A common story among Army grunts and Marines who'd been on the frontlines in countries that didn't want them there.

In Amy's case, a routine patrol ended when an IED, improvised explosive device, blew the front end off her squad's Hummer, killing the driver and taking off part of her face. A firefight took out four more members of her squad before an A10 razed the enemy combatants from overhead.

Amy had been given emergency surgery that made her look like a monster. She'd been discharged on disability. The VA refused further surgeries and put her on meds and psychological counseling.

She'd met Tom during counseling. Years later he'd contacted her and told her he might be able to help. Several surgeries later, she finally felt human again. Now she was helping to find others who needed help and fully supportive of Tom.

The next person was new to the group and had been brought by Amy. He told the group how he'd lost his leg, and a cheap plastic prosthetic was all the VA would give him. He'd met Amy during a counseling session. She'd introduced him to Hope House and brought him all the way from Michigan to here.

The next three people had also been brought by Amy and gave their stories. After a while, the circle reached Nadia. She told a story of betrayal unsurprisingly by the CIA and their minions. She was dishonorably discharged but got a job in security.

Now that job was gone thanks to her loser brother using her house for illegal gambling. The police in her town had used civil forfeiture to take everything she owned except her car. Just like they'd done to Rich.

Hearing her story made Rich feel a little better about telling his story because it couldn't get much more embarrassing than that. Misery loves company, and Rich was about as miserable as it got.

All the other stories gave him a new perspective on his own situation. He began to think that maybe he'd come out of his situation a lot better than others. There were several people who'd lost both legs or an arm and a leg and were still in a better mental state than he was. Maybe it was time for him to snap out of his funk and help Tom make a difference.

The circle reached Tom. Despite the time that Rich had spent with the man, he'd never heard Tom's story. He only knew that Tom was in covert operations. That was just another name for black ops or shadow ops.

"Some of you have heard this story many times, so I'll stick to the short version," Tom said. "I served with a dark ops crew. Our specialty was assassinations and regime change. Our commander had almost a free hand in deciding how we did our jobs."

He sighed. "Unfortunately, one of our team members abused this power. He was using dark rides for his own purposes. For those who aren't familiar, a dark ride is when we exfiltrated our assets and zero questions could be asked about them or anything they brought with them because our unit was completely off the books."

Rich had never heard of such a thing. Even the most secretive operations for the SEALs required oversight.

Tom continued. "One team member was using the dark rides for profit. Someone found out and tipped off the MPs. They opened coffins that were supposed to contain the remains of our honored dead. Instead, they found women who were being sex trafficked."

Some in the circle nodded grimly as if they'd heard it before. Others looked shocked.

"How could the MPs search if no one was allowed to ask questions?" a man asked.

Tom shrugged. "I don't know. Someone high up the chain must have found out and ordered a security override. The end result was that we all paid the price for one person's crimes. Our unit was disbanded, and we were dishonorably discharged."

"I'll bet you found that asshole and made him pay," Nadia said.

Tom shook his head. "I told him I'd kill him the next time I saw him, and I meant it. But he was good at disappearing, and that's just what he did. I haven't seen him since."

That was exactly what Carver had done to Rich. He'd gone off mission and allowed Rich to be captured. Rich had been tortured for two months before being rescued. Not long after that, Carver had been removed from the team without explanation. Rich had hoped he'd been dishonorably discharged, but others speculated that he'd been promoted.

Joe Donnelly knew what happened to Carver, but he never spoke about it. He said it wasn't anyone's business except Carver's. Joe was a great leader, but he had an irrational attachment to Carver and no one could understand why.

So, while Carver had possibly been promoted, Rich had been disabled. Medical had patched him up but they hadn't fixed him. They'd left him seventy percent disabled in his shoulder and knee. They'd told him nothing else could be done. And then they'd discarded him, given him benefits, and promptly forgotten him.

But now Rich saw things a little differently. Everyone in this room had been wronged. Some by fellow squad mates, sure, but all of them had been wronged by the system. The same system that threw them into wars then threw them away when they were done with them.

Tom was finished with his story, but he wasn't done talking. "We all have one thing in common. We all served. We were all betrayed by the people in charge."

People booed and clapped in agreement.

"We might be damaged goods, but we're still alive. And it's time to make the system work for us, not for the politicians or the companies making the weapons."

People stood and cheered loudly. Rich pushed himself painfully to his feet and applauded as much as he could until his shoulder and knee hurt.

"I like this guy," Nadia said. "He talks sense."

"Yeah. And he seems smart enough to follow through." Rich didn't repeat what Tom had told him about getting grants from US agencies. It probably wasn't a secret, but it was Tom's thing to tell.

Tom raised his hands and quieted the room. "I want to thank everyone for coming and for making the long drive." He waved a hand around the gymnasium. "This is not owned by Hope House or any of the many charities we work with. This is owned directly by us. And as such, we invite you to make it your own. Some of you have lost your homes. You've lost everything. This is your chance to make something for yourself."

Rich's heart swelled with gratitude. He and Nadia glanced at each other. They were both in the same situation. Both homeless and hopeless. But now they'd found something more.

Alicia squeezed Rich's hand. "You hear that? You can move on."

"Yeah." Rich liked having options, but another part still clung onto his old life. His parents' house, now stolen by the police. But what else could he do?

Tom was still talking. "I'm going to wrap things up for now. We've converted the back section of the rec center into rooms. There's enough space for everyone to stay the night instead of spending money on hotels."

Everyone cheered.

"Let's regroup in three hours and we'll go to a local pool hall for food, drinks, and relaxation. We'll get to know one another in a different setting." Tom looked around at the group. "Okay, I'm done."

Most people were already standing. The larger group broke into smaller groups and conversations. Rich walked over to Tom and shook his hand. "Man, I really needed to hear that."

"We all need to hear it." Tom patted his shoulder. "Get to know other people. We'll catch up later."

"Yeah, sounds good." Rich returned to his chair. He sat down and massaged his knee. It was hurting something fierce.

Nadia sat next to him. "I don't know what to do."

Rich raised an eyebrow. "What do you mean?"

"I mean, it's great having a place to stay, but that only solves one problem." She sighed. "I don't have a job, but I have car payments. And this area isn't exactly the best part of town to look for work."

"It's something at least." Rich flexed his bad knee to stretch it. It hurt, but it relieved some of the tension. "I want my house back. I want my money back. I want to..." He clenched a fist and stopped himself from saying what he really wanted to do.

"You want to put a hurting on someone, don't you?" Nadia squeezed his hand. "So do I. You don't even want to know the thoughts I've been thinking."

"Murderous thoughts?" Rich said.

She laughed. "Oh yeah."

Alicia sat down. "What are you two talking about?"

Nadia cleared her throat. "Oh, nothing."

Keith sat down on the other side of her. "We're all friends here, Nadia."

Her face flushed. "We hardly know each other."

Keith shook his head. "That's not true. Didn't you listen to our stories? Don't you realize that we all know each other better than anyone else even if we just met?"

Rich nodded. "I know what you mean. We just met but I feel like we're all brothers in arms, you know?"

"Exactly." Alicia squeezed his hand. "We're a family of sorts."

"Almost like a cult." Keith laughed.

Alicia laughed. "Oh, God, not this again."

"It's true!" Keith shrugged. "Anyway, we're here for you guys, okay? You can tell us anything."

"I mean, you already have a lot on me." Nadia stared at Keith. "I just want some good old-fashioned revenge on a few assholes in my life."

"Me too," Rich said. "Especially against those assholes who took everything from me."

"Law enforcement is one thing we don't mess with," Alicia said. "At least not directly. We support local law officers."

"Even if they broke the law?" Rich's face grew hot. "I want to show those assholes what it's like to lose everything!"

"We think it's better to leave that in the past and forge a new path ahead," Keith said. "If we all stick together, we can accomplish a lot."

"Like what?" Rich laughed humorlessly. "What can I do with my physical problems?"

"You let us worry about that," Alicia said. "And if you want help handling someone who's not law enforcement, then we'll help."

"Do you mean that?" Nadia said. "You'd help me with my ex and help me get my kid back?"

Keith nodded. "We can do that."

Alicia nodded too. "Once we're sure you're one of us, then the sky's the limit."

"I am one of you," Nadia said. "One hundred percent."

Rich nodded. "Me too." And he meant it. He had nothing to lose and everything to gain.

This was his new family.

Chapter 24

Carver had a disguise.

He had baggy jeans, a baggy long-sleeved shirt, a ballcap, and a fake beard. And he bought it all for under twenty bucks. That was the power of used clothing stores. He looked like a time traveler from the early 2000s, but it was the best he could do.

The baggy clothing made him look overweight and the thick fake beard looked surprisingly real. With the ballcap pulled low, he hardly recognized himself. It should be enough to fool Rich. Maybe it would fool Jericho. He'd find out real quick if it didn't.

Carver parked down the street from the pool hall and walked the rest of the way. He didn't see any of the vehicles from the rec center parking lot out front. They would start arriving soon. He went into the building and checked out the layout.

The front half of the hall was packed with people. The back half was roped off, leaving ten tables empty. A placard in front of the rope said *Reserved*. The meetup was more organized than it had sounded.

Carver walked along the rope looking for a place to settle in, but all of the tables were taken. The people waiting for pool tables looked miffed that so many tables had been reserved but not miffed enough to leave and go somewhere else.

He went to the bar and waited a few minutes for the bartender to make his way over to him. "I'm with Hope House. Can I go into the reserved area?"

The bartender shrugged and pointed to a hallway. "You'll have to check with Charlie in the office."

"Okay, thanks." Carver ordered a beer. He found an open seat at the bar and settled in there. He hadn't really wanted to go into the reserved area, mainly because he'd be alone there and would stick out like a sore thumb. Once the group arrived, he still wouldn't be able to mingle with them because the group wasn't large enough to hide in.

Alicia was the first to walk through the door. Rich was right behind her. Nadia and Keith came in right after them. Alicia looped her arm in Rich's, talking to him and guiding him to the back. Keith was doing the same with Nadia.

There was nothing romantic about it but using members of the opposite sex to gain comfort and trust was a tried-and-true tactic. That was obviously what was happening here. Then again, Carver was looking at it from a psyops perspective because Jericho was involved. Maybe there was nothing of the sort going on. Time would tell.

Rich and the others went around the end of the rope and claimed a pool table in the back corner. Alicia started racking the balls. Nadia said something and the others laughed. Rich said something and pointed to his bad shoulder. The others shook their heads and pointed at the table. Rich pressed his lips together and nodded.

An old man emerged from the hallway and spoke to them briefly. He nodded a few times and gave them a thumbs up before vanishing back down the hallway. That was probably Charlie confirming they were with Hope House.

Alicia finished racking the balls and pointed at Rich. He blew out a breath and went to the table. Wincing in pain, he awkwardly hit the cue ball and managed a decent break. Nadia clapped him on the back. Alicia rubbed his back and seemed to offer some encouraging words.

Rich grinned and replied. None of what they were saying was important, but it was interesting watching the interactions and trying to figure out if Alicia and Keith were trying to recruit Nadia and Rich for something or if they were genuinely trying to help them.

A larger group of people arrived and joined them in the back. A few more trickled in and filled up the reserved area. Jericho arrived last. His eyes took in everyone and everything in the room. Carver lifted his beer to his lips and pretended to be reading his phone. Jericho's gaze didn't linger on him but that didn't mean anything.

Jericho walked to the back area and greeted the others. He went to a table on the side and spoke with two men. They seemed to know each other well because there were no introductory handshakes or awkward interactions.

Keith, Alicia, and a couple of others swung by the table for a brief talk with Jericho. It looked like they were giving assurances or updates on their wards. At least that was Carver's guess. There was no chance of him overhearing anything. Then they returned to their respective tables and resumed playing pool.

It looked like this plan was going to be a bust. He couldn't get close enough to hear them. About all he could do was watch and read their body language for clues. He didn't have anything else to do that evening, so he settled in and watched.

Rich seemed to be having a good time. He was grinning, laughing, and presumably cracking jokes just like the old Rich used to do. During the downtime between missions, Rich would usually make a humorous observation about something that went wrong during the mission. That would usually break the tension with laughter.

Carver never found Rich particularly funny. Nadia, Keith, and Alicia seemed to find him hilarious, though. It looked like he was bonding. If this was part of Jericho's plan, then it was working well.

Rich hadn't spoken to Jericho since he'd arrived at the pool hall, but it was only a matter of time. It was also only a matter of time until Rich mentioned Carver by name. He would inevitably tell Jericho that he blamed some guy named Carver for being crippled. Then he'd go on to mention that Carver had come to town to warn him he was on an NSA watch list. That would perk up Jericho's ears real fast.

Jericho would tell Rich that Carver was also responsible for what happened to him and other members of Scion. Rich would gladly help Jericho lure Carver in for the kill. There was no way to head that off except by meeting with Jericho and telling him that Leon could confirm the truth about Scion.

That was simply too big of a risk. He would have to get Leon to contact Jericho first and confirm that all was forgiven. Until then, Carver was going to keep an eye on things. A very close eye.

He took a headcount. There were twenty-one people present. That might be everyone, but he wasn't certain. Jericho made his way around the crowd, briefly chatting with everyone. The interactions made it clear who he already knew and the people who were new to the group.

The newcomers were recruits. People like Keith and Alicia were the recruiters. At least, that was how it looked to Carver. This wasn't therapy. It was almost certainly indoctrination.

Jericho was interested in recruiting former soldiers. Alicia, Keith and the other administrators were bringing them to him. Was Hope House in league with them, or were they simply using it to further their goals? More importantly, what was Jericho's end goal?

Carver had to remind himself that it didn't matter. He just wanted to clear the air between him and Jericho and then he could concentrate on getting his money back from the Bickham cops. He'd already fulfilled his duty to Rich. Rich refused his help, and there was nothing more to be done.

Reconciling with Jericho wasn't going to happen until Leon got involved. There wasn't anything else Carver could do tonight and no sense in sticking around the bar. He paid for his beer and left.

He returned to the minivan and climbed in through the sliding door. He considered going to the rec center. It looked like everyone had come to the pool hall, so he could probably search the place if he wanted to.

It probably wasn't a productive use of his time. He had cameras but no idea where to place them in the huge building. His time would be better spent trying to get his money back from the Bickham PD while he waited for Leon to contact him.

Carver mulled over his options for a few minutes and decided to return to Bickham and do just that. He was unhappy with the way they'd treated him. Real unhappy. He wanted to punish them somehow. Make them see the error of their ways. If he did that, he'd have to make sure they didn't know he was the one behind it.

He logged into SecMail. There were no new emails from Leon. He sent another email telling Leon that he'd found Jericho and needed urgent assistance. He sent an email to Paola asking her to light a fire under Leon's ass if she was in touch with him. Hopefully, one of them would check their messages soon.

Carver removed the fake beard and ballcap. He swapped the baggy clothing for cargo pants and a T-shirt. He climbed into the driver's seat and started the car. He drove to the next intersection and turned left. An instant before he rounded the building, he saw headlights blink on just a few spaces back from where he'd been parked.

The headlights got his attention but didn't raise any alarm bells. He drove straight and saw the car the headlights belonged to. It took him a split second to recognize the make and model. The alarm bells started ringing.

The car was an old Chevy Caprice. More specifically, it was Palmer's car, and he wasn't alone. Someone was in his passenger seat. How in the hell had they found him already? He'd known that once Davidson and Morales reported their big haul from the big guy in the minivan that it would be a matter of hours before an APB was placed on the minivan.

He'd expected the lag time to be six to eight hours. Instead, it looked like Palmer had located the van in just over four hours. Maybe because Carver had told Davidson and Morales he was going to Chicago Hope House. That gave them a much smaller search area.

A cop might have found the minivan when it was parked across the road from the rec center. It had been parked right out in open view. He'd called it in. Palmer got word and made a beeline for Chicago. He'd asked Chicago PD to keep an eye on the minivan and tell him where it went.

Then again, they could have spotted him just recently. He'd driven to several stores before going to the pool hall. Then he'd been inside the building for a couple of hours. That was plenty of time for Palmer to get there.

Palmer would have arrived and not been certain where Carver was, so he'd waited outside in the car until Carver showed up. This was getting irritating. Why were these cops so intent on getting him?

Taking all his money should have been enough. He wasn't even in their town anymore. He had no choice. He had to ditch the minivan. The problem was he couldn't afford to replace it. Not unless he got his money back.

His car was marked, but there were ways to handle that. It would be easy to find a nearly identical minivan and swap the plates. That would throw the cops off the scent for a while, or at least until they pulled over the van with his old plate and realized what had happened.

In the meantime, he'd have to lose Palmer and lay low until he found a replacement car. This was going to seriously hinder his efforts to get his money back unless he found a way to turn their plans back on them.

Carver hooked a hard left at the next intersection. He gunned the engine down the residential street and took the next right. He took the very next right, gunned it down the block and took the next right to complete his circle around the block

Palmer's car whizzed past at the intersection ahead. He probably hadn't realized Carver was making a run for it until he caught up at the first turn. By then it was too late. Carver had circled around behind him.

Carver turned off his headlights and watched Palmer's taillights. The Caprice stopped at the next intersection and idled there for several seconds. It pulled into the intersection, made a sharp U-turn, and roared down the road back the way it had come.

At first it seemed Palmer knew Carver had doubled back on him, but Palmer zipped straight past the minivan, ran a few stop signs, and reached the traffic light. He went left when the light turned green.

Carver turned on his headlights and drove to the traffic light. The light was just turning yellow when he turned left through the intersection. He saw the Caprice's taillights about a block ahead and followed them.

Losing a tail was good. Even better was playing a reverse Uno card and following the person who'd been tailing you back to wherever they'd come from. There might be an opportunity for Carver to use it to his advantage.

Palmer drove about twenty minutes to a familiar neighborhood. He parked in front of a house Carver knew well, only because he'd visited it recently. It was Tony's house. There were three other old cars parked out front. An early nineties Ford Taurus, and a real boat of a car Carver didn't recognize.

Carver parked on the side of the road just around the corner. He pulled on a ballcap and got out. Most of the streetlamps were out or dim so there was plenty of darkness to hide him. He stood at the corner and watched Palmer enter the house without knocking.

That was real peculiar. Since when did a hitman let his clients know where he lived? And what made Palmer, a cop, feel so comfortable walking straight in when there were clearly other people inside?

Carver walked down the sidewalk. He got a better look at the big car parked in front of the Taurus. It was a baby blue Ford LTD. A real boat of a vehicle. Probably a seventies model if Carver had to guess. It was in pristine shape. Right in front of it was a new car. A car that Carver recognized right away.

It was Big D's Corvette.

Chapter 25

Carver suddenly had plans for the evening.

He was going to find out what in the hell was going on and who this Big D fellow was. He was going to find out why Palmer and Big D were in a former mafia hitman's house. Since they all seemed to know where Tony lived, it seemed likely there was a lot more to this than a simple business relationship.

The porchlight wasn't on, so the yard was cloaked in darkness. All the interior lights were on. Carver saw people through the windows. He saw Palmer go into the den and talk to Big D. The conversation wasn't pleasant, that much was evident when Big D's face turned red, and he started shouting.

Carver took the walkway between the fence and the neighboring building just like he'd done last time. He went to the back of the house and saw two men in the kitchen. They were drinking from coffee mugs and talking. One of them glanced toward the front of the house and laughed. He was probably getting a kick out of hearing Palmer get reamed out.

The two men were unfamiliar. They weren't wearing police uniforms but that didn't mean they weren't cops. Palmer was dressed like a civilian too. They might be Bickham police, or they might be something else entirely.

Carver eased up to the back door. He could hear the conversation clearly through the old single-pane window. The men were talking about Palmer.

The man on the left shook his head. He was a couple inches under six feet tall, and had a red, veiny face like he drank a lot. "How do you lose a minivan when you've got a souped up Caprice?"

The other guy shrugged and sipped whatever was in his coffee mug. He was a couple of inches shorter than the other guy and looked younger. "We got to get this guy and his buddy, that's for sure. I know they got something to do with Tony's disappearance."

Both men wore cheap looking suits. The heavy drinker's suit was deeply wrinkled and brown. It looked like it came off the rack of a discount store. The other guy's was navy blue and looked a little nicer but not by much.

There was another burst of loud shouting from Big D. Something about Palmer being an idiot and getting his ass back out there looking for the minivan.

The men in the kitchen looked at each other and laughed softly. They probably didn't want Big D to hear them laughing because then he'd ream them out too.

The young woman Carver had seen with Big D at Rich's house walked into the kitchen from the dining room. She smiled at them, but there was a hint of concern in her eyes. Her left eye was swollen and black and she had marks on her throat.

"You got anything to drink? She glanced at the coffee pot. "Besides that?"

"Yeah." The heavy drinker pulled a flask from his back pocket. He took a coffee mug from the cabinet and poured a little something into it.

"Thanks, Georgie." She took the mug and tossed it down. She wrinkled her nose. "You love the cheap stuff, don't you?"

The other guy laughed. "Everything about Georgie is cheap."

"Shut it, Frankie." Georgie poured a little more into the woman's mug. "I got retirement to think about."

"Ah, you ain't never retiring." Frankie opened a cabinet and pulled out a bottle of bourbon. "Tony's got the good stuff and I'm starting to think he won't mind us having it."

Georgie sighed. "Yeah, he never goes this long without reporting in. Something went sideways on the poor son of a bitch."

The men had heavy Chicagoan accents just like the woman. They'd probably all been born and raised in the area.

"You want some more, Betty?" Frankie held out the bottle.

"Yeah." She held out her cup. He poured until her cup was almost full. She laughed. "You trying to get me drunk, Frankie?"

"Nah, you know I would never do something like that." He blushed and looked down.

Georgie tutted. "You know it ain't healthy hitting on the commissioner's girl."

Frankie grinned. "Hey, it's healthier than hitting on the boss's girl."

They all laughed.

"What in the hell is going on in here?" The man Carver knew as Big D stormed down the hallway. "We've got a missing man and the sons of bitches who probably had something to do with it are on the loose."

Betty stepped back behind Georgie and shrank in on herself.

"Look, Commissioner, we searched the house from top to bottom. Aside from Tony's secret playroom, we didn't find anything we haven't seen before." Georgie shrugged. "It doesn't look like he's been home, and the neighbors haven't noticed if he's been home or not."

"Neighbors these days ain't what they used to be," Frankie said. "They don't talk to each other anymore. They're too busy playing with their smartphones and gizmos to care."

"Yeah, well Tony isn't exactly the type who goes talking to the neighbors anyway," Georgie said. "The car he drove to Bickham is still sitting across the road from Hope House, and his daily driver is still sitting in front of the restaurant. It looks like he never even got inside the Hope House building."

Frankie nodded. "We even checked Tony's stash house."

Big D frowned. "Stash house?"

"Yeah, it's an old gas station over on West Seventy-Seventh," Georgie said. "We thought maybe something went down and he hid out there, but it looks like he hasn't been there in a while."

Frankie sighed. "I hate to say it, but Georgie is right. Something happened to Tony."

Palmer walked in behind the others. "Look, there's no way Polaski did this. Carver is his guardian angel. He was probably keeping an eye on his friend. He probably took out Tony before he knew what hit him."

Big D turned on him. "Son, you can't even keep tabs on a man in a minivan, so don't go giving us your professional assessment of the situation." He noticed Betty hiding behind Georgie. "Darling, what are you doing back there?"

"Just staying out of the way, sweetie." She walked around Georgie with a forced smile on her face. "You know I don't like to be in the way of you and your business."

"Palmer ain't wrong," Georgie said. "And how do you expect this guy to keep up with a Navy SEAL?"

"He's a *former* SEAL." Big D barked a laugh. "You think just because someone was in the military that they're hot stuff? Those boys are just like everyone else. They go in, do their job, then come back to civilian life and become just another one of us."

Palmer gave him a doubtful look but didn't say anything.

"I don't think you're right," Georgie said. "But it doesn't matter what I think. It only matters what Vincenzo thinks."

Betty returned to her spot behind him and took a long gulp from the coffee mug.

"Damn it." Big D pounded the flat of his fist on the countertop. "This guy is going to cause us big problems. I want him taken care of."

"I'm trying," Palmer said. "We still have an APB out on his vehicle. He won't be able to hide for long."

"Here's what I don't get." Frankie frowned. "Your men pulled this guy over and took north of fifty grand from him, and he didn't try to stop them. If he made Tony disappear, he could probably make a couple of cops disappear. Maybe he didn't have anything to do with Tony disappearing."

"He's not dumb enough to kill two cops," Palmer said. "Navy SEAL or not, he couldn't take two cops anyway."

Georgie laughed. "You guys are seriously underestimating this guy. At least that's what I think."

"Maybe Vincenzo can send us help," Big D said. "Tony was his man, after all."

"We can ask." Georgie shrugged. "We got a well-oiled machine, but this SEAL guy might be a wrench in the works, and you know Vincenzo don't like wrenches."

"That's for damned sure." Frankie chuckled. "We'll talk to him."

Georgie turned to Palmer. "If you find this guy, keep him alive. I want to break a few of his bones in Tony's honor. Got it?"

"You got it." Palmer ran a hand through his hair. "We'll get him eventually."

"Operations are still smooth?" Georgie said.

"Yes, of course." The commissioner held a hand toward Betty. "Let's go."

She finished off her drink and took his hand. "Where to, baby?"

He jerked her closer to him. "What did I tell you about your heavy drinking?"

"I didn't have that much, baby, I swear!"

"She just had a nip, Bo." Georgie winked. "Nothing to worry about."

Carver finally had a name. A real name. Big D was a commissioner and his name was Bo. He didn't know how that tied in with Bickham, though. Was he their police commissioner? Did small towns even have police commissioners? Maybe he was a county commissioner, the equivalent of a city council member.

He took out his phone and searched for Bickham commissioners. He found the city website. It was clean and professional. It said all kinds of great things about Bickham and the county it was in. It didn't list any city leaders, county leaders, or any names at all. It was about as generic as it got.

The mayor was the only person named on the website and that was because he was front and center. Mayor Grant Steele was a tall, muscular man with a thick head of black hair. He looked like a model and had the name of a main character in a romance novel. He also had a beautiful wife and two lovely kids.

Most politicians weren't attractive, at least not in Carver's experience. The only good-looking politicians he'd met had risen to power through corruption. Mayor Jessica Herrada of El Fuerte was a good example. She'd been a damned good-looking woman and she'd also been a powerful cartel family member who became mayor by taking out the incumbent during an election.

That didn't mean Grant Steele had done the same thing, but the odds were good that he had. That was something a conversation could clear up. Maybe it was time Carver introduced himself to the mayor. He'd have to do it without being taken by the police. One thing was certain, they wouldn't let a little thing like the law get in the way of arresting Carver or worse.

It was also obvious that Bickham officials had an arrangement with the mafia. Vincenzo was a mobster name if Carver had ever heard one. And the fact that Georgie and Frankie looked and acted Italian was another hard clue. That and their fondness for adding "ie" to the end of everyone's names.

Bickham's cleanliness and strict rule of law just didn't jibe with mob connections. Carver had seen plenty of corruption during his time with Scion. Corrupt officials usually didn't care about their towns. What they cared about were kickbacks and bribes from organized crime whether that was from the Russian mafia, drug cartels, or the pimps who ran the prostitutes.

Corruption usually meant high crime rates, and rundown, dirty cities, not sparkling clean towns like Bickham. Nothing about this made sense so far. Maybe the arrangement had something to do with civil forfeitures. Maybe they made millions by taking away money and other assets.

Except that wasn't a long-term strategy for success. If they constantly victimized their citizens, there soon wouldn't be any citizens left. It also seemed that an unusually high rate of government seizures in a specific town would catch the attention of higher authorities.

But maybe it wouldn't, especially if the higher authorities were just as corrupt as everyone else. Maybe they could seize assets like money and real estate, then resell it for a profit. Technically they could make a profit at any asking price since they got it for free.

Once the property was seized, that would leave behind the former occupants of the house. If they targeted lower income people who couldn't afford lawyers, then there would be almost no additional costs incurred.

It didn't seem like a winning strategy, but Carver had seen so many grifts in so many countries that nothing surprised him too much these days. Rich had been the perfect person to target. As a disabled veteran with apparently no other income, he had absolutely zero chance of lawyering up and getting back his property.

There were other options, of course. If there was a chance Rich would take Carver's advice, he would recommend a psyops strategy. Specifically, he would tell him to go to Chicago, talk with the news organizations there, and tell them he was a disabled veteran with low income who had his house seized by an unjust city government because his ex-girlfriend's son had supposedly sold drugs on his property.

Carver would enhance that message through multiple social media channels and major podcasters. The amount of negative press might convince Bickham to return Rich's property or at the very least give him fair compensation for it. At the very least it would put the city in the spotlight and that would put a damper on their out-of-control civil forfeiture grift.

In all likelihood, the civil forfeiture racket was just one stream of income. If they were in league with the mob, they probably had a lot more going on behind the scenes. Carver just had to figure out what it was. Then he had to hit them where it hurt.

Carver was still listening to the conversation inside as he thought things through, just in case someone gave up the particulars of Bickham's dealings with Vincenzo. But they were too focused on finding Carver to talk about anything else.

The quickest way to get answers was by interrogating someone who actually had answers. Palmer probably knew enough to tell him what he wanted to know, and it looked like the meeting inside was breaking up. Palmer might leave soon and that would be the perfect opportunity to have a discussion with him.

There were consequences to catch and release interrogation, however. They would know that Carver knew what they were up to. They would expect him to act against them. That would put them on high alert and make things more difficult.

Carver had no intention of doing anything except recovering his and Rich's money, plus a little something for all the trouble they put him through. Then again, maybe they deserved to be put out of business for being such assholes. He definitely wanted to put a hurting on the two cops who'd taken his money. He wanted them to think real hard before they ever did something like that again.

If he interrogated Palmer, he'd have to kill him. There were no two ways about it. From the moment he took Palmer he would be on a timer until they noticed the disappearance. Taking him in the dead of night would be optimal. Then he'd have maybe ten to twelve hours before they noticed he was gone.

Seeing as how Palmer was integral to the search for Carver, he might have even less time before someone noticed he was missing. They would rightly assume that Carver got to Palmer before Palmer got to Carver and that would put everyone on high alert.

Maybe taking Palmer wasn't the play. He needed someone who wouldn't be missed right away. Someone further down the totem pole.

Carver tuned back in to the conversation inside. Bo was wrapping up. He was telling Vincenzo's men that Carver was almost certainly laying low in Chicago somewhere and to put out an alert with their contacts.

"We'll work the problem from both sides," Palmer said. "This guy won't be a problem for long."

"What's his name again?" Frankie asked.

Palmer shrugged. "Raulerson said he introduced himself as Bert Polaski, Rich Polaski's brother. But Morales and Davidson said his driver's license had the name Chuck Grayson on it."

"You sure he's a Navy SEAL?" Frankie said.

Palmer nodded. "Rich Polaski said some things that indicated the two served together and we know for certain Polaski was a SEAL."

"I mean, they might have just served in the Marines before Polaski became a SEAL," Bo said. "Either way, I don't think that's a factor. We have the manpower to get one guy."

"I'll get back on it," Palmer said. "He was at a pool hall earlier. Maybe there's a reason he was there. I can go check it out."

"You do that," Bo said.

"Maybe he was playing pool with that Rich fellow," Frankie said. "Maybe you could take the guy and use him for leverage."

Palmer shook his head. "When I first encountered them, I could tell that Polaski hates Grayson, or whatever his real name is. I thought the guy would go away but Eddie told me he stuck around and was asking questions, so I knew it might be a problem. That's why I got Tony involved right away."

"Should have just waited for Alicia to do her thing," Bo said. "Maybe Grayson would have gone away on his own."

"Now Tony is dead." Georgie made the sign of the cross over his heart. "Let's handle this better from now on, okay?"

"We will." Bo motioned Palmer out of the kitchen. "Let's go." He grabbed Betty roughly by the arm and dragged her along with him.

Carver watched the interaction and had an idea. Maybe he didn't need to interrogate Palmer at all. Maybe Betty would provide him with answers provided he helped her out of her relationship with Bo. Of course, if she refused to help he couldn't just kill her to keep her silent. He'd have to lock her up somewhere for the time being.

She seemed to go everywhere Bo went. That was a good and a bad thing. It meant she heard everything. It also meant Bo would immediately notice that she was gone. It all boiled down to careful planning on Carver's part. Careful planning required time and patience.

He had plenty of patience, but time was another matter because he had a lot of people looking for him and his minivan. He also had Jericho to worry about because it was only a matter of time before Carver's name crossed from Rich's lips and into Jericho's ears. And that would place Carver right in the center of a vise.

With both sides closing in to crush him.

Chapter 26

Carver unsheathed his survival knife.

He used it to unscrew a license plate from a minivan that was the same make, model, and color as his. It had taken him an hour of driving around to find one. That wasn't too bad, all things considered.

The license plate swap would only work so long. Eventually a cop would run the plates on the other minivan and then an APB would be out on its license plate. Normally, Carver would purchase another vehicle right away, but he didn't have the funds for even the cheapest clunker right now.

Using Tony's burner car wouldn't have been an option either because Palmer would recognize it. But Tony had a stash of cars, according to what Frankie had said earlier. It was in an old car shop on West 77th Street.

Carver checked the map and saw that West 77th Street wasn't nearly as long as the other numbered streets in the vicinity. South Fielding Avenue turned into West 77th and then dead-ended a couple of miles later. Maybe he could find Tony's stash and borrow a car.

He followed the GPS northwest, following South Fielding until it turned into West 77th. It was a residential area with rundown houses and red-brick project homes. He drove from one end to the other and counted three abandoned gas stations. They were all fenced off and boarded up. They were all at intersections.

They were also right next to liquor and grocery stores, the kind that popped up in poor neighborhoods because none of the big brands would build stores in high crime areas. It was late but there were plenty of people out and about, most of them congregating around the liquor stores.

Carver didn't want to get out and investigate all three abandoned gas stations. He opted to drive slowly past them. That drew attention to the minivan, but there were plenty of other vehicles cruising slowly by, many of them playing loud music.

He drove around the block near the gas station at the east end of the street. There were weeds and vines tangled around the chain-link fence and gate. The vines looked unbroken and there were two heavy duty chains wrapped tightly around the gate. It didn't look like it had been opened in a while. The parking lot around the building was empty aside from a rusted-out old truck.

The second location was a couple of blocks west. The gate looked like it hadn't been touched or opened in a while but the driveway leading into the garage looked abnormally clean for something that hadn't been used in a while. The parking lot around the building was packed with old vehicles, presumably ones that had been brought in for repair and couldn't be fixed.

He drove past it and to the last location. There were vehicles in various states of disrepair in this parking lot as well, some of which blocked the driveway into the garage. It looked like a definite no, but Carver drove around the block for a look at the sides and back.

The rear lot was crammed with nonfunctional vehicles. They lined every inch of the fence except for one area where a driveway led to the rear garage door. An old van was parked sideways across the entrance blocking it, but there was an open parking space right in front of it.

It looked like the van could be rolled into the parking spot to clear the driveway. If Carver had to choose between this location and the other one, he'd pick this one.

At least that was what his gut told him. His gut was probably right, but there was a major roadblock that his gut couldn't overcome, the chain and padlock on the gate. He didn't have a bolt cutter anymore. It had been claimed by Mother Nature in North Carolina. He'd have to find a hardware store and buy one. He probably had enough money to afford one.

Carver checked the GPS for the nearest hardware store. There was one twenty minutes away, but it was closed. There was a twenty-four-hour big box store thirty minutes away but there was no guarantee it would have bolt cutters.

He parked the van on the curb and looked around. He was on the back side of the garage and the neighboring grocery store. There was a small crowd of people loitering around the front of the store, but no one on the backside, so he got out of the van and walked up to the rear gate.

The chain link fence was ten feet tall. There was a single gate just a little wider than the driveway leading onto the property. A thick chain and padlock secured the side that opened and the side with the hinges was reinforced with another heavy chain to prevent someone from breaking it open from that side.

Carver's gut feeling morphed into almost absolute certainty that this was the right place. But he wasn't getting a car out of there without bolt cutters or a key. He thought about the keys he'd found in Tony's pocket. The only padlock key had been for the basement door.

There was also another possibility. Nearly every long-term covert mission for Scion required a so-called bugout package. It included money, fake IDs, burner phones, and getaway cars. They kept at least three getaway cars on standby. Some were left in long term parking lots, and some were kept in locked garages.

The ones kept in locked locations always kept a key nearby so the agent could get the car and get out. It was possible Tony kept a key onsite in case he needed a fast getaway. It was also possible that he never carried a key with him and only kept a key hidden onsite.

Frankie had said that Tony's primary vehicle had been left in front of "the restaurant" which almost certainly referred to a primary meeting place for Vincenzo and his boys. He'd parked his car there and taken other transportation here, probably a bus or taxi.

Carver imagined Tony walking down the street. He imagined him looking around to make sure no one was watching him and then retrieving the padlock key from its hiding location. But where would that be?

He walked along the fence, picking up rocks and chunks of broken concrete to make sure they weren't the fake kind people used to hide keys. He didn't find anything. It was starting to look like his theory was wrong. But then he noticed a small section in the chain link fence where the metal was slightly stretched out.

It was almost unnoticeable unless you were looking for abnormalities. The holes in the fence were too small to fit a hand through unless your hand was extremely small. But this one section had been stretched just wide enough to accommodate a hand.

Carver slid his hand through. The fender of a rusting truck was right on the other side. Carver reached under the fender and felt a rectangular object. He tugged on it and it came free. He pulled it out and saw it was a magnetic key case.

He slid it open and found a padlock key inside. He returned to the gate, unlocked and opened it. He closed it behind him and hurried up the driveway to the old van. He walked around the van and examined the garage door. It was secured by another padlock which the same key opened.

He lifted the rollup door just enough to duck under and went inside. His cellphone flashlight gave enough light to see the repair bays inside. There was an empty hydraulic lift in one bay. The rest of the building had been cleared out to make space for six cars.

The cars were all silver, black or white, the most common car colors and the least likely to stick out in a crowd. There was a Chrysler K-car, an 80's era Ford Crown Victoria and a Mercury Grand Marquis which was nearly identical to the Crown Vic, but a touch fancier.

There was a black Chevy conversion van, a Ford F150, and lastly, a silver Mercedes 300 diesel. It was a nice variety of burner vehicles that offered a wide range of options, depending upon what criminal activities Tony was up to.

Carver opened the van. There was a mattress in back with a fitted sheet over it. It smelled like strong laundry detergent. There was a plastic chest on the floor right behind the driver's seat. He opened it and found what could only be described as a kidnapping kit.

There were glass bottles of ether, packs of syringes, and best of all, a box of small pills labeled as scopolamine. Carver knew it as devil's breath. It was dangerous stuff and extremely effective.

He'd been in Medellin, Colombia when he'd first seen it used. Criminals would crush the pills into powder and blow it into the faces of unsuspecting tourists, or they'd slip it into their drinks. The affected person would literally lose their free will and act like they were under strong hypnosis. They'd do anything the criminal wanted.

Judging from the quantity Tony kept in the van, it had apparently become his go-to method for kidnapping his victims, and he used this van to transport them to his house, the last place they'd ever see before he killed them.

Carver closed the chest, exited the van, and looked at the other vehicles. The Ford pickup next to the van had a topper over the bed. The windows for the topper were blacked out. Carver opened the tailgate and saw the metal bed was scratched and rusty. There were traces of broken concrete which made him wonder just what Tony had been hauling back there.

His inspection of the garage answered that question moments later when he found a motorized concrete mixer and a large stack of concrete bags. Next to the bags were stacks of rubber boots. The boots were big even for Carver's feet, but it seemed pretty obvious what they were for.

Tony was old school. So old school, in fact, that he made his own concrete galoshes inhouse and then hauled the unfortunate recipient in his pickup truck to dump into the water. It was likely that he had a boat stashed somewhere and took them out into Lake Michigan where no one would ever find the bodies.

There was a piece of plywood mounted to the wall. There were hooks screwed into the wood and keys hanging from hooks. There was also a heavy metal safe with a combination lock against the wall beneath it. There was a small white sign next to the key hooks with a simple message for anyone who came into the garage with foul intentions.

Smile! You're on camera. Steal anything from here and you will not be prosecuted. I will hunt you down and kill you and your entire family. You can count on that. Thank you.

Carver hadn't noticed any cameras, but he didn't exactly have a powerful flashlight to look around with either. He turned off the flashlight and looked for the telltale sign of an infrared camera. Normally tiny red dots of light would be visible in the dark.

He didn't see anything. He walked to the nearby workbench and found a heavy-duty LED flashlight in the toolbox. It looked like Tony did his own car repairs when necessary. The flashlight illuminated all the dark corners. There were a couple of cameras, but they were ancient relics from the eighties or nineties. They also weren't functional.

After a thorough search, it looked like the threat of a camera was a bluff. It also seemed unlikely anyone would want to steal one of these cars unless they were truly desperate. The only thing that was in danger of being stolen was the safe.

It was easily visible to anyone who walked around the back of the van and the pickup. Carver tried to push the safe, but it didn't budge. It was probably bolted to the concrete floor. Maybe that was why he hadn't hidden it.

The safe was an old Browning model with a combination lock above a large wheel handle. Carver could beat most combination locks with specialized gadgets he had access to during his time with Scion. He, of course, no longer had those gadgets or access to anything like them. Jericho could beat a lock with a stethoscope and a little bit of time.

Carver was no Jericho. The only way he could break into a safe was by brute force. He looked through Tony's tool cart and found several tools that would do the trick. There was a welding torch, a metal cutter, and a heavy-duty drill.

Tony's cars were the main reason Carver had come here, but there might be something useful inside the safe. There might be money or weapons inside. Either would be worth the effort.

The torch seemed like the best tool for the job but it had two gas tanks and Carver had no idea how to use it. One tank was labeled oxygen and the other acetylene. There was a red hose and a blue hose leading into the torch. Each one had a valve. It looked like too much for Carver to figure out on his own, but thankfully he didn't need to.

He opened the video app on his phone and searched for instructions. A man in the first video gave him step-by-step instructions on lighting the torch and how to cut through sheet metal. Carver rolled the cart with the tanks and torch over to the safe, followed the instructions, and got a nice flame going. He went slow and steady over the safe's hinges since that seemed like the logical place to cut.

The flame cut through the hinges easily enough, but they weren't the only thing holding the safe door in place. Apparently, there was more to it than that. He used his phone again and searched for specs on the safe. A man who posted videos about safecracking had the exact same model in one of his videos.

There were four thick rods in the door. When the wheel was turned, they went into holes in the frame, securing the door from all four sides. The man said the rods could be cut with a torch but if there was any paper inside the safe, it would be torched along with the metal.

He suggested another approach which involved shaving the side of the safe if a torch was used. He also demonstrated how he cracked the combination lock, but Carver didn't have the tools necessary for the task.

Carver angled the torch toward the very edge of the left side of the safe and began cutting. He cut a line from the top and then along the front. He couldn't cut the back or bottom because the safe was against the wall and wouldn't move.

That was okay because there was a wrecking bar next to Tony's toolchest. He wedged it into the newly-cut gap and wrenched it sideways. The thick steel slowly bent. He worked at it until he'd bent it wide enough to see what was inside.

There was a shotgun, a handgun, and several boxes of ammunition inside. The edges of the boxes were blackened from the torch. It looked like Carver had come dangerously close to igniting the ammunition.

He pulled everything out that he could reach and shined the flashlight inside to see if he'd missed anything. The only other thing he saw was a red leather book. He reached inside and pulled it out. It wasn't a book. It was a notebook.

The leather binding was old and cracked, and the pages inside were yellowed from age. Inside were names, dates, and numbers. The numbers didn't make sense right away but then Carver realized they were coordinates. The dates went back to the late seventies and the last one was from two months prior.

There were far too many names in the book to be limited to the young men Tony had kept in his basement. This seemed to be a record of all the hits Tony had performed, or at least participated in. Some of the names didn't have coordinates. Instead, there were landmarks or other measurements because Tony apparently couldn't get the coordinates.

There was nothing inside the book indicating why he'd kept such extensive records, but it was likely he'd kept them as an insurance plan in case someone betrayed him, or he had to turn state's witness.

Even though it listed where the bodies were hidden, it didn't incriminate anyone except for Tony because there were no pictures or any other details. He hadn't named any names or listed other perpetrators if they existed.

Carver plugged the coordinates into the map app. The app put red pins at each location. There were a lot of red pins in Lake Michigan. The place was a graveyard.

He decided to hang onto the book. He also decided to take the Ford Crown Vic as his new ride. He opened the trunk and put his new weapons and ammunition inside. Old cars like this had trunks big enough to store three bodies in.

He put Tony's book inside the glove compartment. It might be useful or it might be nothing. It didn't weigh much and it wasn't large, so Carver figured he take it.

Carver removed kidnapping kit from the back of the van and looked over the inventory. In addition to the scopolamine, there was fentanyl, ether, syringes, and a lot of other things that might come in handy, so he put the chest into the trunk.

He opened the rear garage door the rest of the way and examined the Volkswagen van blocking the exit. The van was old and rusty, but it looked functional. He went to the lockbox and found a set of Volkswagen keys. He returned to the van and tried them. The vehicle cranked right up.

He drove the van forward out of the way. He jogged to the road, climbed into the minivan, and started it. He parked it in between two nonfunctional pickup trucks, removed the license plate, and transferred his things to the Crown Vic.

He closed up shop and locked the gate behind him. The minivan wasn't visible from the street. Even if Palmer or one of Tony's other associates came here, they probably wouldn't notice it among the other broken-down cars.

The magnetic key box went back to where Carver had found it. If he needed to ditch this car and get another one, the key would be here waiting. With that done he was ready to start the next phase of his mission.

Getting his money back from the crooks in Bickham.

Chapter 27

Carver drove straight to Bickham.

He needed to put the nighttime hours to good use even though the streets of downtown Bickham were well lit. He parked on a street that ran perpendicular to the road behind the police station so he could watch the place without it watching him right back.

There were cameras on the back gate and cameras at the corners of the walls. There were more cameras mounted on the back of the building. None of the other government buildings had nearly that kind of security.

Carver thought back to the lobby and waiting room inside the police department and the heavy security doors guarding access to the interior of the building. Police buildings required a certain level of fortification because they were designed to temporarily hold prisoners until they could be moved to long-term facilities.

It was possible that they housed long-term prisoners here, but highly doubtful. The last thing a place like Bickham wanted was a prison right in the middle of their downtown. They wanted everything pristine and perfect.

No, what they had going here wasn't necessary unless there was something else they wanted to keep secure behind these walls. Carver had an idea just what that was. This place wasn't built like a prison. It was built like a vault. More specifically, like a bank vault.

He felt certain that somewhere within the confines of that building was a whole lot of cash and other valuables that had been confiscated from citizens. He still didn't know how a revenue stream like that could be maintained long term, but maybe the folks in Bickham had it all figured out.

Maybe Commissioner Bo knew what was going on. Carver suddenly remembered the ornate benches on the sidewalks along Main Street. He remembered the one right outside the town hall and the name on the dedication plate. Beauregard T. Matheson. It was a strange name. And it was almost certainly the full name of the commissioner.

He'd been misspelling the name in his head. It wasn't Bo, it was Beau. He searched the name Beauregard T. Matheson with his phone and found multiple businesses with that name. The car dealerships were all owned by Matheson. Several smaller businesses were also listed with that last name.

But there were no pictures of the man. Nothing specifically about him. Nothing on social media, either. It was as if the man who owned half the town was invisible. It was almost as if he didn't exist.

Beau, aka Big D definitely existed. Carver had seen the man with his own eyes. It was more likely that Beau kept a very low profile. He might have had his name scrubbed from public records. It was easier to run a criminal enterprise that way.

Commissioner Beauregard T. Matheson wasn't Carver's top priority right now. What he really needed was a way inside the police station that didn't involve shooting his way in. Just because there were some crooked cops in the BPD didn't mean that all of them were crooked.

Carver considered a plan of attrition. He sketched it out in his head. It involved taking out the cops he knew were bent, starting with Palmer, Archer, and Sutton. Morales and Davidson were on the list. Raulerson too.

That added up to six cops. Rich had counted nine when they raided his house. That left three others unaccounted for. Facing off against three cops was better than nine, but the preferred number would be zero. He needed to identify all the players, their routines, their patterns, and where they lived.

That was a lot of work for one man with little to no resources at his disposal, but he'd done it plenty of times before under worse circumstances. Plus, it wasn't like he had anything better to do with his time. Once he had all that information, he could form a plan of attack.

Everyone would need to be taken down quickly and efficiently and during a time when no one was expecting to see them for a few hours. That meant taking out as many as possible late at night at home, then moving on to those who were still on duty.

He didn't plan on killing anyone, not unless he was forced to. It would be better to incapacitate them and secure them somewhere. He already knew exactly where he could keep them and how he would get them there.

The van in Tony's garage was the perfect kidnapping vehicle. The kidnapping kit had enough drugs in it to take down a small army. Carver could certainly put that to good use, but he'd have to be extremely careful if he used the scopolamine, aka devil's breath.

Grinding it into powder and blowing it into someone's face worked well, but you had to be damned careful none of it blew back in your face. It was possible to dissolve it in a solution of water and inject someone with it, but you had to hit a blood vessel for an immediate effect. If you got it in the muscle, it could take up to fifteen minutes before it took them down, depending on their size.

Dissolving it into a drink would work well too, but he'd have to have access to something they were drinking and that wasn't feasible. He would look over Tony's kidnapping kit and figure out the best method. Once the drug was in their system, they would comply with whatever he wanted.

He just had to make sure he didn't fall victim to the drug while he was using it, or he'd end up just as mindless as they were. Depending upon the dosage, the effects could last anywhere from four to nine hours. If he accidentally dosed himself, it would be game over.

Carver jotted down a mental list of the things he needed to do next. First was to find the names of all the players. Next was to figure out their schedules and find out where they lived. Then he could plot out the order on a map, collect as many cops as possible and tuck them away in a secure location.

The perfect place to keep them would be at Hope House. He could secure them somewhere in the large unused back section of the building. He added another item to his list, reconnoitering Hope House to find the best room for keeping prisoners.

He moved that item to the top of the list since it would be the easiest to take care of right away. The last item on the list would be infiltrating the police station and neutralizing the remaining resistance. There should be almost no resistance since this would be an early morning op around zero three hundred or shortly thereafter.

By the time he reached the police facility he'd have a keycard or other method of entry into the building. He would just have to make it inside quickly before anyone realized he wasn't one of them and sounded the alarm.

He could probably use Sutton's police uniform, his vehicle and his security card to enter via the back gate. He would be inside well before anyone realized he wasn't Sutton. That was a good plan. He could dose the skeleton crew with scopolamine before they even knew what happened.

He would disable the cameras and erase all the security footage. Beau's men would think it had been done by a professional crew, not by one man. It was possible they wouldn't even consider Carver as a suspect. They would, however, have plenty of reason to think the people from Hope House were involved.

This was a big job for one man. There would be a lot of leg work, and he had to do it in a town where the cops wanted him dead. It wouldn't be the first time he'd had to operate in hostile territory, and it probably wouldn't be the last.

If he was going through this much trouble to get his money back, he wasn't going to limit himself to just his and Rich's money back. He was going to rob these people blind. Rich was going to get his surgery, Leon was going to fix things with Jericho, and Carver was going to go back to the beach.

It was just past zero four hundred. He had a couple of hours before sunrise. Night shift at the police department would probably end around zero seven hundred. He wanted to have a look around Hope House to make sure that one of the backrooms could serve as a temporary prison and get back here to watch the shift change.

That was assuming they had a normal shift change at Bickham PD. Most police and detectives would report to the office at the change of shift. There would be a morning briefing, a task list, and a dismissal. That was about all Carver knew of police work, and most of that was from watching a short video.

Bickham PD might not operate the same way, but it would be useful to know one way or the other. It seemed doubtful anyone on the night shift would be part of the civil forfeiture crew. Those people were probably primarily day shift workers. But it was better not to assume anything.

Carver backed up the car and turned it around. He looped around downtown and headed to Hope House. He parked around the block from the building and walked the rest of the way. He went to the front door and looked inside. The lights were on, but no one was inside. He pushed the front door. It was unlocked.

That jibed with the welcome sign next to the door that said, *Welcome to Hope House. Our doors are always open.* They probably couldn't lock the doors anyway due to the fire code. Since they housed people, they had to provide clearly marked exits in case of a fire.

Carver went inside. He went past the reception desk and into the double doors next to it. The lights were on in the back just as they had been during the tour Alicia had given him. He followed the same route they had because he had a particular area in mind.

He reached the locked metal doors in the back and examined them. They were double doors, but not French doors. These were built to institutional standards like schools and mental asylums. There was a steel frame attached to the concrete block wall and a steel jamb between the two doors.

The doors looked as old as the building, meaning they were probably the original doors. There were multiple layers of peeling paint beneath the topcoat, and dents where it looked like someone had kicked the bottom of the door. Probably a mental patient housed here many moons ago.

Doors like this usually had a push bar on the other side but given that this was a secure facility in its heyday, there might be a regular handle with a thumb lever. Even though the doors opened outward, there was no way to use a slim jim to spring the latch thanks to steel plates extending from the door and over the jamb.

Carver studied the door lock. The brand was one he didn't recognize, probably because it had long since gone out of business. He looked up the brand name Wagner and found out it had indeed ceased operations in the mid-sixties.

He looked up Hope House and found out it was originally called Bickham Institute for the Criminally Insane. It had been built in 1953, closed in the early eighties, and reopened as a regular hospital. A new hospital had been built in the early 2000s, and this one had been closed. It was purchased by the church years later.

Carver looked up the lock in question and discovered it had a major manufacturing flaw that was widespread in many Wagner locks. This discovery led to fewer purchases of Wagner locks and its eventual bankruptcy.

It was interesting that the lock had never been changed despite this discovery. Maybe word hadn't gotten around about the flaw, or the institution never had the funds to get it changed. Carver returned to the reception desk and looked around just in case the key was stored there. It was not.

The desk, a large metal monstrosity with a laminate top, was as old as the building. Carver opened the drawers and found boxes of office supplies that were yellowed with age, and everything from paper clips to rubber bands that were ancient and brittle. He also found a letter opener with spots of rust on the surface.

Carver finished rummaging through the desk and found nothing of use except the letter opener. It would have to do. He returned to the metal doors and attempted to use the manufacturing flaw to his advantage. He watched a video demonstrating the vulnerability. The man inserted a thin and narrow piece of metal a little smaller than the letter opener into the lock. He jiggled and twisted rapidly, and the lock eventually opened.

The letter opener fit all the way inside the lock. Carver emulated what he'd seen in the video. After a solid minute of jiggling and twisting, he was about ready to give up when the lock finally turned. He pulled the door open.

It was dark inside the next room. He slid the letter opener into the jamb to keep the door from latching behind him and went inside. He used the flashlight he'd taken from Tony's garage and revealed a storeroom full of old banker's boxes, filing cabinets, office furniture and chairs.

Carver was a little disappointed in the discovery. He'd hoped for a mostly empty room he could use as a temporary holding cell. This wouldn't do at all. He made his way through the room. It was large but packed from one end to the other with unused furniture and other odds and ends.

There was another set of double doors on the other side of the room. The doors were identical to the ones he'd just come through, but there was one significant difference. The lock was different. It wasn't just an ordinary lock, either. It was a smart lock with a number pad and a biometric reader.

Carver looked up the brand name. It wasn't a military-grade unit, but rather a retail lock anyone could buy right off the internet. That wasn't surprising considering the things a person could purchase these days.

There were no known vulnerabilities or hacks. It looked like he wasn't getting through these doors without someone's fingerprint. It was obvious that there was a lot more to this place than just charity. He should have been surprised, but he wasn't. Jericho was linked to Hope House which meant he was almost certainly using it for some nefarious purpose.

That purpose might be hidden behind this door. Carver was itching to know for sure, but he didn't want to brute force open the lock. He wanted to get in and out without anyone knowing he'd been in there.

Alicia would almost certainly be able to get him into the room but if she was working with Jericho, it wouldn't be easy to convince her to let him in. Not unless he used devil's breath on her. It was also possible Eddie had access, but it seemed doubtful.

Carver studied the ceiling. It used square panels instead of plaster like the rest of the building. He stood on top of a desk and pushed up on the panel. He shined the flashlight inside the space. The plaster wall ran all the way up to the concrete roof slab.

Drywall wouldn't pose much of an obstacle, but plaster and lathe was another matter altogether. It was hard as concrete. He could pound through it with a mini sledgehammer and make a hole large enough to crawl through.

That would make a big mess. But if he cleaned up the mess and put the ceiling tiles back in place, no one would notice the hole. Short of drugging Alicia and using her to open the door, that seemed like the best approach. Tony might even have a tool in his garage that could do the trick.

Carver put a chair on the desk so he could get a little higher and shined the flashlight all around the ceiling cavity. He checked all the walls and didn't see any existing openings. It looked like he'd have to make his own.

He climbed down and put the chair back where he'd found it. He looked around the room in case someone might have stashed a broom and dustpan inside, or possibly even a hammer he could use. All he saw was more furniture and more banker's boxes.

Carver opened one of the boxes and found files dated back to the fifties and sixties. It looked like these were the old patient files. There was nothing useful in the room, so he made his way back to the entrance.

Something caught his attention. He didn't know what it was at first, but he redirected the flashlight beam on the shelf. He realized it was because the boxes on the shelf looked much newer than the other ones in the vicinity. In fact, all the boxes on that shelf looked new and were marked with letters on the front.

He slid the banker's box off the shelf and looked inside. There were files marked only with names and not dates. The surnames all started with the same letter that was written on the front of the box.

There were only four folders in the box marked *H*. He opened the folder for someone named Jacob Hudson and checked inside. There were pictures and documents inside, but it was obvious they were copies and not originals because the pictures were black and white images on regular paper.

There was a copy of a birth certificate, military records, and psychological evaluations inside. It looked like Jacob had been injured in the line of duty and discharged. He'd been required to see the VA shrink to continue receiving benefits. That had been nearly twenty years ago.

Carver glanced at the other folders in the box. The names were different but the circumstances of each were very similar to that of Jacob's. All had been injured and honorably discharged, and all had been required to see a psychiatrist for treatment to continue receiving benefits.

He put the folders back in the box and put it on the shelf. He looked through two more boxes and found similar records but not all of them had been honorably discharged. One had struck a superior officer and been psychologically evaluated. It was determined they weren't fit for duty and had been dishonorably discharged.

Carver suddenly had a thought. He found the box labeled P and opened it. He shuffled back through several folders and found one with a red sticker on the tab. The name on the tab was one he knew all too well.

The name was Rich Polaski.

Chapter 28

Rich was happier than he'd been in a decade.

He was playing pool, even if just barely, he was drinking, and he was talking with people who completely understood his struggles. Everyone was confiding in each other, and it felt amazing to get the weight off his chest.

Nadia had even told him about her encounter with a homeless man in front of Hope House Chicago.

"I didn't mean to kill him, but he attacked me." She shivered violently. "I know I should feel regret, but I don't. I did what I had to do to survive."

"Amen." Rich patted her shoulder. "I'm totally with you."

"We all are," Alicia said.

"When can you help me with my ex?" Nadia said. "These child support payments are killing me!"

"I have a question, and I want you to answer it honestly." Keith put a hand on her shoulder and looked her directly in the eyes. "How badly do you really want custody of your kid?"

She bit her lower lip and looked down.

"Be honest," Alicia said. "You're among friends."

Nadia glanced at Rich then back to Keith. "I don't care about custody. I just don't want the payments." She looked down. "I never wanted kids. Leif is a gutter-dwelling subhuman moron who intentionally broke a condom to get me pregnant. He knew I wouldn't get an abortion."

"He really did that?" Keith said.

"Yep." Nadia clenched her fists. "I married him because I was pregnant and thought it was the right thing to do."

Alicia sighed. "A lot of women fall into that trap."

"Leif is such a weak man. I would never have slept with him if I hadn't been drunk and horny after a long deployment." She laughed humorlessly. "He refused to teach our son how to play sports or how to protect himself from bullies. He was turning our boy into a girly man like himself."

Rich grimaced. "That's the worst."

"Oh, it was. And we fought about it a lot." Nadia rolled her eyes. "One day, I got so mad that I punched him. I nearly knocked his lights out." She laughed. "He fought back. He was stronger than me, but he had no training. He got in a couple of solid licks, but then I put him down on the ground. I put his estrogen-soaked beta male ass down hard!"

"Hell yeah!" Alicia high-fived her.

"I put my foot on his neck and told him that our son was going to be weak like him." The smile faded from Nadia's face. "After I let him up, he spat on me and told me he intentionally broke the condom to get me pregnant because he wanted a woman who could pay the bills."

"Can I have the honor of beating the hell out of this piece of garbage?" Rich raised a fist. "I might be a cripple, but I can still do some damage."

Nadia hugged him so hard that it sent spasms of agony through his shoulder. But he gritted his teeth and bore the pain because the human contact felt so good.

She released him. "I'd be honored to let you beat the hell out of him."

Rich grinned. "Okay. Let's go."

"I forgot to mention that I also have to pay him alimony because he never worked a day while we were married." Nadia smacked her forehead with her hand. "Maybe he was the smart one and I was the idiot."

Keith frowned. "He just stayed home all day?"

"He was in a heavy metal tribute band." Nadia scoffed. "They would play maybe once or twice a month. Their singer and lead guitarist were good, I'll admit that. Leif was the bass player."

"And then you divorced, and he came out smelling like a rose." Rich was starting to hate her ex as much as he hated the Bickham police. "I guess we can't just kill him because then you would be stuck with the child."

"Our son has long hair, he eats with his fingers like a savage, and he plays with dolls." Nadia looked heavenward and sighed. "I think he's a lost cause at this point."

"Does Leif have parents the boy can live with?"

"Yeah, his parents are old-school hippies. I'm sure they'd take the boy in."

"Okay, then let's give this some thought and make a plan," Keith said.

"You're really serious about helping me?" Nadia said.

"Dead serious." Alicia glanced to the side as Tom entered their circle.

Tom grinned. "Hey kids, what's up?"

"Life lessons and murder," Keith said.

"Now that sounds entertaining. What did I miss?"

Keith turned to Nadia. "Tell Tom everything you told us."

She swallowed nervously, then told him about the homeless man and her ex-husband.

Tom didn't look the least bit concerned about anything. "Nadia, I'm glad that you trust us." He glanced at Rich. "You two are very promising candidates."

"Candidates for what?" Rich said.

"Money-making opportunities."

Rich nodded fervently. "Look, I'm willing to do anything whether it's legal or not. I just need to feel something, you know? I want to feel needed again."

Tom laughed. "I like your attitude."

"Hey, me too," Nadia said. "Unless it involves killing animals."

Alicia looked horrified. "Hey, we're not monsters."

"Just tell me what you want me to do," Rich said.

"Well, for starters, we want you to get to know everyone." Tom gestured toward the others. "We asked our team to bring the best candidates to this meetup. Most of you will be qualified to help us in some way. All of you will have the opportunity to make money. And I'll preface it by saying that we're something like domestic mercenaries."

"Kind of like a private military company?" Nadia said.

Tom shook his head. "No. We're not an official company. All of our money is earned below the table because we believe Uncle Sam has taken enough from us already."

Keith raised a fist. "Hell yeah, brother."

Rich scowled. "The government demands everything and gives nothing."

"One hundred percent." Nadia raised a fist too. "Just tell me what to do and I'll do it."

Tom put a hand on her shoulder. "Let's slow down and enjoy the evening first, okay?"

Another question was burning in Rich's chest. He was a little concerned about asking it.

Tom noticed. "What's wrong, Rich?"

"There's just a guy I used to serve with. The guy who's responsible for me being captured and tortured." Rich's mouth felt dry. "I know he was a brother in arms, but I feel like he needs to be taught a lesson."

"We'll review everything and consider it," Tom said. "But we are hesitant to act against our own."

"Normally he's real hard to find, but now he's in town, or at least he might still be."

Tom's grin faded. "He's in town?"

"Yeah."

"What's the name of this guy?"

"Amos Carver."

Tom's right eye twitched. "He's in town right now? Do you know where?"

"Not exactly. He's in Bickham somewhere. I told him to go to hell when I saw him yesterday."

Tom smiled, but it looked forced. "Keith and Alicia, can I have a word with you?"

Alicia looked concerned. "Sure."

Tom led them to the far back corner.

"I wonder what that was about," Nadia said. "Tom looked pissed for an instant."

"No idea." Rich shrugged.

"How did you two meet?"

"I ran into him at one of my psych evals." Rich thought about it. "It was maybe seven or eight years after I was discharged. I had to keep doing it twice a year to keep my benefits."

"God, what a pain in the ass." Nadia sighed. "At least getting a dishonorable discharge means I didn't have to deal with that."

Rich laughed. "Yeah. You said your employer might fire you for your legal problems. They didn't care about the dishonorable discharge?"

"The owner reviewed the facts and said it looked like the CIA burned me." Nadia smiled wanly. "He said the fact that we did what we had to do to survive was all he needed to know."

"Sounds like a good guy."

"Yeah, I think he is." She gulped down the rest of her beer. "You're not a bad looking man."

"Um, thanks, I think."

She laughed. "Sorry, I'm really blunt."

"So I gathered." Rich smiled. "You're a good-looking woman with a killer body."

"You just want to have sex with me, don't you?"

Rich blinked. "I don't even remember the last time I had sex. I haven't had the urge in ages."

"God, you're dense." She tapped his forehead with a finger. "I'm hinting very strongly that I want to have sex. All you have to do is say yes."

"Um, yes. I just hope I'm not a horrible disappointment."

Nadia laughed. "With expectations set so low, I don't see how this could be anything but a success."

Rich burst into laughter. "You're funny. I don't remember the last time someone made me genuinely laugh."

"I like you, Rich." She traced a finger down his chest. "You're raw and unfiltered."

Rich felt things stirring that he hadn't felt stir in ages. He shivered at her touch. "I think maybe my parts are working after all."

She leaned forward and gently bit his ear. She whispered, "Good. Let's find out later."

Rich moaned. "I don't know if I can wait that long."

Nadia laughed. "Anticipation is half of the fun."

It was kind of nice looking forward to something positive for once instead of a string of bland days blurring into one another. Rich had done nothing for years. He'd stagnated. Grown weak and hopeless.

It had made him furious to see Carver not only alive and well, but just as strong and healthy as the last time he'd seen him. He was tanned, muscular, and just as inhumanly strange as ever. Nothing seemed to affect the man whatsoever. Maybe his new friends could change that. Carver needed to feel pain. He deserved to be crippled just like Rich.

"You look angry, Rich." Nadia took his hand. "Let's go meet our new friends, okay?"

Rich shook himself out of it. "Yeah, sorry. Just thinking about Carver."

"Oh, I completely forgot to tell you that some guy named Bert Polaski came by Hope House looking for you."

"What?" Rich frowned. "That's my brother."

"He doesn't look like you at all. He's tall, real muscular, and tanned."

"You've got to be kidding me."

Nadia raised an eyebrow. "What do you mean?"

"My brother looks like me. The guy you just described is Carver." Rich groaned. "He came to Chicago looking for me?"

"Yeah, but Keith and I didn't even know who you were yet."

"I told him to go to hell." Rich ran a hand down his face. "Why would he come here looking for me?"

"No idea. He didn't say anything else, and then we left."

Rich stared blankly at the floor. "Were you followed?"

"Followed?" Nadia blinked rapidly. "By Carver? Why would he follow us?"

"He was looking for me. He must have somehow known I was coming to Chicago with Alicia." Rich bit his lower lip and thought about it. "The man doesn't trust anyone. He might have followed you."

Nadia tilted her head slightly. "Why is he so intent on finding you? Does he want to harm you?"

Rich barked a laugh. "He claims he wants to help me. It's like he's trying to clear his conscience or something."

"He screwed up and cost you everything, now shows up years later and thinks he can make it all right?" Nadia scowled. "This guy deserves what he has coming to him."

"Yeah, he does." Rich shook his head. "We should probably talk to Tom about this. Let him know Carver might have followed you here."

"Yeah, just in case he decides to come in and cause problems." Nadia started walking and paused. "You think he followed us to the old rec center?"

"Well, that was the first place you went." Rich mulled it over. "It seems like if he followed you there, he would have just come in and found me."

"Unless he didn't want you to know he'd found you." Nadia tapped a finger on her chin. "It doesn't make much sense."

"Carver's actions don't make much sense," Rich said. "He was a real weirdo. He never fit into the group no matter how hard Joe tried to make him fit."

"Joe?"

"Yeah, our team leader. He liked Carver for some reason." Rich shrugged. "I could never figure out why."

"He was making do with what the brass gave him," Nadia said. "But like, how was Carver different? Did he follow orders? Did he know what he was doing?"

"Best way I can describe him is like a machine. He did what he was told. He stayed right within the lines until he didn't."

"And that's why you were captured?"

Rich nodded. "Carver was rear guard. I was right in front of him. Then he just vanished. He came running past everyone a few minutes later and told Joe something. Next thing I knew we were in full retreat. I looked back and Carver wasn't there. He was just gone again. Then there was an explosion, and I woke up in the loving care of Rahm Abdul Assad."

"The man who tortured you."

"Yeah." Rich shivered uncontrollably. "Now that's someone I'd love to get my hands on."

Nadia pressed her lips together. "I've never heard of him. Is he a big deal?"

"He's mostly unknown to anyone outside of the intelligence community as far as I know. He's a big mover behind the scenes, but he's not one of the front men who get all the publicity."

"You said there was an explosion. Maybe that separated Carver from the rest of the group." Nadia rubbed his arm as if to comfort him. "Did he ever say what happened to him?"

"No." Rich's thoughts returned to all those years ago. "My team rescued me months later, but I was in bad shape. I was in the hospital for a while, then they let me have visitors. Everyone came to see me."

"Even Carver?"

"Yeah." His throat went dry. "Even Carver. I tried to jump up out of bed and attack him." He laughed. "Just seeing his face filled me with rage."

"Does it still do that?"

Rich shrugged. "When he showed up in Bickham I was already at rock bottom, so it didn't affect me the way it would have years ago."

"Did Joe give a reason why Carver wasn't there for you during the mission?"

"Joe said Carver was blocked off by a cave-in." Rich rolled his eyes. "I told him if Carver had been right on my six like he was supposed to be that wouldn't have happened."

"You're right, it wouldn't have happened." Nadia kissed his cheek. "It sounds like the mission was a complete bust."

"Yeah, it was. But I never got a proper debrief because they put me on disability and took me off active duty within a week of coming home. I lost my security clearance, my job, and my ability to do any other physical work. I went from one of America's elite warriors to a worthless hunk of meat."

"You're not worthless. They can fix your shoulder and knee. Make them almost like new."

Rich scoffed. "The VA wouldn't pay for it, though. And right when I had almost enough money saved up, Bickham PD took it all away."

"Yeah, life's a bitch and then you die." Nadia shrugged. "I'm right there with you. The Allenton cops did the same to me thanks to my worthless ex-husband."

"I think I could take Leif even in my current condition." Rich managed to smile.

"Yeah, you could." She put a hand around his shoulders. "Let's go talk to Tom and let him know Carver might be nearby." Nadia grinned. "Revenge might be closer than you think."

"Yeah. Maybe it is." Rich looked around the pool hall, but he didn't see anyone that looked like Carver. The place was so crowded it was hard to know for sure.

Tom, Keith, and Alicia were still conversing in the corner. Tom saw them approaching and smiled. "We're just discussing your situation, Rich."

"Carver?" Rich said.

"Yes."

"Carver might be closer than I thought. Nadia and I think he might have followed her and Keith to the rec center and maybe even to here."

Tom laughed. "That's good news. Very good news."

"Is it, though?" Alicia looked doubtful.

"It means if he's here, we can find him and drag him out back." Tom ran his gaze over the crowd. "And we'll make sure he knows what real pain is."

Chapter 29

Carver stared at Rich's medical records.

Why in the hell did Hope House have these?

He read through the files. They had everything about Rich's physiological condition, his psychological evaluations, his rejections for elective surgery from Veterans Affairs, and more. There was a page of handwritten notes, but the handwriting was mostly illegible.

Every page was a copy and a low-quality copy at that. That much was evident from the toner stains on the pages. Carver studied the handwritten notes. He realized that the reason they were so hard to read was because they were written in shorthand.

Shorthand was an antiquated mode of note taking in an age where speech to text worked almost perfectly. It was practically another language. That didn't make it impossible to understand, but it certainly made it more challenging.

Carver dug through his phone apps and found one he'd used to decipher foreign languages. It scanned the document with the camera, then ran it through a translator. First, he'd need to convert it from handwriting to typographical symbols, if that was even possible. He searched for the appropriate app and found one that used an AI filter to render even the messiest handwriting into something legible.

The app didn't process the file on the phone. It uploaded it to powerful servers to do that. Hopefully nothing in the file would raise red flags with the government. The odds that would happen were low, but not zero. It could expose Carver's burner phone and allow someone to potentially trace its location.

There didn't seem to be much chance of that happening, and Carver could always ditch the phone if needed. He took a picture of the notes. The app uploaded them to the servers for AI processing. There were two hundred and thirty-three other jobs in the queue ahead of him, giving an estimated time of completion in five hours. He tapped the confirmation button and set it to work.

Carver was more convinced than ever that Hope House and Jericho were firmly linked, and that the organization was wittingly or unwittingly helping him achieve an unknown goal. There was no telling what his goal was, but it probably wasn't going to be good for whoever was on the receiving end.

He found the box with the letter G on the front and opened it. Nadia Garcia's folder was the second one in the box. There were official discharge papers in the first part along with affidavits and testimony from other members of her squad detailing the events of a firefight in northeastern Afghanistan.

It was the same story she'd told during the meeting at the rec center. It was the reason she'd been dishonorably discharged along with other members of her unit. There was a list of requirements she had to follow to avoid a court martial, one of which was a semiannual psychological evaluation. The last psych eval had been completed almost a year ago.

The notes from the psychologist revealed a woman who felt betrayed by the CIA and her country. A woman who had top marks in sharpshooting, close quarters combat, and a person with anger management issues that started soon after she was thrown back into civilian life.

Right around the same time that happened, her husband, Leif Jansen filed for divorce and wanted custody of their son. Nadia had apparently beaten him during an argument, and he decided that was enough.

He claimed she was physically abusive and couldn't be trusted with custody of their child. Since he wasn't employed, he requested alimony in addition to child support. He'd also filed a restraining order against Nadia which had been granted.

There were notes in the margins, all of them in shorthand. Sections were circled with arrows pointing at them, especially the part about the discharge and the divorce. One note in the margin was written in plain English. It simply said *vector*.

Carver searched for shorthand symbols, specifically vector. The word was represented by an arrow. Which meant the high stress points of Nadia's life were considered vectors. But vectors for what?

He opened Rich's file and found arrows around his high stress areas as well. He took pictures of Nadia's and Rich's files so he could review them later because now wasn't the time. He had work to do if he was going to prepare a nice holding area for his soon-to-be prisoners.

He skimmed through the files in the other boxes. Alicia didn't have a file and neither did Keith, but he found pictures of other individuals he'd seen at the group meeting. It didn't take a rocket scientist to realize that Jericho was targeting specific people with specific vectors.

The shorthand notes might be from VA psychologists. Maybe Jericho conned them into giving him insider information so he could more accurately target people. He'd probably convinced them he was doing a government study on PTSD or something and promised to give the doctors credit.

They gave him their notes and he used them to target specific vectors and characteristics that interested him. There were many different definitions of vectors. Biologists used the term to describe disease carriers. In mathematics it was a quantity with magnitude and direction. In combat, it was the path a missile, bullet or other ordnance followed to the target.

In this case, Jericho was clearly recruiting people who fit a certain mold. They were angry at the government, they felt betrayed and discarded by the nation they'd once sworn to protect. They hated their civilian lives. The conclusion seemed obvious. Jericho was finding and collecting these people.

He was manipulating them and twisting their rage to suit his purposes. He'd obviously put a lot of effort into the endeavor. Collecting so much data, public, private, and military, on individuals required privileged access. He probably had a backdoor into a government agency.

There was one government agency in particular that collated information about US citizens and arranged it into dossiers. That agency was the NSA. They wanted to keep their eyes out for potential domestic terrorists so they could prevent major events.

But finding that information required spying on more than just red-flagged individuals. It required spying on everyone. On every phone call, every email, every form of electronic communication. Someone with access to the NSA database could find information on anyone.

What if Jericho was looking for the same thing but for the opposite reason? What if he had access to the NSA's data? Carver couldn't help but be impressed. Jericho was an absolute master at getting what he wanted from systems designed to obfuscate and hide data.

It only underlined just how dangerous the man was. Carver needed to do everything possible to make peace with him, and failing that, kill him or die trying because running and hiding wouldn't work for long.

Carver put the boxes back exactly as he'd found them. He decided that maybe this wouldn't be the best place to stash his prisoners. If Alicia was one of Jericho's inside people, then trying to use this place under her nose would be difficult.

Or maybe, just maybe, that would make it the perfect place. Hope House had some kind of arrangement with Bickham. Carver still didn't know the nature of that arrangement but that didn't matter. If he could make it look like Hope House was the one who pulled off the heist, then it would cause chaos.

Jericho versus the Bickham police would be an entertaining show. One that Carver would break out the popcorn for. Yeah, he liked this idea. He liked it a lot. Maybe the police would take out Jericho and Carver would have one less enemy in the world.

It was a nice thought, but Jericho was hard to kill. Rocker and Menendez used to call Jericho Roach because every time it looked like there was no way out of a situation, Jericho somehow survived.

Carver left the storage room and closed the doors. The hallway continued straight past one more set of doors, but they weren't locked. He opened the doors and found a garage. It was about fifty feet wide and a hundred feet long.

Like the storeroom, this place also served as a graveyard for old furniture. There were rusty metal bed frames, old desks, and other random furniture stacked against a wall. There were no filing cabinets or patient files in this room.

He shined the flashlight around and kept walking. There were two old ambulances parked in the back, both with flat, rotted tires, and a thick layer of dust on them. Otherwise, they looked well preserved from being kept inside.

There were two rollup doors on the back wall. Just inside the doors there were two hydraulic lifts and ceiling-mounted hoists. This had been a repair bay. Carver didn't realize mental hospitals repaired their own vehicles. Maybe that had been a thing back in the day.

He walked to the first rollup door and inspected it. There was a latch at the bottom. He unlatched it and pushed it up. The door creaked and groaned. The edges grated in the railing. It obviously hadn't been opened in a long while. Or maybe it was because Carver was doing it wrong.

He shined the flashlight at the sides of the door and found a chain hanging from above. Carver pulled on the chain and the door rolled up without much resistance. He raised it high enough for him to duck under. As he was going under it, he noticed tire tracks in the dust on the floor. He followed the tracks a few feet in and saw a dark oil stain in the concrete. It looked fairly fresh. Maybe this was where Eddie parked the van.

He went outside. There was a wide concrete drive behind the building, At the end was a small parking lot. The driveway went beneath an awning with a sign on it. The sign read *EMERGENCY* in all caps. The drive continued to the end of the building and turned right. It terminated at the road.

There were yellow arrows painted on the concrete directing the flow of traffic from the street to the emergency entrance and then past the garage where the old ambulances were stored.

The doors once leading into the emergency room were gone, replaced by heavy steel doors with a smart lock. Carver studied the lock and the doors from a distance with the help of his monocular. He wanted to make sure there weren't any cameras watching the area.

There was a strip of trees behind the building. He scanned the trees for cameras. Surprisingly, there were no cameras anywhere, or at least none that he could find. It seemed strange to add advanced security to the doors but not monitor them.

Consumer locks like these sometimes had cameras built in, but this one didn't, according to the information he looked up online. There were also no known vulnerabilities that would allow him easy access.

There were no windows on the back of the building. There were no skylights on the ceiling of the garage which meant there were probably none over the secured section of the building either. A rooftop infiltration might be possible, but he didn't see an easy way up there.

Carver checked the time. He'd already spent two hours investigating Hope House. As much as he wanted to breach the mystery room, it was time to get back to the police station so he could watch the day shift arrive.

There was a normal door leading into the garage. It was a heavy steel door like the others but with a Wagner lock he could easily defeat the same way as the other one. There was a lever to release the rollup door latch from the outside. There was also a lock at the bottom of the rollup door that could be used to secure the latch, but it apparently wasn't being used.

Carver went to the ambulances. He opened their back doors and looked inside. Each one had a foldable gurney and other first aid equipment inside. Removing the gurney and other equipment freed up a lot of space.

That was good. Real good.

Carver closed the ambulances. He ducked under the rollup door, closed it, and latched it from the outside. He followed the emergency driveway around the building to the road, then hoofed it down the sidewalk to Tony's Crown Vic.

He started the car and drove back toward downtown Bickham. The general outline of his plan was solidifying into something more specific. He really wanted to see what was hidden behind the secure doors at Hope House, but his plan didn't require gaining access to that area.

The perfect place to store his prisoners was already easily accessible and available. All it required were some simple modifications and a few additional security measures. He ran through the plan a couple more times in his head and liked what he saw.

Tony's kidnapping van would allow him to carry four or five prisoners easily. He could probably jam all nine cops inside if he needed to, but he'd have to stack them up. He would take them around the rear of Hope House, into the garage, and then divide them up between the ambulances.

Carver considered how to secure the drugged cops in the back of the ambulances. The right dosage of devil's breath would keep them too drugged to do anything for about five to ten hours. That would be plenty of time for Carver to take what he wanted from the police station.

He considered using the cops' own handcuffs to secure them, but rope would be better. He would tie them up, but not too tightly because he wanted them to escape. He wanted them to break out of the ambulances, stumble outside, and see that they'd been held prisoner in Hope House.

They would think Jericho's people had kidnapped them. Then they'd think that Jericho's people had robbed them blind. They would be furious. They would confront Alicia. Ask her what in the hell was going on. She would deny involvement. They wouldn't believe her. They'd kidnap her and demand their money back.

Jericho would tell them his people had nothing to do with it. That someone else had framed them. Beau's men wouldn't believe them. They'd escalate their response. Jericho would have no choice but to respond in kind.

It would be war.

CHAPTER 30

Carver enjoyed sowing chaos.

He especially liked deploying it against people who'd pissed him off. The Bickham police were going to get what was coming to them. Jericho probably didn't deserve it, but this was the best way to keep him busy with other things besides hunting down and killing Carver.

The plan was fairly simple in principle but would require a lot of hard work and luck to pull off. He knew there were at least nine corrupt cops doing Beau's bidding. He had names for six of the nine cops. He needed to find out who the last three were.

There was a lot he didn't know. He didn't know if there were others helping the cops from behind the scenes. He didn't know if the civil forfeiture scam was the only thing they had going, or if it was just an occasional thing they did for extra money and fun.

He might never know the answers to many of those questions. He didn't need to know the answers. He just needed to get the nine cops out of the way and nonlethally neutralize anyone on night shift at the police department.

Carver swung by a diner and got two large cups of black coffee to go. He was going to need them for what came next. He continued into Bickham, circled around downtown and bypassed the street that went behind the police department. The Crown Vic might not stick out to the cameras there, but he certainly would. He drove one block back and turned down the street that ran perpendicular to the rear gate.

Even though most of the houses had driveways and garages, there were still cars parked along the curb. He parked in front of a car with a clear line of sight to the gate.

The cameras on the back gate were angled down to see the area around the gate and the road next to it. Depending on their field of view they might also see parts of the area across the street. They were probably angled that way because they were motion activated, and the cops didn't want traffic in the neighborhood behind the police station triggering the cameras all the time.

From this location, Carver would see anyone approaching the gate from either direction, but he'd see them in profile, not head on. They would be far less likely to see him, but he might have a harder time identifying them.

There were houses across the road from the gate. Any of them would be excellent places for a stakeout but only if no one was home. He decided to sit in the car and watch with the monocular. If it wasn't good enough, then he'd consider breaking into a house.

It was just past zero six thirty. Carver sipped on his coffee and started his watch. A compact car approached the gate at zero seven hundred. The driver was a woman Carver didn't recognize. She wasn't wearing a uniform. She held a card up to the reader and the gate slowly opened.

Once the gate was open, an arm gate lifted and allowed her in. It quickly closed and the gate slid shut. A Toyota Camry appeared at the gate a moment later. An unfamiliar woman in civilian attire was also driving it. She went through the gate the same way as the last woman.

A middle-aged man emerged from the house Carver was parked in front of. Carver leaned his seat back and slumped. The man was too busy staring at his phone to notice anything in the real world. He got into his car and drove away.

Carver raised his seat so he could just see over the steering wheel while keeping as low a profile as possible. The gate was opening. A silver Nissan car left the back of the station once the gate was open.

Carver raised the monocular and studied the woman driving the car. She was middle aged and looked tired. She drove toward Carver's position, went past him, and pulled into a driveway about a block behind him. She was most likely part of the night shift.

At zero seven fifteen, Palmer's Chevy Caprice pulled up to the gate. Palmer was behind the wheel. He was dressed in his police blues, and he was yawning like he'd been up all night. Carver knew the feeling.

Sutton and Archer arrived in their police SUV moments later with Sutton driving. They were both in uniform. It looked like he was the alpha in their relationship. He apparently drove the police SUV as his personal vehicle. Maybe he and Archer were roommates or maybe he picked up and dropped off Archer each day. Despite their sexual harassment of the waitress at the burger restaurant, they might even be a couple.

They were the ones Carver needed to take prisoner first. Palmer needed to be second. They seemed like the top dogs of the nine corrupt officers.

A car pulled out of the next-door neighbor's driveway with a woman behind the wheel. Carver slumped low again as she drove past. Another car departed from the house across the street and went the same way. Neither of them went into the gate.

Carver looked around at the other houses but didn't see anyone else leaving. He straightened and continued watching.

Raulerson arrived at the gate at zero seven thirty. He drove an unmarked Chevy police sedan, a late model Caprice according to an internet search. He wore a brown suit that looked a lot like the one he'd been wearing when Carver met him at the police station.

Right behind him was a blue Chevy pickup with Davidson driving. Just as Davidson was pulling through the gate, a silver SUV driven by Morales pulled up to the gate. Both cops were in uniform.

Those were the six cops Carver knew about. Maybe the women were cops too, but if that was true, why hadn't they arrived in uniform when everyone else had? Besides, Rich had been certain that all the cops raiding his house had been male.

Time kept ticking on. Carver kept waiting. Three more cars departed houses along the block. Carver ducked and waited for them to pass before continuing his stakeout.

He checked out the other houses with a line of sight on him. Most of them had blinds covering the windows and he didn't see anyone staring at him. The last thing he wanted was a visit from Bickham's finest because a nosy neighbor called them.

Around zero eight thirty, Beau's Corvette pulled up to the gate. He had to get out of the car to tap the card to the reader since the vehicle was so low to the ground. The gate opened. He dropped into the car, causing it to nearly bottom out for an instant, and drove inside. It didn't look like his girlfriend was with him.

Was Beau one of the men on the raid? It didn't seem likely. He wasn't in good shape, and he didn't seem like the kind of guy to get his hands dirty. So, who were the other three men and why hadn't they shown up for work yet?

At zero nine hundred, a van arrived at the gate. The sign on the side said *Glenda's Café*. Carver looked it up on the map and saw it was about a mile away. The female driver pressed a button next to the card reader. A moment later, the gate opened.

Carver yawned. He finished off the second cup of coffee and wished he had a third. He wanted to sleep, but he kept waiting and watching. The catering van left about thirty minutes later. Shortly after they left, Sutton and Archer departed in their SUV. A long while after that, Palmer drove out of the gate in his Dodge Challenger police car. Morales and Davidson were minutes behind him in their Mustang.

It looked like everyone got whatever they wanted when it came to police cars. Maybe it was because they had such a small staff that they could oblige. Or maybe it was because they were swimming in dirty money.

No one left or arrived over the next hour. Carver pulled the security cameras from inside his bag. He plugged a USB adapter into the cigarette lighter and plugged a camera into it. He aimed it at the gate and used the camera app on his phone to check the quality.

The footage was high resolution, so it took up a lot of space. He lowered the resolution then checked the footage. Even at the lower resolution he could zoom in and not lose too much detail. It would do for now.

Carver did another quick check of the nearby houses to ensure no one was staring out the window at him, then he leaned the driver's seat all the way back and went to sleep. He slept for three hours and woke up just after noon, feeling rested.

He reviewed the camera footage. Beau had departed around eleven thirty. A car had backed out of a driveway just down the road from him. Other than that, there had been no further activity. That made him wonder about a few things.

Where were the other three cops involved in the raid? Why had only one car with a woman left the police station this morning? Was there only one woman on night shift? From a small-town perspective, it made sense. A town this size didn't need a huge police detail working all night.

It was also possible that any cops working the night shift just went directly home when their shift was over and didn't return to the police station unless they had reason to. That meant Carver would have to watch until later this evening and see if anyone arrived for the next shift change.

There was also the chance that the three missing cops hadn't come in today or for some reason entered via the front door of the police station. Maybe those three didn't drive cars. Maybe they rode bikes or walked their beats. Maybe there was another way to get the information he needed.

His stomach growled loudly. He'd snacked on granola bars for breakfast, but they weren't going to cut it for lunch. Plus, all that coffee he'd consumed was starting to hit his digestive system. He turned off the camera and put it on the seat next to him. He checked the maps app for restaurants and found a diner a few miles away.

He was once again reminded that there were no chain restaurants anywhere within the county. The nearest one was right at the county border. There also weren't any national chain stores. Zero. None. Nada.

Beau and his boys might be crooked as hell, but stepping into Bickham was like stepping back in time. To a day when city landscapes weren't completely covered in national chain restaurants and big box stores. All the stores were locally owned and operated. It was kind of nice in some ways and a real pain in others.

Carver wheeled the car around and drove to Beatty's Diner. They didn't have a drive-through, but they had drive-up dining. Waitresses on skates would take his order from the comfort of his own car and deliver the food moments later.

It wasn't what Carver had in mind, but he needed something in his belly. He put on his ball cap and pulled it low. It was lunchtime and the place was busy, but he found an open parking spot and pulled in.

A teenaged girl took his order with a smile. He paid her and she delivered the order to the kitchen. The food came out about five minutes later. Carver dug into his grilled chicken sandwich. It was good. Real good. The town might thrive off the misery of some citizens, but the food and service were top notch.

Something caught the corner of his eye. Carver saw a police SUV zip past on the highway. He caught a glimpse of Sutton behind the wheel. He put the sandwich in the bag and backed out of his parking spot. He followed the one-way drive around the restaurant and got on the highway.

Sutton was really hauling ass because he was just a faint smudge on the horizon in the thirty seconds it took to get on the road. Carver looked through the monocular. The SUV continued straight along the highway.

Carver passed a nice wooden sign that read, *Thank You for visiting Bickham!* Wherever Sutton was going, it was way outside the city limits. City limits which probably in no way limited Sutton's authority.

The SUV turned right. Carver used the monocular to see which road it was. He kept to the speed limit and turned onto the same road. There were cows grazing peacefully in a pasture to the right and a white house about a quarter of a mile off the road. Sutton's police SUV drove down the long driveway and went around the back of a white barn about a hundred feet behind the house.

Carver drove past without stopping. He kept going until he came to a stand of trees concealing him from view of the house. He looked through the monocular and watched Sutton and Archer walk around the barn and around to the front of the house.

Beau was sitting on the front porch with a glass of amber liquid in his hand. There were three young men with him that Carver hadn't seen before. They all bore some vague resemblance to Beau, or at least enough that it was safe to assume they were related to him. They were certainly all in much better shape than him.

Beau stood. He shook hands with Sutton and Archer, grinning broadly. Palmer exited the house and Beau's expression soured. He jabbed a thumb at Palmer and shook his head a few times. It didn't take a rocket scientist to figure out he was unhappy about Palmer losing Carver.

Beau motioned toward the door and led everyone inside. Carver studied the map of the area. Beau's house was the only one within several square miles. That was common in ranch country, but it looked like he owned almost all the land on this side of Bickham.

Carver drove a little further down the road. There was a pasture road to the right. It went over a cattle gate and followed a barbed-wire fence into the distance. The fence was right on the edge of a long strip of trees that were probably there to serve as a windbreak during the winter months.

They also served as the only cover between Carver and the farmhouse. The land in these parts was flat so he couldn't rely on hills or hollows. He drove until he was past the barn and the house. He wasn't surprised by what he saw behind the barn.

There were three police interceptors parked there, Sutton and Archer's SUV, Davidson and Morales' police Mustang, and Palmer's police Challenger. They'd obviously parked behind the barn to conceal them. Who they were concealing them from was anyone's guess.

It was safe to assume they weren't there for a cookout or an official police matter. They were meeting away from the police station and in a manner that suggested they were up to no good.

Carver focused the monocular on the house and zoomed in. He didn't see any cameras. He focused on the barn. Same deal. That made sense. If they were up to no good, they didn't want to record evidence of their gatherings.

He checked the distance between him and the barn. The monocular gauged it at a hundred yards and some change. There was a whole lot of nothing between him and the barn except a few bales of hay here and there. The hay looked dark and rotten, like it had been sitting there for a long while, but the cows hadn't eaten it. Maybe it had been placed there near the end of winter when the snow melted, and the cows decided to eat grass instead of hay.

Whatever the reason, he welcomed any cover between the trees and the house, because he couldn't pass up this opportunity. He needed to get closer. He needed to find out what in the hell Beau and the boys were up to.

And turn it to his advantage.

Chapter 31

Carver slipped through the trees.

He put a bale of hay between him and the house and sprinted toward it. He was glad the land was so flat because if the house had been built on even a slight rise, anyone glancing out a window would see him.

The hay was the halfway point between him and the house. The next bale was much closer to the barn, but it required him to cut diagonally across the field. He studied the house with the monocular. The window blinds were drawn. He couldn't see in, and they couldn't see out. He dashed toward the other rotting hay bale.

The few seconds it took him to cross the space felt like a small eternity. He kept an eye on the house just in case someone decided to peek out of a window or take a stroll outside. He made it to the other hay bale then he crossed the short distance to the barn.

He went to the police cruisers first. He checked the door handles on each of them. Sutton's SUV was locked. Palmer's was locked. Davidson's was unlocked. Carver slid into Davidson's cruiser and gently closed the door.

Each cruiser was equipped with a laptop. The laptops latched onto a docking station mounted on the center console. The laptop was thicker than most because it was specially designed for law enforcement. There was a laser scanner on the side for checking driver's licenses, and a heavy-duty case to protect it.

A tap on the spacebar turned on the screen. The computer was already logged in with Davidson's username. There were multiple tabs open on the screen, one of which was labeled *Active APBs*. Carver clicked the tab. His minivan was pinned to the top of the list. There was a note that the license plate had been found on another van and the wanted vehicle had the stolen plate. So far, they hadn't found it and probably never would.

Carver went through the other tabs. There was nothing specifically about him which wasn't surprising. They didn't want to announce an official manhunt for someone that they wanted dead. There was also nothing about Tony or Rich.

There was a tab labeled *Internal*. He clicked on that one. Found a list of names and addresses. Some were in Bickham, and others were in towns in the neighboring county. Most of them had question marks next to them. Out of the three that didn't, one had a red exclamation mark next to it and the other two were marked with slashes.

He clicked on the one with the exclamation mark and read the notes.

AC-HH payback referral. Cash laundering. CI had visual confirmation of cash in basement. Est 20 mil unlaundered. Will be transferred Thursday 0200 hours. CI says 0300 Tuesday is best time to raid. Insiders with more information at 2200 Oleander Ln. Retrieve for questioning.

It sounded like a potential civil forfeiture case except that it was one county over in neighboring Thornton, not Bickham. Judging from the notes, it didn't seem like jurisdiction would be a deterrent for Bickham's finest. It looked like they were already primed to hit the place Tuesday at 0300, just a few hours from now.

Carver checked all the other items in the list. The question marks meant the information wasn't confirmed. The slashes meant the targets were no good. The exclamations marks meant they were good to go. It looked like they had confidential informants all over the place and used them to find targets.

There were also targets in Chicago. The names of some of the places in the list told Carver they were owned by other nationalities. Chinese, Russian, and so forth. Like Shen Tao Buffet, or Nikolai's Kitchen. They were almost certainly competitors to Vincenzo. Bickham police were helping the mafia hurt or weed out their competitors, or at least it looked that way.

Why were they specifically helping one group of criminals while acting against others? There was obviously some connection, but it wasn't obvious. Maybe Beau had negotiated something with the mafia in exchange for their help. Stranger things had happened.

Carver took pictures of the list. It looked like they'd be hitting the money laundering operation Wednesday. That was tomorrow. It looked like they had a list of potential targets and a schedule for hitting all of them.

Even though some of the targets looked like ordinary citizens, it was all technically legal and aboveboard. That was why they weren't afraid to have it in the official police database. They could probably easily alter anything they wanted if it became necessary.

Carver found a search function that allowed finding anything by name, case number, and a variety of other ways. He entered *Polaski* into the search function and found Rich's case file. He clicked on the file and opened it.

The file looked a lot different than the list of potential targets. It was a long form filled out with more information than Carver wanted to sort through. There was a field labeled *Perpetrator*.

Rich's name wasn't in the blank. The address and lot number of his house were there instead. There was a mugshot of the house. The casefile read City of Bickham vs Parcel ID 141210. Rich was listed as an unindicted co-conspirator.

The next form listed ninety-two thousand, three hundred twenty-six dollars as the defendant. The form after that listed all assets at Rich's address as defendants. All of the cases were assigned to circuit court judge Nancy Lloyd.

There were scanned images of signed court orders announcing a summary verdict in each case. The assets were all found guilty of being used in criminal enterprises and were thus remanded to the custody of the City of Bickham.

It was one hell of a racket.

He was no expert on the law, but it didn't seem like that was how civil forfeiture worked. Maybe it varied from state to state. Maybe these cops made up the law as the went. One thing was certain. They had all the power and the citizens had none.

Carver had an idea. He ran a search for all civil forfeiture cases. There were only two listed from the current year and five from the year prior. The highest number in one year was twelve and that was three years prior. The lowest number of cases in one year was three.

The cases were all within Bickham City jurisdiction. It was possible they were conducting unsanctioned raids outside of their jurisdiction if the list of potential jobs was to be believed. But it confirmed Carver's suspicion that there wasn't rampant abuse of civil forfeiture in Bickham or the county.

It meant civil forfeitures weren't the sole source of their bread and butter. And it looked like they had justification for many of the cases. Most of them were interstate seizures. In other words, they caught drug traffickers and others during routine traffic stops.

Only a handful of cases involved citizens. Which meant Rich's case was an outlier. It was almost as if he was specifically targeted. Maybe he confided in his ex-girlfriend that he had a huge nest egg hidden under his home. Maybe she told someone else, and that information reached Bickham PD. They saw it as an easy score and took it.

Carver scrolled down and found the case notes, or the lack thereof. All they said was *Request from AC-HH*. What did that mean? He searched for *AC-HH* and found three additional files with the same exact notes.

The other three weren't in Bickham. Two weren't even in Illinois, they were in Michigan and Indiana. The notes said *Request from AC-HH. Coordinate with locals.* It sounded like the Bickham police took the request and somehow relayed it to the police in other jurisdictions.

The other Illinois case was in a town an hour north of Chicago. The town's name was Allenton, but that wasn't what got Carver's attention. It was the name of the homeowner that raised the red flags.

The homeowner was Nadia Garcia.

Someone requested that Rich be targeted. Someone requested Nadia be targeted. Carver had heard Nadia's story at the rec center. She'd lost everything to civil forfeiture just like Rich had, except her case had been a couple of years ago.

Carver looked through the rest of Nadia's file. Like Rich, she was listed as an unindicted co-conspirator. The form listed her as a veteran, though it didn't list the specifics. Rich's form had the same thing. The other two civil forfeiture targets requested by AC-HH were also veterans.

The names and faces weren't familiar. Carver took pictures of them with his phone. He really wished he had a way to download all the information, but he hadn't anticipated having unfettered access to a police computer.

The only file that wasn't a request from AC-HH was the money laundering house. That one said AC-HH payback referral. Did AC-HH request certain jobs and then as payback give Beau tips about cash-rich targets?

Were AC and HH two separate sets of initials for two different people or did the hyphen signify that the first set of initials was a person, and the second set was an organization they belonged to? Another mafia, perhaps? Maybe a government entity?

Carver clicked another tab labeled *Community Service*. There was a very long list of people. Next to the names were their offenses, mostly speeding tickets, littering, and other minor violations of law that landed them community service.

It looked like the minimum amount of service required was forty hours. That was a full work week. It hardly seemed fair for the severity of the crime or the lack thereof. It certainly explained how Bickham remained so clean and on a tight budget.

Lights blinked on in the barn window right in front of the car. Carver quickly exited the windows he'd opened on the computer and selected the tab that had been open when he'd first climbed into the car. He turned off the screen and exited the vehicle.

He heard men talking and laughing. Heard Beau guffawing louder than the others. Carver went to the barn window. It was a narrow window, maybe a foot tall and three feet long. It had the same modern aesthetic often used on cube houses. It was decorative and didn't open from what Carver could tell. But it did the job most windows did and allowed him to see inside.

The barn was wide and spacious. It didn't house farm vehicles or hay or livestock. Instead, it housed an impressive collection of cars. The cars were all the same make and model and only differentiated by years.

They were all Corvettes, and it looked like Beau owned at least one from every model year. There was a black and white Corvette C1 from 1953. That was the best looking one in Carver's opinion. There was a red and white C1 right next to it.

The collection took up the first half of the barn. There was empty space and a wall about fifty feet beyond that. Beau and his men walked past the cars and continued toward a door in the wall. Carver ducked and paced along with them, stopping to look in the windows.

He counted ten men. Beau, Archer, Sutton, Palmer, Raulerson, Morales, Davidson, and the three young men who looked like Beau's sons.

The group entered the door in the back wall. Carver went to the next window and saw that it was blacked out. The rest of the windows on the back half of the barn were the same. There was no door at the back of the barn, and he didn't want to risk going to the other side of the barn where he'd be visible to anyone in the house.

He noticed a sliver of light escaping the last window. There was a narrow slit in the blackness. Apparently, the windows had been painted over from the inside, and something had scratched off the paint.

Carver got his eye up to the narrow sliver and caught glimpses of movement inside. He shielded his eyes from sunlight with his hands and the view clarified. There was a single light on in the room. It was directly over a metal chair. There was a young man tied to the chair. A naked young man.

Judging from the bruises and blood on his body, they'd been working him over for a while. The scabs had to be a day old at least. There was fresh blood on his face. Fresh scratches too. Some of the bruises were dark purple which meant they'd been there for a few hours.

The man looked like he was at the end of his rope. He also looked vaguely familiar, though his features were hard to make out with all the swelling and bruising on his face. Where had Carver seen him before?

Sutton stepped into the light. He wasn't alone. He had a young woman with him. She was also bloody and bruised though not as badly as the man. She looked terrified. She also looked familiar.

The man screamed and strained at his bonds. The chair didn't move because it was bolted to the floor. Carver noticed something dangling under the chair. It took him a moment to realize it was the man's testicles.

Sutton spoke. Frosty breath puffed from his mouth. Was it cold in there? Sutton put a gun against the woman's head. The man shook his head vehemently and spoke quickly. He wasn't audible through the glass, but it looked like he was trying to give Sutton what he wanted.

Sutton pursed his lips. He motioned to someone in the darkness. Archer stepped to the edge of the light. He wrote on a notepad. Made a phone call. He spoke to someone, looked at Sutton and nodded. They had what they wanted.

The man in the chair spoke again. He looked pleadingly at the woman. Sutton ripped open the woman's shirt. He yanked down her pants. Then he pointed at Archer. Archer made a face and shook his head.

Sutton waved his hand toward the other men as if asking if any of them were interested. No one came forward. He looked at the man. Shrugged and shook his head sadly. Then he shot the woman in the head. The man screamed. His screams died an instant later when Sutton shot him. There was no suppressor on the gun, but the sound was muffled. Apparently, the room was well insulated.

It seemed not everything was aboveboard and legal in this operation.

All the lights blinked on, revealing a large space with a concrete floor. There were stainless steel tables, meat hooks connected to a ceiling rail system with pullies, and large cutting machines.

There were partially butchered cows hanging from some of the hooks. There were pigs hanging from the hooks in the area next to that. There were drainage grates running along the floor to capture the blood and funnel it into a containment chamber.

There was a large metal door on the opposite side of the barn. It was the extra thick insulated kind often found on walk-in freezers. That was because this space was both a slaughterhouse and a butcher shop.

It meant they could easily wash away the blood from the dead man and woman and camouflage any evidence that someone had been murdered there. It wasn't the first time Carver had seen a slaughterhouse used for something other than killing animals. In fact, he'd seen variations of it all over the world.

What he wanted to know was what information the man had given them. Did it have something to do with an upcoming job? Was it related to the money laundering house or something else?

Davidson and Morales put on yellow waterproof coveralls and rubber gloves. They pushed a pair of meat hooks along the overhead railing toward the bodies. They stripped the woman naked, strapped her ankles together, and hung her upside down from a hook. They untied the man in the chair and did the same with him.

Morales took a butcher knife and slit the bodies' throats. Blood oozed from opened veins and arteries and poured directly into the floor grates. They were exsanguinating the bodies, draining the blood.

Carver had seen a similar scene in a German slaughterhouse. Government agents had wanted to make a group of internet trolls vanish, so they'd drained their blood, removed their vitals, and then butchered the bodies and made sausage with them. It had been a big joke to them.

Scion had participated in the secret roundup of troublemakers, but the German agents had done the killing and butchering. Jericho found it hilarious. Carver had wondered just how dangerous the individuals had been for the government to want to kill them. Then again, he'd seen governments kill their own people for lesser offenses.

Beau spoke casually to the others while the bodies bled out. He looked happy. Energetic. Like he had something he'd wanted for a long time. Archer and Sutton looked satisfied. Palmer looked grim. He was probably thinking about his failure to capture or kill Carver.

The three men who looked like Beau were smiling and joking with each other. They were even horsing around. Their ages ranged from early to late twenties. They were fit and athletic unlike their father.

Carver felt certain that these were the three cops who'd never come to work, mainly because they weren't cops. They were family. Beau's boys. One of them made finger guns and pretended to shoot the bodies. Beau laughed and nodded approvingly.

Bickham was an amazingly clean and orderly town. It was run like Beau's very own little kingdom, and these men were his enforcers. It explained why the citizens were so afraid of the police. It was because Beau and his men literally owned the town and everyone knew it.

They could target anyone they wanted with impunity, but it looked like they didn't overtly abuse their authority except in specific cases. That way they could avoid attracting too much attention.

Carver suddenly knew where he'd seen the man and woman before. He'd seen them at Hope House in Bickham the first night he'd dropped off Rich. He'd seen them while he was talking to Alicia.

He closed his eyes and pictured them. They looked dirty. They looked a little rough around the edges like they'd been pulled out of a homelessness situation and given shelter. That wasn't surprising given Hope House's status as a shelter.

They'd been arguing about something. Carver had heard the word fentanyl. They were arguing about drugs. Probably about when and where they could get their next hit. Or maybe one of them didn't want to violate Hope House's terms for drug use.

That sparked another related memory. Just before the argument, Carver had been looking at the business cards on Alicia's desk. He'd only glanced at them before being distracted, but he could recall the full name.

Alicia Channing.

Hope House.

Several things crystallized in an instant. AC stood for Alicia Channing. HH stood for Hope House. Alicia must have overheard these people talking about a money laundering operation and referred it to Beau's people. It was a quid pro quo for the requests she had made for them to target Rich, Nadia, and other people.

Beau's men had picked up the couple and tortured them for the information. When they were done with them, they'd executed them and were disposing of the bodies right this very moment.

Hope House and Beau weren't partners. They merely cooperated with each other. It looked like Bickham police requested actions in other jurisdictions at the behest of Alicia, probably because she didn't have any contacts in that area.

Actually, no. The requests weren't from Alicia. They were from Jericho. She was just his proxy. And the implications were disturbing. Not because of the people Beau's men were butchering but because of what Jericho was doing to his own people.

Jericho had sicced the cops on Rich and Nadia.

He was the reason they'd lost everything.

Chapter 32

Rich was drained.

Nadia was naked and curled up next to him in bed. They'd had sex four times in the past twenty-four hours. Once the evening after they'd left the pool hall. Again this morning, again after lunch, and then again a couple of hours after dinner.

They'd spent the time in between getting to know people from other branches of Hope House. They'd gone through another group session and then split into teams to play basketball. Rich hadn't been able to do much except pass the ball to other capable teammates, but he'd still had a great time.

Now it was nearly one in the morning and Nadia was curled up naked next to him. He felt like he was living in an alternative reality. In what world did a woman like Nadia want to have sex with a crippled guy like him?

This was nothing serious. Nadia didn't want a relationship, just sex. He had to remember that. No one wanted a relationship with a cripple. But it was enough to make him stop feeling sorry for himself all the time.

Tom had shown him the light. He still had purpose. He could make a difference in ways that actually mattered. And he could still make a woman happy. Once he had his surgery, he'd be a new man.

He didn't want to get out of bed, but his bladder felt like it was about to explode. He also wanted a shower. The rec center was nice. Really nice. Hope House had converted a section into rooms with queen-sized beds and closets. The showers, however, were communal.

He slid out of bed.

Nadia stirred. Looked at him sleepily. "Hey, you."

"Hey." He grinned. "I've got to take a leak."

"Okay." She rolled over and went back to sleep.

Rich put on shorts and a T-shirt and went into the hallway. He walked to the men's locker room and went to the bathroom. He took a quick shower while he was there. He toweled off and put his clothes back on.

Tom was waiting in the hallway when he left the locker room. "Hey, Rich."

Rich blinked. "Oh, hey. Uh, are you waiting on someone?"

"Yeah, you." He grinned. "We think you're ready for the big time."

"Really?" Rich felt something he hadn't felt in a long time. He felt needed. "What do you want me to do?"

"I'll brief you momentarily." Tom nodded his head down the hallway. "Let's go get Nadia."

"Yeah, sure."

They started walking.

"You two like each other?" Tom said.

"Sure, as, I don't know, friends, maybe?" Rich didn't know how to describe it. "I like her okay."

"You're keeping it casual and that's good." Tom glanced at him. "We're all brothers and sisters in arms here. Casual sex is fine but think of our group as a military cohort."

"No relationships?"

"I don't encourage romance, at least not if you want to be part of the group. Those kinds of entanglements make it hard to focus on the mission."

"I get it. And I promise there's nothing like that with me and Nadia. Honestly, I think she just wanted to blow off some steam."

Tom chuckled. "Oh, I understand that, all right."

"What is your mission, exactly?" Rich asked.

"It's our mission, Rich." Tom stopped walking and put a hand on Rich's shoulder. "We're all about helping veterans and forcing the system to recognize that it's been failing us for too long. It's about bringing the traitors in charge to justice."

"Amen." Rich's fists clenched. "They treat us like we're disposable. Then when we don't conveniently die, they promise us the world and deliver nothing."

"Exactly. These government agencies are riddled with administrators whose only jobs are to delay and deny. They rake in billions for their pet projects and only spend a fraction of that money. The billions leftover end up lining the pockets of politicians and career bureaucrats."

"It's infuriating."

"After being disposed of by the government, I felt lost in civilian life." Tom's gaze went distant. "It's like getting out of prison after ten years and suddenly having to adjust to life on the outside."

"Yeah, exactly." Rich had never heard the analogy before, but it was right. "It's like you've been living on another planet."

"Yep." Tom started walking again. "I had to ask myself, why do I want to live? What's my purpose besides just taking up space?"

"I've asked myself that question a lot." Rich blew out a breath. "I almost ended it all several times."

"But what stopped you?"

"I felt like if I did that, then they won."

"Who is they?"

"Everyone. The idiots who sent us on that mission, the people who dropped me like burning trash, the people who refused to approve my surgeries, and Carver, of course."

"Are you tired of losing, Rich?"

"I'm sick and tired of it."

"You ready to win?"

"Yes." Rich felt something burning in his gut. That same burning desire he felt before every mission during his time in the SEALs.

"Good." Tom stopped outside the door to Rich's room. "Let's go win."

Rich went into the room and found Nadia and Alicia inside. Nadia was already dressed and tying her hair up into a tight bun. She saw Rich and grinned. "We've got a mission."

"Yeah." Rich shivered with excitement. He was still in his broken body, but it felt like the old days again. "I can't wait."

"Let's go." Tom led them down the hallway to a room. Keith was already there dressed in black fatigues and mission ready.

Alicia entered the room last and closed the door.

Tom walked to a corkboard and flipped it over. There were pictures of a man in his late thirties. Pictures of the man with women on either arm at what looked like an extravagant party. Pictures of the man with two different women as he entered an upscale restaurant.

"This is Paul Johnston, head of Illinois Veterans Affairs." Tom pointed to a picture of Johnston with a woman his age. "This is him and his wife." He pointed to the picture of Johnston with the other women. "These are two women who are not his wife."

Laughter echoed in the room.

"He goes to expensive restaurants, parties, and has different women with him every time." Tom pointed to the other pictures. "He's a faceless bureaucrat. No one knows who he is, so he's practically incognito all the time."

Rich raised a hand. "Is he rich?"

Tom smirked. "Johnston entered public service with barely two dollars to rub together. He was a low-level bean counter seven years ago. His immediate supervisor, Gretchen

Linden, was tapped by the governor's office to run an election campaign. No one else in the department wanted the supervisor's job since the pay increase wasn't worth the extra workload. Only Johnston was interested, so he got the job by default."

Tom leaned against the wall. "Johnston took advantage of the role by working from home and doing almost nothing to earn his paycheck. His boss, Terry Jones, however, was doing the same thing so even though little work was being done, there was no one to complain about it."

"Typical," Nadia said.

"Terry Jones died of a heart attack about a year later. All three staff supervisors applied for the position. Gretchen Linden put in a good word for Johnston, so he got the position. He rose through the ranks two more times to reach his current position, consistently failing upward."

Rich laughed. "Is there any other way to get promoted in government?"

"Within two years, he went from a negative net worth to being worth two million dollars. That has since grown to sixteen million dollars." Tom sighed. "I think you can do the math from there."

"Did he even serve in the military?" Nadia asked.

"He was in the state national guard for two years when he was eighteen." Tom rolled his eyes. "He claims that he's a five-year veteran despite working only one weekend out of every month over that five-year period."

"So, what do we do about it?" Rich said. "Capture him and fly him to Yemen?"

"I wish." Tom laughed. "We are simply going to trim the fat and get VA resources channeled back to where they should be going."

"I'm in," Rich said. "Just tell me what to do."

Tom pointed to black fatigues neatly folded on a shelf at the back of the room. "Go get geared up and meet back here in ten."

"Yes, sir." Rich picked up the fatigues. Nadia was right behind him. They went to the locker room and got dressed. They met back in the briefing room.

Tom nodded approvingly at them. The group walked down the hallway. Tom stopped at a door with a biometric lock and put his thumb on it. The door unlocked and they went through it. They exited another door and entered a utilities room.

There were large pipes, electrical trays and cables, and more running along the ceiling. There was large machinery that looked as if it hadn't been used in recent memory. It was everything that was once needed to provide HVAC, swimming pool pumps, and more for the rec facility in its heyday.

Now it was being used as a garage. There were two black high-top vans parked in the space. Alicia climbed into the driver's seat of the nearest van. Tom opened the back door and everyone else piled onto the bench seats on the sides.

Tom got in last and closed the doors. He sat down and rapped his knuckles on the side. Alicia started the van and drove to the garage door. She hit a button, and the door rolled up. The van pulled out and got on the road.

Keith pulled a tablet from the pocket on the back of the front seat. He turned it on and turned it toward Rich and Nadia. There were pictures of a high-rise building in downtown Chicago. "This is one of Johnston's residences. Officially, he has only a house on the Gold Coast, but this is one of his favorite places to host women he meets at the clubs."

Rich scowled. "Swanky."

"How did he get so rich?" Nadia asked. "I get that he's stealing, but how is he doing it?"

"Oh, it's insidious." Keith set the tablet on his lap. "As the head of the state VA, he receives federal funds that are channeled into various veteran programs. He has ultimate discretion as to how to allocate funds. Rather than directly help veterans, he instead channels the money to charities to help vets."

Nadia frowned. "Yeah, but how does he get the money?"

"One of those charities is a fundraising arm of a political party. They take the funds and give them to veterans that also happen to be ranking members of the political party." Keith clenches a fist. "Not a one of these people saw combat or even came close to it. But they get hundreds of thousands of dollars each. Johnston, as a vet, takes a cut of the disbursements and filters them through shell companies to make it harder to track."

"Wow, what a dirtbag." Nadia's face clouded with anger. "How did you track it?"

"We have a few inside people at the right agencies. Veterans who want justice to be served." Tom smiled coldly. "And we will serve justice."

Keith raised the tablet again. "Johnston is home alone tonight. We will be entering the building through a back entrance and using the service elevator to reach his floor."

"Is he in the penthouse?" Rich asked.

Keith shook his head. "No. He's got a two-bedroom condo on the fortieth floor."

Nadia nodded. "What are we going to do to him?"

"You'll see." Keith turned off the tablet and put it away.

Moments later, Alicia pulled into a loading zone behind the building. It was the dead of night, nearly zero one hundred hours. The streets were empty. She backed the van up a ramp to a rollup door and stopped a few feet shy of it.

Tom opened the rear doors and hopped out. He entered a code into the keypad. The door rolled up quickly. He hopped back into the van and rapped on the side. Alicia backed it inside the door and into the receiving area.

She put the van in park. The door closed in front of the van. Tom pulled his mask on. He hopped out again. He drew a pistol, aimed, and fired it twice then motioned the others out. Rich got out and looked around. He saw two cameras in the corners, both blinded by splotches of red.

Tom lowered his mask and showed him the gun. "Paint gun. Easiest way to disable cameras."

"Nice." Rich had used high-tech equipment for the same thing. The SEALs usually used complicated gadgets even though there were plenty of low-tech solutions to problems. "How did you defeat the keypad?"

"I watched someone open it and used their code." He went to a large cargo elevator and punched in a code. The elevator hummed to life. "Same code for this."

"Civilian security is a joke," Keith said. "Then again, so is military security if you know the weaknesses."

The elevator doors slid open. There was padding on the walls to protect them. It was used for moving furniture and other large items to condos and for maintenance or janitorial workers to use so they didn't occupy the same elevators as the people who lived here.

Tom pressed a button. The doors closed. The elevator rose rapidly, seemingly much faster than any elevator Rich had been in.

Keith laughed when the elevator jolted upward. "I guess they don't care about smooth rides for the service people."

"Nope." Alicia drew her handgun. She popped out the magazine, cleared the chamber. Put the loose round back in the magazine and chambered it again.

"What's the purpose of that?" Rich asked.

She shrugged. "Nervous habit before a mission."

Rich didn't even have a gun. Neither did Nadia. Not that they would need them against a single unarmed target. He wasn't even sure what they would do to the target. Hurt him? Scare him? Kill him?

He'd always felt it was best to purge the world of bad guys, and this Johnston guy was clearly a bad guy. Maybe he wasn't blowing people up or robbing people at gunpoint, but he was indirectly killing lots of people. Mostly vets.

The elevator stopped. Tom held up a fist. He peered into the corridor. Held his hand flat and motioned it forward. Alicia and Keith stacked up behind him. Nadia mimicked them and Rich took rear guard.

They moved smoothly down the hallway. Rich was surprised by how quickly he picked up the tempo and how he automatically reacted to Tom's hand signals. It was like he'd never left the service.

Tom stopped outside the door at the far corner. He tapped a fob to the door lock. There was a faint beep and a click. He turned the handle and disengaged the deadbolt. He slowly turned the handle and opened the door.

They filed inside, quiet as ghosts. Rich eased the door shut behind him. The overhead LED lights were on but dimmed to nightlight mode. They stood in a nice kitchen with fancy cabinets and a granite countertop.

There was a den with a huge television on one side and a sectional couch on the other. There were several doors in the kitchen, probably to a pantry and closets. There were doors on either side of the den.

Tom raised his mask over his face again. The others did the same. Tom opened the door on the left and shined a flashlight inside. There was a desk with a laptop inside. He pointed to the door on the right side of the den. Turned toward Rich and motioned him closer.

Tom whispered, "You and Nadia get him out of bed and bring him to the office. Keep it quiet."

Rich shivered with excitement. He felt whole again. He felt needed again. He had found his home.

Chapter 33

Carver should have been surprised.

He wasn't. Jericho had manipulated events to put Rich in the very predicament he was supposedly helping him out of. He'd offered Beau not only Rich's nest egg and house, but also the keys to a money laundering operation that had millions in cash on location.

The cops could take that money and spend it however they wanted. No taxes, no limits, no questions asked. It was a real nice arrangement. Jericho must have found out about Beau's ties with the Vincenzo family in Chicago and realized these cops were most definitely for sale.

Something else was also clear. They were almost certainly going to raid that cash house tonight and probably right around the recommended time of zero three hundred hours. Trying to do it Wednesday would be cutting it too close.

Carver watched as one of Beau's sons disemboweled the woman's bloodless body. Another of his sons brought over a meat saw and began dismembering her. Beau was talking excitedly with Sutton and Archer. His eyes were bright and eager.

Yeah, he was ready to go. They were going to do this tonight for sure. Carver didn't need to hunt these people one by one. He could take them all at once. It would be riskier this way. If he missed his chance, it might be game over.

He also had to consider something else. These people weren't playing games. The crimes they committed weren't bloodless. So, why should he have a less than lethal approach when they almost certainly wouldn't?

They'd even tried to renege on their deal with Jericho by using Tony to kill Rich. They apparently thought using a hitman would fool Jericho into thinking they had nothing to do with it.

There were a lot of variables to consider, but for now, it was time to go. Dusk was settling in. It would be dark soon. If Carver's gut instincts were right, Sutton and the others would be gearing up for their raid on the money laundering house within a few hours.

Nine men had raided Rich's house. That meant Beau hadn't gone with them. He probably wanted to stay away from the action where it was safe. Maybe he waited here at his house. Maybe he waited at the police station. It seemed most likely that he'd be at his house. It was where he felt most comfortable.

Carver watched Beau's sons carve up the body of the man. They were good at it. Efficient. He ducked away from the window and hustled back across the field, using the hay bales as cover even though it was past twenty-one hundred hours and dark. He got back to his car and watched the house with the monocular.

The cops exited about thirty minutes later. Beau was with them, talking and gesturing excitedly. He was excited about the haul, but why? He already had plenty of money. Hell, he practically owned the entire town. So why would more money make him so excited?

Carver decided he was overthinking it. Money was the most important thing in the world to some people. They could never get enough of it. They could never get enough new things or really be happy.

Maybe it was the hunt for more money that excited Beau. Maybe unearthing the next big score was what got him up in the morning. Maybe he could finally afford to add another Corvette to his personal collection. It was hard to say. He didn't look like the kind of man to do his own detective work. He left that to his personal police force. He wouldn't go on this raid either.

Maybe his partnership with the mob wasn't a two-way thing. Maybe he owed them a lot of money, and this would settle the score. There were a lot of possibilities, but in the end, none of them mattered. Beau and his men would do their thing and Carver would do his.

Somehow, Carver needed to take care of Beau's men. That was going to be a major challenge even if he went with lethal options.

Taking them out when they left the police station or while enroute would be impossible unless he found a spare rocket launcher or land mine laying around.

It might be possible to take them out while they were at the money laundering house. That was much easier said than done. They'd arrive in a truck and stack up on the door before moving in and clearing the rooms one by one.

They'd be alert and fully geared up. Unless Carver gained access to hand grenades or a minigun, taking out nine fully armed and armored men would be impossible. He had Tony's shotgun, his Sig, and another handgun. That just wasn't going to cut it. He really wished that MP5SD hadn't been broken.

Was the target location even a house? Carver hadn't checked the map to find out exactly what the place looked like. He opened the map app. The address was still in the search bar. He zoomed in on the property.

The target house was a three-story property. It was a cube house, the kind that resembled a community college more than a family residence. The road view showed a Dodge Ram TRX parked next to five other cars in the driveway.

At a hundred grand, the TRX was the cheapest car there. The Lamborghini Urus was probably the most expensive. The others were all in between. Whoever was running the money laundering business was bad at it. Really bad. Having all those expensive cars in the front was like waving a big red flag.

People would wonder who lived in the house and what kind of job they had so they could afford all those cars. Someone might even report them to the IRS or the police. Jealousy was a powerful motivator and the government's best friend. It made neighbors tattle to the authorities on each other.

The dossier said just two people were running the operation. They didn't have guards because extra security would draw more attention to them. At least they had that part right.

The dossier didn't say who the money belonged to. Did it belong to a cartel? The Yakuza? The Triad? The Russian mafia? None of the above? Beau's men didn't seem to care. Rich had said that there was nothing identifiable on the cops when they raided his house. And the van they used didn't have any markings either.

That was why they weren't worried. They would slip into Thornton, raid the house, take the money, and vanish. The targets would have no idea who did it because the men would be masked and wearing uniforms without identification.

They were smart. Carver would have to be careful not to underestimate them. He would have to plan everything out precisely. And most importantly, he'd have to know the lay of the land.

That meant going to the target house in person and looking it over. Beau's men had parked right in front of Rich's house. They'd stormed inside quickly and efficiently, yanking him out of bed before he was even fully awake.

They'd almost certainly take the same approach with their current target. If there were only two people in the house, it would be a simple matter to roll up to the front gate in the dead of night, force it open, then burst through the front door.

The dead of night was ideally between zero three and four hundred. Unless the occupants of the house stayed up all night playing video games or partying, then that would be the ideal times to strike.

Carver's ideal time to strike would be heavily dependent on several factors and what he could conjure up to help him take on nine armed men. A grenade would be great. A rocket launcher would be even better.

He didn't have any of those things, but he did have Tony's kidnapping kit and all the drugs in it. Devil's breath could be used as an airborne agent. He could crush it into a fine powder and distribute it through the air vents of the house. If only it was that easy.

The movies made it look easier than it really was. Most modern HVAC units had heavy duty filters built right into the main unit. You had to remove the filter and then dump the powder directly into the fan. Even then, the powder might not make it through all the vents.

A house this new probably had ceiling vents as opposed to floor or wall vents. Some people put filters in the vents themselves. Some vents would be closed, and the agent wouldn't disperse into rooms with closed vents. It would be different if it the agent was a gas and not a powder.

These were factors Carver couldn't know without infiltrating the house. Infiltrating the house undetected on such short notice would be next to impossible, though he could use the scopolamine on whoever answered the door and walk right in.

Another option was to hide near the gate. When Beau's men rolled in with the van, they would disembark via the back door. There would be an opportunity to toss a drug bomb into the truck and close the doors before they could get out.

Provided they all inhaled the drug, they would be disabled before ever getting out of the van. Carver could drive them back to Bickham, lock them up at Hope House, and go about his business.

That would likely start the conflict between Bickham and Hope House and create the chaos Carver had originally wanted to go with. But hitting them before they exited the truck was harder than it sounded.

Sutton, Archer, and the others were probably experts at raids like this. After all, they targeted dangerous people and needed to be in and out of a building before there was a meaningful response. Which meant they'd be out of the van within two or three seconds. They'd come out of van so fast that there was no way Carver could throw in a drug bomb and shut the doors before they were out.

Carver went to the trunk of the Crown Vic and disabled the taillights and reverse lights. He didn't want them to be visible when he started driving. He got in the car, turned around on the pasture road, and went to the highway.

The GPS led him to Thornton about forty minutes away and to the target house. The house looked mostly the same as it had in the maps app street view image. There were three cars in the driveway, none of which were Lamborghinis or Dodge Rams.

There was an Audi R8, a Tesla Cybertruck, and a Mercedes G Wagon. It was an odd combination of vehicles. The people running the money laundering business probably got bored and swapped cars a lot. Maybe they didn't even own the cars and just rented them.

Carver parked just down the street. The other nearby homes were older ranch houses. The mini mansion the launderers lived in was probably a remodel or a tear-down and rebuild. The front lawn was overgrown with weeds, and the house looked like it needed some repairs. The occupants clearly didn't take care of the place.

The front gate was broken and hanging open. Beau's men wouldn't even have to break it down. They could just drive right in. The house was only fifty feet off the road and the front door was easily accessible.

The outside lights either weren't on or weren't working. The windows were blocked by blackout curtains. The only light escaping the house came from the sidelights on the front door. There was a doorbell camera on the front door, but no security cameras elsewhere.

For a place that supposedly had millions of dollars in cash, it didn't have much basic security. Cameras and motion detectors might not be as effective as a squad of armed guards, but they would draw a lot less attention.

The garage door was closed. Carver wondered if there were more cars inside or if it was full of junk. Maybe it was full of cash. There was only one way to find out for sure. Carver hadn't planned on infiltrating the house without doing his due diligence, but it didn't look like there was much to stop him.

He used an app to scan for Wi-Fi signals used by wireless cameras in case there were any hidden in the trees. He picked up several nearby wireless access points, but no cameras. There was no home across the street from the target house, and the wooden fence around the property concealed much of the property from neighbors.

The doorbell camera was the only security device to worry about and it was easy to avoid because the gate was on the left side of the driveway just out of view of it. He could simply skirt through the left side of the driveway and go around the house.

Carver returned to the Crown Vic. He opened the trunk. Tony's kidnapping kit was inside. There were several bags of scopolamine pills inside. He figured one bag was probably enough. There was a manual coffee grinder in the kit. It was slim with a plastic container on the top, a glass jar on the bottom and a handle on the top.

He dumped the pills into the coffee grinder. There was a lever on the side that was already set to the finest grind level. He rotated the handle until the pills were reduced to a fine powder in the lower half of the grinder.

The Crown Vic was parked in a relatively secluded spot on the road next to a strip of trees and bushes. It was also nearly two in the morning, but he looked around to make sure there weren't pedestrians or nosy neighbors watching him. It looked like he was in the clear, so he continued his work.

There was a respirator outfitted with P100 filters in the kit. Carver put it on to avoid drugging himself and carefully poured the powdered scopolamine into a rubber bulb. The fine powder mostly went into the bulb but some of it clouded the air around Carver. Without the respirator, he'd probably be in dreamland by now.

The rubber bulb was designed to puff boric acid and other fine powders into hard-to-reach spaces for pest control. In Tony's case, it was used to puff powdered drugs into the faces of unsuspecting victims.

Once all the powdered drug was transferred, Carver screwed the metal tip onto the rubber bulb. He pointed the tip away from him and gently pressed the bulb. A cloud of devil's breath burst from the tip, forming a cloud large enough to engulf a man's head. The range was about three feet. That should be ample enough.

The tip was hinged in the middle and could be bent down to effectively close it to prevent any accidental discharges. He bent it down and put the puffer into a small side satchel from Tony's kit. He strapped the satchel onto his waist for easy access.

Carver closed the car trunk and walked toward the target. He remained vigilant, scanning the area in case someone happened to be out and about at this late hour. He walked past the target driveway and studied the house with his monocular for a moment.

There were blackout curtains on the windows, so it was impossible to tell if there were any lights on inside. He entered the left side of the gate and cut left to follow the fence. The front fence was wrought iron, but the fence down the side and back of the house was the cheap wooden kind with thin pine slats.

The fence was heavily weathered and rotting in places. It was a visual barrier and only a minor inconvenience to anyone who wanted to break through one of the rotted sections. Carver was glad it was there to hide him from the neighboring houses.

He continued following the fence down a steep slope into the back yard. The windows on the side and back of the house were covered by blackout curtains just like the front. He used the monocular to look for cameras and found none.

The back yard was level with the basement. Stairs led up to a wooden deck that was even with the main floor, so he slowly climbed them to minimize creaking wood. There was a stainless-steel grill on the deck and a variety of bamboo patio furniture. The grill was dented and dirty, and the furniture was moldy.

Carver eased up to the French doors that led into the house. The windows were covered with blackout curtains like all the others. The occupants apparently hated daylight with a passion, or maybe they just wanted privacy.

He went back down the deck stairs. There was a single steel door beneath the deck, presumably leading into the basement. He slid a slim jim into the jamb and sprung the latch. He pushed gently and the door opened inward. He stepped into darkness and used night vision on the monocular to light the way.

He was in a large basement with thick plastic covering a dirt floor. It smelled musty. There was a rusty old lawnmower, a pile of lawn tools, and other random things here and there, but no cash. There were scuffmarks on the plastic and square indentations where it looked like something had been sitting for a while, but no clues as to what it had been.

There were footprints leading into and out of the door. There was no telling if the foot traffic was recent or not. Something had been stored down here, then moved out. Maybe the cash had been stored here and was already gone. Or maybe it had simply been moved.

He checked the rest of the basement. He found square indentations in the plastic all over the place but no traces of what had been there. There was nothing here. It was time to move upstairs. He left the basement and closed the door. He went up the deck stairs, walked past the French doors, and went to the single steel door that presumably went into the garage.

He jimmied the door open and went inside. It was a three-car garage but there were no cars inside. Instead, there were pallets lined up in neat rows. The cargo on the pallets was wrapped in translucent plastic wrap. Carver couldn't see through the plastic, but he didn't need to. It was easy to guess what the square blocks on the pallets were.

He unsheathed his survival knife and sliced the plastic at the bottom of a pallet. He looked underneath and found stacks of twenty-dollar bills. The bills were bundled into cubes. Judging from the size of the cubes, each one contained about a million dollars.

It took fifty thousand twenties to make a million dollars. US bills weighed about a gram each. A million dollars in twenties would therefore weigh about a hundred and ten pounds. It would be no problem to carry out a million bucks right now.

It was easy. Too easy. It was so easy, in fact, that Carver wondered if this might be a honeypot trap. Sometimes it was better to make a target come to you, so you set up a fat, juicy target, one they couldn't afford to ignore. The honey would attract the flies, and once they took the bait, the trap closed around them.

This place had all the tells of a setup. The cars in the driveway, the broken gate, the pallets of cash. There was one thing that made Carver think it might not be a honeypot. Well, two things. Two people, actually.

The people in Beau's slaughterhouse had been tortured and killed trying to protect this place. The entire point of setting up a honeypot was to make sure the target had all the information they needed to find it. You had to make it easy but not too easy or they'd suspect something.

Getting two people killed to convince them the target was legit was not a sound strategy. Maybe the couple that Sutton shot had nothing to do with this place. Maybe Carver was barking up the wrong tree.

But he was almost certain this was the right tree. The information on Davidson's police computer painted this place as a ripe target ready for plucking. Maybe this wasn't a honeypot. Maybe those people had died trying to protect it because they knew their bosses would kill them if they didn't.

Carver went to the door and looked outside. He scanned the area with infrared. He didn't see an army of federal agents closing in from all angles. The backyard was clear. This almost certainly wasn't a trap, at least not yet. But if Carver had his way, that would change.

This was going to become his honeypot.

Chapter 34

Rich went toward the target's bedroom door.

Nadia followed him and stepped to the left side of the doorway. She looked at Rich. He nodded. She twisted the doorknob and pushed the door open. Rich shined the flashlight inside. He had a clear line of vision to the bed.

His knee was killing him, but he ignored it and stepped inside the room. He saw a walk-in closet with a laundry basket inside. He grabbed a sock out of the basket and went to the bed.

Johnston was snoring peacefully. Rich made sure no one else was in bed with him, then jammed the sock in the man's mouth and shined the flashlight in his eyes. Johnston's eyes fluttered open.

Rich grabbed Johnston's right arm with his left hand and yanked him upright. Nadia did the same from the other side. They hefted him out of bed and dragged him from the room before he could fully wake up. He tried to shout, but the sock muffled his cries.

He tried to plant his feet, but he was a short man who probably hadn't worked out a day in his life. Even with his bad knee, Rich had no problem overpowering Johnston with Nadia's help. She was strong as a bull and Johnston was still half asleep.

They shoved him into the computer chair. Alicia wrapped a nylon strap around Johnston's neck and the bottom part of the headrest and zipped it tight. Tom stood in front of him, his eyes dark above his mask. He pulled a knife and touched the tip to Johnston's throat.

Johnston froze. His eyes widened. Tom held a finger to where his lips would be under the mask. Johnston nodded in understanding. Tom nodded at Rich. Rich pulled the sock from Johnston's mouth.

"Log onto your computer," Tom said. His voice was deep and electronic. He was apparently using a voice disguiser under the mask.

Johnston shivered. "Who—"

Tom put the knife against his neck. "No questions. Only compliance."

Johnston did what he was told. Tom continued giving instructions. He seemed to know exactly what he was looking for because within minutes, Johnston was logged into a dozen bank accounts all over the world. The man had accumulated far more than ten million in assets. He had access to literally billions of dollars.

"Who are you laundering money for?" Tom asked.

"I don't know." Johnston shivered violently.

"Do you have a handler?"

"I think so. I don't know if it's one person or many."

"How hard is it to move the money?"

"Please don't make me do that. They'll kill me."

"That's not my problem." Tom pressed the flat of his knife to Johnston's throat. "They're stealing money from us, from vets. They don't seem to understand that if they bite us, we can bite back."

"Please don't make me do it." Tears pooled in Johnston's eyes. "I can still make you rich."

Rich was confused. How did this guy have access to billions of dollars and why was he laundering money? He had so many questions, but he didn't talk. He just let Tom do his thing.

Something beeped. Tom turned away from Johnston and pulled up his shirt sleeve. He looked at his smartwatch and tapped on it. Then he covered the watch and turned back to Johnston. "Keep talking."

"This is just a drop in a bucket," Johnston said. "It's only twenty billion. Someone, maybe one of their other launderers, accidentally gave me access to other parts of their funding network. The total assets are in the trillions."

"I know," Tom said. "There's no other way to fund the kinds of things they fund." He stared at the screen. "The money comes from the government and goes into USAID and other government agencies. It is then sent to NGOs all over the world in places with little to no accountability or tracking."

"What's an NGO?" Nadia hissed.

Tom turned. Put a finger up to silence her. "Non-governmental organization. It's a fake corporation used to launder federal money." He turned back to Johnston and picked up where he'd left off. "The money is spent on items purchased from various organizations at heavily inflated prices. It then goes into bank accounts and is transferred to bank accounts all over the world."

Johnston's mouth gaped. "How do you know so much?"

Tom's eyes brightened. "Because I used to work for them."

"Used to?"

"Yes. Then I found out what they were doing. How they were hurting vets. I decided to put a stop to it." Tom tapped an account on the screen. "Let's start small. The next time you move money you will put half a percentage point into one of our accounts. You will continue to do this as if this account is one of your laundering accounts."

"I can't make a transfer alone. I type in a code, then two other people have to approve the transfer. If they see money going to another account, they won't approve it."

"It sounds like they added extra security since the last breach." Tom's jaw moved under his mask. "We'll have to approach this from another angle." He stared at the laptop for a moment. "Are they still using domestic cash houses?"

Johnston didn't answer right away. Then he looked at Tom's blade. "Y-yes."

"What's the nearest one?"

"I don't know. The locations rotate frequently."

Tom raised an eyebrow. "Show me."

Johnston typed with trembling fingers. He opened a spreadsheet and copied a long string of characters, probably encrypted. He pasted them into another website. That site decrypted a set of coordinates. He entered the coordinates into a maps program, and it returned an address.

"That's the closest one. Thirty minutes away."

"How much is there?" Tom asked.

Johnston opened another spreadsheet and went through a similar process of decrypting information. "Several million dollars. It's scheduled for dispersal soon, though."

Tom nodded. "How does that work?"

"There are all kinds of ways, but in this case, most of the money will be given to individuals who will then donate it to a political action committee because the mayoral election is this year."

"Typical." Tom turned to the others. "Did you know selling art and political action committees are the two easiest ways to launder money?"

"I did not," Alicia said. "But it makes sense."

Tom sheathed his knife. "From now on, you're my inside man, Paul. You're going to help me locate cash houses like these. But don't worry, we'll keep it random enough that they won't suspect you're the one giving them up."

Johnston gulped. "They're going to figure it out."

Tom patted his shoulder. "We know there are at least three people who know about the cash houses, right? You and the other two people who approve transfers?"

"Um, I guess so, yeah."

"Who else might know?"

"I really don't know. I don't even know who the other two people are."

"Well, that's not important anyway." Tom gripped Johnston's hair and yanked his head back. "All that's important is that you keep me informed or the next time we come for a visit, it won't be nearly so pleasant."

Johnston shivered. "I'll do it, I promise."

Tom squeezed his shoulder hard enough to make the other man wince and cry out. "Do you believe that I can find you anywhere anytime?"

"Yes."

"Good. That's all you need to know." Tom patted him on the head. "You're mine now. Got it?"

"Yes."

"That's yes, sir to you."

Johnston trembled. "Yes, sir."

"Good boy." Tom sprayed something in Johnston's face. The other man recoiled. His eyes glazed over and within seconds, he slumped in his seat. Tom turned to Rich and Nadia. "Tuck him back in, okay?"

"Yes, sir." Rich and Nadia hefted Johnston and put him back in bed. They laid him on his back and pulled up the covers. They didn't say a word to each other, but they didn't need to. Nadia's eyes glowed with excitement.

Rich hadn't felt this excited, this happy in a long time. Tom wasn't running amateur hour. This man was the real deal. They rejoined the others in the den and exited to the hallway. They went back to the service elevator and exfiltrated the building the same way they'd come in.

Alicia drove the van out of the service area and got on the road. She drove slowly. "Where to, sir?"

"Hang on a minute." Tom took out a USB drive and plugged it into a laptop. "I used one of my gadgets to capture everything from our new friend's computer. Decrypting some information will be a challenge, but I think we can figure it out."

"I've got contacts who can probably decrypt anything," Keith said. "But we won't have access to their bank accounts."

"We don't need that kind of access," Tom said. "At least, not right away. Let's start small." His watch beeped again. He looked at a notification and tapped it.

Nadia pursed her lips. "Are cash houses considered starting small?"

Tom nodded. "Exactly." He opened a spreadsheet on the laptop. "How about we start tonight?"

"I'm in," Alicia said.

Keith nodded. "Same."

Rich grinned. "You don't even have to ask me."

"Same." Nadia clenched a fist and held it up. "I'm ready."

"Good." Tom closed the laptop. He put the address into his phone and checked the distance. He checked the time. "Let's go to the shop and gear up. We leave at zero two thirty."

"Don't we need to reconnoiter first?" Keith said.

Tom shook his head. "The file Johnston decrypted told me everything we need to know. I'll brief you on the way back to the shop."

Alicia took a sharp turn. "Headed back to the shop."

Tom leaned back in his seat. "The target is a storage unit in a moderately secured facility. We'll just need to bypass a keypad at the door and a keypad in the elevator. We can use the carts onsite to bring the cash down to the van."

"That easy?" Keith said.

Tom nodded. "That easy."

Nadia's eyes widened. "And how much money is there?"

"It says eighteen million in the file."

Rich whistled. "Man, that could pay for my surgery and a boob job."

Nadia laughed. "I think you need to get rid of your man boobs, not make them bigger."

The others laughed. Rich laughed the hardest. It felt good to be needed. To be wanted. To have the camaraderie of the squad again.

They arrived back at the shop, as Tom called the rec center. They got out of the van and walked to the building. "Wheels up in fifteen," Tom said.

"We have a chopper?" Alicia said with a grin.

Tom laughed. "Not yet. But we'll be able to afford one after this."

"Hell yeah." Keith clapped his hands once. "I'm sick of commuting in traffic."

"What about the other people who were at the meeting earlier?" Rich said. "Will they be part of this unit too?"

"Maybe," Tom said. "Not all of them passed tonight's eval."

Nadia's eyes widened. "Tonight was an eval?"

"Yep." Keith grinned. "And you two passed with flying colors."

Rich frowned. "What was the criteria?"

"A willingness to do more. A lot more." Tom patted Rich on the shoulder. "Let's leave it at that, okay?" He checked his watch. "Go to the bathroom. Get some water. Report back here geared up and ready to leave in fifteen, okay?"

"Yes, sir." Rich resisted the urge to salute.

He used the head and hurried back to meet the others. He was as excited as he'd been before his first SEAL mission. There was new gear waiting for him in the locker room, a pair of SIG P365 Legions and holsters.

Rich stared in awe at the new handguns. He looked through the aimpoints. Checked the chambers. Ran a hand over the cool metal. There was no serial number where it should be.

"Nice, huh?" Nadia stepped inside. She was already wearing both guns on her thigh holsters. She rotated, slowly. "What do you think?"

Rich whistled. "Hot."

She grinned. "I know, right?"

Rich strapped the holsters to his thighs rather than the waist since it was easier to reach them there. He had trouble reaching the buckle with his bad shoulder, so Nadia helped him. "I can't wait to get my shoulder fixed."

She tightened the strap. "Can you reach the gun?"

Rich pulled the gun and holstered it again. "Yeah, it's perfect, thanks."

She smacked his butt. "My pleasure, sailor."

He laughed. They went outside through the rear door and found the others waiting next to the van.

Tom nodded approvingly. "Looking sharp, people."

Rich gripped his hand. "Thanks for the Sigs."

"My pleasure. Can't have us going into the field unprepared." He opened the back of the van and took out a hardened case. "One more thing." He opened the case to reveal several HK416s.

Rich whistled. "Man, where did you get those?"

"I've been saving them for a rainy day." Tom placed a suppressor on the muzzle with a half twist. He handed the rifle to Rich. "How does that feel?"

Rich put the rifle to his right shoulder. It hurt to bend his shoulder that much, but it was a good pain. He looked through the aimpoint. Switched from night vision to infrared. He held the rifle as steady as he could for a few seconds. "Feels like a million bucks."

Tom grinned. "Excellent." He handed Nadia her rifle and opened a hardened case with loaded magazines inside. "Gear up."

Everyone was locked and loaded within a minute. Rich felt his old instincts coming back. He felt like his old self again. Ready to take on the world. They loaded into the van and Alicia headed for the target destination right on schedule.

They arrived at the address thirty minutes later. The storage facility was there, but it was obvious that the mission was a bust. The six-story building was a burned-out husk. It looked like it had burned down recently, and there was nothing left.

"How the hell does a building made of metal and concrete burn like that?" Alicia said.

"Not without help." Keith looked grimly at it. "The stuff stored inside burns well enough, especially if it's cash."

Tom looked at his laptop and laughed. "If our new friend had bothered scrolling across the spreadsheet, he would have seen that this location was marked as compromised and assets were moved to a new location." He gave the address to Alicia. "Let's go there."

She plugged it into the GPS. "ETA twenty minutes."

Tom tapped on the laptop. His eyebrows rose. "Looks like a cash house." He turned the laptop to show the street view in the maps app. "Take a look at those cars."

There was a Lamborghini and other exotic cars parked in the driveway.

"Wow!" Nadia whistled. "Can I keep one?"

"We don't do flashy cars," Keith said. "We don't want to draw undue attention to anyone."

She sighed. "Well, a girl can dream."

Tom chuckled. "Don't worry. We'll have company vacations. Then you can rent flashy vehicles."

"I can live with that," she said.

Rich studied the target house. The driveway was gated but the gate was broken and the fence around it was wooden. The place looked like an easy infil. "Any idea how many people are inside the place?"

"The spreadsheet says two. They keep a minimal detail in places like this, so it doesn't arouse suspicions." Tom shook his head. "Apparently, the occupants didn't get the memo about not attracting attention with expensive cars."

"Idiot civvies," Keith said. "This should be easy."

Tom nodded. "We're going to do it by the numbers."

"ETA three minutes," Alicia said.

Rich trembled with excitement. This was going to be fun.

Chapter 35

Carver had a trap to set.

Beau's boys were coming. They could be here any minute. It was zero two twenty-five already. The dead of night. The perfect time to strike an unsuspecting target. He had to secure multiple objectives before he'd be ready for them.

There was an entry door to the house in the garage, but it was blocked by pallets loaded down with cash. They must have been hiding them in the basement and relocated them to the garage since they were being picked up tomorrow.

Since he couldn't get in that way, he went out to the deck and to the French doors. He put an ear to the glass and listened. He didn't hear a television. Didn't hear voices. Didn't hear anything. That was to be expected at this hour of the night. It was late and everyone was probably asleep.

Like most French doors, this one had wooden latch plate extending from the left door to protect the jamb. He put his foot at the bottom of the door without the protection and pushed it in while simultaneously pulling out on the other door.

There was enough play in the door to give his slim jim some wiggle room. He slid the thin metal into the crack and sprang the latch within a few seconds. The door popped open with a rattle. He winced and slipped inside.

It was dark inside the house. He used his monocular to scout the dark room. There was a huge television mounted on a wall. A dingy sectional couch with food stains on it. A pair of end tables with dirty dishes and old food wrappers on them. The place reeked of marijuana.

Thankfully, it didn't smell like dogs. That was a little surprising. People who liked flashy cars tended to like big flashy dogs, like pit bulls. Judging from how lazy these people were about putting away dirty dishes and tossing out the trash, keeping a dog was just too much for them to handle.

Carver remained still near the back door and scanned the place with his monocular. He looked for infrared cameras, motion sensors, or anything else that would detect him.

He didn't see any of that. This was definitely no way to run a criminal enterprise, but he wasn't going to complain.

The den and kitchen were one large room. There were two other empty rooms. Probably a dining room and an office. He cleared the entire first floor within seconds. He went upstairs next.

The stairs led to a balcony that wrapped around the top of the den. The south side offered a great view of the front door. That might come in handy when it was time. There was a loud rattling coming from the bedroom at the north end of the hallway.

It sounded like a metal fan. That was probably the master bedroom. He'd check that room last. The loud fan would mask any sounds he made while he cleared the other rooms. That was good for him and bad for the occupants.

He started with the bedroom on the south end. There was a huge television with multiple gaming consoles connected to it. There were shelves full of Blu-ray movies and video games. There was an industrial-sized trashcan that was full to overflowing in the back of the room.

A sliding glass door led to an outside balcony that ran down the entire length of the house. It might be a good escape route if it came down to that. He went back into the bedroom. Walked down the hall and entered the next room.

There was a cheap laminate bookcase inside. It was loaded down with bottles of expensive booze. It was so heavily loaded that some of the shelves were bowing inward and causing the bookcase to lean heavily to the side.

The next bedroom was filled with boxes. Some of the boxes had logos printed on the side for a place called EZ Storage. It looked like the boxes had been emptied and tossed aside. There were piles of comic books and other random items in a pile next to the boxes. There were also twenty-dollar bills scattered around. The comic books were recent editions, not collectibles.

That combination of things told Carver a lot. The cash had been stored in these boxes. The comic books and other items had been packed on top to hide the cash. The boxes had been purchased from a storage facility named EZ Storage and stored in the same place.

The cash had been moved from there to here. It had probably sat in the boxes until it was time to move the cash elsewhere. For some reason, they decided to put the cash on pallets and wrap it in plastic rather than keep it in the boxes.

Carver couldn't guess why they'd do that. He didn't know why they'd bring the boxes upstairs, unpack them, take the cash downstairs to the basement to load on pallets, and then bring the pallets back up to the garage. It seemed like a whole lot of unnecessary work, but he wasn't an expert at money laundering. He knew the basics and that was all he'd needed to know

The next room was the master bedroom at the end of the hallway. The door was unlocked, so he eased it open and looked inside with the monocular. There was a king-sized mattress on the floor, trash, condom wrappers, and more delights tossed like landmines all over the place. The room stank of marijuana, unwashed bodies, and stale food.

A male and female were on the mattress. The male was on his side and the female was cozied up to him like she was glued to his back. A stained comforter lay halfway on and halfway off the couple.

Carver spotted the source of the rattling. It was an oscillating fan on the left side of the bed. It rattled loudly as it rotated back and forth. It was loud enough to wake the dead, but some people needed that kind of noise to fall asleep.

He cleared the bathroom and walk-in closet and felt certain that the only occupants of the house were asleep on the mattress. There was a Glock on the floor next to the male occupant of the bed. He picked it up and shoved it into his back pocket.

Carver covered his face with a cloth mask. He unplugged the oscillating fan. He turned on the lights. The couple kept snoozing. He gave them a few seconds. The woman stirred first. She rubbed her eyes. Looked up at the light. She groaned and sat up. Saw Carver. She gasped.

Carver pointed the Sig at her. "Wake up your boyfriend."

"Who are you?"

"A friend. I found out you're going to be raided tonight."

"Raided?" She gasped. "Are you with the company?"

The man pretended to sleep while his hand slowly reached toward the place where the Glock had been. He found nothing but an old condom wrapper.

"Remove the comforter and sit up," Carver said.

The woman pushed the comforter away. The man sat up and scowled at Carver.

"Do you know who we work for?" the man said.

Carver ignored the question. "What are your names?"

The woman answered. "I'm Darla and this is Greg."

"Shut up!" Greg said.

Darla grabbed his arm. "He said the house is going to get raided tonight and wants to help us."

"Say what?" Greg stiffened. "Who the hell are you?"

"Let's just say that I'm helping you out of my own self interests." Carver looked around in case there were other weapons he'd missed. "The people who are coming to raid the house are my enemies."

"So, you want to kill them?" Greg said.

"Probably." Carver wasn't completely sure. Killing even crooked cops would raise a real stink, but he could probably get away with it. "Was there another man and woman helping you here?" Carver described the couple that Sutton had executed.

Darla shook her head. "No, it's just us. Sometimes they send some guys to help when we have to move things fast."

Greg shook his head too. "Never heard of them. What happened to them?"

"The people coming here tortured and murdered them. I thought it was for information about this house." Carver shrugged. "Guess I was wrong."

Darla gripped Greg's arm. "When are we being raided? What are we supposed to do?"

"Your choices are simple." Carver checked the time. "Any time now these people will arrive. They will storm through the front door, systematically clear all the rooms, and probably kill you. Then they will take the cash in the basement."

"Do they know it's counterfeit?" Greg said. "The company has been sitting on the stash for a long time because the bills aren't good enough to pass muster. They're picking it up tomorrow to take it to an incinerator."

Carver couldn't stop the grin crossing his face. "The bills are fakes?"

"Yes!" Greg ran a hand down his face. "They're going to kill us for counterfeit dough!"

It was tragic and funny, at least according to Carver. Maybe Beau's men deserved to die for counterfeit money. They certainly deserved it. Unfortunately, there was one major hurdle to overcome. One that Carver hadn't figured out yet.

How could he ambush and neutralize nine armed and armored men? The moment they stormed the house they'd probably split into groups of threes. They'd clear the first floor, try to enter the garage, and find it blocked.

One group would go outside to the garage door and find the money. The other two groups would rush up the stairs and quickly and quietly clear the bedrooms. They'd reach the master bedroom, burst inside, and kill or capture the occupants.

At least, that was how Carver would do things if he had a nine-man squad behind him. But as usual, it was just him. Even with the help of Greg and Darcy, it would be impossible to neutralize even three heavily armed and trained men.

They would be wearing armored helmets and vests. The only way to take them down would be with leg shots. That wouldn't stop them from shooting back. There was no place to take cover. Drywall wouldn't stop bullets. The marble wall tiling in the bathroom wouldn't either.

The Bickham cops would unload on the room, killing everyone inside.

The upstairs balcony would be a good ambush spot if he had six men of his own. The only bottleneck was the front door. Once the cops entered, they had plenty of room to spread out and plenty of rooms to hide in.

The stairs also formed a bottleneck but the stylish glass balustrade at the top wouldn't conceal anyone trying to hide at the top. The bedrooms were the only places with hiding spots for an ambush.

Carver looked around the room. This would have to do. The main variables were Greg and Darla. They might help him. They might turn on him. He didn't want to take chances with a pair of unknowns.

He pointed to the pillows on the floor. "Put those under the comforter to make it look like someone's in the bed."

"I can do even better." Darla stood. "Can I go to the closet?"

"Let's all go," Carver said.

She sighed. "I'm helping you, I promise."

Greg stood. "Yeah, we'll help you. Like I said, there's nothing of value here. If these people are smart, they'll figure that out fast."

"What's in the closet?" Carver said.

"My wigs and a sex doll."

Greg nodded. "Yeah, I got one of them realistic sex dolls. We can use it in the bed."

Darla smiled. "He plays with it when I'm not in the mood."

Carver had seen a lot of horrors during his time in the military. Picturing these two going at it would probably rank right up there with the worst of them.

"Let's do it." Carver followed them inside the walk-in closet. Sure enough there was a fairly realistic sex doll inside, its rubber mouth hanging open like a receptacle.

Darla grabbed a wig and Greg grabbed the doll. They put the doll on its side on the mattress. Darla bunched up pillows next to it and arranged a wig to make it look like someone was there.

With that done, Carver motioned them into the bathroom. There was a big cast-iron clawfoot tub inside the shower stall. "I want you to lay down in the tub and stay there until this is over."

"Can't you just let us run away?" Darla said. "We don't want to be here when they come."

Cutting them loose wouldn't work. They'd run straight to a phone and call their bosses. He also didn't want them free to run around during a firefight either. He pulled out the puffer with the scopolamine in it. He hadn't properly tested it.

"What's that?" Greg said.

Carver puffed a dust cloud at him and his girlfriend. The effects were instantaneous. Their faces went slack and expressionless. They stood in place like zombies. He put on the respirator just to be safe, then took Darla's hand and pulled her toward him. She walked slowly, like someone half asleep.

"Get in the bathtub, Greg."

Greg got into the bathtub and stood there until Carver told him to lie down. Once he was situated, Carver turned to the woman. "Your turn, Darla."

She stared blankly at him.

"Get in the tub, Darla."

Like an automaton, she got in the bathtub.

"Lie down next to Greg." She did it slowly but without hesitation.

Carver was impressed. This stuff was scary effective. He wondered just how far he could push someone. Could he make them kill themselves? Make them kill someone else? He was tempted to find out, but he had other things to do.

He took off the mask and hooked it to his satchel. He closed the nozzle on the puffer and put it in the satchel. He looked outside to make sure no one was storming the gates just yet, then quickly gathered what he needed for the ambush. He grabbed one of the storage boxes, a roll of the packing plastic they'd wrapped around the pallets of counterfeit money, and some packing tape.

He set everything up in the bedroom. It was a simple plan. The best ones usually were. But it required proper timing. That meant he'd have to be right in the thick of things and hope nothing went sideways.

Carver went through the sliding glass door and out on the balcony. It was the same one that stretched down the side of the house to the other bedrooms. There was a collapsible fire escape ladder bolted to the side of the balcony that was tastefully hidden inside a planter.

Carver lowered the ladder. It would be his Plan B if everything went sideways. He went back into the house and put the final touches on the trap. He looked everything over one more time and turned off the bedroom lights.

With that done, he returned to the balcony, crouched behind the wall, and watched the road. If Beau's men were sticking to the case file notes in the laptop, they'd be here right at zero three hundred.

The unmarked SWAT truck appeared at zero two fifty-nine and drove past the broken gate. It stopped just outside the front door. The engine ran quietly for a diesel. Most truck engines were loud enough to wake the dead. This one was probably surrounded by thick insulation to muffle the sound.

The back doors opened. Nine men swarmed out and formed up at the front door. Carver lost sight of them under the front awning, but he heard them ram open the door. Carver went through the French doors to the second bedroom, through the bedroom door, and looked over the stairway balcony.

Beau's men quickly and efficiently moved through the house clearing the first floor, their rifle-mounted flashlights sweeping the area. They didn't say a word or make hardly a sound. They were really good at this.

Carver backed away from the glass balustrade and went back out onto the balcony. If they cleared the balcony, he'd slip inside the master bedroom to hide, then duck back out to the balcony when they were back inside.

He'd cracked open the curtains on the windows in each room so he could see when the room was swept. A flashlight blinked in the window at the far end. Moments later, it blinked in the next bedroom. Each room had a bathroom and a walk-in closet. Empty rooms would take just a few seconds to clear, but he anticipated the room with the boxes and dollar bills on the floor would take a few seconds longer.

Beau's men reached the room with the boxes. They took an additional ten seconds to sweep it. They were good at staying on objective. Carver couldn't see them, but he envisioned them stacking up outside the closed door to the master bedroom. They knew that this would be the only room with anyone in it.

Carver cracked open the balcony door. He grabbed a strip of the packing plastic on the other side. The rattle of the oscillating fan was the only thing he heard. The door slowly opened. Flashlights aimed at the bed. A suppressed rifle coughed four times, striking the sex doll and the pillows.

The lights came on inside the room. Men rushed through the doorway. It was time to spring the trap.

Carver yanked on the packing plastic. It ran along the floor and was taped to an upside-down storage box. Under the box was a stack of Blu-ray movie cases. They were stacked high enough to place their payload directly in the path of the fan.

The payload was a pile of devil's breath.

A thick cloud of powdered scopolamine filled the room. The invaders hacked and coughed. They wore masks to cover their faces, but it wasn't enough protection. Someone shouted a warning and dove to the side, but it was too late. They'd already been exposed.

Carver counted six men. He'd been right to assume they'd follow protocol and send one group of three to find the money. Four of the men were still standing. They went slack, some dropping weapons on the floor and others managing to hold on to theirs.

The two men who'd tried to dive out of the way lay on their sides unmoving aside from the rise and swell of their breathing. Six men were neutralized, but three were somewhere else in the house.

He needed a security badge from one of them, but the dust cloud of scopolamine was still thick, and he didn't trust the respirator a hundred percent. It should be just fine, but he didn't want to take any chances, especially not with three of Beau's men still on the loose.

He didn't know who the disabled men in the room were due to their masks. The two smaller figures were probably Davidson and Morales. Two were tall and big. They might be Sutton and Archer, or they might be Beau's two older sons who were just about the same size.

It didn't matter. Taking out three men would be much easier than taking out nine.

He hurried down the balcony to the room furthest from the master bedroom and quietly entered the sliding glass door. He peeked into the hallway. No one else was there. He crept downstairs and saw no one, but the French doors leading outside were open.

They were probably in the garage. Probably gawking at the pallets full of cash. He went to the open doors and peered outside. No one was on the deck. The rear garage door was open, and the lights were on inside, confirming his suspicions.

He looked through the door and saw Palmer. The other man's rifle was leaning against a pallet of cash. His mask was down, and he was holding a wad of money. He grinned at someone Carver couldn't see and threw the money in the air.

"Man, this is a massive score!"

"Hell yeah," a familiar voice said. "Let's connect with the others and get the truck backed up to the garage so we can load it."

"Can we even fit all this on the truck?" another familiar voice said.

"We can make two trips if we have to," Palmer said.

"We'll probably need three," one of the other men said.

They laughed. Carver couldn't blame them. They were possibly looking at the biggest score of their lives. They were riding high on a successful mission. But it was all a mirage. The bills weren't just fakes, they were bad fakes.

The moment they tried to pass them they'd be in trouble. They could probably explain it away as a counterfeit bust, but they were going to be real upset when they discovered the truth.

Carver was doing them a favor. A big favor. He was going to spare them the embarrassment and disappointment of finding out.

Palmer stepped toward the presumed location of the other men and disappeared behind a pallet. Carver gave him a second, then slipped inside and pressed his back to a pallet. He slid around the side.

Palmer and the other two men were talking and laughing. It sounded like they were cutting off the packing plastic so they could more easily move the cash bundles. Carver peered around the corner and was pleased by who he saw.

He'd been mistaken about the identities of the men upstairs, because his three favorite Bickham cops were standing right in front of him, Palmer, Davidson, and Morales. Their masks were off, and their guns were slung across their backs. They were also blocked in on all sides by pallets of counterfeit money.

Their body armor was the main issue. Carver had used all the powdered scopolamine to take down their friends upstairs, so he didn't have any left in the puffer. His Sig would do okay, but what would do even better was Palmer's rifle leaning on the pallet of cash just a few feet away.

Unfortunately, he'd have to step into the open to get it. The men were preoccupied with the cash, but they might see movement in their peripheral vision and instantly be on guard. Carver could move slowly and maybe avoid that altogether.

He took two slow steps into the open. Grabbed the rifle. It was already locked and loaded. It was an M4 CQB variant with a large suppressor on the end. He aimed it at the men just as Palmer seemed to realize something had moved.

Palmer turned toward Carver. Carver pulled down his mask and smiled. "Does anyone else smell marijuana in here?"

Davidson and Morales spun toward Carver, hands reaching for sidearms. Carver fired a shot that struck Davidson's sidearm. The bullet pinged off the metal.

"I'd appreciate it if you raised your hands," Carver said.

They raised their hands.

"What the hell do you think you're doing?" Palmer said. "We're officers of the law carrying out a search and seizure."

"You're bent cops working for or with the mob." Carver shrugged. "I saw what you did with those people in Beau's slaughterhouse."

Their eyes widened. "How in the hell did you see that?" Palmer said.

"Who were they?" Carver asked. "Were they connected to this house?"

Palmer stared sullenly at him.

Carver aimed low. "I can shoot off your foot if that'll make you talk."

Palmer licked his lips nervously. Clearly, he wasn't used to being on this end of a rifle. "We had intel they knew about the security on this place, so we picked them up. They claimed they didn't know anything."

"And you killed them anyway?"

"They saw our faces," Palmer said. "No choice."

"Because you're idiots." Carver sighed. Turned to Davidson and Morales. "I definitely smell marijuana. Looks like I'm going to have to seize everything you own."

"Look, maybe we can work something out," Davidson said. "You can have your money back plus interest, and we go our separate ways."

"You know, you're pretty good at butchering humans." Carver raised an eyebrow. "It makes me wonder how many people have been chopped up in Beau's slaughterhouse. Is that the only reason he had that place built?"

Palmer huffed. "What the hell do you want, Grayson, Bert, or whatever the hell your name really is?"

"Well, first of all I wanted to tell you that the money on these pallets is counterfeit." Carver pulled a bill from the pallet to his right. He hadn't seen the bills in the light, but now that he could, it was obvious that the paper was wrong, and it was missing the anti-counterfeiting strip. "I'm surprised you haven't realized that yet."

"He's lying," Morales said. "There's no way this is fake."

"Oh, it's fake, all right. And just so you know, I'm going to get all my money back tonight with interest. All I need from you is a security badge." He held out a hand. "So, toss them over."

"We didn't bring them inside, you idiot." Palmer laughed scornfully. "They're in the truck."

"Good to know." Carver figured he could question them all night, but he only had one more question to ask. "Where is the money stored and what kind of security do you have?"

"Go to hell," Palmer said. He shook his upraised arms back and forth. Moved his upper body while he spoke. It was a bad attempt at keeping Carver's attention focused on him while Davidson and Morales made a move.

The other men lunged for their rifles. Carver put Davidson down with a bullet through the bridge of his nose. He put a shot through Palmer's throat and struck Morales in the arm. Morales went down with a shout of pain.

Carver walked up to him. Their rifles were out of reach, so he pulled the man's sidearm out of the holster and tossed it. He rolled Morales over onto his back and jumped back in case the man had a knife.

Morales did indeed have a knife. The same one he'd used for cutting the plastic. He flailed wildly with it. "I'm going to kill you!"

Carver trained the rifle on him. "Tell me what I want to know, and I'll spare you."

"I don't believe you."

"Talk in five seconds, or it's over."

"Go to hell!" Morales climbed to his knees and lunged. Carver kicked him in the face. The knife fell on the floor with a clatter. He booted it to the side. Looked down at Morales. "One more chance."

Morales spat at him. Carver put a bullet in his head. He hadn't planned on them being so reluctant to give up information. He also hadn't planned to spare them if they told him what he wanted to know. It was better to put crooks like this out of other people's misery. Or something like that.

Carver slung the M4 on his back. He searched the bodies. No security badges. Palmer had been telling the truth about that. He'd have to go out front to the truck to get one. Then he could neutralize the other men and leave.

He could probably frame it as a firefight between the cops and Greg and Darla. A firefight that a couple of potheads had miraculously won without a scratch. It would be a masterful bit of misdirection.

He left the garage and closed the door. He went inside through the French doors. As he was stepping inside, something caught his peripheral vision. He crouched just inside the doorway and aimed the M4. He looked through the scope in night vision mode.

Five people were creeping up the deck stairs on the west side of the house. They wore black fatigues and were armed with HK416 rifles. They stacked up against the garage door. The leader twisted the handle.

They rushed inside. Suppressed rifles coughed. Apparently, they didn't realize the garage occupants were already dead or maybe they just wanted to be sure. One thing was certain.

Someone else was here and they weren't taking any prisoners.

Chapter 36

Carver quickly and quietly made his way up the deck stairs.

He didn't know who the newcomers were, and he didn't want to find out. He needed to get a security badge from the cops' truck. The pallets of cash might keep the newcomers occupied long enough for him to do that.

First, he needed to go upstairs and get a bird's-eye view of the situation on the ground outside. He hurried upstairs. He cut through the first bedroom on the right and took the balcony to the master bedroom. The six men were still there, still standing or lying where'd they'd been when he left.

The small pile of powdered scopolamine was gone, and the cloud had dispersed. Hopefully there wasn't anything in the air or Carver might end up drugging himself. He pulled his mask back up even though it wasn't designed for air filtration.

He went inside and tugged down the masks of the men. Archer, Sutton, and Raulerson were all there next to Beau's sons. None of them would be coming home for breakfast.

Carver searched their pockets. They probably weren't carrying their security badges, but it was best to check just in case. It'd save him a trip to their truck. Raulerson's wallet was in his front pocket.

Archer and Sutton weren't carrying anything. They'd probably left their personal items in the truck. He tucked Raulerson's wallet back into the man's pocket, then hurried to the balcony for a look at the front yard.

Something caught his ear. Something he couldn't quite put his finger on at first. He realized it was a faint whining. A very familiar whining. The whine of an electric motor. He looked up.

Carver put his monocular to his eye and saw several drones hovering in the air above the house. The drones had specialized baffles around their propellers to muffle the whine of their motors. The people who'd stormed into the garage were federal agents. No one else had access to this kind of tech.

They were watching Carver right now. He looked at the front driveway. A black high-top van had been backed in through the gate and parked next to the cops' SWAT truck. The back doors were open. That was the van the agents had arrived in. Someone was remotely controlling the drones and probably reporting Carver's position to them right now.

Had the feds planned to raid this place already and Carver had the bad luck of choosing the same date? It seemed unlikely. It seemed more likely that someone had been keeping an eye on him and followed him here.

He ran back into the house. Sutton stood there gazing blankly at the wall. The others were doing mostly the same thing. Carver tried an experiment. "Go outside and shoot the drones."

Sutton's mouth dropped open and a long string of drool stretched from his mouth to his chest. None of the others moved.

Carver tried something else. "Walk forward."

Raulerson took a step forward and fell onto the mattress. They'd either been overdosed, or the drug didn't work the same on everyone. Carver raised Sutton's rifle. "Hold it there." He released it and Sutton held it in place.

He turned off the bedroom lights. He went outside, targeted the nearest drone through the night vision scope on Palmer's rifle. Fired. The drone flipped sideways and tumbled out of the air.

Carver took aim at the next one. He shattered a propeller. The drone dropped into the trees. The last drone dipped and dodged. It dropped out of sight on the other side of the house. Carver checked for other drones and saw none.

He heard footsteps coming down the hallway. He strapped the M4 to his back and slid down the fire escape ladder to the ground. He'd go into the truck for a security badge, then book it down the street to the Crown Vic.

He ran to the truck and jumped into the back. There were unlocked locker boxes beneath the bench seats. He opened them one by one and found Sutton's and Archer's wallets, security badges, and two sets of keys inside the last one. He stuffed them in his satchel.

There were no extra uniforms inside. That was inconvenient, but he could find Sutton's address from his driver's license and pick up a uniform from there. He jumped out of the back of the truck and considered ramming it through the wooden fence.

Taking the truck back to Bickham would be better than the Crown Vic because no one would give it a second look if they saw it entering the rear gate at the police station. Anyone watching the camera feeds would immediately flag the Crown Vic as suspicious. Or maybe they wouldn't.

An engine roared. Seconds later, the rear end of a black van smashed through the wooden fence on the west side of the house. Another one smashed through from the east side. More federal agents were arriving. Why they were so late to the party was anyone's guess.

Carver ran around the side of the house. Taking the truck was no longer an option. His only option was to climb over the back fence. Even if he made it, it was probably too late. They probably had him boxed in from all sides.

A rifle coughed. A bullet splintered the fence to Carver's left. He rolled sideways under the balcony. He smashed open a window with the butt of the M4, not because he was going inside, but because he wanted them to think he had.

Men shouted from the front yard. Someone up on the balcony shouted in surprise. "Who the hell are they?"

Two things got Carver's attention. The first was that the first group of newcomers didn't know who the second group was. The second was that he recognized the voice.

Carver took a gamble. "Rich, is that you?"

"What the hell?" Rich said. "That's Carver!"

"Is Jericho with you?"

"Who?"

"You know him as Tom."

A new voice spoke. "Hello, Carver."

"Jericho, I know we didn't part on the best of terms, but I suggest a temporary alliance until we get out of this. Agreed?"

He didn't hesitate. "Agreed."

"I suggest rear exfiltration."

"They probably have it covered."

"There were three drones. I took down two of them."

"I took down the third." He paused. "We'll come to you."

"Use the fire escape ladder at the north end of the balcony, but hurry."

A moment later, he saw five figures hurrying down the ladder. The last one was having a hard time sliding down the ladder. That was probably Rich. They hurried to him. There was no sign of the latest newcomers. They were probably forming up at the front, playing it safe before rushing around both sides of the house.

Jericho reached him first. "Sitrep?"

"Six men in the house incapacitated. Three deceased in the garage. I noticed drones overhead and thought they were yours."

"Not ours. Probably NSA."

"NSA?" Carver frowned. "Why would a money laundering house be an NSA target?"

"Could be the FBI," Jericho said, but it didn't sound like he believed it.

"Agreed." Carver hurried to the back fence and looked for rotten slats that would be easiest to break through. Going over the top would just leave them open to anyone waiting on the other side. Going through a hole would let them remain low to the ground.

"Drone," a female said. Her face was hidden, but it sounded like Alicia.

"If you have a shot, take it," Jericho said.

"It went behind the house before I could shoot. They have our location."

Carver rammed a shoulder against the old wood. Two planks broke off. He found a newer fence just on the other side. Apparently, the neighbor had built a fence of his own. Bullets splintered the fence not far from them, but they were way off target.

A voice rang out through a megaphone. "You are surrounded. By order of the US government, you will surrender yourselves now."

"How many?" Jericho said.

Rich was suddenly in Carver's face. "Carver, what in the hell is going on? Why are you here?"

"That's not important right now. Survive first, talk later." Carver turned to Jericho. "Two vans one on either side of the driveway. Probably ten men in each van."

"No visual."

Carver shook his head. "No visual."

Jericho looked up. "We need an eye in the sky."

"On it." Alicia ran up the stairs to the back deck. She jumped up, grasped a window ledge. Jumped up and grabbed the gutter. She pulled herself up to the flat roof and dropped low.

Carver saw the drone peeking over the house again. He aimed and fired on pure reflex. The bullet winged the drone, and it went down before it was high enough to see Alicia on the roof.

"You always were a good shot," Jericho said.

Carver watched Alicia through the scope. She vanished from sight, then returned a moment later. She flashed ten fingers and pointed toward the front left of the house. Flashed ten again and pointed to the front right. She pointed directly back and to the sides and made a circle with her hand.

Jericho held up his fist to signal for her to wait. "We're not surrounded. They think they have us fenced in."

"They think right," Rich said. "We can't shoot our way through ten federal agents even if we wanted to."

"Maybe we don't have to." Carver had an idea. "Be right back."

"I'm coming with you." Jericho turned to his team. "Hold tight." He signaled for Alicia to come down. She met them on the deck.

"What's on the other side of the fence?" Carver asked her.

"The back fence is blocked by the neighbor's fence." She wiped sweat from her forehead. "The east and west sides are clear."

Jericho nodded. "Make a hole on the east side but wait for our signal."

She frowned. "What will the signal be?"

"You'll know it when you hear it." Carver stepped into the house.

Jericho laughed. "That's cliché even for you, Carver."

The voice echoed on the megaphone again. "You have one minute to comply with our order. Then we will come for you and use lethal force."

Carver ran upstairs, Jericho right on his heels. He went to the master bedroom. It was pitch black inside. He went to the big picture window and shoved the curtains aside. Light poured in from a spotlight outside.

Jericho crouched next to Raulerson and checked his pulse. "What in the hell did you do to these men?"

"Ancient Chinese secret." Carver reached a hand to Raulerson. "Take my hand." Raulerson took his hand. Carver yanked him to his feet. "Get the others on their feet."

Jericho went to the other two men on the floor. Carver grabbed the mattress and dragged it out of the way so there was a clear path to the windows. He arranged the docile men into a line. He turned them toward the large windows on the north side of the bedroom overlooking the front yard.

"You used devil's breath on these poor bastards, didn't you?" Jericho looked amused. "Nothing else works like this."

"Yes, but I think I overdosed them."

Jericho's grin grew wider. "I see where you're going with this."

Carver went to the drugged men. "Raise your rifles."

The men raised their rifles. Archer and Sutton raised them into firing position. Raulerson didn't move. Beau's sons looked like they were trying but having difficulties.

"Man, they're so high and in the worst way." Jericho laughed. "Damn, it's been a while since I've had this much fun."

"Walk to the window and fire your guns at the glass," Carver said.

Archer, Sutton, and Raulerson moved stiffly forward like robots. Beau's two oldest sons trudged forward. The youngest son stood still and drooled. Carver gave him a gentle push forward and he started walking.

Sutton and Archer started shooting at the window. Tempered glass puckered and crumbled. Raulerson started shooting a moment later. The other three didn't seem capable of pulling their triggers.

Return gunfire started almost immediately. Archer fell over backward, his finger stuck on the trigger. His rifle fired full auto until the magazine went empty. Sutton spun and went down with a dozen holes in his armored vest.

Raulerson walked right up to the broken glass and fell through it, plummeting out of sight. Beau's sons shook like puppets whose strings were being controlled by someone having a seizure. Despite that, they went down without even a cry of pain. It was eerie as hell.

Someone outside was shouting to cease fire, but it took a few moments before the trigger-happy agents complied. There was a command to breach the front door. Carver and Jericho were already running down the hallway, downstairs, and out the back.

Alicia and the others were huddled behind the bushes near the fence. There was a ragged hole in the wood. She saw them coming and grinned. "I heard your signal."

"Let's go." Jericho waved them toward the hole. "I think the feds will be busy for a while."

Nadia pulled down her mask. "What the hell happened?"

"Talk later." Jericho ducked through the hole.

Carver went to the hole, but Rich got in his way and put a hand on his chest. "You can go last."

Carver didn't have time for idiocy, so he grabbed Rich and threw him bodily through the hole, then went through after him. Rich was in a heap on the other side. Carver stepped over him and went to Jericho. "Before you decide to follow through on your promises, we need to talk."

"Promises?" Jericho grinned. "You mean about killing you the next time we met?"

"Yeah."

"As much as I'd like to gut you, it can wait."

Carver nodded. "Leon can give you some information that might change your mind."

"Leon?" He raised an eyebrow. "You're still in touch with the kid?"

"From time to time. He's doing his own thing now."

"Apparently, so are you." Jericho looked at Rich and back to Carver. "Meet me at Hope House and we'll talk."

"Which one? Bickham or Chicago?"

"You already know about the rec center, don't you?"

"Maybe."

Jericho chuckled. "Meet there at noon tomorrow."

"The cash in the house is counterfeit, by the way."

"Yeah, I figured it out within a minute of inspecting a bill." He shook his head. "All that for nothing." He didn't seem all that disappointed, but that was just Jericho being Jericho.

"Okay." Carver started walking backwards, not quite willing to take his eyes off Jericho. "See you at noon."

"Yep. High noon." Jericho made finger guns and fired them at Carver. He circled a finger above his head and his group hurried away through the neighborhood.

Carver circled back around to the Crown Vic. It looked like the invading feds had taken the bait and were all inside the house. They'd figure out real soon that the bodies inside weren't the ones they were looking for.

In fact, Carver knew exactly why they were there and who'd sent them. The only question was how they knew where to find him. He hadn't been followed, at least not by car. He wasn't being tracked, at least not with something stuck to a car or in his phone.

It was more likely that he'd been tracked by satellite or high-altitude drone. Carver was good at evading tracking but only if he knew about it. He probably should have considered it as a possibility given the interaction that triggered this entire visit.

Carver didn't know if the Crown Vic was a burned asset, so he didn't get into it or drive it away. He focused instead on the black SUV parked across the street from the target house. He dodged through back yards and went to the back of the house the SUV was parked in front of.

He saw a figure jogging across the road to the SUV. It wasn't a fully armed special agent. It was a guy in a suit. A guy Carver knew. The man got inside the SUV. Carver used night vision on his monocular to confirm the man was alone.

He kept to the darkness at the side of the house and low walked to the SUV. He opened the passenger side door and pointed his Sig at the man inside. The man's eyes went wide as dinner plates.

"What the hell?"

Carver got in. Closed the door. "Hello, Barry. Let's go for a ride."

Chapter 37

Rich was pissed.

They were crossing through the woods just across the street from the money laundering house and he was already exhausted.

"We had Carver right there!" Rich stopped to catch his breath. "Why didn't we take him out?"

"Because I gave him my word." Tom crouched and looked around. He stared at the agents swarming the house they'd just escaped from.

"We don't owe him anything," Rich said. "We should have taken him prisoner at least."

Tom shook his head. "We formed a temporary alliance to survive, and now it's over. Don't worry, okay?"

"I just don't like it." Rich huffed. "Are we going to teach him a lesson tomorrow?"

Tom peered through his rifle scope. He watched the activity around the house. "Alicia, go to the next street over and find us new wheels. The rest of you go help her. I'm going to keep an eye on things here."

"Yes, sir." Alicia turned north. "Let's go."

Rich begrudgingly turned and followed her. They hustled through the woods to the next road over. There weren't many vehicles parked on the road because most of the houses had driveways or garages.

Keith finally spotted an old construction truck with a crew cab and an eight-foot bed. He looked it over and nodded. "Nineteen eighty-three Chevy. I can hotwire one of these."

"Not exactly hard to do," Alicia said with a grin.

Rich didn't know how she could smile. The operation had been a total bust. And why were none of them talking about the Bickham cops being there? Had Carver lured them there and killed them? None of it made any sense.

Keith slid a slim-jim between the truck's window and door frame and popped the lock within seconds. He got inside, stripped some wires with his knife, and touched two wires together to start the engine.

Everyone piled in. He drove them down the street. A figure emerged from the woods on the right-hand side and got in. It was Jericho and he was grinning.

"How can you look so happy at a time like this?" Nadia said. "This mission was FUBAR!"

"Things don't always work out." He turned to Keith. "We have a stash about ten minutes away. Let's go there and pick up our wheels."

"Yes, sir." Keith checked the maps app on his phone and plugged in an address.

"Is no one going to answer my question?" Nadia said.

"I have the same questions," Rich said. "What in the hell is going on?"

"Sometimes things don't work out." Tom turned to look at them in the back seat. "We'll debrief later."

Rich worked his jaw back and forth. "Do we call you Tom or Jericho?"

"Tom is best for now," Tom said. "No more questions for now. We'll sort this out later."

"But—"

Tom's face grew deadly serious. "Rich, do you want to continue to be a part of this operation?"

"Yes, sir."

Tom nodded. "Then follow orders."

Rich saluted. "Yes, sir."

Nadia squeezed Rich's hand once and released it. It looked like the ride back to Chicago would be long and quiet.

Carver aimed his Sig at Barry.

He should have known better than to trust anyone from the NSA even if they claimed to be a friend of a friend.

"Start driving, Barry. We need to talk."

Barry tried to play it tough. "You realize I've got a whole unit with me, Carver? That I can have them on you in seconds?"

"I realize that you could be dead in a split second if you don't start driving right now."

Barry worked his jaw back and forth. He shifted into drive and accelerated. "Look, I can explain—"

"I know you can. But first, I want to know what you've done with Liana." The only reason Carver had listened to Barry in the first place was because he supposedly had a message from Liana. He'd been lying. Pieces of the truth were already falling into place, but he wanted to hear it straight from Barry's lips.

"Liana is fine."

"She's alive?"

"Yes."

"I want proof. I want to know where you're holding her."

"What makes you think we're holding her?"

Carver pointed to an empty parking lot at a strip mall. "Pull over here."

"Why?"

Carver drew his knife and pressed it to Barry's leg. "Because I said so."

Barry pulled into the parking lot.

"Get out."

Barry struggled to undo his seatbelt. Carver slid out and hurried around the front of the car. Barry jumped out of the vehicle and reached for the holster on his waist.

Carver waggled a finger. "Don't test me."

Barry stopped reaching for his sidearm and held up his hands. Carver took the pistol and tossed it into the SUV. He grabbed Barry by the back of the neck.

"Ow!" Barry whimpered. "Not so hard!"

Carver ignored his pleas and guided him around the back of the strip mall and next to the dumpsters.

"You are going to tell me everything. You are going to tell me the truth. If you don't, they'll find your body in this dumpster." Carver pressed the tip of his knife against Barry's throat. "Understood?"

Barry gulped. "I'm trained to resist torture. I'm not a vanilla civilian."

"It's okay. I've had experience with all types." Carver grabbed Barry by the throat and slammed him against the dumpster. "Where is Liana being held?"

Barry gasped in pain. "I don't know. That's the truth!"

"Who knows?" Carver tightened his grip on Barry's neck.

"Operations division manager, Esther Childs," Barry gasped. "I'm just the field agent assigned to this operation."

"Who's your primary target? Me or Jericho?"

"Jericho is dead!" Barry's eyes went wide as if he was surprised.

Carver knew better. "Don't play games. You put him on the list as deceased because you wanted me to think he was dead.

Barry trembled. "What makes you think Jericho has anything to do with this?"

"Because you knew where I was all this time. You could have come for me whenever you wanted." Carver narrowed his eyes. "You knew that telling me Rich Polaski was on the watchlist would trigger a response. You knew he was the only one on the list that I would try to warn."

Carver continued. "Jericho manipulated Rich's life. He arranged the civil forfeiture and probably other events leading up to Rich joining his group of mercenaries or whatever they are. You knew about the civil forfeiture seizure and timed it so I would arrive right after that crucial event. You knew Jericho would be somewhere nearby and wanted to use me as bait because you know he wants to kill me."

Barry said nothing.

Carver slammed him against the dumpster again. "How close am I?"

"You're close, okay?" Barry gasped. "Shortly after Scion was disbanded, Jericho began investigating on his own. He wanted to find out what really happened. He thought you were involved as a pawn in a bigger scheme. That maybe you got paid to do it."

"And what did he discover?" Carver said.

"We don't know. He was working a lot of angles we didn't even know about. He somehow got lists of former soldiers with PTSD and other issues. He knew they were required to go to VA psychologists, so he'd visit various VA hospitals and find people he could radicalize."

Carver wasn't surprised. "Sounds like something Jericho would do."

Barry pried Carver's fingers. "Can you let me breathe?"

Carver released his throat. "Keep going."

"Jericho used disgruntled military vets to carry out attacks against people he thought were involved in the conspiracy that caused Scion to be disbanded. He has since expanded operations to create an entire network of specialists, operators, and more who will gladly die for him. He's a domestic terrorist that needs to be stopped."

"He's a threat to Enigma and other shadow organizations like them." Carver shrugged. "Not a terrorist."

"He's a bigger threat than Leon Fry." Barry massaged his throat. "We found out how he was recruiting people. We found out that Rich Polaski was on his list and that he was getting ready to harvest him, so to speak, by making a deal with the Bickham cops to raid and seize all his property. They would then direct him to Hope House and the radicalization would start there."

Jericho always played the long game. He started small, planting ideas in people's heads and letting those ideas grow and fester for years before manipulating events to send them off the deep end. Once that happened, he was in control of them.

It was insidious, but genius. Carver didn't have the patience for that kind of thing. Some people played the long game. Jericho played an even longer game. Carver folded his arms over his chest. "You knew Jericho hated me so you sent me in hoping that would cause him to make a mistake."

Carver thought about the events at the house. How Jericho's crew had been completely surprised by the NSA raid. Jericho had remained calm. He seemed to be having fun. A very big puzzle piece clicked into place.

Carver blew out a breath. "Son of a bitch." He backed up and looked around. "Jericho, where the hell are you?"

Jericho walked around the corner, a grin on his face. "How did you know?"

"You both used me as bait, didn't you?" Carver holstered his gun. Jericho could have killed him at any time over the last few minutes and he hadn't. Plus, he probably wasn't alone. Shooting his way out wasn't the answer. Not yet anyway.

"Maybe." Jericho's grin widened.

Carver looked from one man to the other. "Barry used me to find Jericho. Jericho used me to draw out the people hunting for him. Looks like you both won."

Barry shrank back. "Carver, don't leave me with him. I'll tell you anything you want to know."

"Hope House provided the Bickham cops with the tip about the money laundering house." Carver shook his head. "You were luring the cops there. What I don't get is how you knew I'd be there too."

"You give me way too much credit, Carver." Jericho laughed. "When I found out the cops tried to kill Rich, I decided to kill them. I have a contact who provides me with insider information about government money laundering. He told me about the counterfeit money at one of these cash houses and I decided to use it as bait."

"You planned to draw them out, kill them, and make it look like a bust gone wrong?"

"More or less." He grinned. "Hell, I even put on a good show for the others. We broke into the man's condo and interrogated him. He played his part flawlessly."

Barry gasped. "You did that to trick your own people?"

"Alicia and Keith are in the know. But I like to test my new recruits." Jericho shrugged. "I had other plans for you, Carver. Yes, I wanted to use you to lure out any federal agencies looking for me, but the last thing I expected was to arrive at my own bait house and find out you were already using it."

"Sorry to ruin your plans." Carver was relieved to know he'd surprised Jericho. "I still managed to do what you wanted. I got the NSA to expose themselves."

"Yes, you did. Just at the completely wrong time." Jericho burst into laughter. "That was fun, though, wasn't it? Drugging the cops with scopolamine and making them commit suicide by NSA agent was a genius move."

"You did what?" Barry looked horrified. "Those were cops my men shot?"

Carver ignored him. "That wasn't my plan. I was going to frame it as a bust gone wrong, just like you'd planned."

"Yeah, well I guess we all learned a valuable lesson today, didn't we?" He glared at Barry. "Even the best laid plans don't always pan out." He laughed. "Barry played you, Carver. I played Barry and Rich. But in the end, you sniffed out all the bullshit and came out smelling like a rose."

"Did I?" Carver wasn't so sure just yet.

Barry shivered. "Maybe we can work something out."

"I don't think so." Jericho slid a knife from somewhere on his thigh. Probably a sheath woven into the black fatigues. "First, I'm going to take care of Carver, and then you."

Barry's face went sheet white. "B-but—"

"Shh." Jericho put a finger to his own lips. "Wait your turn, Barry boy."

"I don't want to fight you." Carver didn't draw his knife. "I want to know where Liana is. I want her released unharmed, and then I'll go back to living on the beach and you can do whatever it is you're doing."

"I don't think so," Jericho said.

"Rocker and Menendez framed me for the sex trafficking." Carver held out his hands. "I'm not the reason Scion was disbanded."

"Carver, you were a pawn. A paid henchman. Of that, I am certain." Jericho whirled the knife in his hand. "I want to know how involved you were with the plan. I want to torture it out of you just for fun."

Carver shook his head. "I wasn't a pawn in anyone's plan. I was a patsy. Like I said, Rocker and Menendez were the ones who set it up. They did it as part of a broader plan to privatize U.S. special forces. Companies like Breakstone were right at the center of it."

Carver looked around. Jericho might have his people surrounding them already. There might be nowhere to go. "Leon can confirm everything."

"Leon's an impressionable kid with a heart of gold. He'll want to protect you no matter what." Jericho shook his head. "Don't worry, Carver, I didn't bring along anyone else. I can handle this on my own." Jericho moved with lightning-fast speed and swept Barry's feet from beneath him. He flipped the man on his stomach and hogtied him with nylon straps.

Jericho leaned down and spoke into Barry's ear. "You NSA types think you're so smart, don't you? You think all that fancy surveillance tech gives you an insurmountable advantage. But it doesn't." He stood and brushed off his hands. The knife suddenly appeared in his grasp again. "Barry, we'll have a long, painful talk after I finish this."

Barry wriggled. "No, please!"

Carver sighed. Maybe it was best to finish this here and now, no matter the outcome. He drew his knife. Braced himself for Jericho's first move. It came an instant later, a quick strike toward his stomach.

The knife was in Jericho's other hand, not the one coming at Carver's stomach. It was a feint. A trick Jericho used many times to force his opponent to block low while the knife came in high. Carver didn't block. He sidestepped. The fist missed his midriff, and the knife missed his throat.

Jericho's knife switched directions, going for Carver's chest. Carver thrust out a forearm and struck Jericho's wrist. He simultaneously thrust out with a knee and caught the other man on the hip. It was a glancing blow, but it was more than enough to throw Jericho off balance.

Jericho stumbled but quickly recovered. He spun. Ducked. Rammed the knife toward Carver's thigh. Carver shifted away but not fast enough. The knife sliced open his pants and carved a line in his flesh.

They danced and parried each other, each time Jericho avoiding injury while delivering a nick or cut to Carver. Carver gritted his teeth. The cuts hurt, but that wasn't why he was gritting his teeth. He was getting angry. Frustrated. He'd sparred with Jericho. Fought the man. It was like trying to grab a greased pig except the pig had a weapon.

Jericho flipped the knife to his other hand and slashed upward. It slashed open a tear in Carver's other pants leg and left another long cut. Jericho grinned and backed up a step. He whirled the knife as if it were a natural extension of his body.

"You're big and strong, Carver, but brute force can't win against speed and cunning." Jericho paced around him. "You're going to bleed out before you ever get your hands on me."

Carver checked his wounds. So far, Jericho hadn't struck an artery. Probably because he was just playing with him. Jericho was much smaller and lighter than Carver. He was much faster. He was better trained at martial arts.

Jericho dashed toward him. Carver fended off a flurry of attacks but came away with cuts on his arms and a new hole in his shirt. He was bleeding from multiple wounds now, none of them major in and of themselves, but together, they would start to drain him.

Blocking the attacks was just postponing the inevitable. Sometimes, the only way to defeat an enemy was to accept a certain level of injury. That wasn't something Rhodes or Joe had told him. He couldn't remember where he'd heard it. Maybe he'd read it somewhere. Maybe he'd just made it up on the spot.

There had been times when he'd faced a superior opponent. Someone who could fight better or had the upper hand. His only choice had been to go down swinging. Just like Tony had. That was why he had scars from bullet wounds. He was going to have a lot more scars by the time this was over.

Jericho came at him again. Carver didn't block this time. He lunged straight at the other man, not even trying to avoid the next attack. What would have been another slash from Jericho's knife went straight into Carver's side. The blade dug into Carver's flesh but glanced off his rib bones like God intended.

Carver wrapped Jericho in a bear hug and squeezed. Jericho gasped and flailed. Carver squeezed harder and harder until he heard bones cracking. The knife clattered on the asphalt.

Carver released Jericho but immediately punched him in the gut. The other man doubled over and went down. He rolled onto his side, gasping for breath. He laughed and groaned. "You lucky son of a bitch."

"It's not luck." Carver was starting to feel a little lightheaded from the blood loss. He looked down at his rib. There was a lot of blood. The glancing blow had still done some damage. His thigh was bleeding a lot too.

A white cloud puffed from a slash in his satchel. Apparently, some of the scopolamine powder had spilled out of the puffer and into the satchel. He opened the satchel and saw that the puffer bulb had been cut open. It apparently still had a pinch or two of the drug still left in it.

Carver stood over Jericho. "I had nothing to do with sex trafficking women. I was a patsy, not a pawn, not a henchman."

Jericho struggled to rise. "I don't believe you."

"I don't care." Carver took a pinch of devil's breath from the sliced puffer bulb and sprinkled it in Jericho's face.

Jericho went slack. His eyes turned glassy. He was down for the count.

Carver groaned. He stripped off his shirt. Tugged down his pants. He tore his shirt to strips and formed a tourniquet. It looked like a deep cut in his thigh was bleeding the heaviest. The other wounds weren't a threat.

He tightened the tourniquet just enough to stanch the bleeding. He didn't want to cut off all circulation to his leg. He walked around the corner of the building and found the car Jericho had arrived in. It was a black Tesla Model X, an electric vehicle. That was why he hadn't heard it coming. There was no engine noise to these things. They were whisper quiet.

It looked like the one Alicia had driven to Chicago, but the windows were tinted darker, and the wheels weren't as sporty. The tires were also all terrain.

Carver rolled Barry onto his side. "Hi."

Barry looked wildly around. "I thought you two were going to kill each other."

"That would save you a lot of trouble, wouldn't it?"

"No, you don't understand at all, Carver." Barry grimaced in pain. "We want Jericho dead, but we want to recruit you."

Carver laughed. "I'm supposed to believe that now?"

"Yes, because it's the truth."

"Then tell me what happened to Liana."

Barry winced. "She's in custody, but she's fine."

"You assholes told her she could return to her job. That everything was fine."

"We kind of lied."

"There is no kind of to it." Carver stood. "Wait here."

"What are you going to do to me?"

"What do you think I'm going to do to you?"

"Wait!" Barry struggled to move but being hog tied prevented him from doing much except squirming. "It's the truth! They plan to use Liana as leverage to get you to join us. We need your help rooting out Enigma."

Carver stopped walking He turned around. "What do you mean by that?"

"Enigma had the run of the agency for a while, but things have been changing thanks to you and Leon Fry." Barry craned his neck to look at Carver. "They're still everywhere, but there are some of us who aren't beholden to them. If we had an outside agent, we could turn this around completely."

Carver went to Jericho's car. The door handles were flush with the door panel. He didn't see a way to pull them open. He pushed on the handle to see if it tilted inward. It didn't, but the door opened all the way automatically. The car wasn't locked because the keycard was sitting on the center console.

The handles on the back doors were also flush with the door panel. He pushed on the handle and the door opened out and up like a giant wing. It was spacious inside. Apparently, the second row of seats had been taken out and the third row had been replaced by hardened nylon weapons crates that could double as a bench seat.

It had been reconfigured into a troop carrier that could hold six people in the back. Not only was it whisper quiet, but the wing doors made it easy for people to get into and out of. It still wasn't nearly as good as a van, but it certainly was much quieter than anything with a combustion engine.

That wasn't the only reason Jericho had chosen this vehicle. It blended into traffic. It looked like a normal civilian vehicle. People might look twice at it, but not for the wrong reasons. They'd look at it because it was sleek and luxurious. Windowless vans tended to draw people suspicions.

There were straps bolted to the floor. Straps that were obviously designed to secure prisoners for transport. Carver couldn't pretend to understand everything about the vehicle's purpose, but he didn't need to.

He drove the car around the building to Jericho and Barry. He strapped Jericho down to the floor. The man stared blankly. He was drooling slightly, bleeding, and it looked like he had a broken rib from Carver's hug, but he'd survive. Carver put Barry on the floor next to him.

It was time to get some answers.

Chapter 38

Carver parked the Tesla out of sight behind a dumpster.

The front bucket seats had been modified to swivel around, so he turned the seat to face Barry.

Barry spoke first. "Carver, what do you think about our offer?"

Carver ignored the question. "How did you find me at Myrtle Beach, and how long did you know where I was before you approached me?"

"I don't know."

Carver drew his knife. "I'm going to cut pieces off of you until you start answering my questions."

"I'm telling you the truth!"

Being hogtied meant Barry's hands were bound behind his back and connected to his ankles so he couldn't see his own hands. Carver grabbed Barry's hand. He pressed the dull side of the knife against the pinky finger and started cutting.

Barry screamed. "Stop! Stop! I'll tell you!"

"I'd better like the answer," Carver said.

"We got lucky. You walked in front of a bank window with high-resolution camera on the inside. The camera was pointed toward the window. That was the only time you were caught on camera, so we only knew that you were in town. It took two months to finally lay eyes on you." Barry whimpered. "I came up with the idea to recruit you because you were the only person who'd put a hurting on Enigma."

"Why are you against Enigma?" Carver said.

"Because they killed my girlfriend when I wouldn't play ball." He trembled violently. "I was approached by some low-level analyst who told me that he was my new handler and made it clear that I would do what I was told or suffer consequences."

"You refused?"

"Yes. And they killed my girlfriend of two years. Framed it as an overdose of fentanyl." He sobbed. "She never touched drugs in her life."

"Why are you holding Liana then?"

"Because I'm not the boss. My director thinks Liana is a threat unless you're on our side."

"I think you're lying. You want me to come in willingly. Liana is collateral, yes, but not the way you're framing it." Carver tried to consider all the angles but there were too many. "What about Jericho? Do you want him dead?"

"He's a former shadow asset gone rogue. He's one of the most dangerous people in the world besides..." He trailed off.

"Besides who?"

Barry worked his jaw back and forth. "Besides you and Leon Fry."

Carver laughed. It was a genuine laugh because that was the craziest thing he'd ever heard. "I'm a full-time beach bum. I'm not dangerous at all."

"Unless someone bothers you or prods you into action." Barry stared at him. "Scion was a legend in intelligence circles. It was one of the most successful units in history with some of the most dangerous people. And then someone killed the goose that laid the golden eggs."

"So, you know who was behind the bloodbath in the shadow ops community?"

Barry shook his head. "No, we only know who the lower-level players were. Sam Rocker and Tony Menendez were the rats in your unit. That was when Enigma and several other oligarch-backed groups began attacking the fabric of not just our country, but other western nations. We need help turning it around."

"Maybe Jericho or Leon would help you."

"We don't think anyone can control Jericho. He needs to be taken out. And Leon has been impossible to find or contact." Barry glanced at Jericho. "I still can't believe you beat him. Will you kill him?"

"No, I don't think so, even though it would be the smart move." Carver looked at Jericho. The other man was on his back staring blankly at the ceiling. "Jericho, tell me your plans."

Jericho looked at him. His face was slack, emotionless. "I plan to kill you." He said it in a monotone voice. "I plan to destroy the organization you worked for."

"How?" Carver said.

Jericho blinked. "I can't remember right now."

"How did you find me here? Did you follow me the entire way?"

"I saw you and Barry in the SUV. I put a magnetic GPS tracker on it. My crew stole a truck and took us to a local stash. I took this car and came to you."

Carver liked how well the scopolamine worked as a truth serum. He decided to see if it would allow him to make a suggestion or implant an idea in Jericho's head like hypnosis.

"Jericho, I did not help anyone destroy Scion. Sam Rocker and Tony Menendez did that. I was framed for everything. You will believe that."

Jericho blinked slowly. "I don't believe you."

"You will believe me," Carver said firmly.

"I do not believe you."

Apparently, scopolamine didn't work like hypnosis, but at least it had been worth a try.

"What the hell did you do to him?" Barry said.

Carver didn't answer. He rotated the driver's seat back to the front. "Jericho, where are Rich and the others?"

"They are headed to Hope House in Bickham. I told them I would meet them there."

"Okay." Carver still had a lot to do. He still had to decide if Jericho was going to live. He didn't want the man Barry described as the most dangerous person in the world coming after him, but he also hated to kill someone as skilled and valuable as Jericho. He was an S-tier operator. You didn't just discard people like that especially when your goals were somewhat aligned.

Carver dug out the drivers' licenses he'd taken from the Bickham cops. He plugged Sutton's address into the GPS and aimed the Tesla in that direction. He reached the house forty minutes later. It was on the outskirts of town not far from Beau's place. There were no cars in the driveway and the house was dark.

Sutton's little slice of Bickham was a white, two-story farmhouse with board and batten siding. There was a detached three-car garage to the side. It was a real nice place. Too nice to afford on a small-town cop salary. Sutton probably hadn't paid a dime for it. He might have gotten it for free through civil forfeiture.

"Where the hell are we?" Barry said.

"Quick stop. I'll be right back." Carver examined the house for cameras. There were none that he could see. The doorbell was just a normal doorbell. He used the keys he'd taken from Sutton's truck locker and opened the front door.

The house was nice and modern. It looked and smelled newly renovated. Either the furniture was new, or it was hardly used. Carver kept a mask over his face just in case there were cameras and went to the master bedroom.

The room was clean as a whistle. The bed sheets were neatly made and tucked tight as a bunk in a military barracks. The closet was nice and neat too. There were multiple sets of patrolman blues and multiple sets of SWAT fatigues like what the cops had worn to the cash house. Those would do just fine.

He went to the bathroom and checked out his wounds. Jericho had gotten him pretty good. He had slashes all over the place. Only the cuts on the thigh and ribs were deep enough to worry about. Carver searched for something to dress his wounds because he didn't want to get his new clothing bloody.

There was thick cotton gauze, liquid bandage, and medical tape under the bathroom sink. A lot of it. Why Sutton had so much was a mystery. Did he have his own dirty secrets like Tony had? Having seen the way he casually shot that woman and her boyfriend in Beau's barn, it wouldn't surprise Carver in the least.

Carver took a quick shower to wash off the dried blood. He dried with one of Sutton's towels and got blood all over it. He didn't like leaving DNA behind, so he'd have to take the towel with him.

He dressed the rib and thigh wounds with liquid bandage to keep them from bleeding, then taped gauze over both wounds. He used liquid bandage on the smaller wounds as well until he wasn't bleeding anymore. Then he cleaned up the mess and tossed everything into a kitchen garbage bag.

Carver returned to Sutton's closet. He tried on the black cargo pants. The stretchy material fit like a glove. The shirt fit perfectly too. He grabbed a suitcase from the shelf and put all the SWAT uniforms into it. He took what little civilian clothing there was as well.

He looked through the rest of the house. There was a large gun closet with three M4 carbines inside, all identically configured to the one Carver had taken from the cops. There was a long duffel bag folded inside the gun case. Carver put the weapons and ammo into the bag and took it as well.

There was a black iron door at the back of the gun closet that was locked. Carver unlocked it with a key on Sutton's keychain and flipped on the light switch on the other side. Stairs led down to a basement. He heard what sounded like an air conditioner running loudly below.

Carver had flashbacks to Tony's basement. He went downstairs and into a large open basement. The walls and floor were painted glossy white. The surface felt slick. Like it was more of a coating than paint. Probably made cleanup easy. But cleanup for what?

A large white tarp covered something with a distinctly cube-like shape in the middle of the room. A long flexible duct ran from beneath the tarp and over to what looked like a portable air conditioning system against the wall. The AC unit was the source of the loud noise he'd heard.

He pulled the tarp off the cube. Beneath it was a large plexiglass box. More accurately, it was a cage. There was a girl inside. A girl with cuts and bruises and a lot of gauze and bandages all over her.

Carver knew the girl. It was Jen from the diner. She covered her eyes and winced as they adjusted from the total darkness beneath the tarp to the brilliant basement lights. There was a heavy metal bar over the cell door. He slid it off and opened the door.

"Please, no more!" She cowered in the corner. "Please! I'll do whatever you want, just let me go." She started sobbing.

"I'm not Sutton." Carver knelt next to her. "I'm the guy from the diner the other day."

She blinked and shielded her eyes. Her forehead furrowed. "The big guy?"

"Yeah." He didn't touch her. That was probably the last thing she wanted after being abused by Sutton for however long he'd had her here. A day at least.

She flung herself at him and hugged him. "Oh, God. I thought I was going to die down here." She sobbed uncontrollably. "Help me."

Carver picked her up in a cradle carry. She was thin and light. He carried her upstairs and took her into the garage. He didn't want her to see what he had inside the Tesla. He didn't want her to remember him at all, but it was probably too late for that.

It turned out Sutton did have a personal vehicle. It was an SUV identical to the police interceptor, except it was completely civilian. Carver found the keys. He put Jen in the passenger seat, then got into the driver's seat. He backed the SUV out of the garage, past the Tesla, and onto the road. He closed the garage door with the remote.

He turned to Jen. "It's really important that you drive yourself home, okay? And it's important that you never tell anyone that I saved you. If you need to give a description, make something up."

She looked confused. "But, why?"

"Because the cops in this town are crazy, okay? I don't want to be a target."

"Yeah, they are. And Sutton is going to come after me again once he realizes I'm gone."

"Can you leave town? Maybe go stay with relatives somewhere else?"

She shook her head. "No. If we leave, they'll hunt us down. We have to be one big happy family, or they'll hurt us." She started sobbing again.

Carver gripped her arm. "Jen, Sutton and the others are dead, okay? They tried to raid a drug money house earlier and died in a firefight. They're all dead."

She gasped. "What? Are you serious?"

He nodded.

Her tears dried. She started laughing. "They're dead?"

"All of them."

"Oh my God, I can't believe it!" She laughed hysterically. "This can't be real!"

"It is real. You need to drive yourself home and do what I told you, okay? Forget all about me. Never mention me. Got it?"

She stopped laughing and nodded fervently. "Whatever you want, Mister. I owe you my life."

Carver got out. Jen slid into the driver's seat. She blew him a kiss then drove away. Carver went back into the house. He put the tarp back over the plexiglass cube. He closed and locked the basement door. He sprayed bleach cleaner in the shower and around the sink to eliminate as much of his DNA as possible.

He took the kitchen bag with his bloody clothes and towel and used gauze out to the car. He took the duffel bag and everything else he'd liberated from Sutton's house to the car. Then he locked up the house behind him. He opened the rear door and put everything inside the Tesla.

"Where in the hell have you been all this time?" Barry said. "You've been gone thirty minutes."

"My stomach was upset, so I had to make a pit stop." Carver backed out of Sutton's driveway and aimed for his next destination.

Barry struggled against his restraints. "I heard another car. I heard you talking to someone. Who was it?"

Carver didn't answer. He pulled into the circular drive at Hope House ten minutes later. He checked the magazine in Sutton's M4 to make sure it was full. Rich, Alicia, Keith, and Nadia exited the front door and stared at the Tesla as if they'd been expecting it to arrive.

The windows were darkly tinted so they couldn't see inside. Carver could see them just fine. They looked worried. Probably because Jericho had split from the group to do his own thing, or maybe because their op at the cash house had gone so badly.

Most importantly, none of them were armed. Carver got out.

"What the hell?" Rich nearly fell over backwards.

Carver hurried around the front of the Tesla, the M4 at the low and ready.

Keith put his hands up. "Is Tom dead?"

Tears filled Alicia's eyes. "You son of a bitch!"

"You mean Jericho?" Carver shook his head. "He's fine."

Rich stared the bandages on Carver's arms. "Did Tom do that?"

"Yep." Carver nodded at the Tesla. "Open the rear passenger door."

Rich pressed the handle. The door rose up and out like a wing. Jericho was still lying on the floor staring blankly. Barry was hogtied right next to him.

"What the hell?" Rich stared at Carver. "What's wrong with him?"

"He's just a little drugged. Nothing big."

"Nothing big?" Rich started loosening Jericho's bonds. "He looks catatonic."

Carver checked the time. He needed to speed things along. "Jericho, did you have an agreement with the Bickham police to raid Rich's house and seize his assets?"

"Yes," Jericho said.

"Have you been manipulating the lives of veterans so they'll join your cause?"

"Yes."

Rich staggered back like he'd been struck.

Nadia gasped. "What the hell?" She got in Jericho's face. "Did you manipulate my life too?"

"Yes," Jericho said.

"He's on some kind of truth serum," Rich said.

Carver waggled a hand. "Something like that." He noticed Alicia and Keith weren't shocked by the revelations. "Are you in on it or just okay with it?"

"Tom—Jericho tried to manipulate me, but I caught on," Alicia said. "I told him I'd willingly help destroy our broken system. Nothing has changed."

"Jericho told me what he'd done." Keith shrugged. "I told him he broke me out of an endless cycle of depression and self-pity. He gave me a new life and I'm thankful for it. Nothing you say about him will change that."

Rich glared at Carver. "You know what? I'm fine with it too. My life was crap until Tom intervened. I'm with him no matter what."

Nadia looked uncertain but nodded. "Yeah, me too. Regardless of how I got here, I like Tom, or whatever his real name is." She looked at Jericho. "What's your real name?"

"Thomas Jericho," Jericho said.

Rich hauled Jericho out of the car. He groaned and winced in pain, struggling against his bad shoulder and knee.

"He can stand on his own," Carver said.

"Okay, so why did you bring him back to us?" Alicia strode toward Carver. "You know damned well he wants to kill you." She nodded at the bandaged wounds on Carver's hands and arms. "Looks like he was taking his time with it."

Carver lowered the M4. "I just don't want to kill him. He's a rare individual. An agent of chaos."

Rich frowned. "Sounds like you admire him."

"I do, but not in the way I admired Joe or my former commander, Rhodes."

"You realize he'll still want to kill you?" Keith said. "He went through a lot of trouble to lure you here."

"I know." Carver held up Sutton's security badge. "The reason I brought him back is because I need help. We can leave him here and you can come with me for a quick operation."

"You've got to be kidding me." Nadia laughed. "We're not following you anywhere."

"Hold on." Alicia took the badge and studied it. "You've got the keys to the kingdom, don't you?"

"Yep." Carver pulled the suitcase out of the car. "I got us uniforms too. Might be a little big, but they'll work okay."

"Not necessary." Alicia gave him a look of superiority. "We already have uniforms we planned to wear for the very same job."

"You planned to hit the police station tonight?" Carver said.

"Yes. Jericho had planned on taking out the cops at the fake cash house and then we were going to steal their badges and go in."

"Apparently, you had the same idea," Keith said. "Man, I've never seen that kind of chaos before. It was insane."

"It was FUBAR," Nadia said. "And what the hell do you mean about the cash house being fake?"

"We'll debrief you later when Tom is back to normal." Alicia nodded at Barry. "What about the spook?"

"I'll leave him with you. Jericho can decide what to do with him."

"Carver, are you insane?" Barry wriggled helplessly. "They'll kill me!"

"Doubtful," Carver said. He turned to Alicia. "So, you're okay with me leading the police station job?"

She nodded. "Yeah. I trust you as far as that goes."

Keith nodded. "I trust her judgement."

"Good, then let's get a move on. We've got a few hours at most before the night shift finds out everyone on the day shift is dead."

Nadia sighed. "Guess I'm in too."

Keith cracked his knuckles. "Let me take care of Tom first." He took Jericho by the arm. "I'll tuck him in bed and gear up."

Alicia headed toward the doors. "Let's get suited up." She nodded at Barry. "Bring him inside, please."

Carver cut the zip ties holding Barry's ankles together. That freed his ankles from his wrists so he could stand. Carver helped him out of the Tesla and toward the building.

"Carver, they're going to kill me." Barry was sweating and shaking. "Please, just let me go. I'll do anything you want. I'll be your inside man."

"They won't kill you." Carver pushed him inside the front doors. "Jericho is smarter than me. He'll know what to do with you."

"I can help you find Liana. I think she's at one of our dark facilities. I know all the locations. I can find out which one is holding her."

"The moment you get back safely into the fold, you'll renege on that promise." Carver shook his head. "I will, however, let you deliver a message to your director. What's her name?"

Barry hesitated. "Deputy Director Rachel Evans."

Carver knew the name from somewhere, but he couldn't put a finger on it. "Tell her that if Liana isn't released and allowed to go about living her life then there will be trouble."

"Coming after the NSA is treason, Carver. Not even you are crazy enough for that."

"Maybe. Maybe not." Carver shrugged. "Jericho might be crazy enough."

Barry licked his lips nervously. "You might be right."

Alicia joined them in the hallway. She was dressed in a black SWAT uniform that looked close enough to pass as the ones he'd taken from Sutton. "Follow me." She led Carver to the secure room in the back. The same one he'd broken into earlier. She led him across the room and through the doors he hadn't been able to get through.

There were weapons crates stacked from floor to the ceiling against one wall. There were racks of equipment, weapons, ammunition, and more. There was also a heavy iron cage. Alicia put Barry inside and locked it.

She gave him a sandwich and water. "Sit tight, and we'll get back to you later."

"I'm claustrophobic!" Barry moaned. "Let me out of here!"

Alicia ignored his pleas. She looked around and sighed. "Guess we'll have to relocate our shop now that it's burned."

"We already knew about this place," Barry said.

"Yeah, but we knew that you knew and used it to our advantage. Now you know that we know." She shook her head. "Time to pull up roots."

Carver and Alicia returned to the front. The others were in SWAT uniforms and ready to go. There was even a SWAT truck parked in front of the building. It looked nearly identical to Bickham PD's truck.

Jericho had certainly planned more thoroughly than Carver had, but he also had an organization at his back. Carver was alone and making do with what he could find. He wasn't sure if he'd come out on top through dumb luck or skill.

Maybe he owed all this to Joe. Joe had told him to never give up on his brothers in arms. To always help when they needed it even when they claimed they didn't want it. It was a principle that Carver followed despite what his instincts told him.

Then again, Joe's advice was what got him into this mess in the first place. It pulled him right into Jericho's trap. It cost Carver a lot of money and a pretty decent minivan. At least all of that was about to be paid back in full.

Alicia climbed into the driver's seat. Carver took shotgun. The others got in the back. She set course for the Bickham police station.

"You really screwed up our plans tonight," she said. "Jericho had big plans for you once we did the Bickham police job."

"Back at the pool hall when I mentioned Carver to Tom, he acted surprised," Rich said. "Was that an all act?"

"Yeah. He was building up to a big finale." Alicia shrugged. "You win some, you lose some."

"It's obvious Jericho planned to double cross the Bickham cops even before they tried to kill Rich." Carver rapped his knuckles on the dashboard. "You can't just pick up one of these at an auction."

Nadia leaned forward. "Wait, the cops tried to kill Rich?"

"They have ties to a Chicago mafia. They hired a hitman to take out me and Rich." Carver shrugged. "I took out the hitman. Dumped the body in a homeless encampment."

Alicia laughed. "That sounds like something Jericho would have done."

"Just because you saved my life doesn't change things," Rich said.

"Jericho's plans for Carver put you in the crosshairs," Nadia said. "I know Carver is responsible for you being captured and tortured but give the man a little credit."

"Maybe." Alicia shrugged. "But only a little."

Rich didn't reply.

Alicia pulled up to the gate behind the police station. She used Sutton's security badge on the card reader and the gate slid open. She pulled into the parking lot. There were two more SWAT trucks parked nearby along with a variety of brand-new patrol cars. There was even a black Corvette police interceptor. Probably for Beau.

Palmer's old Caprice was there alongside his patrol car. Sutton and Archer's patrol SUV was there too. It looked like Bickham PD was going to have to hire a lot of new staff.

Alicia parked the truck near the metal door in the rear. She gave Carver a smartphone in a rugged rubber case. "Use the signal disruptor app to make the camera feed fuzzy." She showed him the app.

Carver got out of the truck and pulled up his mask. He kept his head down and walked beneath the camera then activated the app. A message appeared on the screen. *Signal disruption successful.* He unlocked the rear door with the security badge.

The others got out of the truck, and they filed inside. There was a long hallway ahead. Carver didn't see any cameras mounted on the wall. He started walking. "Where are we going?"

"No idea," Alicia said. "We never could get a map of the interior. About all we know for sure is that there's just two women answering phones and one officer on patrol."

Carver hoped they were right. Otherwise, this operation was going to get real complicated real fast.

Chapter 39

Carver kept his rifle at the ready.

Alicia walked alongside him. "Are you always this paranoid, Carver?"

"I'm still alive, aren't I?"

"No reason to let our guard down," Nadia said. "Just in case."

Rich kept his rifle to his shoulder. "Agreed."

Alicia didn't look convinced. "There's only a skeleton crew here. All their big boys are dead."

"Rich was supposed to be the one to kill the cops who made his life miserable," Keith said. "Not Carver. It was part of his redemption arc."

"Yeah, you took that away from him," Alicia said.

"Seriously?" Rich huffed angrily. "You were just going to play act everything tonight to keep manipulating me?"

"It was going to be your reward," Alicia said. "But Carver ruined it."

Rich glanced at Carver. "I was looking forward to putting a bullet in Raulerson's smug face."

Nadia shivered. "What about me? Did you have big plans for me?"

"You were going to help Rich kill the cops and bond over it." Keith shrugged. "Then the two of you were going to kill your ex-husband. Carver ruined everything."

"Carver has a way of ruining even the best laid plans," Rich said.

Carver couldn't deny that.

"How about you never manipulate us again or we put bullets in you?" Nadia said.

"Fair enough." Alicia stopped in front of another heavy metal door.

Carver unlocked it with Sutton's security badge. He stepped through the door and turned on the light to reveal an evidence room the size of a warehouse. The shelves weren't loaded with files and boxes of evidence. They were loaded with treasure.

Nadia gasped. "My God, it's like finding a pirate's hideout!"

There was ornate furniture, vases, paintings and other art. There were boxes of jewelry, loose gems, and gold bars. There were fancy weapons, baseball cards, boxed toys and other collectibles. But most importantly, the shelves were packed with cash.

Keith whistled. "Merry Christmas."

Nadia picked up a handful of gemstones. "Have they been robbing jewelry stores?"

"God only knows." Alicia looked around. "No cameras in here. Nothing." She opened a duffel bag and tossed folded bags to everyone.

"Makes sense." Carver unfolded his bag and started stacking cash inside of it. "They don't want anything recording their stash."

"They've got more money than a bank!" Rich slid stacks of bills into a bag. "Man, I could get my whole body rebuilt with this much money."

Nadia laughed. "You want to become the Bionic Man?"

"Hell yeah!"

They stuffed the bags with cash and took them to the truck, then came back for more. No one from the night shift disturbed them. The night workers probably didn't even know about this place.

The stacks of cash were sorted by bill denominations. They filled bags with hundreds and fifties until they ran out of bags. They found more bags in the vault and used them too but still didn't have enough room for all the cash.

Nadia looked longingly at a diamond necklace. Rich tried on a gold Rolex watch.

Alicia shook her head. "Don't ever wear jewelry like that. It just draws attention and raises questions."

Rich put the Rolex back where he'd found it. "I wish we could clean this place out."

"The truck is half full already," Keith said. "We've got millions of dollars. I think that's good enough for now."

"Yeah." Alicia checked the time. "We've been at this for two hours. The day shift is supposed to arrive in an hour. I want us to be long gone by then."

They locked up the room and left. They carried their last loads outside and tossed them into the truck. The rear gate rattled and began to slide to the side.

"Shit." Alicia motioned everyone behind the truck. "Make sure the camera is still disrupted."

Carver checked the app and confirmed the camera above the door was still disabled.

A loud engine rumbled. The gate slid aside, and Beau's Corvette drove in and screeched to a stop next to the Corvette police car. He struggled to get out of the low car, his generously sized belly a major impediment.

Carver pulled up his mask and walked around the corner of the truck. Betty wasn't in the passenger seat. That was good.

Beau finally got out of the car. He saw Carver and held up his hands in an angry gesture. "Why the hell didn't you radio in and tell me you were back? I was so excited I hardly slept last night. Are you unloading the cash now?"

"More or less." Carver lowered his mask. He smiled. "We're unloading your cash."

Beau's eyes flared. He snorted like a surprised pig and went for a big flashy revolver on the holster at his waist. Carver put a bullet through his hand. Beau squealed like a stuck pig. Carver turned to Rich. "He's the ringleader. Do you want the honors?"

"Hell, yes." Rich pulled down his mask and grinned at Beau. "Hey, you son of a bitch. Remember me?"

Beau tucked his injured hand under his other arm. He was whimpering and crying. "I can bring unholy hell down on you, you bastards."

"Bad news," Rich said. "All your crooked cops are dead."

Beau's eyes went wide. "My boys?"

"They died in a firefight with the NSA," Carver said.

Alicia put a hand on Rich's shoulder. "We've got to go."

Beau howled in agony. "Not my boys!"

Rich pulled the trigger. His cries abruptly went silent and his brains splattered on his white Corvette. He flopped on his back spread-eagled and a pool of blood formed under his head.

Carver looked at Rich. "Feel better?"

Rich nodded. "Yeah. I feel like a million bucks."

"Well, that's great." Keith sighed. "Federal agents killed the other cops at the cash house. How are we supposed to link Beau's death to that?"

"We could be feds for all they know. The cameras outside the gate saw us coming and will see us going." Carver tossed a bag of cash into the back of the truck. "Nothing has changed."

"He's right," Alicia said.

"Thanks for letting me kill him." Rich hobbled into the back of the truck. "A pity kill was just what I needed."

They got back in the truck. Alicia drove them back to Hope House and parked in front. She turned to Carver. "Take a bag of cash and go. I think it's best if you're gone by the time Jericho comes to his senses."

"Speaking of which, how long will that be?" Keith said.

Carver checked the time. "Another couple of hours at least. I didn't hit him with a heavy dose."

"What did you use on him?" Alicia said. "Sodium thiopental?"

Carver didn't reply. He got out of the truck. Walked to the back and took two bags of cash. He put them in Jericho's Tesla next to the guns he'd taken from Sutton's closet. He opened the glove compartment and found the car's paperwork. It was registered to Matt Simpson in Maine.

"Is this registration legit?" Carver said.

Alicia nodded. "It's one of our burner cars. You can keep it."

"Already planned to. Does it have a tracker?"

"No. Even the onboard computer's GPS and cell service is encrypted to prevent tracking." She shrugged. "It does get free supercharging though."

"Not sure if I believe you, but I'll keep it for now."

Alicia pursed her lips. "You know, maybe we could talk Jericho out of killing you and into bringing you onboard. The movement could always use people like you."

Carver made a face. "I'm not interested in joining causes. I suggest you take your newfound riches and enjoy life instead of fighting it."

Nadia nodded. "I like that idea."

"I don't." Rich walked up to Carver and prodded him in the chest. "You're the last person I want joining us. Maybe you don't deserve killing, but you deserve to know the pain I went through."

"Maybe," Carver said. "The Akim Jabar mission was a setup. We were sent there to fail. I did my best to get us out of there, but an explosion caved in the ceiling and separated me from everyone else. I should have stuck closer to you. I should have done a better job. But I didn't and it is what it is."

Rich reared back and punched Carver in the face with his left hand. Carver saw it coming from a mile away and let it happen. He let Rich get in two more licks before he backed up and rubbed his jaw.

"Feel better?"

Rich shook his head. "No. Truth is I never liked you, Carver. You're an easy man to hate. You're just naturally good at things that I had to work my ass off to get good at. I'll never like you no matter what. But I guess I can admit that part of it comes from jealousy."

"I can live with that," Carver said. "Hopefully the money will help you get patched up." He closed the Tesla door. "Give Jericho a hug for me when he's back to his normal self."

Alicia barked a laugh. "Will do."

Carver paused. "Ask him to interrogate Barry and find out what happened to Liana. She's a friend."

"You want to help her?" Alicia said.

Carver nodded. "Yeah. I guess I do." He gave her his secure email address. "Contact me there with anything you find."

"I'll do that." Alicia shook his hand. "Take care."

"You too." Carver got into the Tesla and drove away. He had no idea where he was going, so he turned east towards the coast and the beaches. He really just wanted to relax, but now it looked like he'd have to find out what happened to Liana and help her.

He'd lived with her in that mountain cabin in western North Carolina for a while. They'd become friends. She'd wanted more than anything to return to her job at the NSA as if nothing ever happened. Carver hadn't liked the idea, but it was her life.

They'd lured her back in and probably interrogated her. Probably promised her a lot if she'd help them find Carver. She hadn't done that, so they'd locked her up and started looking for him themselves.

Carver was going to find them. Ask them nicely what they'd done with his friend. And they'd better have answers he liked, or bad things were going to happen to them. They'd taken their shot at Carver and failed.

Now he was going to return the favor.

BOOKS BY JOHN CORWIN-

Books by John Corwin
Want more? Never miss an update by joining my email list and following me on social media!
Join my Facebook group at https://www.facebook.com/groups/overworldconclave
Join my email list: www.johncorwin.net
Fan page: https://www.facebook.com/johncorwinauthor

PSYCHOLOGICAL THRILLERS
The Family Business
AMOS CARVER THRILLERS
Dead Before Dawn
Dead List
Dead and Buried
Dead Man Walking
Dead by the Dozen
Dead Run
Dead Weather Days
Dead to Rights
Dead But Not Forgotten
CHRONICLES OF CAIN
To Kill a Unicorn
Enter Oblivion
Throne of Lies
At The Forest of Madness
The Dead Never Die
Shadow of Cthulhu
Cabal of Chaos
Monster Squad

Gates of Yog-Sothoth
Shadow Over Tokyo
Into the Multiverse

THE OVERWORLD CHRONICLES

Sweet Blood of Mine
Dark Light of Mine
Fallen Angel of Mine
Dread Nemesis of Mine
Twisted Sister of Mine
Dearest Mother of Mine
Infernal Father of Mine
Sinister Seraphim of Mine
Wicked War of Mine
Dire Destiny of Ours
Aetherial Annihilation
Baleful Betrayal
Ominous Odyssey
Insidious Insurrection
Utopia Undone
Overworld Apocalypse
Apocryphan Rising
Soul Storm
Devil's Due
Overworld Ascension
Assignment Zero (An Elyssa Short Story)

OVERWORLD UNDERGROUND

Soul Seer
Demonicus
Infernal Blade

OVERWORLD ARCANUM

Conrad Edison and the Living Curse
Conrad Edison and the Anchored World
Conrad Edison and the Broken Relic
Conrad Edison and the Infernal Design
Conrad Edison and the First Power

STAND ALONE NOVELS

Mars Rising

No Darker Fate
The Next Thing I Knew
Outsourced
Seventh

About the Author

John Corwin is the bestselling author of the Amos Carver Thrillers, Overworld Chronicles, and Chronicles of Cain. He enjoys long walks on the beach and is a firm believer in puppies and kittens.

After years of getting into trouble thanks to his overactive imagination, John abandoned his male modeling career to write books.

He resides in Atlanta.

https://www.facebook.com/groups/overworldconclave

Join the Overworld Conclave for all the news, memes and tentacles you could ever desire!

https://www.facebook.com/groups/overworldconclave

Or get your fix via email: www.johncorwin.net

Fan page: https://www.facebook.com/johncorwinauthor

Printed in Dunstable, United Kingdom